Katherine Mansfield and *Bliss and Other Stories*

GW00570428

KATHERINE MANSFIELD STUDIES

Katherine Mansfield Studies is the peer-reviewed, annual publication of the Katherine Mansfield Society. It offers opportunities for collaborations among the significant numbers of researchers with interests in modernism in literature and the arts, as well as those in postcolonial studies. Because Mansfield is a writer who has inspired successors from Elizabeth Bowen to Ali Smith, as well as numerous artists in other media, Katherine Mansfield Studies encourages interdisciplinary scholarship and also allows for a proportion of creative submissions.

Series Editor
Dr Delia da Sousa Correa, *The Open University, UK*

Editors
Dr Gerri Kimber, *University of Northampton, UK*
Professor Todd Martin, *Huntington University, USA*

Reviews Editor
Dr Aimee Gasston, *Birkbeck, University of London, UK*

Katherine Mansfield and *Bliss and Other Stories*

Edited by
Enda Duffy, Gerri Kimber and Todd Martin

EDINBURGH
University Press

Edinburgh University Press is one of the leading university presses in the UK. We publish academic books and journals in our selected subject areas across the humanities and social sciences, combining cutting-edge scholarship with high editorial and production values to produce academic works of lasting importance. For more information visit our website: edinburghuniversitypress.com

Edinburgh University Press Ltd
The Tun – Holyrood Road, 12(2f) Jackson's Entry, Edinburgh EH8 8PJ

Typeset in 10.5/12.5 New Baskerville by
Servis Filmsetting Ltd, Stockport, Cheshire,
and printed and bound by CPI Group (UK) Ltd,
Croydon, CR0 4YY

A CIP record for this book is available from the British Library

ISBN 978 1 4744 7730 7 (hardback)
ISBN 978 1 4744 7732 1 (webready PDF)
ISBN 978 1 4744 7731 4 (paperback)
ISBN 978 1 4744 7733 8 (epub)

Contents

Contents

List of Illustrations

Acknowledgements

The editors would like to extend particular thanks to the judging panel for this year's Katherine Mansfield Society Essay Prize: Professor Enda Duffy, University of California Santa Barbara, USA, and Chair of the Judging Panel; Professor Marilyn Reizbaum, Harrison King McCann Professor of English, Director of Gender, Sexuality, and Women's Studies Program, Bowdoin College, Maine, USA; and Professor Sarah Cole, Parr Professor of English and Comparative Literature, Dean of Humanities, Columbia University, New York, USA. The winning essay, 'The Well-Tempered Story: Experiments with Sound in "The Man Without a Temperament"' by Richard Cappuccio, is featured in this volume.

The editors would also like to thank the following organisations and individuals: the Alexander Turnbull Library, Wellington, New Zealand, for permission to reproduce images of Francis Carco's postcard to Katherine Mansfield; the Society of Authors as representatives of the literary estate of Katherine Mansfield, for permission to reproduce copyright material; Susan Wilson, for allowing us to use her painting *Prelude*, commissioned for the Folio Society edition of *Katherine Mansfield's Short Stories* (2000), on the front cover of this volume (Susan Wilson is represented by Browse & Darby, 19 Cork Street, London W1 www.susanruddwilsonartist.com); Professor J. Lawrence Mitchell and the J. Lawrence Mitchell Collection, Cushing Library, Texas A & M University, for the images of the first edition of *Bliss and Other Stories*; and La Gonda Studio for reproducing paintings and sculptures by artist Terry Stringer featured in this volume.

Abbreviations

Unless otherwise indicated, all references to Katherine Mansfield's works are to the editions listed below and abbreviated as follows. Diaries, journals, letters and notebooks are quoted verbatim without the use of editorial '[*sic*]'.

CP
The Collected Poems of Katherine Mansfield, eds Gerri Kimber and Claire Davison (Edinburgh: Edinburgh University Press, 2016)

CW1 and CW2
The Edinburgh Edition of the Collected Works of Katherine Mansfield: Vols 1 and 2 – *The Collected Fiction*, eds Gerri Kimber and Vincent O'Sullivan (Edinburgh: Edinburgh University Press, 2012)

CW3
The Edinburgh Edition of the Collected Works of Katherine Mansfield: Vol. 3 – *The Poetry and Critical Writings*, eds Gerri Kimber and Angela Smith (Edinburgh: Edinburgh University Press, 2014)

CW4
The Edinburgh Edition of the Collected Works of Katherine Mansfield: Vol. 4 – *The Diaries of Katherine Mansfield, including Miscellaneous Works*, eds Gerri Kimber and Claire Davison (Edinburgh: Edinburgh University Press, 2016)

Letters 1–5
The Collected Letters of Katherine Mansfield, 5 vols, eds Vincent O'Sullivan and Margaret Scott (Oxford: Clarendon Press, 1984–2008)

Notebooks 1–2
The Katherine Mansfield Notebooks, 2 vols, ed. Margaret Scott (Minneapolis: University of Minnesota Press, 2002)

Dust jacket of the first edition of *Bliss and Other Stories*, 1920. Cushing Library, J. Lawrence Mitchell Collection.

Introduction:
Achieving Bliss

Enda Duffy

After a century, it can now at last be said: Katherine Mansfield's *Bliss and Other Stories* ranks as one of the greatest short story collections in the English language. If we accept – as we must – that the short story, with its fast-fiction, briefly told burst of narrative impressions, is *the* modernist literary genre, then *Bliss and Other Stories* must be taken to rank as one of the greatest works of modernist Anglophone fiction. Literary criticism of modernist work, which has only slowly disengaged itself from the tremendous and highly persuasive self-publicity projects of the various modernist movements and coteries, and their many boosters, is only now, a century after the works themselves were produced, gaining the critical distance necessary to make these evaluations.[1] At this remove, Mansfield's *Bliss and Other Stories* emerges as not only brilliant, but also pivotal. To commemorate its publication a century later is to celebrate a masterpiece.

It may be said that if each new era or artistic episteme has its own characteristic art form, the one which was invented for and epitomises modernism, then, surely was film. If we confine our critical horizon to the written word, however, then the short story must be seen as the characteristic literary form of the long 'modernist moment'. The short story[2] owed its rise to the needs of the new, now relatively mass-distributed periodicals that appeared in the latter half of the nineteenth century; it therefore had, from the start, a hand-in-glove, practical business relation to modern mass-media and publishing developments. Given that the new magazine media ecology catered to increasingly broader audiences, it is appropriate that the short story had its modern origins in subcultural and pop forms. The detective stories of Poe, Sue and Conan Doyle, for example, themselves inheritors of the 'true-crime' accounts and popular fascination with crime and its containment that had earlier

1

found expression in broadside ballads, were notable avatars of the modernist accounts of urban anomie among the *flâneurs* and *flâneuses* strolling through western cities which we encounter in the works of the high modernists. At heart, these stories, like their high-art successors, are quintessentially urban fictions: they tell their readers how to navigate the physical, infrastructural, social, cultural and emotional terrains of the new and increasingly middle-class megalopolises and suburbs, from London to Los Angeles. In a short and fast tale, the short story builds on such forms as the detective story and the romance tale, could bring worlds into confrontation, have people of different classes and conditions meet, collide or near-collide, record strange stimulations and annotate reactions, all while elucidating the alertness and a keener sense of danger and opportunity needed to make the most of the lively city. The modernist short story, in other words, was the perfect medium in which the writer could communicate to her reader how to be productively and excitingly modern. Here Mansfield, her somatically attuned prose a kind of telephone exchange charged to pick up signals of every strength and resonance, excelled.

It is not simply that *Bliss and Other Stories* ranks with some of the other great, and occasionally more famous, early twentieth-century short story collections, although in that company it holds its own. James Joyce's *Dubliners*,[3] for example, ends on the long and profound note of 'The Dead', while *Bliss and Other Stories* might be thought instead to peter out with only the more jittery discordant brace of set pieces, 'Revelations' and 'The Escape'. Yet *Bliss* opens with what may be Mansfield's own masterpiece, 'Prelude', which achieves an impressionistic liveliness which outdoes all but the best of Virginia Woolf, offers a modernist portrayal of childhood[4] which outdoes Joyce in the opening sections of *A Portrait of the Artist as a Young Man,* and which marshals in its twelve sections a kaleidoscope portrayal of a whole minor world more complex than the nocturne of 'The Dead' and composed at a level of modernist orchestration which Joyce would achieve only in the 'Wandering Rocks' episode of *Ulysses.* Yet comparing Mansfield's *Bliss and Other Stories* to the work of some of her great contemporaries – D. H. Lawrence's *The Prussian Officer and Other Stories* (1914) (which included 'Odour of Chrysanthemums'), Edith Wharton's earlier *Crucial Instances* (1901), or work as varied as that by Henry James, Gertrude Stein or Ernest Hemingway – only convinces us of the vast variety and sophistication which the form had achieved by the end of the second decade of the twentieth century. Rather, one might dwell on the way in which Mansfield's work, in retrospect, reveals itself as pivotal.

On the one hand, her stories are transmission points in which the great earlier work of the European developers of the form – notably Chekhov, beloved of Mansfield, and also Maupassant – had their influence made apparent in Anglophone writing. On the other, we can think of Mansfield – whose smart and modish modernist realism, stretched and energised into an elastic vitalist vehicle though it is, never crossed over into the fully fantastical modernist mythmaking of, for example, Djuna Barnes – as the keeper of the borderland zone between the old realism and the new experimentalism. Furthermore, it is clear that the many projects at this crossing point were influenced in profound ways by the gender, and gender-consciousness, of their authors. Here, Mansfield's feminist modernism, with her ever-present awareness of the oppressions of women's lives under patriarchy, seems much more fully revolutionary than the experimentalism (often in the cause of reaction) of such figures as Wyndham Lewis. Next, Mansfield's New Zealand birth and experience places her at the starting-point of a whole new range of short fiction that represents the experiences of people, and especially women, from beyond the metropolitan centres of Britain, Europe and North America. All of this is to say that Mansfield, more than many of her peers, has had an enormous influence on the progress of the short story since 1920. Whether it be the more realist works of Alice Munro or the fantastical feminist fables of Angela Carter, in accounts of women's lives in particular – in the century when the subservient and silenced roles assigned to women have been radically contested – Mansfield's influence is undeniable.

Mansfield, in other words, in *Bliss and Other Stories* and beyond, strikes us today as fully and wholeheartedly modern in ways few of her peers can equal. This modernity leads us to compare the collection to other glittering modernist artworks in a multitude of forms, all created by women around the same moment during or after World War I: the house E-1027 (1926–7) by the Irish–French architect and designer Eileen Gray,[5] the costume and set designs for Tristan Tzara's *Le Cœur à Gaz* by the Ukrainian–French painter and textile designer Sonia Delaunay,[6] or the chapbook *The Book of Repulsive Women*, published by Djuna Barnes in 1915.[7] In each case, these brilliant artists' marginal, contentious and, until recently, only grudgingly accepted relation to the modernist -isms of their day gave their work in each case an extraordinary avant-gardist edge. In each of these works, the artists flipped their estrangement from hegemonic, often male, versions of modernism into a peculiar and pungent strength. So it was also with Mansfield in *Bliss and Other Stories*. Her characters, her innovative stylistic experiments, her manipulations of the various *ressentiments* that, for both characters and readers, are produced by the oppressions rampant in modern life, are never less than intensely modern. In her portrayal of rush, flash and energy, in stories such as 'Psychology' (about two fashionable writers) or 'The Man Without a Temperament' (about a woman on holiday with her impatient, vulgarian husband) at the centre of the volume, she out-does the Italian Futurists, since her grasp of the double-sided nature of human vitalism is much more nuanced than theirs. In tales such as 'Je ne parle pas français' she offers a portrait of the bohemian demi-monde which casts its blighted vacuity in terms that would be equalled only in the work of Jean Rhys. In 'The Little Governess' and in 'The Escape' she offers a portrait of modern patriarchal sexual relations which shows up even Joyce, in comparison, as a kind of sentimentalist. In 'Bliss' she offers a portrait of lesbian desire hardly equalled at that point in modern British fiction. In story after story, her portraits of middle-class marriage are more unequivocally harrowing and psychologically astute than anything in Eliot's 'The Waste Land'. Above all, in 'Prelude', she grants us her version of a Proustian memory palace and, implicitly, a post-World War I survivor story, cast, necessarily now, as a full-scale modernist montage or repetitive idiom, its series of movements repeat-ing, again and again, with an insistence that reminds us of Cézanne's repeated attempts to portray Madame Cézanne[8] or Wallace Stevens' attempt, in the poem 'Thirteen Ways of Looking at a Blackbird', to try over and over to portray something as simple as a small songbird – in order almost to convince herself, or us, that even a past that was trou-bled by the multiple micro-aggressions of enforced patriarchy offered sufficient ballast for a post-war modernist subjectivity and even collectiv-ity going forward.

Bliss and Other Stories, therefore, in its concentration of modernist preoccupations and the stylistic verve it displays in response to them, is utterly modern. Happily, the essays assembled in this volume of criticism and creative work on the occasion of the centenary of the publication of the short-story collection draw our attention to, as they illuminate, each of the collection's strengths. The prize-winning essay, Richard Cappuccio's 'The Well-Tempered Story: Experiments with Sound in "The Man Without a Temperament"', drawing our attention to the fact that Mansfield, before she turned seriously to writing, had worked in earnest to become a cello player, reads her work as a cacophonous, vividly modernist soundscape. He not only offers an arresting read-ing of 'The Man Without a Temperament', collating its extraordinary assemblage of rings, pings, bangs, echoes and cascading sonorities, but, in the process, alerts us to the utterly vivid ear for the symphonies of sounds which Mansfield voices, and then, like a director, orchestrates in every one of her stories. It is common to place Stravinsky's *Rite of Spring*

as the defining moment at the heart of modernism;[9] likewise, it is often
stated that, for modernists such as Joyce, the Sitwells or Mina Loy, the
writers' interest in music meant that their experimental texts trafficked
in sounds in a way never attempted in prose before this.[10] Cappuccio,
in his reading of a single story, makes clear that Mansfield was the most
musically sophisticated and possibly had the most discerning ear for
sounds, timbres and temperaments of any literary writer in the modernist musical galaxy. This essay, further, is a door into *Bliss and Other Stories*
as a glorious sensorium, a series of experiments – of taste in 'Psychology',
of sight in 'Prelude' – which not only makes for a new kind of writerly
immediacy and a post-Fauvist recasting of literary impressionism, but
more, in its assemblage of sense impressions represented and relayed to
the reader with an urgency and directness not achieved in the same way
prior to this in English prose, offers us texts which achieve in relation
to each of the senses what it had taken a painter such as Cézanne to do
in relation to sight, which Stravinsky achieved in relation to sound, and
so on. This is not merely a new achievement in synaesthesia, but, rather,
a new literary discovery that prose can annotate, and illicit, sensory
attunements and reactions in a way that outdoes the ability to focus on a
single sense implied in other art-forms. Sensuous modernism finds one
key entrée to modernity in the pages of *Bliss*.

Inevitably, such sensuous vividness has a gendered component, and
is deployed in each story in ways which suggest that new ways of sensing,
and then reacting and taking action, necessitate a new politics of gender.
Eleri Anona Watson lays out what is at stake here in her essay, ' "We
were a nothingness shot with gleams of what might be. But no more":
Katherine Mansfield, Virginia Woolf and the Queer Sublime', when she
shows how the Burkean category of sublimity was recast by modernist
writers such as Mansfield in the service of a radical queer politics of narrative. Mansfield's modernist queerness, in Watson's terms, produces
her intensely queer narratives: that is, her narrative strangeness is at
the service of a queer politics which emerges, unequivocally in stories
such as 'Bliss', against a background of endless pent-up frustration on
the part of the heroine and the text itself in the face of the hypocritical
surface glamour of the prevailing patriarchal order. This essay, which
places Mansfield's work over against a range of recent advances in queer
theory, shows how the charge of sublimity, which had motivated many of
the romantics towards a rethinking of the subjective and the personal, is
reworked by modernists such as Mansfield in the service of the relational
and the communal. Marlene Andresen, in her essay 'Seeking Blissful
Ignorance: Katherine Mansfield's Child Protagonists in "Prelude" and
"Sun and Moon" ', then shows how Mansfield's profound interest in

portraying the sensory and cognitive terrain of childhood befits a writer who wished keenly to consider sensory evidence, especially one who is delighted to amplify, rather than repress, the queer potential within all such experience. (In this vein, the scene in 'Prelude' of the beheading of the duck by the Irish servant Pat, and the child Kezia's reaction to it – her repeated screams of " 'Put the head back' . . . until it sounded like a strange hiccup" (CW2, p. 87) – is the opening salvo to which every subsequent scene in *Bliss and Other Stories* responds.) Argha Kumar Banerjee's essay, 'Of "Trust" and "Mistrust": Reading the Mind of a Predator in "The Little Governess" ', offers a new and timely reading of the encounter of male predator and teenage girl in the story 'The Little Governess', limning a sexual politics which Mansfield has laid out with Zolaesque inevitability. Banerjee reveals the story for what it is: a tale about sexual harassment. In the European metropolis, a 'world full of old men with twitching knees', women (CW1, p. 432), whether Mouse in 'Je ne parle pas français' or Miss Ada Moss in 'Pictures', are in danger from the male predators who circle round them. Mansfield is the first writer to bring this reality of gender relations for the modern working woman into the light of literature.

At the same time, as Gaurav Majumdar reminds us, when he too, like Eleri Watson, discerns a revised version of sublimity emerging in Mansfield's work, and when he shows how 'the correlation between ecstatic pleasure and plot-based pain, if you like, remains evocative' in her fiction (p. XXX), *Bliss and Other Stories*, despite its Chekhovian realism, does not succumb to despair or any totalising angst of modernity. Monica Tyrell, the heroine of 'Revelations', may 'suffer[] from her nerves' (CW2, p. 213), and Ada Moss, in 'Pictures', is an out-of-work, past-her-prime singer who spends her day trudging the streets of London, hungry and alone, but even such pathetic reminders of goodness as the withered bunch of violets in 'Psychology' or the soft-falling snow seen through the window of the Parisian café in 'Je ne parle pas français' do not fail to register a trace of utopian longing. As in the aloe plant in 'Prelude', the pear tree in 'Bliss' and the tree which the husband sees on the very last page of the collection in the story 'The Escape', in its images of organic life, even vegetable life, Mansfield's modernism is profoundly hopeful:

> There was something beyond the tree – a whiteness, a softness, an opaque mass, half-hidden – with delicate pillars. As he looked at the tree he felt his breathing die away and he became part of the silence. It seemed to grow, to expand in the quivering heat until the great carved leaves hid the sky, and yet it was motionless. Then from within its depths or from beyond

there came the sound of a woman's voice. The woman was singing. (CW2, p. 221)

This voice is perhaps Mansfield's own: refusing silence, singing as a woman, sounding notes that appeal to a better nature and the possibility of actual bliss. The collection's keyword, emblazoned in its title, testifies to the utopian possibility which every story here attempts to have us reach.

The final two essays on *Bliss and Other Stories* in this collection attest to the broader intellectual and geopolitical arcs within which Mansfield's stories were written, and in which their mixture of cold-eyed critique and utopian longing intervene in lives lived in the real world. Marilyn Reizbaum's deeply informed essay on the way in which decadence and savagery are figured in Mansfield, 'The "Little Savage from New Zealand" in "Bliss" ', begins by tracking the profound influence of Wilde on the young writer and leads us to consider how decadence, degeneration and the animal are front and centre in Mansfield's work.[11] This essay is a notable contribution to a new area of critical attention in modernist studies: the significance of animals, and the fraying of the human–animal distinction, in modernist writing. The essay by Maurizia Boscagli and myself, 'Refrigeration, *Bliss* and the Modernist World Order of Imperial Culture', works to place Mansfield's interest in food (and its freshness), and in time and the attempts to 'conquer' it, in the context of Mansfield's New Zealander origin as a (post-)colonial writer. Just as in the case of the friable boundary between the human and the animal explored by Reizbaum in Mansfield's stories, so too the appetite for food (and even more, food in a world of compressed time) in stories such as 'Psychology' turns out to be an index of the stories' geopolitical import.

As always in this series, the essays on the given topic are complemented and enriched by a cornucopia of other work: reports, poetry, fiction and a review essay. Janet Wilson supplies a characteristically insightful piece on Mansfield's transitional wartime story, 'An Indiscreet Journey', delineating how its (concealed) autobiographical origins matter to the text. Robin Woodward writes on Terry Stringer's late 1960s and 1970s sculpted portraits of Mansfield, and sees in them the making of a valid New Zealand cultural icon at the moment when New Zealand was loosening ties with Britain. Most exciting of all, Martin Griffiths reports on his discovery of a potential new story (and with it, the possibility of a series of other stories), 'The Thawing of Anthony Wynscombe', by 'Katharine R. Mansfield', published in the *Star* in Sydney on Saturday, 25 June 1910. The story is reprinted here.

In further work, Lee Garver reviews four books with strong Mansfield connections, including Helen Rydstrand's innovative *Rhythmic Modernism* and a new book by Roger Lipsey on G. I. Gurdjieff. There is a whole mini-anthology of Mansfield-inspired and related poems here, by Erica Stretton, Gerardo Rodríguez-Salas (a translation from the Spanish in collaboration with Lizzie Davis and Carmel Bird), Jackie Davis, Jessica Whyte, Julie Kennedy, Kirsten Warner, Maggie Rainey Smith, Mark Pirie, Melissa Browne and Suzanne Herschell. There is a moving short story, 'Mari', set in a New Zealand valley at the time of Queen Victoria's death, by Paula Morris. New work by Mansfield is potentially still being discovered, then, while her powerful stories, resonating across the century, continue to inspire sculpture, poetry and many more short stories. Mansfield's legacy is still contested and shows no sign of shedding its power to generate controversy, passion and new ideas. This is apt, because *Bliss and other Stories*, while refusing to deny the dream of its title, makes clear that any dream of bliss has to be struggled and fought for by those denied it, articulated, worked for and brought into focus in modern, improvised and often inadequate lives, if it is to ever be achieved.

Notes

1. A most notable recent example of this move has been in the realm not of literature but of modernist visual art: the reorganisation of the displays at the Museum of Modern Art in New York to include a range of modernisms alongside the long-familiar canonical one. See, for example, Holland Cotter, 'MoMA Reboots With "Modernism Plus"', *New York Times*, 10 October 2019, p. 1.
2. The classic, original critique here, complete with a grudging respect for the work of Mansfield, is the Irish short-story writer Frank O'Connor's *The Lonely Voice: A Study of the Short Story* (Hoboken, NJ: Melville House, [1963], 2004). For an overview of more recent work, see Adrian Hunter, *The Cambridge Introduction to the Short Story in English* (Cambridge: Cambridge University Press, 2007). For exciting recent work on the form, see, for example, David Trotter, 'Dis-enablement: Subject and Method in the Modernist Short Story', *Critical Quarterly*, 52: 2 (2010), pp. 4–13.
3. For one of the best recent rereadings of *Dubliners*, which also offers a meticulous review of previous criticism, see Margo Norris, *Suspicious Readings of Joyce's 'Dubliners'* (Philadelphia: University of Pennsylvania Press, 2011).
4. For the best recent work on modernist childhood in geopolitical context, see Jed Esty, *Unseasonable Youth: Modernism, Colonialism, and the Fiction of Development* (New York: Oxford University Press, 2012).
5. There is now a burgeoning critical attention to Gray. See, for example, Jennifer Goff, *Eileen Gray: Her Work and Her World* (Dublin: Irish Academic Press, 2015).
6. See Anne Montfort, *Sonia Delaunay* (New York: Harry N. Abrams, 2015).
7. See Djuna Barnes, *The Book of Repulsive Women and Other Poems*, edited by Rebecca Loncraine (New York: Routledge, 2003).
8. See Dita Amory (with contributions by Philippe Cézanne and others), *Madame Cézanne* (New York: Metropolitan Museum of Art, 2014).

9. See Modris Eksteins, *Rites of Spring: The Great War and the Birth of the Modern Age* (Boston: Houghton Mifflin, [1989] 2000).

10. See Josh Epstein's highly engaging *Sublime Noise: Musical Culture and the Modernist Writer* (Baltimore: Johns Hopkins University Press, 2014).

11. This essay builds on the project developed in Marilyn Reizbaum's book, *Unfit: Jewish Degeneration and Modernism* (New York: Bloomsbury, 2019).

CRITICISM

The Well-Tempered Story:
Experiments with Sound in
'The Man Without a Temperament'

Richard Cappuccio

From a musician's perspective, Kate Kennedy explains the virtuosity of Katherine Mansfield: 'She offers us writing [. . . with] the cadences and shapes of musical phrases. In short, she writes as she plays, and we can sight-read her writing, with an aural performance in mind.'[1] Kennedy's observations are not very different from Mansfield's own when she writes about playing music. In a poem composed in her teens, 'This is my world' (1903), Mansfield recognised not just the power of music, which she describes as 'Heaven to me', but, more importantly, the power realised in the subtlety of expression: 'And that is my 'cello, my all in all / Ah my beloved, quiet you stand, / – If I let the bow ever so softly fall, / – The magic lies under my hand' (CW3, p. 22). By 1920, shortly after she had finished writing 'The Man Without a Temperament', which she included in *Bliss and Other Stories* (1920), Mansfield's expression had expanded from a tightly written quatrain to a greater consideration of the complex relationships of sound, silence and, with a modernist awareness, noise. In fact, her poetic not only had developed to the point that her scoring of the story exhibited her well-developed ideas about the role of traditional music in her writing, but it also allowed her to experiment with musical ideas that would not be articulated until later in the century.

Mansfield was a musician before she was a writer: she started her musical studies in Wellington, and, as Gerri Kimber writes, when still in her early teens, her 'musical talents [. . .] developed rapidly; she practiced hard and was soon a proficient player, eventually playing a repertoire not dissimilar to that of young Tom [Trowell]'.[2] At Queens College, London, Ida Baker

would often go to Katherine's room to listen to her playing the cello, and formed a quartet with the three [Beauchamp] sisters – Chaddie singing, and Vera playing the piano. Both Katherine and Vera had real musical gifts – though Vera acknowledged Katherine's superiority.[3]

Mansfield was focused on a career in music; in 1907, she scheduled six hours of cello practice each day;[4] some of her early writing included song lyrics, and throughout her *œuvre*, music performance is integrated into her stories. Even after Mansfield had given up her goal to pursue the cello professionally, she still had a piano in her flat. When she and John Middleton Murry moved to Runcton Cottage in Sussex in 1912, she moved her piano to their country home.[5] In her private papers, Mansfield's manuscripts include scribbles that indicate the correlation of her writing and music. Helen Rydstrand notes that, next to a thought about adding a letter from Beryl to Nan Fry in 'Prelude', Mansfield's

> sentence is flanked by a cluster of treble clefs and followed by a sketch of a cello and a musical ensemble hovering above a scribbled-out bar of music in the bass clef staff, consisting of a violinist, cellist, a pianist, [and] possibly a bassist and a singer.[6]

Writing to Richard Murry, Mansfield carefully explained the relationship between the rhythmic nature of her writing and her musical background while writing 'Miss Brill':

> I chose not only the length of every sentence, but even the sound of every sentence – I chose the rise and fall of every paragraph to fit her – and to fit her on that day at that very moment. After Id written it I read it aloud – numbers of times – Just as one would *play over* a musical composition, trying to get it nearer and nearer to the expression of Miss Brill. (*Letters* 4, p. 165)[7]

It is certain that with this attention to the musical nature of her writing she would have been aware of the importance of using musical diction as well. Her most obvious choice was to rename *'The Aloe'* as *Prelude* when it was published by the Hogarth Press (1918). The title sums up the piece as both a beginning for certain characters in the story and a comment on the musical nature of her episodic structure. She returned to a musical term for the title 'The Man Without a Temperament'. Originally entitled 'The Exile', her revision embraces multiple meanings: while the word 'temperament' refers to the character's disposition, it is also a word that refers to musical tuning. J. S. Bach's study of tone and colour in the two volumes of his *The Well-Tempered Clavier* consists of preludes and fugues in each major and minor key. Bach was aware that the way in which an instrument was tuned would affect its harmonics when moving from key to key. In writing for the instrument that is *wohltemperiert*,

14

he writes to accommodate every key without sounding out of tune.[8] Those with specialties in fields other than music might be confused by the difference between methods of temperament and, despite being devoted listeners to music, might not hear what would be more obvious to musicians trained in performance. But Mansfield was exact when she spoke about the importance of sound, especially as she compared it to the writer's need to use the same method in choosing her words. Mansfield's attention to sound was with a trained ear; she knew the well-tempered sound that she heard in Shakespeare and Marvell:

> Musically speaking, hardly anyone seems to *even understand* what the middle of the note is – what that sound is like. Its not perhaps that they are even 'sharp' or 'flat' – its something much more subtle – they are not playing on the *very note itself*. (*Letters* 1, p. 205)

Mansfield was even more aware of the abrasiveness of sound. In a notebook, she compares her writing with her struggles with music:

> Whenever I have a conversation about Art which is more or less interesting I begin to wish to God I could destroy all that I have written & start again: it all seems like so many 'false starts'. Musically speak[ing] it is not – has not been – in the middle of the note – you know what I mean? When on a cold morning perhaps, you've been playing & it has sounded alright – until suddenly you <u>realise</u> you are warm – you have only just begun to play. Oh how badly this is expressed! How confused and even ungrammatical. (*Notebooks* 2, p. 137)

Mansfield satirised musical expression that lacked nuance. In 'The Modern Soul' (1911), for example, she starts with the image of the pompous Professor Windberg, a trombonist of questionable sensitivity: he describes his 'blasts on "liebe"' that leave his 'throat as dry as a railway tunnel' (CW1, p. 214). Mansfield's descriptions sound a lot like those in her youthful correspondence to Garnet Trowell: 'Oh, dear, next door someone has started scales on the trombone – curiously like a Strauss Tone Poem of Domestic Snoring' (*Letters* 1, p. 62). The harshness of Professor Windberg's interpretation, even for those who are not familiar with the dynamics of Grieg's 'Ich Liebe Dich', amplifies his *fortissimo* personality and leaves the reader wondering why this piece was being played out in the woods. Why is he competing with the sounds of nature, the 'pine trees [. . .] accompaniment' and their 'sighing delicacy' (CW1, p. 214)? Outwardly silent, the narrator records the Professor's bodily sounds as he consumes cherries; those disturbing noises sum up his overbearing nature: 'He chewed [. . .] and spat' (CW1, p. 214). The Professor's reaction to Fräulein Sonia's recitation at the pension's talent showcase highlights his self-congratulatory narcissism with a staccato rhythm: ' "What did I say?" shouted the Herr Professor [. . .] "tem-per-ament!" ' (CW1, p. 218).

In January 1920, when Mansfield was writing 'The Man Without a Temperament', she was living in Ospedaletti and going through a dark period of emotional turbulence, coupled with worsening health. She had already written her will the previous September. It was also a time when she not only questioned Murry's response to her illness, but had recently received news that her father had just remarried her mother's friend, Laura Bright. When Harold Beauchamp had visited with her just weeks before, he had been silent about any such plans. Her body, on the other hand, was not still: she recorded that consumption had left her with 'a great deal of moisture (& pain) in my BAD lung' (*Notebooks* 2, p. 171). In a few months' time, she would describe her illness in greater and more disturbing detail: 'I cough and cough and at each breath a dragging boiling bubbling sound is heard' (*Notebooks* 2, p. 219). That description of her suffering is among the most chilling and poetic of her writing as she describes the details of her chronic cough with an alliterative use of hacking sounds: there is not just a harsh musical sound in the repetition of the word 'cough', but she describes, as well, the sound and sensation in her lungs as 'boiling [and] bubbling', which echoes the chant of a Shakespearean prophecy. As she slowly drinks and pauses to spit, the accented monosyllables tick like a clock marking her time. The unsettling use of three stressed monosyllables at the end of the following line illustrate Mansfield's rhythmic scoring: 'I feel that my whole chest is boiling. I sip water, spit, sip, spit' (*Notebooks* 2, p. 219).

This use of a triple accented metrical foot, 'spit, sip, spit', is one that Mansfield made great use of in her poems and stories, including 'The Man Without a Temperament': there she writes that Jinnie Salesby 'sipped, sipped, drank . . .'; after those three monosyllabic, accented words, where a composer would score a rest or a poet would have added a line break, Mansfield inserts an ellipsis. After the musical rest, she repeats the word 'drank. . . .' and ends the sentence with a long silence (CW2, p. 201). Mansfield was expert in employing this uncommon metrical foot.[9] She knew how to exploit that unusual, weighty rhythm, largely unused by poets, to indicate an underlying disquiet in a character or situation. Her musical training would have given her the experience with such a dynamic: she knew its percussive power became more manifest with the shift to the silence of the ellipsis. Just as Professor Windberg's bodily sounds grate on an outwardly silent character, Jinnie Salesby's bodily noises result in her husband's silence; more importantly, they are thunderous to the reader.

These, and other noises in the story, are scored against periods of silence. For the critic Jill Johnston, the function of silence traditionally 'served music only to punctuate a phrase; it was, in other words, the invisible servant in the form of a pause that gave dramatic emphasis to an otherwise constant stream of sound'.[10] In preparing 'The Man Without a Temperament' for publication, Mansfield was concerned with the effect of the silences she had included in the story. In a letter to Murry, she is adamant that every aspect of the story be printed as she has prepared it:

> I must see the proofs myself before it is printed. If its typed 10 to 1 there will be mistakes and at any rate I cant expect anyone to go through it as I must go through. Every word matters. This is *not* conceit – but it must be so.
>
> Will you promise to send the proofs to me if he prints the story? Ill send them back express the same day. If you did not live at such racing speed I would beg you to go through the typed copy with the MSS and see that the *spaces* were correct – that where I intend a space there is a space. Its sure to be wrong [. . .]
>
> Will you please answer this when you write. (*Letters* 4, p. 204)

Mansfield's insistence that the printer correctly include the silent interludes speaks to her need, like that of a musical composer, to control her score. While it is easy to claim that she might just be using the traditional rests that are integral to musical composition, she is constructing silence in a manner similar to the most experimental ways employed by composers later in the twentieth century. As Johnston articulates, John Cage reverses 'all traditional practices of composing music by making silence the material of music as well as sound'.[11] The spacing that Mansfield insisted on in the published version both indicates her toggling between the present time and flashback, and marks the movements into which the story is divided.

Mansfield opens with an image of silence: 'He stood at the hall door turning the ring, turning the heavy signet ring upon his little finger while his glance travelled coolly, deliberately, over the round tables and basket chairs scattered about the glassed-in verandah' (CW2, p. 199). She establishes the soundless leitmotif: Robert Salesby turning his ring. The words themselves, however, establish the musical nature of Mansfield's prose through her careful assonance: the 'o' in stood, door, upon, cooling and round, as well as the 'i' in turning, signet, little, finger and glassed-in. Everything in the opening lines, however, imitates silent action: 'He pursed his lips – he might have been going to whistle – but he did not whistle' (CW2, p. 199). The actions imply that music will start, but it is not in the predictable form, very much in the way that John Cage's *4' 33"* (1952) also works. Cage's piece is still often misread

17

as a composition in which the musician walks to the piano and sits quietly for the duration of the piece. Those who read the composition differently, however, see and hear the performer

> deploying his arms three times in ways that suggest the work might have three distinct movements [. . .] Cage's piece implies that the 'music' consists of all the accidental noises in the room, whether humanly produced or not. Therefore, whereas a spectator originally observed that the piece contained no music at all, once he grasps the implications of *4' 33"*, he can infer that literally everything he hears within that frame of four minutes and thirty-three seconds belongs to the piece.[12]

As Cage would later pioneer in his music, Mansfield creates a story in which any sound, especially when amplified against the background of silence, is itself music. In 'Prelude' she had already teased out this idea with Linda's thought that if she were 'quiet, more than quiet, silent, motionless, something would happen [. . .] she seemed to be listening with her wide open watchful eyes [. . .] watching for something to happen that just did not happen' (CW2, pp. 68-9).

Mansfield writes about the unsettling silence in her journal. As her own breathing, the most primal ambient sound, becomes more laboured, she is upset by Murry's reaction:

> And I can't expand my chest – it's as though the chest had collapsed. Life is – getting new breath. Nothing else counts. And Murry is silent, hangs his head, hides his face with his fingers <u>as though</u> it were unendurable. 'This is what she is doing to me! Every fresh sound makes <u>my</u> nerves wince'. (*Notebooks* 2, p. 219)

Mansfield builds on the tension of quotidian sound and silence in 'The Man Without a Temperament', adding a musical element. When Robert goes back to the room to fetch his wife's shawl, he interrupts the

> servant girl singing loudly while she emptied soapy water into a pail [. . .] When she saw him her small impudent eyes snapped and her singing changed to humming [. . .]
> 'Vous désirez, Monsieur?' mocked the servant girl.
> No answer. He had seen it. He strode across the room, grabbed the grey cobweb and went out, banging the door. The servant girl's voice at its loudest and shrillest followed him along the corridor. (CW2, p. 200)

Not only does Mansfield mark the chambermaid's singing as *forte*, Mansfield also adds Robert's dour silence to a mix of ambient sounds, and in doing so she creates a particularly modernist score: water being poured into a pail, humming, a solo voice with a mocking question, a banging door, and a *fortissimo* echoing of the original theme. In addition, Mansfield's words indicate that if the servant's anger could sound a percussive snap with her eyes, they did. Perhaps Mansfield had heard of or read about Jean Cocteau's addition of the sounds of a typewriter, milk bottles and even a pistol to his arrangement of Erik Satie's *Parade* (1917) for the Ballets Russes.[13] Most certainly, as Claire Davison writes, 'When Luigi Russolo was writing a manifesto to celebrate *The Art of Noises* (1913), Mansfield was composing stories to orchestrate the musical and environmental soundscapes of her century.'[14] Included in Mansfield's orchestration is Robert, who, like the pianist in the John Cage piece, moves but is silent.

The addition of discordant, chaotic and offensive sounds, what can commonly be categorised as noise, is 'a key metaphor for the incommensurable paradoxes of modernity', according to David Novak.[15] One can think of the effectiveness that Virginia Woolf achieved when adding 'the drone of the aeroplane' in her story 'Kew Gardens' (1919) as an example Mansfield would have known after praising that story in her review in the *Athenaeum*.[16] The noises of modernity interrupt images bathed in light and, as Mansfield wrote, help in 'heightening the importance of everything [. . . in a] world [. . .] on tiptoe' (CW3, p. 474). Mansfield had already discovered what Cage would later articulate about the nature of noise: 'Wherever we are, what we hear is mostly noise. When we ignore it, it disturbs us. When we listen to it, we find it fascinating.'[17]

While readers are accustomed to Mansfield's innovations in the use of indirect discourse and flashback, in 'The Man Without a Temperament', Mansfield pushes this new technique of modernism – intrusive sounds that add a complex, tonal meaning to the narrative. She integrated onomatopoeic phrases into her earlier work: in 'Carnation' (1918), for example, Katie hears the mechanical repetition of the 'Hoo-hor-her! Hoo-hor-her!' of the water pump as an accompaniment to the rhythms of poetry (CW2, p. 162). Mansfield's experiments with the importance of such sounds in 'The Man Without a Temperament' include using noise to exploit the effect of tonal colour and demonstrate what Russolo articulates: 'Noise has the power to bring us back to life.'[18] This is the case even if the characters in the story often let the noise go by unacknowledged.

That power to reanimate the reader is rooted in the metrics of Mansfield's language. Aimee Gasston sums up Mansfield's creative process: 'European culture had become too cultivated, lacked vivacity, and needed to rediscover its own barbarism to be rewarded with fecundity.'[19] From her days at *Rhythm*, Mansfield subscribed to the belief that '"Before art can be human it must learn to be brutal."'[20] By this point in

Mansfield's writing life, she was well aware of the impact of sound. Aside from the chambermaid's singing, Mansfield inserts traditional music on only one other occasion in 'The Man Without a Temperament': 'The lights from the *salon* shine across the garden path and there is the sound of the piano' (CW2, p. 208). Here Mansfield takes a cue from Woolf to tie sound and the visual image, and the piano remains in the background as the story tiptoes in the ghostly scene between life and death. Nature is out of one's control, but buzzers and bells and other mechanical sounds intrude because they are created for, it seems, no other reason than to grate on the ear. There is a clear distinction between the rational sequence of formal music and the random and brutal nature of noise.

Mansfield's experiment with animal sounds in 'The Man Without a Temperament' might at first seem to be an exception. However, those noises are unlike her later use of the intentional imitation of animals by the children with sounds that replicate their personalities in 'At the Bay' (1921). 'The Man Without a Temperament' uses those sounds to add a rhythmic interruption: when the lapdog Klaymongso yelps, it seems out of character for the passive, domesticated animal. Most often in the story, Mansfield's repetitions of rhythmic noises include the animal sounds that she associates with the General who doesn't appear until Robert Salesby briefly escapes the Pension Villa Excelsior's grounds. As Robert steps aside to allow the General and the Countess to pass in their carriage, the Countess nudges her husband, and he 'gave a loud caw and refused to look' (CW2, p. 204). Twice afterwards, Mansfield includes cawing for the General's reaction: after Robert's walk, as Klaymongso yelps, the General adds to the cacophony with a more aggressive 'Caw! Caw! Caw!' (CW2, p. 206). Mansfield's ambitious limiting of the General to his oft repeated cawing is not simply to create a caricature of him, but is more intuitively drawn to what Jacques Attali explains: 'music theory in the West is tied, through its discourse, to the ideological reorganization necessitated by the emplacement of repetition'.[21] Mansfield's repetition is not just in the sounds of the crow, but in her use of that unsettling triple metre of the General's squawks. Unlike Mansfield's earlier experiments with the molossus, she does not limit it to the harsh sounds of an ominous crow; she repeats it in the saccharine public interaction in the honeymoon couple's spat over which fish each caught earlier in the day: ' "No it's not. Yes, it is. No it's not" ' (CW2, p. 207). The playful squabble ends with the same measured cadence of childish laughter, ' "Tee! Hee! Hee!" ' (CW2, p. 207). The disruptive metrical weight of each monosyllabic word creates a rhythm that outweighs the meaning, whether it be a projected animal sound, childish bickering or an exaggerated laugh. The power and imbalance of Mansfield's triple metre can never be confused with the waltz rhythm of a dactyl.

Mansfield controls her sound by contrasting predictably regular sounds with arbitrary rhythms of industrial noises. Rydstrand, looking at Mansfield through the lens of Henri Lefebvre, explains that there is a 'rhythmic theory of the ordinary in which harmony, or eurhythmia, functions as a measure of health and peace in opposition to discordance, or arrhythmia'.[22] Mansfield amplifies disruptions in the story by introducing arrhythmia in the quotidian sounds that are most easily defined as noise. For example, when Robert leaves the room with his wife's shawl, he exits, 'banging the door' (CW2, p. 200). There is also a regular return to the sounds of measured time, the 'clock that struck the hours at the half-hours' (CW2, p. 200). These sounds have a measurable and rational but irregular rhythmic quality, striking an incremental number on the hour but alternating with a single chime on the half-hour. Mansfield, however, returns to the weight of the molossus in her description of the event: 'A clock struck' (CW2, p. 205).

Mansfield expands her rhythmic experiment in the sounds that Robert hears while on his walk. When he passes women doing their laundry in a nearby stream, Mansfield writes, 'two old hags were beating linen. As he passed them they squatted back on their haunches stared and then "A-hak-kak-kak" with the slap, slap, of the stone on the linen sounded after him' (CW2, p. 205). There are, in fact, several tonal and rhythmic effects that Mansfield achieves: poetically, there is the assonant onomatopoeia of the women's labour, 'a-hak-hak-hak', that is translated into a more conventional sound in the spondaic 'slap, slap'. Musically, it adds another level of rhythmic complexity as Mansfield scores a pick-up beat[23] with the 'a', followed by a triple metre in the 'hak-hak-hak' and then switches to the duple metre in the 'slap, slap'. The disruptive rhythms align with what Murry would later assert: 'there is no *order* in modern experience, because there is no accepted principle of order'.[24] Rydstrand explains its 'rhythmic modernism': ' "The Man Without a Temperament" explores the interruption of ordinary rhythm [and . . .] brings to the fore Mansfield's ongoing fascination with arrhythmia – with pathological or malign rhythms.'[25] If Robert can briefly escape the sounds of his wife's illness, he cannot escape the echo of those rhythms on his walk.

In addition to Mansfield's use of arrhythmic noises, she also emphasises an element that is the most revolutionary and most commonplace in twentieth-century music, the lack of tonality that expanded traditional definitions of music. Jacques Attali writes, 'Since the abandonment of tonality, there has been no criterion for truth or common reference for those who compose and those who hear.'[26] When Mansfield adds the sound of the lift, ' "hoo-e-zip-zoo-oo!" ', she combines both the elevator's arrhythmia and dissonant tonality (CW2, p. 199). Until that point, she focuses her descriptions on unvoiced communications of the guests at the villa: 'a foreign little shrug' and the wave of 'an understanding biscuit'. The intrusion of the industrial is accomplished with a few syllables, each one signifying a sound of varying duration and colour until the final cadence, 'The iron cage clanged open' (CW2, p. 199).

After his walk, Robert wants to return to the room with his coughing wife: 'She sat down on one of the red plush chairs while he rang and rang, and then, getting no answer, kept his finger on the bell' (CW2, p. 206). The dominance of noise disturbs the peace with a constant grating pitch which upsets everyone. The General starts to caw, and 'a Topknot darts out with one hand to her ear' and shouts for the manager, whose name is similarly shrill-sounding: ' "Mr. Queet! Mr. Queet!" ' (CW2, p. 206). While, for Robert, holding down the elevator call bell expresses impatience, it incites others to join in a dissonant chorus. By the next time Robert wants to use the lift, someone at the villa has disconnected the call bell, and the manager apologises with feigned ignorance: ' "I'm sorry the bell won't ring, it's out of order. I can't think what's happened" ' (CW2, p. 207).

There are intrusive noises that are more difficult to control. Mansfield includes two insect metaphors in the story: first, she describes 'The black insects [that] "zoom-zoomed" ' against the 'open, motionless' flowers outside the villa's dining room that give an image of the larger world (CW2, p. 203). These pests are fast and loud with an audible, repetitive sound. As Mansfield brings the story to its conclusion, she shifts to a single mosquito inside the shroud-like netting that covers Jinnie's bed. If the sound from the elevator, with its arc from disturbing to alarming to unnaturally silent, exemplifies Jinnie's condition and foreshadows her death, Mansfield's language gives the mosquito its own musicality in the final measures of the story: when Jinnie wakes Robert, she tells him, 'I can hear him singing' (CW2, p. 209). This droning sound alternates with silences, first as Robert 'hovers' and then when he kills the insect. That death is also without sound and recalls Emily Dickinson's fly, whose buzzing foretells the 'Stillness in the Room / [. . . and] the Stillness in the Air'.[27] The exact moment, however, is marked when Robert declares, ' "got him" ', and acknowledges that he was ' "a juicy one" ' (CW2, p. 209). The fly, like a clock, may be an often used image, but unlike the clock, its sound repeats and finally ends unpredictably, like the mortality it portends.

With Mansfield's attention to the tonal range from harmony to dissonance, her ending produces varied readings. Robert's final word, ' "Rot" ', leaves readers divided as to the grammatical meaning of the word: Murry told Antony Alpers that he thought Salesby's character is 'drawn with loving admiration';[28] Pamela Dunbar contends that Salesby's final word 'is a terse command to his wife – something in direct contradiction to his apparent gentleness'.[29] Rydstrand focuses on its modernist

> polysemy for its emotional complexity [. . .] In the popular vernacular of the day, he has described her qualms as nonsense, while more literally, he uses the verb in its imperative form, thus encapsulating the ambivalence he has been displaying throughout the story.[30]

However one opts to interpret the ending, one must factor in that Robert's final word comes after Jinnie turns his ring. While Robert might see supporting his wife as the dutiful action of a just man, Jinnie asserts a power over his ring of Gyges, the mythical ring that not only empowers one with invisibility but tests one's character in the process. Mansfield's language does what music cannot: it encompasses both visibility and invisibility, compassion and apathy, bonding and disruption.

Inspired by a new vision of sound, Mansfield in 'The Man Without a Temperament' fulfils her earlier vision of art. Mansfield knew the effect of the changes in modern music, in those 'strange Macdowell, Debussy chords', or in the music for the Ballets Russes that overturned the conventional popular music of the West End (*Letters* 1, p. 80).[31] Jacques Attali sums up its power:

> Music is prophecy. Its styles and economic organization are ahead of the rest of society because it explores, much faster than material reality can, the entire range of possibilities in a given code. It makes audible the new world that will gradually become visible, that will impose itself and regulate the order of things; it is not only the image of things, but the transcending of the everyday, the herald of the future.[32]

Mansfield understood that transcending the quotidian in writing meant demanding of herself a higher level of concentration to avoid what she referred to as 'so many "false starts" ' (*Notebooks* 2, p. 137). In attending to the music, the rhythms, the silences and the noise in her writing, she kept to her goal, her 'strange ambition [. . . to] Revolutionise and revive the art of elocution – – – take it to its proper plane [. . .] the side of *art*'. She goes on to explain her desire 'to study *tone* effects in the voice [. . .] and express in the voice and face and atmosphere all that you say. *Tone* should be my secret – each word a variety of tone' (*Letters* 1, p. 84). She did not want her art to be routine, like the practice sessions of musicians she heard through her walls: 'Above me a woman is practicing the drum – not an inspiring instrument. It sounds like the growling of some colossal dog, and I know I shall have dreadful nightmares' (*Letters* 1, p. 62). Instead, she wanted her writing to always be 'in the middle of the note' as she had 'begun to play' (*Notebooks* 2, p. 137). 'The Man Without a Temperament' is a performance piece, much like the sole manuscript she sent to Murry: 'The MSS. I send is positively my only copy. I cannot possibly repeat it. May I beg you to see that it is not lost?' (*Letters* 3, p. 174). Mansfield's willingness to post the lone copy of her manuscript can be read as either naïve trust in the international mail, or her faith in both the risk and reward of life itself. Her musical experiments in the story take the combination of language, music and rhythm to its proper plane, reflecting and also predicting the democracy of sounds in twentieth-century music. Her temperament captures the musician's knowledge that 'I possess the power of holding people' (*Letters* 1, p. 84).

Notes

1. Kate Kennedy, 'Sight-reading Katherine Mansfield', originally published in *Landfall* (Otago: Otago University Press, 2010). The quotation here is from a pdf copy supplied by the author, p. 1.
2. Gerri Kimber, *Katherine Mansfield: The Early Years* (Edinburgh: Edinburgh University Press, 2016), p. 95.
3. Kathleen Jones, *Katherine Mansfield: The Story-Teller* (Edinburgh: Edinburgh University Press, 2010), p. 58.
4. Claire Tomalin, *Katherine Mansfield: A Secret Life* (New York: Knopf, 1988), p. 42.
5. Antony Alpers, *The Life of Katherine Mansfield* (New York: Viking Press, 1980), p. 149. While it is unclear, Mansfield may have either sold or abandoned the piano as she and Murry moved back to London in November 1912, when they took a one-room flat in Chancery Lane due to the financial difficulties they faced because of Stephen Swift.
6. Helen Rydstrand, *Rhythmic Modernism* (New York: Bloomsbury Academic, 2019), p. 112.
7. Mansfield was not rigid about spelling and punctuation in her private writing, and the quotations reflect that.
8. Bach did not reveal his tuning system; the harpsichordist Lillian Gordis explains, Bach 'found a system that works [. . .] He doesn't give you the answer. He doesn't write it out for you. He gives you a huge corpus of music and he's like "Well, I have the answer."' *Now Hear This: The Riddle of Bach*, Harry Lyndi, dir. [Arcos Film, 2019], 38:01–40:51.
9. The term for the triple accented foot is molossus. Mansfield employs the device regularly: see 'Ole Underwood' (CW1, p. 321), 'Jangling Memory' (CW3, p. 84) and 'Marriage à la Mode' (CW2, p. 337).
10. Jill Johnston, 'There Is No Silence Now', in *John Cage*, ed. by Richard Kostelanetz (New York: Praeger, 1970), p. 146. Johnston was the dance critic for the trend-setting weekly, *The Village Voice*.
11. Johnston, p. 146.

12. Richard Kostelanetz, 'Inferential Art', in *John Cage*, pp. 107-8.
13. *Rhythm* publicised the Ballets Russes in both reviews (see 2: 6, p. 57ff.) and images (see Anne Estelle Rice's drawing of the Ballets Russes in 2: 7, p. 84).
14. Claire Davison, 'Foreword', in Gerri Kimber, *Katherine Mansfield and the Art of the Short Story* (New York: Palgrave, 2015), p. ix.
15. David Novak, 'Noise', in *Keywords in Sound*, ed. by David Novak and Matt Sakakeeny (Durham, NC: Duke University Press, 2015), p. 125.
16. Virginia Woolf, 'Kew Gardens', in *The Complete Shorter Fiction*, ed. by Susan Dick (New York: Harcourt, 1989), p. 95.
17. Kostelanetz, The Future of Music – Credo', in *John Cage*, p. 54.
18. Luigi Russolo, *The Art of Noises*, trans. by Robert Filliou (New York: Something Else, 1967), p. 9.
19. Aimee Gasston, 'Katherine Mansfield, Cannibal', in *Katherine Mansfield and the (Post) colonial*, ed. by Janet Wilson, Gerri Kimber and Delia da Sousa Correa (Edinburgh: Edinburgh University Press, 2013), p. 19.
20. 'Aims and Ideals', in *Rhythm*, 1: 1 (1911), p. 36.
21. Jacques Attali, *Noise: The Political Economy of Music*, trans. by Brian Massumi (Minneapolis: University of Minnesota Press, 1985), p. 112.
22. Helen Rydstrand, 'Ordinary Discordance: Katherine Mansfield and the First World War', in *Katherine Mansfield and World War One*, ed. by Gerri Kimber, Delia da Sousa Correa and Todd Martin (Edinburgh: Edinburgh University Press, 2014), p. 56.
23. The pick-up beat or upbeat, as it is commonly referred to, is one or more unaccented notes that lead into the accented note of the next measure. Some band leaders indicate this as 'and a' before counting out 'one, two three'. A more technical but equally precise term is anacrusis.
24. John Middleton Murry, 'The "Classical Revival" ', in *Defending Romanticism*, ed. by Malcolm Woodfield (Bedminster: Bristol Press, 1989), p. 179.
25. Rydstrand, *Rhythmic Modernism*, p. 140.
26. Attali, p. 113.
27. Emily Dickinson, '591', in *The Poems of Emily Dickinson*, ed. by R. W. Franklin (Cambridge, MA: Belknap Press, 1999), p. 265.
28. Alpers, p. 305n.
29. Pamela Dunbar, *Radical Mansfield* (London: Macmillan, 1997), p. 126.
30. Rydstrand, *Rhythmic Modernism*, p. 140.
31. See Mansfield's reference to Harold Fraser-Simson's *Maid of the Mountains* in 'Marriage à la Mode', CW2, p. 335.
32. Attali, p. 11.

Refrigeration, 'Bliss' and the Modernist World Order of Imperial Culture

Enda Duffy and Maurizia Boscagli

On 15 February 1882 a clipper, the *Dunedin*, sailed from Port Chalmers, New Zealand, carrying a frozen cargo of 4,331 sheep and 598 lambs, all sown in calico sacks, 22 pig carcasses, 246 kegs of butter, hare, pheasant, turkey and chicken, and 2,226 sheep tongues. When it arrived in London ninety-eight days later, it became the first ship ever to carry a refrigerated cargo successfully across the world's oceans. There had been mishaps: 10,000 sheep had originally been slaughtered, but before the sailing the refrigerator apparatus crankshaft broke and reloading was needed. The Bell–Coleman compression system, which cooled the entire hold to 40 degrees Fahrenheit below the local temperature, worked well in New Zealand but was strained in the tropics: the *Dunedin*'s captain, entering the hold to cut air holes, almost died of exposure. Yet when the New Zealand and Australian Land Company's profit on the voyage proved to be £4,700, it at once converted a second ship (both had originally carried emigrants to New Zealand). The modern economic prosperity of New Zealand as an industrial-scale supplier of food to Britain, which continued for over eighty years, was launched. Furthermore, the specific version of colonial relation to Britain granted New Zealand – its version of 'settler colonialism' – was thoroughly connected to its role in Britain's food-supply chain. The *Dunedin*'s voyage marked a turning-point in New Zealand's value as colony to the British Empire, in the colony's economic vitality, and in the history of global trade and of the reorganisation of cheap global food supplies. Possibly even more than the 1840 Waitangi Treaty between the British Crown and Māori chiefs, or the assumption of dominion status in 1907,[1] the *Dunedin* announced New Zealand's modern place not only in the British Empire, but in the world supply system.

What does the availability of New Zealand lamb in Britain since 1882 have to do with the quality of the short stories published in London by New Zealander Katherine Mansfield in the small volume *Bliss and Other Stories* in 1920? If we are to historicise the uniqueness of Mansfield's literary achievement fully, the answer is: everything. If we believe, as has been said, that culture is what will remain when all else about a society and social order has been forgotten, then it behoves us as evaluators of the specific power of Mansfield's work to comprehend not only how it was sparked by that specific place, New Zealand at the close of the nineteenth century (where the writer was born Kathleen Mansfield Beauchamp in 1888), but how it represented not merely that place, but the network of global relations of power, demand and profit that enabled it and that it needed to function successfully. What, then, were the specific structural underpinnings enabling the conditions of New Zealand society as the young Mansfield experienced them, and how did she represent them in her works, wherever they were set? Did she import these structures into the perceptual apparatuses of her stories – even, and especially, into her New Zealand stories, but also into those set in Germany, Paris or London itself? It is common to speak of Mansfield as a writer who never forgot that as a student newly arrived in London, she was sneered at as 'the little colonial'; here we want to insist that it would be a mistake merely to imagine that this provided her with an off-kilter, alienated perspective that granted her modernism its specific flavour of ennui, and that gave her extra perceptiveness on the matter of race-based exploitation, even if these turn out to be true. Rather, a materialist reading of Mansfield's stories as (post-)colonial texts, one that reads her as a new voice in world literature, demands that we recognise in her modernist innovations structures of perception, of affect, of consciousness and of representation that allegorise, homologise or otherwise replicate the political and economic structures out of which she came and within which she found her audience. This goal of a total view of Mansfield's post-colonial modernism is the horizon at which we hope to pitch this essay.

There is by now a considerable body of critical work on Mansfield and colonialism, culminating in *Katherine Mansfield and the (Post-)colonial*, edited by Janet Wilson, Gerri Kimber and Delia da Sousa Correa in 2013.[2] This work engages with the politics of Mansfield's prose in a series of registers. The first grapples with the implications of what we might call the biographical presumption: the claim that Mansfield's birth and upbringing in a British colony increase the depth of her insight into colonialism and its power structures. First, much work considers her attitude to the Māori, the inhabitants of New Zealand displaced by the European colonists. Essays in this register refer to Mansfield's youthful diary accounts of a trip to Urewera country in the North Island,[3] home to the Tuhoe, whom one critic calls 'the Māori peoples with the fiercest and most sustained resistance to the white man and civilization'.[4] They turn to such stories as 'How Pearl Button Was Kidnapped', where the encounter with racial others is the focus. Second, Mansfield's insight into the 'settler colonial' culture of Anglo New Zealand[5] is canvassed: here, critics might turn to 'The Woman in the Store' or 'The Garden Party' to consider the treatment of the different conditions of settler life. In the next register, the contrast between Mansfield's own 'settler colonial' youth in New Zealand and her cosmopolitan, bohemian, heart-of-empire career in London is cast as the basis for her modernist ambivalence. In more complex accounts, this doubleness of her identity, and, presumably of her consciousness, is then laid over the hybridity which is taken to characterise settler–native relations in the colony. Mansfield's double-consciousness, enabled by the rift between her colonial origins and her cosmopolitan success, is seen as making her a writer whose modernist *ostranenie* (defamiliarisation) deconstructs the colonist–native binary. Mansfield's modernist style, rather than any trace of authorial intentionality, is thereby decoded as the index of the author's anti-colonial deconstruction of binaries. (Notably, she is almost invariably cast by critics as implicitly anti-colonial: almost no one accuses her work of being in any sense imperialist, and few discuss how her anti-colonial inclinations compare with liberal doctrines of her day.)[6] This work richly illuminates the origins of the intricate strangeness inherent in many of Mansfield's stories, and the development of her own political consciousness. Yet they remain determinedly attuned to culture: working to demonstrate the power of a particularly brilliant instance of modernist high culture (Mansfield's stories), they risk relinquishing any critique of the reality (colonialism) in its economic, territorial and power-asserting aspects that gave licence to such readings in the first place. In this essay, we will consider how colonialism's basic economic aims and effects insinuate themselves into just one Mansfield story and the worldview it promulgates.

This recourse to a foundational materialist reading inevitably invokes a pivotal and controversial essay of 1986, Fredric Jameson's manifesto for post-colonial literary criticism and a strong call for a totalising materialist critique, 'Third World Literature in the Era of Multinational Capitalism'.[7] This text was critiqued by, among others, Aijaz Ahmad,[8] for foisting upon post-colonial literatures from diverse cultures a single global cultural imperative: to represent, more than the literature of any western nation ever could, the political realities of the subaltern nation from which it came. Yet the heated critiques of its globalist (not to say post-modern, soft imperialist) decree must not blind us to how Jameson's more crucial task in this ground-breaking work is to advance allegory, or homology, as the vocation of any literature worthy of a political vocation, regardless of origin. He deployed a logic adapted from Lukács's essay 'Reification and the Consciousness of the Proletariat',[9] to claim that the colonial writer, having experienced imperial oppression, could be more conscious than could her western, cosmopolitan counterpart of the homology between a represented scene of a family, a couple or a community, and the broader workings of not merely national, but planetary politics and power distributions. Seldom has the totalising theorem – the suggestion that a literary work's greatness comes from its power to suggest the sum total of power relations informing it – been enunciated more forcefully. Together with his concept of 'the political unconscious',[10] which demolishes the lingering backward glance at authorial intent and instead claims that the literary work, possibly despite its author's intentions, will represent in its form the power structure of both its nation and the global power networks in which the nation functions, and his essays (particularly 'Modernism and Imperialism'), later gathered in *The Modernist Papers*,[11] Jameson called, at the outset of post-colonial criticism, for a materialist post-colonial critique whose horizon – no matter how local the text being read – would be the globe itself, and its organisation by world economic interests. For this task, of always reading the text in the final instance with the horizon of global economic forces in view, he deemed necessary the strong critical weapon of allegorical interpretation.

The expansion of post-colonial literary criticism since has also resulted in a radical rethinking of the formerly monolithic 'modernism' as a much more dispersed collection of localised modernisation initiatives; one spectacular example is Susan Stanford Friedman's *Planetary Modernisms*.[12] The concept 'colonialism' too has increasingly been applied to areas other than ex-colonies, including the west itself and its endocolonisations. Less investigated, especially by scholars of culture, are the many different versions of colonial and post-colonial power which have been exercised throughout modern economic and political geohistory. Colonial regimes differed because of imperial methods, the state of politics in the imperial metropolis, and national realpolitik: Britain's colonial rule in Nigeria, for example, with a 'Governor's Advisory Council' that, after 1914, admitted six African members, differed from that of Italy's occupation of Abyssinia after the invasion of 1935, or Belgium's '*bula matari*' ('break rocks')[13] post-1908 regime in the Belgian Congo. They differed also because of different timescales of invasion, conquest and rule: British control of South Africa and what is now Zimbabwe after the Boer War, for example, was different to its control of New Zealand, even if both were part of the British Empire. These differences are acknowledged under such terms as 'direct rule' and 'settler colonialism', the (apparently) softer application of imperial might implied by 'spheres of influence', or, after the western powers' takeover of Ottoman territory after World War I, the 'mandate system'. To consider the reasons for these differences will lead us to question why the global imperial system reached its zenith around 1890, and why it had crumbled – again, in a multitude of ways – by about 1960. We need to be specific about the differences between the lived conditions experienced under different colonial regimes if we as critics are to account for varieties of (post-)colonial cultural expression. To limn the politics of any (post-)colonial literary text, we must grasp the specificity of the imperial regime out of which it came.

Hence, in reading 'Bliss', refrigeration. The ability to supply Britain efficiently with abundant lamb is key to the specific condition of the colonial regime which existed in New Zealand at the turn of the twentieth century. New Zealand mattered to British imperial prosperity, first, as a site to which considerable numbers of people who were surplus to the requirements of Industrial Revolution capitalism in Britain could emigrate: it was part of the 'spatial fix' which David Harvey[14] describes as a key reason why nineteenth-century western capitalism could overcome its successive crises. By the dawn of the new century, however, further possibilities for that spatial fix were growing limited: Halford Mackinder's essay, 'The Geographical Pivot of History'[15] of 1904, pointed out that at that moment, in the planet's history, a limit-point had been reached: the whole world had now been mapped, and there was now no unknown territory to conquer. Not long before, for the British settlers in New Zealand, all available land had likewise been taken. This, in itself, meant that, in the realm of culture, the dreams of exotic 'other spaces' that had sustained fervid imperial fantasies, and the motif of adventure which had portrayed marching into such places as the acme of western masculine endeavour, were now radically undercut and had to revamp themselves. (The work of Jules Verne in France, of Henry Rider Haggard[16] in Britain and of Edgar Rice Burroughs[17] in the USA exemplifies a male cultural hysteria regarding this development.) At the same time, the world's soil was being re-evaluated as a resource to be exploited in a massive global reorganisation of the food supply, mainly to feed the new urban bourgeoisie of the sprawling cities and new suburbs of Europe and the US. As early as 1859 the physicist Justus von Liebig had written of how the land of Europe was being leached of nutrients by over-intensive farming,[18] nutrients which were being replenished by guano imported from Peru. The sugar cane plantations of the Caribbean, the pampas of South America, the wheat-lands of the North American Midwest and eastern Europe, the banana plantations of Central America, and the cattle and sheep ranches of Australia and New Zealand: in all of these sites, industrial-scale agriculture was imposed, in conjunction with the facilities for the movement of sugar, grain and meat by rail and ship over planetary distances. In New Zealand's case, 'settler colonialism' involved the large-scale displacement of the Māori to enable agriculture on this scale as the basis of the colony's prosperity. In a global perspective, this was a new phase of large-scale planetary-resource extraction, put in place to provide the nutrition necessary to sustain the urban armies of the western industrial workforce and the cadres of the state and financial bureaucracies – the western working and middle classes.[19] If the imperial endeavour of post-Enlightenment western modernity is thought of as the western project for the exploitation of the whole planet (in the era of the Anthropocene or 'capitalocine'),[20] then, like the other stages of modern imperial resource extraction, from the 'gold rushes' of California and Australia to the establishment of the grand oil companies, Standard Oil in 1870, the Anglo-Persian Oil Company (now British Petroleum) in 1908, and Royal Dutch Petroleum's merger with Shell in 1907, this was one component of a newly ruthless programme of planetary energy-sourcing, the world-wide capture of resources convertible to energy. (Joseph Conrad, former merchant seaman, was writing of the trade in ivory in *Heart of Darkness* (1899), and of that in silver in *Nostromo* (1904), in the same period: glamorous allegories, perhaps, for foodstuffs and for oil.)

Trade, as commercial activity, and colonialism, as political regime, entered at this moment a new level of efficient alignment, facilitating larger-scale transfers of wealth and resources. The *Dunedin*'s pioneering use of refrigeration in a cargo ship's hold placed New Zealand at the forefront of the global adoption of new technology to make such transnational transfers feasible on a hitherto unimaginable scale. Refrigeration, by freezing the perishable cargo, overcame the problem of time as duration. A notable example of modern 'time–space compression', theorised by Paul Virilio and David Harvey, among others, was achieved.[21] Some of the key technological advances of the turn of the twentieth century, such as the motor car and aeroplane, conquered space and compressed time through speed; refrigeration, instead, suspended time's effects upon the commodity shipped for the duration of the voyage. The time of transport, literally, now did not matter: it was lost, negated, overcome. It was not stopped, but its effects were nullified. If this suspension, this modern magic of suspending the effects of time, can be considered the secret of the success of the New Zealand agricultural, food-exporting colonial and neo-colonial economy for the following ninety years, then we can explore how this crucial elision of time's effects infiltrated every aspect of colonial culture. Britain – or 'home', as it was often referred to by upper-class New Zealanders – was far away and took a long time to reach (in a journey that meant passing through a series of the new time zones adopted after the International Meridian Conference of 1884).[22] If, however, the time of that voyage, in the case of the commodity which supplied the colony's wealth in exchange for the energy source it delivered to the centre of empire, could effectively be nullified, then the wealth itself not only further accrued the abstraction that is the basic quality of all money, but also was further abstracted since its source was made possible by the technological conquering of time.

It is one thing to sketch this nexus of colonialism, capital, technology, global food supplies, wealth flows and energy transfers in the case of late nineteenth-century New Zealand; it is another to ask how this is refracted in the fictions of Katherine Mansfield. To put it another way, how, when most of the lived realities of late colonial New Zealand experience will be forgotten, will Mansfield's stories continue to signify the realities out of which the author developed her particular style of representation? For it is in that style, rather than in any mere hints about colonial realities tracked down and read symptomatically, that are imprinted the structural effects of New Zealand's specific colonial role in the late imperial capitalocene. When we reread Mansfield's stories keeping in mind all that ship refrigeration represents, we in fact find everywhere the expression of its effects.

Specifically, the new model of industrial-scale agriculture being practised in New Zealand, based on the mass export of frozen food to the imperial centre, represented a new relation to nature for the colonial hinterland. Likewise, a few decades later, we find this uncanny version of nature being represented, and experimented with, in Mansfield's texts. Second, as food itself, in its new transportability across the globe, becomes not only the basis for New Zealand's *raison d'être* in the imperial world order, to which the inhabitants of the territory offered obeisance, but also a cypher in the global economy of the energy needed for growth, especially economic growth, then the relation to food also alters. Aptly, the representation of food and its meanings turns out to be up for grabs in story after story of Katherine Mansfield. Third, as the reworking of the idea of nature, and the new relation to food, are both made possible by a technological innovation which effectively conquers time, it turns out that time too is literally shattered and recomposed in

many of Mansfield's stories. There is, of course, a whole constellation
of effects, especially political ones, resulting from the colonial–imperial
power regime that are not captured in this trio, and that undoubtedly
leave their imprints upon the lineaments of Mansfield's prose. Many of
these, however, exist in every colony. It is the specific constellation of
effects operating in the New Zealand colonial context around 1900 that
we must attend to here, and these, this essay claims, find their homolo-
gies in Mansfield's work in the first instance at the level of content and
its representation, but in the final instance, at the level of style. Thus
this historicising and world-political reading of Mansfield can, perhaps
paradoxically, illuminate what is unique and individual to her: the specific strategies of modernist defamiliarisation (to use Bakhtin's phrase)
which characterise her prose.

* * *

If we turn to the first edition of Mansfield's *Bliss and Other Stories* and open
it at its centre, we come upon the story 'Psychology'. If we consider this
story in the light of the three 'theatres of representation' just outlined,
our three topoi which, this paper claims, have been altered for the New
Zealand writer because of how the New Zealand late colonial situation
has radically recast them – nature itself, the significance of food, and
the immense predictability of the progress of time – then 'Psychology',
we realise at once, radically recasts each of them. In 'Psychology' the sil-
liest and most incidental of food is accorded an intense attention almost
to caricature: ' "Do you realize how good it is?" she implored. "Eat it
imaginatively. Roll your eyes if you can taste it on the breath." '[23] At a key
moment, as we shall see, there is also a significant turn to the question
of freshness, and withering, as the indices of nature's power. However,
it is *time* – time as unnervingly elastic, taut, tense and stretched-to-its-
limit medium – that laps at the plot's margins, is mentioned constantly
and obsessively, and is toyed with by both the story's characters and the
text's structure. 'Psychology' is a tale that, like the best lyric poems from
Keats to Dickinson to Wallace Stevens, often seems to want to be about
almost nothing, to be as light as air. This urge towards abstraction,
which would be achieved in the post-World War II minimalist painting
of Agnes Martin or the plays of Samuel Beckett, is incipient in the works
of high modernism. In this tendency, as displayed in 'Psychology', *time* is
enlisted as an ally, a medium that can be stretched, drawn out, twanged
(like Miss Douce's elastic garter in the 'Sirens' hotel scene in Joyce's
Ulysses),[24] which then, when released, flies back into something (time-)
less, almost not-there. Just as refrigeration would kill time to create the
basis for New Zealand's prosperity, in 'Psychology' time gets battered,

BLISS

AND OTHER STORIES

BY KATHERINE

MANSFIELD

LONDON : CONSTABLE
& COMPANY LIMITED

Fig. 1 Inside title page of the first edition of *Bliss and Other Stories*, 1920.
Cushing Library, J. Lawrence Mitchell Collection.

its dilations and compressions cancelling each other out, until it is nullified. Time, in this story, is not allowed to pass. The consolation, as in the case of the New Zealand money-for-energy voyage, is that this compression will repeat itself.

'Psychology' is therefore not so much a story awash in time imagery as it is a story of the abduction of time. Time theft is its topic, propelling its plot, impelling its style. The story, utterly simple, tells of an afternoon visit of an unnamed man to an unnamed woman in her flat. Together they feast on tea and cake, contemplate 'the thrilling quality of their friendship' (p. 146), and discuss the psychological turn in contemporary fiction. He leaves, the moment passes; the woman is visited by, and refuses entry to, an old, and elderly, friend. When 'he', the male protagonist, first arrives, his slowness, his promiscuous wasting or expenditure of time, becomes the chief interest, the strangeness we are initially invited to remark upon:

> He laid aside his coat and hat gently, lingeringly, as though he had time and to spare for everything, or as though he were taking leave of them forever and came over to the fire and held out his hands to the quick, leaping flame. (p. 144)

The flame is 'quick', the visitor notably languorous. While this is the studied languor of modern ennui and boredom, in the manner of T. S. Eliot's 'In the room the women come and go / Talking of Michelangelo',[25] it is also contested here, countered by a regimen of nervy busy-ness on the part of his host. The story is ostensibly an account of a passionate encounter foregone, a possible sexual connection unrealised and unachieved because of . . . over-politeness, indecision, a failure of 'nerve'? In this scenario, the visitor's slowness, his desire to dawdle, communicates his hint that he wishes to savour a deeper experience, a more intense, prolonged encounter with all that is suggested by the quick flame.[26] Moments after, however, this apparently easeful dilation of time contracts, as the woman 'buys time' now, by making tea:

> And yet she couldn't hurry. She could almost have cried 'Give me time'. She must have time in which to grow calm. She wanted time in which to free herself from all these familiar things with which she lived so vividly. (p. 146)

For her, it appears, extra time will enable disengagement from 'things with which she lived so vividly'; for him, in their subsequent conversation, it emerges that time is a flux in which 'I don't know the names of things a bit – trees and so on – and I never notice places or furniture or what people look like' (p. 148). For him, the simile of the journey in which time is cancelled is specifically invoked: 'He was like a man in a train who wakes up to find that he has arrived already at the journey's end' (p. 148). His success as a novelist, and proponent of 'psychology', is based on the same logic as that which underpins the success of New Zealand's model of the colonial economy: the ability to cancel out the journey, to overcome the distance, as long as the freshness is delivered at the end. For her, however, this brittle talk is a frustrating concealment which merely leaves her uncertain about the efficacy of this suspended time:

> They were off and all was as usual. But was it? Weren't they just a little too quick, too prompt with their replies, too ready to talk each other up? . . . His heart beat, her cheek burned and the stupid thing was she had not discovered exactly where they were or what was happening. She hadn't time to glance back. (p. 149)

Once time is suspended, she seems, with panicked awareness, to grasp, you cannot buy it back. Therefore, this is a story of a short duration (Bergson's *durée*)[27] of lost time, or lost opportunity in time.

'Psychology' is so saturated with time references, from the clock that 'struck six merry little pings' to the 'smile that undid them, it had lasted so long' (p. 151), that it is unquestionably a story about modern, clock-parcelled time, and how the little of it that the modern person has might be stretched and snapped to make possible an authentic moment. That kind of moment is named here as 'the boundless, questioning dark' (p. 149) – apparently, a time region outside of clock time. With its clock, its visit fitted into a schedule, its endless busyness, its non-stop sense of rush, its notation of each of the characters' nervous attempts to stretch out, if only slightly, the short time available, it is supremely modern. Both characters are at once bored ('And he was so utterly bored' [p. 151]), and champing at the bit of the time they have. The keywords of this tale may be 'Quickly! Quickly!' (p. 149). These so-modern people 'have no time'. In this sense, it might be asked, is this not a story about the modern dilemmas of time in general? How can it function, therefore, as a very distant reflection, homology or allegory, of the way in which the refrigerated cargo ship conquered time and launched the great stage of New Zealand's late colonial prosperity? The answer: the overcoming through technology of the time imposed by distance in late imperial trade was certainly just one aspect of an across-the-board and transglobal reordering of time, and its increased abstraction, that took place in this period. Refrigeration's overcoming of time's effects in order to nullify colonial distance was one aspect of a revamping of time's significance that also led, for example, to the institution of the worker's eight-hour day, to the mass popularity (with a boost from the need to synchronise the fatal 'over-the-top' moment in World War I battles) of the modern wristwatch, and eventually to the inauguration, in 1982, of Air New Zealand flights from Auckland to London via Papeete and Los Angeles, a journey that could now be measured in hours rather than days. Philosophers of the day, especially Henri Bergson in such works as *Matter and Memory* (1896),[28] were also adducing new philosophical approaches to time. To separate out the overcoming of time's effects in the colonial food trade is to prioritise the material and the economic as primary determinants. Yet the story 'Psychology' makes clear that, while it is, in the best manner of bourgeois discretion, coy about who has paid for the cakes and the rent on the dramatist's flat, it is supremely interested in the *material* and its nature as the possible victim of the regime of time. (In many other stories Mansfield shows herself to be the most class-conscious of the modernists, especially in such servants–master tales as 'The Life of Ma Parker'. She may be modernism's supreme class warrior, her class-consciousness one reason for the suspicion she garnered from snobbish modernists such as D. H. Lawrence.[29]) This interest in time's effects on matter makes its appearance in 'Psychology', first, aptly, in terms of food, and then, poignantly, in terms of nature itself – represented by an organic nature that is no longer fresh: a bunch of wilted flowers.

The counterpoint to Mansfield's representation of modern time is found in the work of T. S. Eliot ('And indeed, there will be a time to wonder / Do I dare?'),[30] yet her nervy, stressed-for-time modernist time-keeping strikes one as much more modern than his, which reads as marching to the cadences of an elegy for cyclical, repetitive, not to say epic and other superseded timescales. Similarly, her literary counterpoint on the matter of food is James Joyce, whose paragraph-length description of every item of food and drink available for the dinner in 'The Dead' is matched by the minute attention to food, flavours and digestion throughout *Ulysses*, culminating in Bloom's burgundy and gorgonzola cheese lunch in 'Lestrygonians'.[31] Yet, here again, Mansfield seems more completely the modern artist: whereas for Joyce the allure of food emerges against a background of the earlier Irish reality of food shortage (his food writing may be haunted by the social memory of the 1845–9 Irish Famine, itself an effect of colonial food production regimes in transition), Mansfield's food world is one in which food consumption, or the thought of it, is invariably imbued with a theatrical or spectacular quality, as in a play or an advertisement. This advertisement mode of presenting food appears even in the story 'Pictures', which follows 'Psychology' in *Bliss and Other Stories*; in this tale of an out-of-work woman who wanders the streets of London all day without the means to buy a meal, when she awakens hungry we are told that, as if she were watching it in film, 'A pageant of Good Hot Dinners passed across the ceiling, each of them accompanied by a bottle of Nourishing Stout' (p. 156). In 'Psychology', food is merely a matter of the delicacies served with afternoon tea, but it is served with an emphasis on longing so ostentatious that it reeks of how appetite is incited by an advertisement:

'Are you longing for tea?'
'No, not longing.'
'Well, I am.' (p. 145)

This advertising idiom (served with a dash of imperialist racism, when the visitor tells his host that 'You're a perfect little Chinee' [p. 147]) is accentuated with a relapse into an almost pornographic food focus:

Carefully she cut the cake into thick little wads as she reached across for a piece. 'Do you realize how good it is?' she implored. 'Eat it imaginatively. Roll your eyes if you can and taste it on the breath. It is not a sandwich from the hatter's bag – it's the kind of cake that might have been mentioned in the Book of Genesis. . . . And God said, 'Let there be cake. And God saw that it was good.' (p. 147)

The reader might assume that this intense desire on the part of the woman not just to eat her cake but to savour it, and have her visitor do likewise, is a simple transfer from sex to food (with a reminder of Eve and Adam added, in the reference to Genesis). Yet the food here is indeed wonderful,[32] an intense experience in itself, at least for the visitor: '"You needn't entreat me", said he. "Really you needn't. It's a queer thing, but I always do notice what I eat here and never anywhere else"' (p. 147). In Joyce's 'The Dead', when the succession of minor incidents is interrupted by the paragraph which enumerates every item of food lined up for the feast, the chief impression is of bourgeois self-satisfaction with food's plenitude, not unlike the feeling of the German villagers before their laden tables in the early Mansfield story, 'Frau Brechenmacher Attends a Wedding'. Here, however, in Mansfield's more wholly modernist work, the food, itself frivolous, becomes almost surreal. It is food, as in an advertisement, in close-up. The cake, in its 'thick little wads', is not simply sustenance, as the host notes (p. 147). Neither is it merely symbolic (of sex, for example). Furthermore, the attention given it is not quite ironic: the point is not that it is, in fact inferior or over-ostentatious. Rather, despite its arrival in the story with the advertisement-like language of longing, beseeching the guest to enjoy, it lands there – in very much the same way as Mrs Sheridan's masses of lilies are attended to in 'The Garden Party' – as a zone of intense sensuousness, a dream of a more perfect intensity. Those 'thick little wads', like the lilies for Laura in 'The Garden Party', are really all the heroine has. The rest of the story, circulating around this food offering, is stress, jumping up and down, not connecting, needing time.

Is it too much to see, behind those 'thick little wads', the thousands of sides of frozen lamb sewn into sacks in the hold of ship after ship leaving New Zealand for Britain, returning with the money from trade, the very trade that made the Beauchamps rich and which financed New Zealand as it transitioned from colony to 'Commonwealth status' as an independent nation? Perhaps. Yet if food is the actual material which supplies the colony's wealth, and if that food is the vast export *surplus*, the portion of the resource created that is massively excessive of the needs of the local population, then one can see how food needed to be imaginatively reconfigured in New Zealand (and global) culture. On the one hand, food is the earth's resource which, after air and water, supplies our most basic need – the need to live. On the other, food as exported wealth-generator is food abstracted, removed from any actual knowledge of its origins, and transformed into the most abstract element of modernity, money. In other words, food, the most basic satisfier of human needs, is commodified, and, as Marx devotes the magisterial Chapter I of *Das Kapital* to explaining, the commodity is, in modernity, the most mysterious and important version of matter of all. Industrial-scale agriculture that makes its fortune by exporting food across the globe is at once a species of resource extraction and the complete commodification of nature. Once that basic resource has, through the system of planetary late imperial global trade, had to cross the world in order for that commodification to occur, then this commodification is of a more complete and intense order still. For a writer whose own comfortable life as she grew up was built upon this activity, food itself, consumed even in the most intimate of social settings, begs to have its commodification noted, dissected, attended to.

In this attention, the trope of freshness is key. The glamour of the food's commodity form – its celebrated flavour – is in its freshness, which is what hides the fact that the work of extraction and production occurred far away. It is this apparent freshness that is enabled by refrigeration. Technologically enabled refrigeration, therefore, does not merely nullify time, in order to deliver an energy source that was extracted in the colony: by delivering the food in question apparently *fresh*, it supplies the allure of its commodification as well. When the female protagonist of 'Psychology' presents the tea and cake to her visitor in terms of the longing broadcast in advertising – presents it, that is, as intensely commodified – one can say that the unconscious awareness of intense commodification wrought by a global system of late imperial trade, arising from Mansfield's own closeness to that system arising from her New Zealand origins, inheres in the almost surreal version of sensuousness that Mansfield here, and in all the nutrition attention in her work, brings to food. In 'Psychology', those 'thick little wads' of cake must be flavourful; for the New Zealand colonial food trade enabled by refrigeration, the food must be fresh. Then, to prove beyond doubt that this sensuousness of the commodity is no substitute for a true sensuous connection between human beings, and indeed diverts them from it, 'Psychology' supplies at its close a stinging supplementary fable, in which a further failure of human warmth is signified, reproachfully, by organic matter that is no longer fresh: a bunch of withered violets.

The main story has not disputed the cake's sensuous flavour; it leaves it as a given, a kind of reverie for what might have been between the couple, since the experience of eating it does not allow them to connect. Their encounter alienates them more. In Marx's terms, this is a standard relation under capital: mediated by the commodity, it leaves the subjects alienated, in the very definition of reification. The story tells of a missed connection between alienated people over the frivolity of tea and cake. After the male visitor leaves, we are once again reminded of the manipulation of the time of modern ennui, in the brilliant, comic phrase: 'After a long time (or perhaps ten minutes)' (p. 154). Then the story of a potential connection is repeated with a second visitor, this time a woman, described as 'An elderly virgin, a pathetic creature' (p. 154), from whom the heroine usually accepted a 'bunch of slightly soiled-looking flowers' (p. 153). When this friend is told, with a lie, to go away, we read:

> 'I was just passing and I thought I'd leave you some violets'. She fumbled down among the ribs of a large old umbrella. 'I put them down here. Such a good place to keep flowers out of the wind. Here they are', she said, shaking out a little dead bunch. (p. 154)

The withered violets, ' "really nothing. Just a little thrippenny bunch" ' (p. 154) in their soiled state, their price (unlike the price of the cake) openly given, become the mark of an authentic effort to connect with another person – an effort deemed pathetic in the up-to-date, ever-fresh world in which the female protagonist moves. (Crushed violets had also featured as emblems of the pathos of inadequate love-links in Mansfield's early story 'In a Café'.) In case we miss any of this, the introduction of the umbrella as the storage place for the flowers adds, again, a surreal kick. The umbrella with its dead violets is, literally, surreal: we might be reminded of the most famous formula of all for a surrealist image, de Lautréamont's line from *The Songs of Maldoror* about 'A chance meeting of a sewing machine and an umbrella on a dissecting table'.[33] Or we might think of how Robinson Crusoe, in Defoe's novel of 1719, which might well be thought of as the paradigmatic origin fable of 'white settler' colonialism and the original modern novel of bourgeois life, celebrates as his greatest technological feat the construction of his very own umbrella. For us, reading the late colonial modernist Katherine Mansfield of two centuries later, the umbrella holding the withered flowers exists as a resounding image of the late colonial surreal, an image of the failure of freshness so estranging that it achieves a late modern pathos, a rush of human fellow-feeling that led the heroine to fold her arms around her friend 'more tenderly, more beautifully, [. . .] held by such a sweet pressure, and for so long' (p. 154). The heroine has lied, but she is still 'fearful of making a ripple in that boundless pool of quiet' (p. 154). The time test and the freshness test have both, for a few moments at any rate, been vanquished, and, by implication, been exposed as the impostors they are.

Is Mansfield, then, a modernist writer against empire, even in a story that apparently has no empire in it almost at all? In a sense, the key to the answer to this is contained in the story's title. 'Psychology' refers to what the two not-quite-lovers, over tea and cake, decide is to be the future direction of British fiction and drama: that is, literature will be valorised to the extent that it probes further and further into 'inner' life, using the tools and tactics of the new mind science, psychology. To the extent that the story itself traffics in its own characters' psychologies, however – that is, to the extent that it puts on display their own attempts to live out their destinies as merely 'psychological' – it charts only failures. In this urban-scape of missed human connections, lost opportunities for tender communions, and, with the exception of the brief hug between the women at the end, the achievement of any perceptibly authentic human connections, the culprits appear to be, first, the modern arrangement of timescales and schedules, and second, the mediation of commodities – fresh food and withered flowers – whose presence is more tangible than the actual lives of the characters themselves. Both tight time arrangement and the commodification that is central to reification are the lived conditions of all capitalism – and are lived most completely and, for the bourgeois subject, most comfortably, accompanied by the greatest level of compensatory pleasures, in the metropolitan centres of empire. They have been experienced most comprehensively, however, and therefore can be adumbrated if only unconsciously, by the person who has lived them in the colony. Mansfield,

41

who had arrived in London from a colony enriched by a technologically enabled colonial trade, and who wrote chiefly in England, grasped in her work both of these realities. This is the imperial-metropolitan *and* colonial global context from which her dual images of the 'thick little wads' of cake and the 'dead little bunch' of 'slightly soiled-looking flowers' arose. These are the (modest) imageries of late colonial surrealism. Circulating around them exists a world and a way of living that, in their tragic reification, are undeniably modern – but that owe their existence to nothing less than a planetary regime of imperial food production and transfer, and to the versions of the material world, and sustenance itself, only graspable within the context of this imperial global trade.

Notes

1. For an economic history of New Zealand, see Gary Hawke, *The Making of New Zealand: An Economic History* (Cambridge: Cambridge University Press, 1985). For a recent history, see Giselle Byrnes, ed., *The New Oxford History of New Zealand* (Auckland: Oxford University Press, 2009).

2. Janet Wilson, Gerri Kimber and Delia da Sousa Correa, eds, *Katherine Mansfield and the (Post-)colonial* (Edinburgh: Edinburgh University Press, 2013).

3. See, for example, Michelle Elleray, 'When Girls Go Bush: Katherine Mansfield Ventures Out', *New Literature Review*, 38 (2002), pp. 19–27.

4. Anna Snaith, *Modernist Voyages: Colonial Women Writers in London, 1890–1945* (Cambridge: Cambridge University Press, 2014), p. 125. Snaith places Mansfield in the context of Olive Schreiner, Una Marson, Christina Stead and others.

5. See Bridget Orr, 'Reading with the Taint of the Pioneer: Katherine Mansfield and Settler Criticism', *Landfall*, 43: 4 (1989), pp. 447–61.

6. On modernism's liberalism, see Gabriel Hankins, *Interwar Modernism and the Liberal World Order: Offices, Institutions, and Aesthetics after 1919* (Cambridge: Cambridge University Press, 2019).

7. Fredric Jameson, 'Third World Literature in an Era of Multinational Capitalism', *Social Text*, 15 (Autumn 1986), pp. 65–88.

8. Aijaz Ahmad, 'Jameson's Rhetoric of Otherness and the "National Allegory"', *Social Text*, 17 (Autumn 1987), pp. 3–26, reprinted in Ahmad, *In Theory: Classes, Nations, Literatures* (London: Verso, 1992), pp. 95–112.

9. Georg Lukács, 'Reification and the Consciousness of the Proletariat', in *History and Class Consciousness*, trans. by Rodney Livingstone (Cambridge, MA: MIT Press, [1923] 1971), pp. 83–222).

10. Fredric Jameson, *The Political Unconscious: Narrative as a Socially Symbolic Act* (Ithaca, NY: Cornell University Press, 1981).

11. Fredric Jameson, *The Modernist Papers* (London: Verso, 2007).

12. Susan Stanford Friedman, *Planetary Modernisms: Provocations on Modernity Across Time* (New York: Columbia University Press, 2015).

13. See Osumaka Likaka, *Naming Colonialism, History and Collective Memory in the Congo, 1870–1960* (Madison: University of Wisconsin Press, 2009), p. 56.

14. See, for example, David Harvey, *Justice, Nature and the Geography of Difference* (Oxford: Blackwell, 1986), and David Harvey, *Spaces of Capital: Towards a Critical Geography* (Edinburgh: Edinburgh University Press, 2001).

15. Halford Mackinder, 'The Geographical Pivot of History', *The Geographical Journal*, 23: 4 (April 1904), pp. 421–37.
16. See Wendy Roberta Katz, *Rider Haggard and the Fiction of Empire: A Critical Study of British Imperial Fiction* (Cambridge: Cambridge University Press, 2010).
17. See John Newsinger, 'Lord Greystoke and Darkest Africa: The Politics of the Tarzan Stories', *Race and Class*, XXVIII: 2, 1986, pp. 61–4.
18. Justus von Liebig, *Letters on Modern Agriculture* (London: Walton and Maberly, 1859).
19. See John Bellamy Foster, *Marx's Ecology: Materialism and Nature* (New York: Monthly Review Press, 2000) for a detailed history of nineteenth-century thinking on agriculture and how it influenced Marx's concept of nature.
20. See, for the use of this term (as opposed to 'anthropocene') in recent materialist debates on the environmental crisis, Jason Moore, ed., *Anthropocene or Capitalocene? Nature, History and the Crisis of Capitalism* (Oakland, CA: PM Press, 2016).
21. See David Harvey, *The Condition of Postmodernity: An Enquiry into the Origins of Cultural Change* (Oxford: Blackwell, 1990), and Paul Virilio, *Speed and Politics*, trans. by Mark Polizzotti (New York: Semiotexte, [1977] 1986).
22. See Stephen Kern, *The Culture of Time and Space, 1880–1918* (Cambridge, MA.: Harvard University Press, 1983, especially Ch. 1, 'The Nature of Time', pp.10–35. For one interesting recent discussion of how this consciousness entered literature, see Charles Tung, *Modernism and Time Machines* (Edinburgh: Edinburgh University Press, 2019).
23. Katherine Mansfield, 'Psychology', *Bliss and Other Stories* (New York: Alfred A. Knopf, 1929), pp. 144–55 (p. 149). Subsequent references to this story will refer to this edition, with page numbers given in parentheses in the text.
24. James Joyce, *Ulysses* (New York: Vintage, 1986), p. 219, Episode 11, pp. 410–11: 'Smack: She set free sudden in rebound her nipped elastic garter smackwarm against her smackable a woman's warmhosed thigh.'
25. T. S. Eliot, 'The Love Song of Alfred J. Prufrock', *Collected Poems, 1919-1962* (New York: Harcourt Brace and Company, 1963), pp. 3–7.
26. For an interesting reading of the story in terms of male and female versions of *jouissance*, see Allan Pero, ' "Jigging Away into Nothingness": Knowledge, Language and Feminine Jouissance in "Bliss" and "Psychology" ', in *Katherine Mansfield and Psychology*, edited by Clare Hanson, Gerri Kimber and Todd Martin (Edinburgh: Edinburgh University Press, 2016), pp. 100–12.
27. See Henri Bergson's *The Creative Mind: An Introduction to Metaphysics*, trans. by Mabel L. Andison (New York: The Philosophical Library, 1946), pp. 11–14. The best-known attack in English on Bergson's approach to time is by Wyndham Lewis in *Time and Western Man*, ed. by Paul Edwards (San Francisco: Black Sparrow Press, [1927] 1993). On Mansfield's debt to vitalism, see Clare Hanson, 'Katherine Mansfield and Vitalist Psychology', in *Katherine Mansfield and Psychology*, pp. 23–37.
28. Henri Bergson, *Matter and Memory* [*Matière et mémoire*] (New York: Zone Books, [1896] 1990).
29. Modernist class-consciousness has received little attention; one outstanding exception is Sean Latham, *Am I a Snob? Modernism and the Novel* (Ithaca, NY: Cornell University Press, 2003).
30. Eliot, p. 6.
31. Joyce, p. 144.
32. For another, fascinating, reading of Mansfield and food, see Aimee Gasston,

'Katherine Mansfield: Cannibal', in *Katherine Mansfield and the (Post-)Colonial*, pp. 15–28.
33. Comte de Lautréamont, *Maldoror and Poems* [*Les Chants de Maldoror*], trans. by Paul Knight (New York: Penguin, [1868–9] 1988), p. 10.

The 'Little Savage from New Zealand' in 'Bliss'

Marilyn Reizbaum

My title does not propose a biographical reading of Katherine Mansfield's famous story, 'Bliss' (1918). Instead, it raises the spectre of Mansfield's topic in that story, and elsewhere in her *œuvre*, that may be found in the epithets attributed to the writer in her brief writing life.[1] This 'little savage' from an outpost of the empire was often characterised in animalistic terms, and these terms are often to be found in her stories, along with 'pet' names, sometimes literal: Monkey, Duck, Mouse, Face, Mug, Sun, Moon, much like her own 'Tig' or 'Wig'. There have been a number of critical approaches to the figure of the animal in her stories, as, for example, fairy-tale populace or Darwinian menagerie. I am interested in the latter, less to make the case, as Thomas Dilworth does, for the displacements of evolution that the story 'Bliss' observes, but rather for the degenerative impulse in Mansfield's work.[2] In my focus on 'Bliss', I will be arguing that 'savagery' is overwritten by the ecstatic performance of bliss, a blind for both the reader and the character. This is not to say that savagery trumps blissfulness, since one of the challenges of the story is its shifting emotional and conceptual terrain (not to mention that some of these 'pets' seem more domesticated than savage). In effect, in the terms put forward by degeneration theory, they are one and the same: Bertha's ecstasy is a measure of her 'savagery', in its expression of bodily or sexual excess and its delusional aspect – both of which may be read as a sign of Bertha's derangement (or hysteria). I have organised this chapter in categories that are both distinctive and sometimes overlapping as markers of the degeneration thesis, overdetermined as it is.

Wilde Degeneration

'Bliss' deploys the terminology of degeneration, a set of theories devolving from Darwinism that affected all areas of knowledge, including the arts, from where the concept of literary decadence emerged. Max Nordau would decree that modernist art was a sign of the author's 'disease', moral, physical and mental; and of course, Oscar Wilde was one of his targets. Mansfield was a great admirer of Wilde's – several critics have explored this connection. As the editors of her letters comment: 'Katherine Mansfield's early notebooks, as well as several of her early stories, are drenched in Wildean influences.'[3] Their note glosses a letter that Mansfield writes to Ida Baker about being 'subject to the same fits of madness as those which caused his [Wilde's] ruin and decay'. Those 'fits of madness' are synonymous with the 'picture of his exact decadence', which is how Mansfield describes Wilde when she thinks of him, resonant, of course, of his novel, *The Picture of Dorian Gray*, and of sexual desire. At one point, in recording her attraction for a female friend, Mansfield exclaims: 'O Oscar, am I particularly susceptible to sexual impulse?'[4] Mansfield worried that her 'mind was morally unhinged' and considered suicide, which she took to be another sign of her 'degradation'.[5]

Referring to her queer desire as 'exact decadence' might seem to the modern reader veiled, but in the period they were overtly synonymous. Bertha's expression of her physical desires, that for her husband and Pearl Fulton and for her baby – to hold her physically – is mediated through the feeling but also the word 'bliss' – 'a burning sensation sending out a little shower of sparks into every particle, into every finger and toe? . . .' The ellipses gnomonically account for what cannot be expressed, either because disallowed or because, as the next line in the story glosses – 'Oh, is there no way you can express it without being "drunk and disorderly?"' Much has been made in the critical responses to the story about the metaphor Bertha next uses – 'the rare, rare fiddle, shut up in a case' – for her sense of deprivation. Bertha immediately disavows that metaphor as 'not quite what I mean', but is unable to finish the thought 'because – ';[6] instead, she runs up to the nursery to attenuate her almost unbearable feeling of anticipation. She returns to the thought when vying for possession of her baby with the nanny who occupies her child. The baby is 'kept – not in a case like a rare, rare fiddle – but in another woman's arms' (p. 146). How would Bertha have filled in the blank? She seems to object to the rarefication contained within the metaphor of the fiddle. After all, such instruments should be protected from mis- or overuse, like and unlike a woman's

46

body, which Bertha is attempting to redefine and rediscover. Perhaps one way she does that is rhetorically, 'demeaning' the violin by colloquialising it as a fiddle, just as her baby's rarefication into a 'rich girl with a doll' is countered by herself as the 'poor girl' watching. I think it is a mistake to read Bertha's desire here and elsewhere in the story as angled socially upward. Although her feelings are exuberantly ascendant, she also seems earthbound, in touch with material objects and sensations, and falling in symbolic and literal ways (in love, on the couch). Further, the second iteration of the metaphor might provide what's missing or necessarily displaced – 'another woman's arms'. Sydney Janet Kaplan observes Richard Ellmann's assertion that 'Wilde recognised that homosexuality was the great undercover subject', and wonders if Mansfield felt this way, too. Her technique would suggest yes. And no.[7]

Woolf Woolf

In Ali Smith's marvellous piece about the relationship between Mansfield and Virginia Woolf, in a volume of illuminating essays on that subject, she discusses the 'rivalrous' relationship between them. She quotes Woolf's initial response to 'Bliss' after reading it in the *English Review*: 'She's done for! Indeed I don't see how much faith in her as a woman or writer can survive that sort of story [. . .] her mind is very thin soil'; but then thinks better of it, perhaps reflexively, by ending the same entry with a worry that personal criticism of Mansfield is being read into her story, criticism that Woolf herself purveyed.[8] Smith also gleans from Woolf's reflections on Mansfield that she liked to read her as 'creaturely or itinerant', as 'barren or marmoreal', as 'cheap' but also (sometimes) admirably promiscuous sexually: 'Dogs, cats, hogs, so many representatives of the animal kingdom – I think always related to the possibility of otherness in Woolf's writing – crowd Woolf's first reactions to Mansfield.'[9] Smith then quotes an oft-cited diary entry where Woolf refers to Mansfield on first impression as 'stinking like a civet cat that had taken to street walking'.[10] Smith concludes that Mansfield '*gets Woolf's goat*'. This is a play on Woolf's nickname (which was goat), by which Smith means that Mansfield piques Woolf, but also that they had a profound sympathy with one another, mediated through these ambiguous emblems of their desire.[11]

Before I come to say more about the role of animals in 'Bliss' – the horrible civet cats and so on – I want to observe not only Woolf's framing of animality as the possibility of otherness (one might think of *Orlando*'s example), but also Woolf's discomfort with the 'animal' instinct. Mansfield is well known to have created characters in the image of those in her circle (in 'Bliss', for example, a reference to an 'Alpha show' made by the guests is cited in a note as a satirical reference to Vanessa Bell's Omega Workshops, for contemporary interior design (p. 151, n. 4); and it is striking to see a moment in 'Bliss' that is almost an exact extraction from a letter written by Mansfield to Woolf in 1917:

> My God, I love to think of you, Virginia, as my friend. Don't cry me an ardent creature or say, with your head a little on one side, smiling as though you knew some enchanting secret: 'Well, Katherine, we shall see.'[12]

Compare this to a moment in 'Bliss':

> Was there anything beyond it? Harry said 'No.' Voted her dullish, and 'cold like all blond women, with a touch perhaps, of anemia of the brain.' But Bertha couldn't agree with him; not yet, at any rate.
> 'No, the way she has of sitting with her head a little on one side, and smiling, has something behind it, Harry, and I must find out what that something is.'
> 'Most likely it's a good stomach,' answered Harry.
> He made a point of catching Bertha's heels with replies of that kind . . . 'liver frozen, my dear girl', or 'pure flatulence', or 'kidney disease' . . . and so on. For some strange reason Bertha liked this, and almost admired it in him very much. (p. 148)

As we soon discover, Harry protests too much here. His flip, sardonic characterisation of Pearl Fulton, his paramour, and Bertha's love interest – 'Bertha had fallen in love with her as she always did fall in love with beautiful women who had something strange about them' (p. 147) – is a cover for both of them, articulated in the crudest gender stereotype but importantly pathologised in the currency of degeneration: she a dumb blond, vacuous, except for some rotting organs, further evidence of her degradation. Bertha 'almost' admires her husband for his unchivalrous portrayal, inexplicably, reassured somehow by his dismissal of her mysterious guest or by the unsavoury image. Their encoded exchange is well represented by the head tilted to one side with something behind it, an image of Woolf with whom Mansfield has clearly fallen in love despite, and perhaps because of, the ambivalence she experiences through the pretension of the Bloomsbury set, who often spoke of her as Harry defensively speaks of Pearl Fulton.[13] The image is repeated when 'Miss Fulton, all in silver, with a silver fillet binding her blond hair, came in smiling, her head a little on one side' (p. 151). Bertha will soon protest too much in her own terms, by enumerating everything she 'really – really – has' with every cliché of domestic bliss: 'adorable baby, didn't have to worry about money, satisfactory house and garden' and so on (p. 148). She does this just before her guest, Mr Norman Knight – or

Mug – provides the contest to this form of bliss with his allusion to Cyril Connolly's famous dictate: 'There is no more sombre enemy of good art than the pram in the hall.'[14] Woolf would not fall prey to this 'enemy'; her purported wish to have a child was complicated, at least in part, by an assessment of her depression as a symptom of degeneration.[15]

Creatural

Mansfield was fond of assuming and ascribing animal monikers to characters in her stories and in life: Tig, from 'Two Tigers'.[16] In her essay, 'Katherine Mansfield's Menagerie', Melinda Harvey argues that the prevalence of animals in her work is more than a corollary of her identification with the underdog, but is productive of a kind of 'zoopoetics':[17] 'primarily a consequence of her theory of literature – her deep held convictions regarding its impulses and imperatives [. . .] Mansfield's sense of "Life" is clearly anti-anthropocentric.' 'It is also possible to read Mansfield's stories as a 'safehouse for endangered species human and animal [. . .]'.[18] But Harvey's insights, while illuminating, a bit too quickly override the import of the 'underdog' in the work in favour of the more salutary or romantic view of Mansfield's view of nature and animals. Moreover, their often ambiguous role in the work, I would argue, is central to the theory of literature. In the course of her essay, Harvey adjusts the word 'menagerie' in her title in order to specify Mansfield's collection of small animals, which are 'small enough to be ignored, innocuous enough to remain uncaged, or unsavoury enough to avoid to be eaten [. . .] diminutive and unostentatious'.[19] These attributes underscore their role as negligible, bottom of the evolutionary scale, and thereby signal the discourse of degeneration through typologies of breeding – the pure-bred versus the mongrel, for example.[20] Returning to Woolf for a moment, I would point to Derek Ryan's essay on '*Orlando*'s Queer Animals', where he discusses Woolf's 1940 unpublished story 'Gipsy, the Mongrel', and reminds us that the concept of the mongrel, which is synonymous with 'Mischling' (in German referring to Nazi designations of racial miscegenation, Jews and Aryans, in particular), whether cross-species or by the 'co-shaping of sexuality and animality' among humans, was very much present not only in Woolf's work, but as a background and frame for modernist work more generally.[21] In Woolf's story, Gipsy the dog runs away to the gypsies, recalling Orlando and where he runs just before his transformation, and calling up a typological interface between 'mongrels' and gypsies; 'mongrel', which, like the animals that appear in Mansfield stories, represents both the liberatory and also the unsavoury and dangerous. For both Woolf and

Mansfield, then, animals performed the double work of representing radical non-conformity – 'the proper subject of the artist is the unlikeness to what we accept as reality'[22] – and an expression of ambivalence toward the 'unlikeness' as both thrilling and viscerally disgusting.

In 'Bliss', the reader's first encounter with animals comes during Bertha's ecstatic inspection of her garden and the pear tree (though, before this, there is mention of a 'strange dog', whose ear Nanny lets baby tug because it is assumed to be tame):

> A grey cat, dragging its belly, crept cross the lawn, and a black one, in shadow, trailed after. The sight of them, so intent and so quick, gave Bertha a curious shiver.
>   'What creepy things cats are!' she stammered, and she turned away from the window and began walking up and down . . . (p. 148)

Woolf's streetwalking civet cat comes to mind, as though Mansfield had read her diary entry. Certainly, she had been privy to some of the ways in which she had been savagely vilified by her detractors. These 'creepy' cats disrupt her idyllic vision here; they represent a danger she cannot certify until at the conclusion, when they return, personified by Pearl and Eddie, the latter trailing the other as they leave the house, and, again, in connection with the pear tree, whose function is hard to assess. The cats, too, are hard to read: they are 'creepy' but quick; the 'curious shiver' they give Bertha is also ambiguous, it being a word that can convey both pleasure and dread (p. 148). Or, in its own ambiguous way, 'shiver' suggests illness. Throughout the story, Bertha's discomfiture and passion are expressed in double-entendres, or in pairings of agitation and delight. These cats with their dragging bellies and ominous blackness are on the prowl – Pearl for Harry and Eddie Warren for fame – but seeing Pearl and Eddie this way after the revelation of the affair between her husband and Pearl, and Eddie's fatuously trendy utterances, seems also to be Bertha's narrative act of derisive retribution. Even Harry's visage metamorphoses into a 'creepy' animal in the revelatory moment – 'Harry's nostrils quivered; his lips curled back into a hideous grin' (p. 155).[23]

The guests are all animal or human specimens in a Darwinian plot: Mrs Norman Knight arrives in her 'orange coat with a procession of black monkeys around the hem and up the front' (p. 149). Bertha refers to it as 'amusing' (just after she emerges in her own outfit resembling the pear tree). Mrs Norman Knight would appear to be radically chic, but even with her coat off Bertha perceives her to look 'like a very intelligent monkey' (p. 149). Norman is wearing a 'tortoise-shell rimmed monocle' and, by way of introduction into the party, recounts the shocked reaction of fellow train travellers to his wife's outfit – ' "The cream of it was when she, being full fed, turned to the woman beside her and said: "Haven't you ever seen a monkey before?" ' (p. 149). Eddie Warren enters '(as usual) in a state of acute distress'; he is fey – 'lean, pale', with an 'immense white silk scarf and white socks to match'. Bertha finds these latter 'most charming'; Mrs Norman Knight refers to them euphemistically as 'happy socks' (p. 150). Eddie's flustered first appearance is due to a *dreadful* experience with his taxi driver, whom he describes as *sinister, bizarre, crouching*, with a *flattened* head – all words italicised in the text as though referencing a lexicon of degenerate types (p. 149). The description recalls that of Mr Hyde – 'troglodytic', Mr Utterson says.[24] The Knights' nicknames for each other, 'Face' and 'Mug', certainly reference the Lombrosoan forensic physiognomy that emerged in this period. As Bertha watches her guests eating and gossiping, Harry among them, she perceives them as 'dear', 'delightful' and 'decorative', reminding her of a play by 'Tchekof' (p. 151). The observation sets them apart from the blazing fire of bliss that Pearl ignites, and yet, the tip at the end about Chekhov renders this eye jaundiced – in good Chekhovian style, the narration mocks these characters while presenting or being invested in them as charming. At the same time, as Brian Richardson has observed, Bertha's gloss disguises 'the lives of futility, failed ambition, marital disappointment and sexual frustration' that often typify Chekhovian characters, and that, counter to the story she tells herself, reflect her own.[25]

The vacillating regard for these 'dear, dear, decorative' creaturely guests points to Bertha's uneasy recognition of her sexual impulse, reminiscent of Mansfield's 'lament' of 'susceptibility to sexual impulse', synonymous with 'decadence'. Thomas Dilworth invokes 'the cliché of the "Hairy Ape" '. Mansfield was familiar with Frank Norris's work, referencing *McTeague* in her letters. Orality, animality, class and biological determinism are the staples of Norris's naturalistic themes. Norris, writing a generation before Mansfield, provides, unlike her, little ambiguity about his degenerate type. The decadent gene is on display, as Mansfield, too, would worry about her own.[26]

Speech would be among the issues that contribute to Mansfield's self-consciousness about being a 'little savage', and it is also signal in the taxonomies of degeneration. While the reader is several times thrown into a conversation where it is difficult to discern who is speaking, Eddie Warren is always identified by his verbal emphases and enunciative hyper-correctness of 'lit-tle', a signal in this instance of his theatrical pretension. He uses it three times, once in his characterisation of the troglodytic taxi driver, once in reference to the *French Review*, and once in a very unsettling description of a ' "*dreadful* poem about a *girl* who was *violated* by a beggar *without* a nose in a lit-tle wood . . ." ' (p. 153). This latter comes a few conversations after one in which a woman, who is impugned for being *All About Eve*-like (an arriviste), is described as having had what seems like cosmetic surgery.

> 'I met her at the Alpha show – the weirdest little person. She'd not only cut off her hair, but she seemed to have taken a dreadfully good snip off her legs and arms and her neck and her poor little nose as well.' (p. 151)[27]

In a kind of invocation of hairy apes, the corrective for her appearance presents as interspecial.

This curious but insistent reference to missing or snipped noses is in keeping with all the other physiognomical references, but more than this, it seems to point to a nose fetish; in Freudian terms, the nose is a stand-in for the penis, which here, snipped, would amplify the circumcised penis and thereby the 'violating' degenerate as Jew.[28] The move toward rhinoplasty or 'nose bobbing' was in place as early as the late nineteenth century for Jews who wished to remove what was determined to be their identifiable feature.[29] The *dreadful* poem with the assailant beggar is referenced only a few lines after the mention of the Jacob Nathans, who remain unidentified except that they are somehow mockingly worthy of a room with a fish and chips 'scheme' (a seeming reference to the Omega Workshop and fashionable design), and by their name, as obviously Jewish. In her essay 'Powers of Disgust: Katherine Mansfield and Virginia Woolf', Maud Ellmann considers Mansfield's story 'Je ne parle pas français' and Woolf's story 'The Jeweler and the Duchess' to show how 'disgust disgusts'.[30] Though Woolf was persuaded to remove any direct identification of the corrupt jeweller as Jew, 'nonetheless, his Jewishness remains "under erasure", in Jacques Derrida's sense, in that the revisions failed to wipe out the original'.[31] Ellmann points out how the identifying feature of the long nose is made apparent in Woolf's story with its 'curious quiver at the nostril', to which Mansfield, it seems, is directly alluding in her description of Harry at the moment when Bertha apprehends his amorous relationship with Pearl (p. 155).[32] And, of course, there is Leonard Woolf's earlier story 'Three Jews' (1917), one of whom – the Jewish cemetery keeper – has the 'shiny nose' of Freud's paradigm.[33] In all these ways, Mansfield, who unreservedly counted among her friends the 'Bloomsbury Jews' Samuel Koteliansky and the painter Mark Gertler, seems to be indicting British society, and Bloomsbury in particular, for its very own savagery.[34]

Disease

Ellmann writes:

> In Woolf's and Mansfield's writing, disgust is also associated with the indigestible, but it expands into the social and political domain, where revulsion is a means of 'othering' the undesirable. [. . .] Woolf turns up her nose at the common, the 'vulgar' and the 'cheap' – to quote some of the slurs she flings at Mansfield, claiming to be shocked at her 'commonness' [. . .] Mansfield on the other hand, is revolted by the bourgeoisie [. . .] a [*sic*] distaste for the 'Blooms Berries' – presumably a sour, indigestible, or even poisonous fruit. In her writing as in Woolf's, disgust defaults to food; both writers show a queasy, even anorexic attitude to eating, their nausea exacerbated by the sight and sound of other masticating jaws.[35]

This 'distaste' is omnipresent in Mansfield's writing and is notable in 'Bliss', where the social indictments often dissolve into literal distaste and grotesquerie. Drawing on Sianne Ngai's work in *Ugly Feelings*, Ellmann makes the connection but also the distinction between desire and disgust: 'disgust is never ambivalent about its object', whereas 'desire can be ambivalent and vague'.[36] 'Bliss' provides many instances of eating and/or conflations of desire and food: as the guests discuss the 'weirdest little person' who has trimmed her offending body parts, Bertha as narrator observes them, 'spoons rising and falling – dabbing their lips with their napkins, crumbling bread, fiddling with the forks and glasses' (p. 151); Harry talks about food suggestively, 'to glory in his "shameless passion for the white flesh of lobster" and "the green of pistachio ices – green and cold like the eyelids of Egyptian dancers"' (yet another suggestive reference to being eaten, as was Face by the train travellers consuming her monkeys and bananas apparel) (p. 149); Bertha's desire for Pearl – her thought that she might 'give a sign' – is displaced into a focus on the etiquette of her own role as hostess.

> What she meant by that she could not know, and what would happen after that she could not imagine.
> While she thought like this she saw herself talking and laughing. She had to talk because of her desire to laugh.
> 'I must laugh or die.'
> But when she noticed Face's funny little habit of tucking something down the front of her bodice – as if she kept a tiny, secret hoard of nuts there, too – Bertha had to dig her nails into her hands – so as not to laugh too much. (p. 152)

Her expression of desire or passion in the story often pains her and is connected with thoughts of illness. Early in the story, as she arranges the fruit she has purchased for the dinner party, she gets carried away by her aesthetic delight, which she worries is an act of hysteria – again, activated by an impulse to laugh, itself a nervous tic. Then there is the literal and metaphorical presentation of the stomach as diseased: Harry impugns Pearl on the basis of her diseased organs – her 'good' stomach, 'liver frozen', 'flatulence', 'kidney disease'; the name of a play the guests are discussing about a suicide is jokingly referred to as 'Stomach Trouble' (pp. 146, 148, 151). As Ellmann observes of Mansfield's story 'Germans at Meat', she 'plays disgust for laughs'.[37] But she also plays it for disgust at what 'polite' English society will or will not stomach, or countenance, for that matter.

Mansfield was already ill in 1917 and it has been noted that Woolf, among others, read this as a sign of the inferiority of her overall constitution – she was 'feeble', 'crawling'.[38] Mansfield describes her tuberculosis as the sensation of 'UTTER cold', which recalls the 'shiver' Bertha feels when she sees the cat, 'dragging its belly'.[39] But the double work that word 'shiver' does speaks to the ambivalence toward creaturely desire, also reflected in the bisexuality at the core of 'Bliss'. In this regard, Bertha's passionate desire for both Harry and Pearl is legitimately present and both give rise to a kind of hysteria. Woolf was ambivalently admiring and forthrightly critical of Mansfield's promiscuity, which would be a marker of her 'commonness',[40] and perhaps this accounts for her lack of sympathy for an illness that – however ironically, given her own penchant for 'yielding to temptation' – she might have attributed to Mansfield's dissoluteness. Mansfield struggled to live up to Wilde's exhortation in *The Picture of Dorian Gray* to get rid of temptation by yielding to it, worrying about her decadence all the while.

Triangulation

While the spectre of bisexual desire is present, the critical opinion over the aim of Bertha's 'true' desire has been as multifarious as that of the symbol of the pear tree, if it is a symbol at all.[41]

Sydney Janet Kaplan has pointed to Mansfield's probable familiarity with Otto Weininger's notorious work on bisexuality in *Sex and Character*, either through D. H. Lawrence or just generally, given the prevalence of those theories in the literary milieu of the time.[42] The impact of Weininger's work on writers in this period was profound. Weininger would both underscore the essentially bisexual nature (both sex and sexuality) of all human beings, but also disparage 'W' as such for being the negative aspect (in referring to the womanly aspect in this way, he also tellingly implicated himself with the first letter of his name). Weininger claimed that a 'woman's inclination to lesbian love is precisely a *product of her masculinity, which is in fact the prerequisite of her* superiority'. Weininger speaks of degrees of complementarity in the choice of sexual partners and in the constitution of sex of the individual. He uses physiognomy, among other external measures of evidence, to prove his case.[43]

In another context, Kaplan writes,

> Katherine Mansfield's aesthetics are grounded in a precocious recognition of the self and many selves – male/female being only one of the several possible polarities. She had a very early experience of *multiplicity* [. . .] the breaking apart of something that was once whole.

This productive variation on Weininger's ideas, furthered by figures like Edward Carpenter and Magnus Hirschfeld, is useful in thinking about how Mansfield's work resists the Weiningerian model and/or produces a more volatile model.[44]

Both expressions of desire for Harry and Pearl are undeniable, but the contexts for that expression change the interpretive calculus. The medium of these contexts is Bertha's consciousness, which in part accounts for the misunderstanding or misinterpretation. As I have tried to suggest, the ambivalence is less a product of Bertha's obtuseness and more that of the ambivalence that attends the 'undercover subject' of queer desire. In this way, as Dominic Head suggests, the story reveals the ideology [of social taboo] under which it operates.[45] The story is saturated with degeneration, 'unlikeness', and exact and inexact decadence. Its narration tests the difficulty of discernment.

Thinking that Miss Fulton 'gave the sign' by asking her about her garden, Bertha, trance-like, takes her to view the quivering, flowering pear tree through the long windows, inserting all the symbology of sexual excitement in seemingly normative terms – the flames growing taller to touch the moon:

> How long did they stand there? Both, as it were, caught in that circle of unearthly light, understanding each other perfectly, creatures of another world, and wondering what they were to do in this one with all this blissful treasure that burned in their bosoms and dropped, in silver flowers, from their hair and hands. (p. 153)

But this is Bertha's reverie, which she soon recognises – 'or did Bertha dream it?' Key to this passage is the *un*ambiguous alterior space of their creatureliness. What follows this moment when 'the light snapped on' is the discussion of the 'dreadful' poem about rape, and immediately after Bertha's desperate thought about needing to convince Harry about

Miss Fulton's wonderfulness and about her other need: 'I shall try to tell you when we are in bed to-night . . . what she and I have shared' (p. 154). The proximity of the reference to rape and to her shared bed with Harry leads to the last significant textual break in the narrative (there are four such breaks in the story): 'Something strange and almost terrifying' darts into Bertha's brain – 'the warm bed . . . ' (p. 154). The thought is so terrifying that she has to interrupt it by running to the piano and making a request for someone to play. It is unclear whether what follows the interruption continues the revelation or alters it to make it more digestible:

> For the first time in her life Bertha Young desired her husband.
> Oh, she'd loved him – she'd been in love with him, of course, in every other way, but just not that way. And equally, of course, she'd understood that he was different. They'd discussed it so often. It had worried her dreadfully at first to find that she was so cold, but after a time it had not seemed to matter. They were so frank with each other – such good pals. This was the best of being modern. (p. 154)

With all the pieces in place, the encrypted language seems legible. In marriage, Bertha's body has been encased. The reference to playing on the piano, which disrupts her terrifying thought, would appear to correspond to the encased fiddle, fiddling too being a kind of playing – 'What a pity someone doesn't play' (p. 154). Harry's desires needing to be met – they do have a child – Bertha would have to submit. The welling up of her creaturely desire for Pearl is triangulated through the site of the sexual act – 'the warm bed' – and articulated in her sudden desire for Harry. This triangulation perversely occurs again, when she witnesses Harry mouthing the words 'I adore you' to Miss Fulton while she responds with the 'moonbeam fingers' and 'sleepy smile' that Bertha thought was a sign of Pearl's feeling for her, reserved for her (p. 155). When Miss Fulton refers to the 'lovely pear tree' at the very conclusion, as she departs, Bertha considers it might be another sign and runs over to view where they had stood together earlier, but unlike before, where its stillness burned, here the image may be read as a return to a life unchanged by bliss and perhaps even savaged by it, even while the tree is flowering. The image that directly precedes this is that of the creeping, seemingly lascivious cats.

It is difficult to discern what the narrative break at the very moment of Bertha's epiphany has effected. The description of the unsexual nature of Bertha's and Harry's marriage comports with what Virginia Woolf's diaries revealed about her marriage with Leonard. Of course, it was not an exclusive scenario in the history of compulsory heterosexuality.

Bertha's understanding that 'he was different' seems an acknowledgement of Harry's active sexuality and heterosexuality, attested to by his affair with Pearl (p. 154). But the suggestion that Bertha and Harry have a modern marriage would indicate that theirs is an open marriage and that neither is surprised by the other's pursuits or inclinations. Kate Fullbrook has argued that, 'betrayed by both male and female, and part of a set that would not recognise Pearl and Harry's affair as betrayal at all, Bertha's distress must be masked by the hypocrisy of a social posture of openness'.[46] In short, the story remains an 'open closet', wherein 'a radical uncertainty about its subject remains flush with the text of its exposition'.[47] This is Mansfield's 'picture of exact decadence', hidden, and not so plainly in sight.

Notes

1. Carey Snyder, 'Katherine Mansfield, *Rhythm*, and Metropolitan Primitivism', *Journal of Modern Periodical Studies*, 5: 21 (2015), pp. 138–59 (p. 139). 'The appellation was given her by the principal of Queens College in London, where she simultaneously acquired the social finishing deemed desirable for young colonials and was initiated into metropolitan prejudice.'
2. Thomas Dilworth, 'Monkey Business: Darwin, Displacement and Literary Form in Katherine Mansfield's "Bliss"', *Studies in Short Fiction*, 35 (1999), pp. 141–52.
3. *Letters* 1, p. 90. See also Sydney Janet Kaplan, *Katherine Mansfield and the Origins of Modernist Fiction* (Ithaca, NY, and London: Cornell University Press, 1991), and Angela Smith, *Katherine Mansfield: A Literary Life* (Hampshire and New York: Palgrave, 2000).
4. *Letters* 1, p. 90. Also in Kaplan, p. 22. Both are quoting from Mansfield's *Journal*, ed. by John Middleton Murry (London: Constable, 1954), p. 14.
5. The letter from which the quotations come was written in 1901. The editors are guessing that it was written before April and to Ida Baker. *Letters* 1, pp. 89–90.
6. Katherine Mansfield, 'Bliss', in *Selected Stories*, ed. by Vincent O'Sullivan (New York and London: W. W. Norton & Company, 2006), p. 145. All further references to Mansfield's stories are to this edition and references placed parenthetically in the text.
7. Dominic Head, *The Modernist Short Story: A Study in Theory and Practice* (Cambridge: Cambridge University Press, 1992), pp. 29–31. Head discusses Mansfield's indirect style in 'Bliss' as a result of Althusser's notion of relative autonomy.
8. Quoted in Ali Smith, 'Getting Virginia Woolf's Goat', in *Katherine Mansfield and Virginia Woolf*, ed. by Christine Froula, Gerri Kimber and Todd Martin (Edinburgh: Edinburgh University Press, 2018), pp. 131–54 (p. 144).
9. Ali Smith., p. 143.
10. Woolf, *Diary*, 11 October 1917, cited in Smith, p. 143.
11. Smith, p. 144.
12. *Letters* 1, p. 313.
13. See, for example, Richard Cappuccio, 'An Invitation to the Table: Katherine Mansfield's "Cup of Tea" and Literary London', in *Katherine Mansfield and the Bloomsbury Group*, ed. by Todd Martin (London and New York: Bloomsbury, 2017), pp. 219–34 (p. 229).

14. Cyril Connolly, *Enemies of Promise* (Chicago: University of Chicago Press, [1938] 2008), p. 116. 'She will know at what point domestic happiness begins to cloy, where love, tidiness, rent, rates, clothes, entertaining and rings at the doorbell should stop and will recognize that there is no more somber enemy of good art than the pram in the hall.'

15. Julia Briggs, *Virginia Woolf: An Inner Life* (New York and London: Harcourt, 2005), p. 40. Mansfield would have a miscarriage.

16. Mansfield's husband, John Middleton Murry, assigned them the monikers Tig and Wig, as he would refer to her for the rest of her life – see Melinda Harvey, 'Katherine Mansfield's Menagerie', in *Katherine Mansfield and Literary Modernism*, ed. by Janet Wilson, Gerri Kimber and Susan Reid (London and New York: Continuum, 2011), pp. 202–11.

17. Harvey, p. 203.

18. Harvey, pp. 205, 209.

19. Harvey, p. 207.

20. One might go to Cesare Lombroso's work on criminal anthropology, where he connects human 'abnormalities' to primitive, animalistic tendencies, marking them as atavistic throwbacks. Lombroso's theories accounted for many of the physiognomical measures used in degeneration theories. Cesare Lombroso, *Criminal Man*, trans. by Mary Gibson and Nicole Han Rafter (Durham, NC, and London: Duke University Press, 2006).

21. Derek Ryan, '*Orlando*'s Queer Animals', in *A Companion to Virginia Woolf*, ed. by Jessica Berman (Chichester: Wiley Blackwell, 2016), pp. 109–20. See also Derek Ryan, 'Katherine Mansfield's Animal Aesthetic', *Modern Fiction Studies*, 64: 1 (2018), pp. 27–51; Kirstie Blair, 'Gypsies and Lesbian Desire: Vita Sackville-West, Violet Trefusis, and Virginia Woolf', *Twentieth Century Literature*, 50: 2 (Summer 2004), pp. 141–66. Blair writes: 'In British culture and beyond, fictional gypsies maybe have been seen as romantic Bohemian artists, but real gypsies were often regarded as dangerous foreigners, notable for criminality. Lombroso famously classified gypsies in the late nineteenth century as inherently degenerate types, "the living example of a whole race of criminals", and of course they were to be a prime target of Nazi racial policy' (pp. 161–2). Deborah Epstein Nord writes importantly on this topic in ' "Marks of Race": Gypsy Figures and Eccentric Femininity in Nineteenth-Century Women's Writing', *Victorian Studies*, 41: 2 (Winter 1998), pp. 189–210.

22. Cited in Harvey, p. 206.

23. This horsey description of Harry seems a direct reference to Woolf's Jewish jeweller in 'The Duchess and the Jeweler', first published in *Harper's Bazaar*, 1938. Virginia Woolf, 'The Duchess and the Jeweler', *The Complete Shorter Fiction of Virginia Woolf* (Orlando, FL: Harcourt, 1989), pp. 248–53: 'That was so; he was the richest jeweler in England; but his nose, which was long and flexible, like an elephant's trunk, seemed to say by its curious quiver at the nostrils (but it seemed as if the whole nose quivered, not only the nostrils) that he was not satisfied yet, still smelt something under the ground a little further off' (p. 249).

24. Robert Louis Stevenson, *Strange Case of Dr Jekyll and Mr Hyde*, ed. by Martin Danahy (Toronto: Broadview Editions, 2015), p. 43.

25. Brian Richardson, 'Dangerous Reading in Mansfield's Stories and Woolf's "The Fisherman and His Wife" ', *Katherine Mansfield and Virginia Woolf*, pp. 117–27 (pp. 119–20). Eddie Warren's name was originally 'Wangle', to which Murry objected, saying it was 'a Dickens touch – you're Tchehov' (*Letters* 1, 6 March 1918, p. 127).

26. Dilworth, p. 144. The image would soon have dramatic currency in Eugene O'Neill's *Hairy Ape* (1922), a contemporaneous work providing context for the story, even if post-dating it.
27. For an explanation of the 'Alpha show' reference, see n. 4, p. 154 of 'Bliss'.
28. See Sigmund Freud's 1927 essay, 'Fetishism', and *The Interpretation of Dreams* (1900). Jay Geller provides an excellent discussion of this topic in ' "A Glance at the Nose": Freud's Inscription of Jewish Difference', *American Imago*, 49: 4 (Winter 1992), pp. 427–44.
29. See Sander Gilman's discussion of 'The Jewish Nose', in *The Jew's Body* (New York and London: Routledge, 1991).
30. Maud Ellmann, 'Powers of Disgust: Katherine Mansfield and Virginia Woolf', *Katherine Mansfield and Virginia Woolf*, ed. by Christine Froula, Gerri Kimber and Todd Martin (Edinburgh: Edinburgh University Press, 2018), pp. 11–28, p. 18.
31. Ellmann, p. 20.
32. See n. 23 above.
33. Leonard Woolf, 'Three Jews', in *Two Stories*, written and printed by Virginia Woolf and L. S Woolf (Richmond: Hogarth Press, 1917).
34. For more on these connections, see Galya Diment, *A Russian Jew of Bloomsbury: The Life and Times of Samuel Koteliansky* (Montreal, London and Ithaca, NY: McGill-Queens University Press, 2011). Ellmann also references this text in her discussion of Woolf.
35. Ellmann, p. 13.
36. Ellmann, p. 17. See Sianne Ngai, *Ugly Feelings* (Cambridge, MA: Harvard University Press, 2005).
37. Ellmann, p. 17.
38. *Notebooks* 2, p. 219. As cited in Cappuccio, p. 229.
39. Cappuccio, p. 229.
40. Cappuccio, p. 228.
41. Kate Fullbrook describes the pear tree as a 'bisexual emblem of her [Bertha's] just discovered sexual need', in *Katherine Mansfield* (Bloomington and Indianapolis: Indiana University Press, 1986), p. 101.
42. Kaplan, pp. 134, 107.
43. Otto Weininger, *Sex and Character: An Investigation of Fundamental Principles*, trans. by Ladislaus Löb, ed. by Daniel Steuer with Laura Marcus (Bloomington and Indianapolis: Indiana University Press, [1903] 2005), p. 58.
44. Kaplan, p. 169. See, for instance, Wen-Shan Shieh, 'Katherine Mansfield's Art of Changing Masks in "Je ne parle pas français" ', *Journal of Literature and Art Studies*, 16: 8 (August 2016), pp. 869–81.
45. Head, p. 30.
46. Fullbrook, p. 102.
47. See Joseph Valente's discussion of the concept, in *Quare Joyce* (Ann Arbor: University of Michigan Press, 2000), pp. 68–72.

Sublimity and Mansfield's 'Subjective Correlatives' in 'Bliss'

Gaurav Majumdar

Katherine Mansfield's 'Bliss' (1920) keeps indeterminate the precise relations between past experience and current sensations or thoughts. Especially when the story presents Bertha Young's negotiation of intense experience (ecstasy in the case of this discussion), the correlation between ecstatic pleasure and plot-based pain, if you like, remains evocative, rather than specific. These relations are not literalised by a simple causality but linked to a sense of overwhelming, a sense linked to the grandeur or largeness, coupled with terror or pain, that classical and Enlightenment theories emphasise as a signature of the sublime. While there is no grand heroic gesture or encounter with an immense natural force in 'Bliss', Mansfield's story, nevertheless, deftly fuses evocations of the sublime with a scalar departure from the grandeur associated with sublimity: it convolutes the direct proportion or implicit equivalency of, on the one hand, the size of sources displaying sublimity, and, on the other, the intensity of the ecstatic pleasure or bliss that they provoke.[1] This essay will focus on the complex workings of this convolution in 'Bliss'.

Feeling 'a little shower of sparks' radiate from her ecstasy at the beginning of 'Bliss', Bertha Young traces the source of the shower to a sensation of having 'suddenly swallowed a bright piece of the late afternoon sun'.[2] In this strange mapping of sensation, Bertha feels not as if she has swallowed the sun itself, but a part of the sun that remains active within her: the 'bright piece [. . .] burned in your bosom, sending out a little shower of sparks' (p. 145), which recurs in images of fire and burning across the story.[3] The sense of derangement and natural displacement here reflects the confusion that Bertha senses has no adequate expression in standardised language and formal sobriety: immediately after feeling the sparks of bliss, she wonders, 'Is there no way you can express it without being "drunk and disorderly?"' (p. 145). Considering intoxication as the only condition of expressive adequacy to describe the sublime, the question evokes the confused imagination that the ecstatic experience catalyses. Bliss produces not only a sense of inadequate representation, but also disorientating inversions of scale – as is further evident in Bertha's ensuing contemplation of a table that seems to 'melt' into dusky light and a glass dish (p. 146).

Processing this sense through a series of inconsistent images, Bertha is overcome by this strong, ineluctable sensation of bliss, but she also feels as if she herself has 'swallowed' its source. Thus, she thinks of herself as being the container of the source, but at the same time under its power and unable to contain its overwhelming force. Jean-François Lyotard reminds us in his famous appendix to *The Postmodern Condition* (1979) that, for Immanuel Kant, the sublime sentiment is 'a strong and equivocal emotion: it carries with it both pleasure and pain'.[4] Lyotard adds, 'Better still, in it, pleasure derives from pain [and] this contradiction, which some would call neurosis or masochism, develops as a conflict between the faculties of a subject, the faculty to conceive of something and the faculty to "present" something.'[5] However, while we can indeed conceive of sublime immensity or infinity, our imagination cannot present such vastness to us, producing an epistemological crisis that resembles Bertha Young's own failures to find correspondence for her vertiginously fatiguing internal 'crises' in the facts of her 'external' life.

Classical literary criticism on the sublime confirms this sense of disorientation in encountering the sublime. According to Longinus, the sublime ecstasy that grandeur produces in us overwhelms – rather than persuades – us, drawing from us 'amazement and wonder' that 'get the better of [us]'.[6] There is a manifest violence to such overwhelming: As Longinus puts it, 'Sublimity tears up everything like a whirlwind . . . at a single blow.'[7] In other translations, 'thunderbolt' or 'bolt of lightning' replace the word 'whirlwind'.[8] The violent effect is, none the less, linked with grandeur in the sublime. The sublime oration or poetic moment can convey itself or heroic action as embodied, physical action, and further, as Stephen Halliwell suggests, as 'an intrinsic "greatness of mind/spirit" [that] requires an intuition of eternity to function in this context as a symbolic correlate of the unlimited powers of the human mind, the infinite (extra-cosmic) reach of thought itself'.[9]

In the *Critique of Judgment* (1790), Kant divides this possibly joint signification of infinity and physical grandeur from sublime objects into two kinds: the 'mathematical sublime' – related to vastness or profusion, producing a feeling of infinitude in quantity – and the 'dynamic sublime' – related jointly with a feeling of vulnerability in terror before overwhelming force and pleasure because such terror is experienced from a safe vantage. In 'Bliss', Bertha struggles with variants of these two categories for sublimity: bourgeois prosperity as the mathematical sublime, which works through serial accumulation, and sexual or sensuous freedom as the dynamic sublime. Her concomitant sense of inadequacy partly reflects that of the viewer's or listener's sense of inadequacy before the sublime (as noted by Longinus, Kant and Edmund Burke), as well as an awareness of wholes unavailable to human imagination and representation (as noted more recently by Lyotard and Neil Hertz).[10]

Such unavailability aggravates Bertha's perplexity not only through gestures of dizzy exultation or overwhelming vastness: Mansfield questions the latter through an inversion of scale, repeatedly evoking the removal of *small* details, both through Bertha's responses to others and through the gaps in her evaluation of her own experience. 'Bliss' shows how such elision abets the production of grandeur, as well as the confusion in presumed ecstasy and bourgeois bliss. As Bertha tries to reconcile these, she lacks what Hertz calls 'a compensatory positive movement' in the Kantian encounter with the sublime – 'the mind's exultation in its own rational faculties, in its ability to think a totality that cannot be taken in through the senses'.[11] Bertha's exultation collapses *en route* to thinking a totality: the obliviousness in her bliss brings her to repeated interpretive exhaustion, which she then reads unidirectionally, either as a problem in her own character or as an appreciable sign (see my discussions below of her self-descriptions as 'absurd' and 'too happy', and of her responses to Harry's buoyancy). However, 'Bliss' itself is insistently aware of the paradox in claiming bliss or ecstatic pleasure in the face of the disorientations that Bertha's sense of domestic sublimity provokes.

Burke's theorisations of the sublime implicitly display this paradox in *A Philosophical Enquiry into the Order of Our Ideas of the Sublime and the Beautiful* (1757).[12] Even in this work from an early stage in his career, magnitude signals greatness for Burke. Evoking science, Burke argues in the *Enquiry* that, if the rays a retina receives

vary their nature, now to blue, now to red, and so on, or their manner of termination as to a number of petty squares, triangles, or the like, at every change, whether of colour or shape, the organ has a sort of relaxation or rest, but this relaxation and labour so often interrupted, is by no means productive of ease; neither has it the effect of vigorous and uniform labour.[13]

It is, instead,

> a teasing [*sic*] fretful employment, which at once wearies and weakens the body [. . .] by continually altering [its] tenor and direction [to] prevent that species of uniform labour which is allied to strong pain, and causes the sublime. The sum total of things of various kinds [. . .] should equal the number of uniform parts composing some *one* entire object.[14]

Importantly, Burke's accommodation of variety comes with a demand for the uniformity of parts to compose a greater whole. Size matters here not only because a work ethic that stretches itself has its reward in sublimity, but because Burke sees a lack of magnitude as equivalent with a lack of effect and worth:

> The mind in reality hardly ever can attend diligently to more than one thing at a time: if this thing be little, the effect is little [. . .] the mind is bounded by the bounds of the object; and what is not attended to, and what does not exist, are much the same in effect; but the eye or the mind (for in this case there is no difference) in great uniform objects does not readily arrive at their bounds; it has no rest, whilst it contemplates them; the image is much the same every where [*sic*]. So that every thing great by its quantity must necessarily be one, simple and entire.[15]

There is a literalism driving Burke's theses, one that prefers size and wants greatness externalised, seeking merit manifest in size. The effect of the little is little, within the logic here. This is overwhelmingly the case, even when Burke notes that,

> as the great extreme of dimension is sublime, so the last extreme of littleness is in some measure sublime likewise [. . .] we become amazed and confounded at the wonders of minuteness; nor can we distinguish in its effect this extreme of littleness from the vast itself.[16]

Burke's gesture to the possible sublimity of 'littleness' is lost with that final clause: 'we distinguish in its effect this extreme of littleness from the vast itself'. The absence (or difficulty) of the effort to maintain an awareness of this difference allows Burke to reinstate the predominance of the large in his valuation of greatness by quantity. This greatness not only is immense, but it is 'necessarily one, simple and entire'. The ironic coexistence of uniformity and a lack of perceptual rest justifies Burke's equation of size, simplicity and greatness. Bertha's own thoughts reflect this 'uniformising' view of plenitude when, eliding the very possibility of alternatives or exceptions to the satisfactions of her bourgeois life, she thinks, 'Really – really – she had everything' (p. 148).

Hypnos *and Hypnosis*

For Kant, '*the sublime is that in comparison with which everything else is small*'.[17] According to this logic, sublime feeling dominates our experience, overwhelming registration as a Longinian 'whirlwind' or 'thunderbolt'. Overwhelmed, we do not register the small: we suspend nuanced reading and ignore details, as is evident in 'Bliss', when Bertha verges on recognising or even expressing helpful details but is unable to reach such insights as she faces the versions of sublimity that agonise her. Rather, she seems to intuit her inability when contemplating the mathematical sublimity to which she has access and thinks, 'I'm absurd. Absurd!' (pp. 148-9). Such indication of aporiae equips 'Bliss' to trace subtly – rather than state explicitly – what is unavailable in Bertha's experience. Mansfield, thus, reveals the *lack* in sublimity that classical depictions see as semiotic plenitude that exceeds or renders superfluous the registration of the small in the aggressive flood of sublimity. Affect, rather than conscious thought, is Mansfield's critical aid in such mapping of absence. Longinus discourses on the spoken sublime – that is, sublimity in spoken or narrated forms; Mansfield attends to the unspoken, the unconscious and the *felt*, rather than the seen. Lacking the exteriority of performative display, Bertha's sense of the sublime gains a psychological urgency in 'Bliss'.

The story makes clear that, within Bertha's circumscribed world, the sublime functions as the misread; it is not so much a source of pleasure as a sign of what is unavailable to Bertha. Mirroring the experience of the sublime that imposes a sense of our representational limits, Bertha experiences sublime ecstasy when both sensing and more self-consciously considering norms of bourgeois domestic success as the sublime. The *Oxford English Dictionary* gives the etymology of 'ecstasy' as follows: 'to put out of place – the classical senses of ἔκστασις [*ekstasis*] are "insanity" and "bewilderment"; but in late Greek the etymological meaning received another application, viz., "withdrawal of the soul from the body, mystic or prophetic trance"'. If the very etymology and classical connotations of ecstasy suggest that an ecstatic mind is 'put out of place', then Bertha's ecstatic experience in her home – in her proper 'place', if you will – offers a telling irony. Combining opposed emotions, its supposed transportive power serves only to make Bertha feel more constrained and astonished by pain. Aggravating the problem, there is no single or clearly identified source or force that is responsible for the sublime pain and panic acting upon Bertha in 'Bliss': the fluctuating and conjoined pressures of marriage, domesticity, property, maternity, repressed sexuality, bourgeois social interactions and consumer culture obviate a simple transfer of correspondences between causes and effects.

Sublimity's unbrookable surfeit of signs (which Burke and Kant rationalise into uniformity) does not permit its audience temporal or intellectual sufficiency to trace such correspondence, making the audience's 'knowledge' inadequate and partial, at best. Such a view effects the reduction of the subject experiencing the sublime and the hyper-formalisation of the sublime itself into largeness and even grandeur, as it is for Longinus. The asymmetry produces the reduced subject's sense of inadequacy, restlessness and desperation that, as I will show later, the formal sophistication of Mansfield's story reflects as an ethical argument to unpack the grandeur of privileged form in classical and bourgeois models of happiness. Intense sensation agitates Bertha into an evaluation of her emotions: she reads such sensation against the standards of a received index of happiness, as emblematised in her inventory of bourgeois satisfaction. A strenuous happiness in her conscious thoughts loses repeatedly to her bewilderment about her life.

The Greek word for the sublime, *hypnos*, shares an etymological node with the words 'hypnosis' and 'hypnotised': the combining form of the Greek ὕπνος or 'sleep'. This etymological genealogy hints that the strong sensation of sublimity is the result of something like stilled curiosity, a curiosity that the vacuity and evacuations of strong feeling in bourgeois domesticity deny to Bertha. After she considers the intense smell of jonquils in her living room, she enters a simultaneously aesthetic and introspective evaluation of sensation: 'How strong the jonquils smelled in the warm room. Too strong? Oh, no. And yet, as though overcome, she flung down on a couch and pressed her hands to her eyes' and, immediately, she murmured, 'I'm too happy – too happy!' (p. 148). At this juncture of confused emotions and overwhelming sensation, the story tellingly links Bertha's sense of inadequacy to a sense of excess: the 'too strong' jonquils are a marker that she has violated some border of optimal happiness and is, therefore, undeserving or unable to bear the happiness she feels. Through the leaps and gaps in Bertha's self-implicating interpretation, Mansfield makes clear that Bertha's 'excessive' happiness is defined by hasty reading.

The 'Hertzian Sublime': 'Un-insulating' Dissatisfaction

In short, Mansfield conveys psychological and semiotic mobility by exploring the immobilisation and separation of smaller nuances in Bertha's evaluation of her circumstances. The story shows such immobilisation of signs within the local or the domestic when it suggests

Bertha's neglect of Harry's fondness for ostensibly candid crudeness – with his offhand references to 'pure flatulence' or 'kidney disease' – and of a cannibalistic aspect to his appetites – for 'the white flesh of the lobster' or 'pistachio ices' that remind him of 'the eyelids of Egyptian dancers' (pp. 148, 152). Such scenes turn habitual response stasis into figural explorations of what is unspeakable and inescapable, at the same time. Bertha reads her own affective intensity through figures: 'a little shower of sparks' and a 'bright piece' of the sun, emerging from a 'bright glowing place' in her bosom (p. 145). As her helpless focus on *parts* suggests, interpreting or narrating sublime experience is an attempt to link metonymically aspects of the overwhelming semiotic rush that sublimity unleashes. This is overt in her list of metonyms for bourgeois satisfaction (which peaks with her cook, who makes 'the most superb omelettes'), each metonym becoming a figure for the larger sublime force acting upon her.

Reading the relation between sublime and figurative language in Neil Hertz's redefinition of sublimity, Jonathan Culler explains in his essay 'The Hertzian Sublime':

> The indefinite plurality, threatening to the integrity of the self, is tropo-logically reduced to a single opposing force which can be recognized in a one-to-one confrontation and give rise to the dialectical recuperation . . . But Hertz shows that this is a specular rather than a dialectical process. The reduction is sought by consciousness to master an epistemological threat to the status and integrity of the subject by misrecognizing it as a structured conflict *between* subjects. The compensatory positive movement of the mind that has been checked is not just a *result* of the confrontation of the sublime but its telos, what the mind was seeking in the first place.[18]

Culler proceeds to identify this 'brilliant conversion of the Longinian and Kantian sublime to an economy of the sublime that pervades the most trivial scenarios of the self' as 'the Hertzian sublime'.[19] Noting Hertz's interest in Longinus's 'transfers of power' from the sublime actions of gods and heroes to the sublime articulations of the texts or poets that describe them, Culler writes that, within instances of sublim-ity in Longinus's text, 'the subtle metonymic echoes between one cita-tion and another . . . work to build up a pattern of linkage between the actions of gods and heroes . . . and the sublime speech acts of poets'.[20] Given the objects in her list of things worth having (a marriage between 'pals'; money; 'modern' friendships, garnished with books and music; house and garden; and a new, skilled cook), Bertha Young has the metonyms for bourgeois mathematical sublimity to transfer to herself in 'Bliss' (pp. 148-9). However, instead of directly conveying the sublime into her life, Mansfield puts Bertha in the position of a reader interpreting the accumulated material of bourgeois 'sublimity'. Bertha is trying to gauge why she feels the burning pain of her assumed ecstasy – in one of the story's prominent ironies, she tries to interpret what such bourgeois bliss *lacks* at the same time as she thinks, 'Really – really – she had everything' (p. 148). The moment points to the contradictory temporal dimension of material ownership that Sara Ahmed has analysed as follows:

> If objects provide a means for making us happy, then in directing ourselves toward [an] object, we are aiming somewhere else: toward a happiness that is presumed to follow. The temporality of this does matter. Happiness is what would come after. Given this, happiness is directed toward certain objects, which point toward that which is not yet present.[21]

This is the view of happiness that 'Bliss' asserts. Mansfield's deft relation of parts gives her story an enthymemic form – a form that asserts its arguments evocatively, rather than explicitly. This stands in subversive contrast to the violence of the sublime, a violence that guarantees the sundering of our interpretive capacities from sublime thunderbolts, *a priori*. For the text itself, Bertha's unease and confusion provide ways of implying, rather than explicitly stating, an ethics of dissatisfaction.[22] Dissatisfaction appears as Bertha's yearning for change, but not as an *acknowledged* appetite for surprise, in the story. From the beginning of 'Bliss', Bertha craves unfamiliar experience: She has an 'air of anticipation, waiting for something . . . divine to happen . . . that must happen . . . infallibly' (p. 145). Surrendering her agency to formulaic domesticity, she faces her burning agitations through nervous maternity, presumed marital bliss and its devastating rupture, amid an anxious yearning for the certainty of unimaginable change. Her checklist for successful bourgeois life and her own estrangement from her baby provide metaphors for the confusion in these priorities,[23] as well as a negative inventory for the intensity of experience unavailable to her – an intensity that might indeed produce sublime pleasures, were it not pre-empted by Bertha's oscillations between ecstatic vagueness and painful, though always incipient, analysis.

'Subjective Correlatives': Sedation and Strong Feeling

Against such vague happiness or painful frustration, Mansfield pits small detail and nuance, fleeting moments and expressions as sources of the metaphysical and semiotic excess that Longinus, as well as Kant and Burke, attribute to the large. This is not to say that the smallness to which Mansfield gives such importance lacks *semiotic* immensity: rather, it is to say that Mansfield's version of the small compacts what Stephen Halliwell describes as the 'interlocking elements'[24] of the Longinian sublime: intuition, emotion and metaphysics. In light of this inversion of scale, Mansfield's version of sublimity operates on a kind of geo-metrical paradox: minutiae function as triggers for intuitive, emotional and metaphysical immensity in 'Bliss'. This counterintuitive immensity alone, although alongside other factors (among them cultural diagno-ses, gender relations, and national and international histories), rebuts T. S. Eliot's patronising compliment that it is Mansfield's skilful use of 'minimal' material that renders her work 'feminine'.[25]

For Eliot,

> The only way of expressing emotion in the form of art is by finding an 'objective correlative'; in other words, a set of objects, a situation, a chain of events which shall be the formula of that *particular* emotion; such that when the external facts, which must terminate in sensory experience, are given, the emotion is immediately evoked.[26]

In giving the location of emotion such emphasis and such restriction simultaneously, Eliot both stresses the importance of psychology and simplifies it. His stress on correlatives as *objective* delimits their semi-otic possibilities within his interpretive system, which Mansfield pries open with her symbolist shifts, associative subjectivity and uncertain-ties. In Mansfield's work, however, these 'external facts' or forms of 'surplus' (dissatisfactions or unease as oblique signs of social pressure, for instance) are ethical assets, suggestive artistic engines that propel stories such as 'Bliss'.

In the story, the pear tree operates as an emblem of stasis and devasta-tion in Bertha Young's life, with an unattributed speaker (presumably, but not necessarily, Bertha's consciously speaking self) echoing Pearl's murmured phrase:

> 'Your lovely pear tree – pear tree – pear tree!'
> Bertha simply ran over to the long windows.
> 'Oh, what is going to happen now?' she cried.
> But the pear tree was as lovely as ever and as full of flower and as still.
>   (p. 155)

The tree, which Pearl explicitly mentions to Bertha, has a vertiginous series of associations in the story: the story's formal associativity and mobility are emphatic analogues for the conditions that Bertha lacks. Sharply contrasting the restrictions of the Eliotic 'objective correlative', Mansfield employs sublime ecstasy as a fertile 'subjective correlative' in 'Bliss', relating through impressionistic but figurative details and vivid 'correlatives' that do not follow the one-to-one correspondence that Eliot orders, but, nevertheless, clarify and nuance the relations of Bertha's ecstasy or bliss with her anxiety and misconstrued reasons for disappointment at herself. For Eliot, such excess is, paradoxically, a deficiency, an artistic shortcoming; for Mansfield, it is an asset, an artistic engine that propels stories such as 'Bliss'. In a scene rich with metaphorical potential and nuance, to Bertha the pear tree seems immune to both immaturity and decay: 'Bertha couldn't help feeling [. . .] that it had not a single bud or a faded petal' (p. 148). Alongside this figure of the 'natural' or the unmediated or the undamaged,

> [d]own below, in the garden beds, the red and yellow tulips, heavy with flowers, seemed to lean upon the dusk. A grey cat, dragging its belly, crept across the lawn, and a black one, its shadow, trailed after. The sight of them, so intent and so quick, gave Bertha a curious shiver. (p. 148)

That the cats have both intention and quickness seems to provoke Bertha into stammering, ' "What creepy things cats are!" ' (p. 148). Soon after this paragraph, Bertha thinks her white and green outfit for the party 'wasn't "intentional" ' (p. 149). At these moments, Mansfield signals the absence or lack of intention as the absence of a will to action. Such absence functions as a pivot for her exploration of normalised behaviour and entrenchment in the familiar versus proscribed, but liberating, choices that signal decisive, quick erotic intention, mobility, and desires that might be deemed animalistic or even feral.[27]

'Bliss' implies that the antidote for Bertha's pain lies in risking the strange or the unfamiliar, and erotic alternatives to Bertha's established life: the cold of Pearl Fulton's arm signals the erotic pull of the unfamiliar, offsetting the painful heat that persists in Bertha. This is a pull that, Bertha recalls, she 'always' feels from 'beautiful women who had something *strange* about them' (my emphasis, p. 149). Mansfield leaves ambiguous the precise connotations of the word 'strange', but the sentence obviously employs the word to underscore Bertha's unspoken erotic investment in the non-normative or the unaccustomed.

Bertha's potential relationship with each of these women is stifled by – presumably –heteronormative prohibitions on homosexual 'inclination', to borrow Adriana Cavarero's term. Evoking Hannah Arendt's 1965 lectures on Kant at the New School (entitled 'Some Questions of Moral Philosophy'), Cavarero stresses Arendt's note that ' "every inclination turns outward, it leans out of the self in the direction of whatever may affect me from the outside world" '.[28] Arendt's point not only reminds us that 'the meaning of the word inclination points to a geometrical imaginary; it also, above all, clarifies that, in the theater of modern philosophy, center stage is occupied by an I whose position is straight and vertical'.[29] In a description that would render Bertha's homoerotic fascination with 'strange' women altogether 'horizontal', Cavarero observes, 'The "upright man" of which the tradition speaks, more than an abused metaphor, is literally a subject who conforms to a vertical axis, which in turn functions as a principle and norm for its ethical posture.'[30] Establishing norms as functions of his posture, the upright man admits to no deviation from probity in thought or action. In 'Bliss', Harry's buoyant candour and zest are mimetically 'modern' performances of such probity that his furtive affair with Pearl Fulton reveals to be not only false, but also the negative of Bertha's nervous but unrealised extra-marital sexual interest in women. The inertia silencing this interest partly fuels Bertha's anxieties – she does not *express* such interest nor her suspicion that Pearl Fulton's frankness was limited (p. 148) – and, as corollaries, her disappointments and uncertainties, as well as her deflections of her own desire. We see the first sign of such deflection near the story's beginning when she asks (in free indirect discourse), 'Why be given a body if you have to keep it shut up in a case like a rare, rare fiddle?' and answers herself with 'No, that about the fiddle is not quite what I mean' (p. 148). Bertha's self undergoes an unsettling that further explains the absent attribution for some pieces of speech in 'Bliss' – the absence of attribution reflects a non-attributable self, as Bertha faces, in Cavarero's words, a 'thrust of inclination [that] knocks the I from its internal center of gravity and, by making it lean to the outside[,] undermines its stability'.[31]

In a sense, Bertha herself considers her own experiences as external to her, as reflected in yet another of her thoughts about the pear tree: 'And she seemed to see on her eyelids the lovely pear tree with its wide open blossoms as a symbol of her own life' (p. 148). The tree appears here as after-image and rationalised analogue, which the story gradually seems to offer as an emblem (with its 'wide open blossoms') of what Bertha's life lacks, as well as the sedated quality of her life, if we note the story's closing description of the tree ('lovely as ever and as full of flower and as still') and if we (following Bertha) read the tree as 'becalmed' (p. 155). As such, it offsets Bertha's own emotional upheavals while seeming to be forcibly calmed.

Submitting to sedation – agreeing to a process that renders one 'becalmed' – is submitting to the action of allaying and assuaging, of another force *making* the agitated subject calm or quiet. This is a condition of mediated, sometimes enforced, calm that might offer itself as a route to ecstasy – but only with the numbing of the senses. The false offer produces the interpretive impasse in which Bertha finds herself at story's beginning and ending. Bertha considers the process of sedation itself – a sedate life – the source of sublimity while intuiting the lacunae and unavailability of alternatives in her life of putative bliss. The story clarifies the alternatives before her through a kind of negative logic. She could indeed experience not the Kantian dynamic sublime, but a dynamic pleasure, were she to engage details more closely, and – in the logic of the story – to consider, appreciate and risk a break from the metonyms for her dissatisfaction: the marriage between 'pals'; money; friendships marked by sniping gossip, self-absorption and pretensions to cultural refinement; property; and the domestic sequestration of her priorities. The apparent absence of alternatives for Bertha in her paralysis reflects the impasse in her life of insulated interpretations, neglect of 'littleness' or detail,[32] and imagination, leaving an intuitive excess in the subjective correlatives of Bertha's ecstatic experience. This ecstasy produces an effect that recalls the Late Greek etymological nuance for the word 'ecstasy': 'withdrawal of the soul from the body, mystic or prophetic trance'.[33] As the ending of 'Bliss' repeats Pearl Fulton's comment on the pear tree from earlier in the story, Bertha's paralysis seems prophetic. The canonical theorisations of Longinus, Kant and Burke do indeed associate the sublime with immensity, pleasure and pain, but not with anguish – a sense verging on bereavement or terminal loss – as Mansfield does in 'Bliss'. In the absence of detailed recognitions, Bertha is at an imaginative loss by the story's ending. If the sublime agitates feeling, Mansfield, in contrast, leaves her story suspended amid subjective correlatives that evoke the loss (the pear tree, Bertha's unattributed penultimate comment, and the ending's resonance with Bertha's obliviousness, earlier in the story), with a foreboding that verges on decidedness. The story's last word, of course, is 'still' (p. 155).

Notes

1. Mansfield's early poem, 'This is my world, this room of mine', anticipates this strategy, extending the perspectival defiance of some eighteenth-century works, such as Xavier de Maistre's *Voyage Around My Room* (1794). For Mansfield's poem, see CP, p. 22.
2. Katherine Mansfield, 'Bliss', *Katherine Mansfield's Selected Stories* (New York: W. W. Norton and Co., 2006), p. 145. Hereafter, all references to Mansfield's story are to this edition and page references placed parenthetically in the text.
3. The specific recurrences of fire imagery are on pages 147–8, 150–3 and 155. The fact of numbing repetition is crucial for Bertha's stupefaction in the story, producing in Bertha what Sianne Ngai has called 'stuplimity', rather than the classically conceived pleasures of the sublime: see Ngai's *Ugly Feelings* (Cambridge, MA: Harvard University Press, 2005), esp. pp. 248–97.
4. Jean-François Lyotard, *The Postmodern Condition: A Report on Knowledge*, trans. by Geoff

Bennington and Brian Massumi (Minneapolis: University of Minnesota Press, 1989), p. 77.

5. Lyotard, p. 77.
6. Longinus, 'On Sublimity', in *Classical Literary Criticism*, trans. by D. A. Russell (Oxford: Oxford World's Classics, 2008), p. 143. Acknowledging the obscurity of Longinus's identity that makes classical scholars frequently render his name in quotes, I consciously employ his name without quotation marks here.
7. Longinus, p. 144.
8. The former appears in Longinus, 'On the Sublime', in *Aristotle/Horace/Longinus: Classical Literary Criticism*, trans. by T. S. Dorsch (Harmondsworth: Penguin, 1965), pp. 97–158; the latter, in Longinus, 'On the Sublime', in *Aristotle, Poetics; Longinus, On the Sublime; and Demetrius, On Style*, ed. and trans. by W. Hamilton Fyfe, revised by Donald Russell (Cambridge, MA: Harvard University Press, 1995), pp. 161–305.
9. Stephen Halliwell, *Between Ecstasy and Truth: Interpretations of Greek Poetics from Homer to Longinus* (Oxford: Oxford University Press, 2012), p. 357.
10. For the latter, see Jonathan Culler, 'The Hertzian Sublime', *MLN*, 120: 5 (December 2005), pp. 969–85.
11. Neil Hertz, *The End of the Line: Essays on Psychoanalysis and the Sublime* (New York: Columbia University Press, 1985), p. 40.
12. My commentary here compacts, with obviously different emphases, my larger reading of the colonialist priorities that Burke's theory of sublimity houses: see Gaurav Majumdar, *Migrant Form* (New York: Peter Lang, 2010), esp. pp. 7–9, 21–3 and 41–2.
13. Edmund Burke, *A Philosophical Enquiry into the Origin of Our Ideas of the Sublime and Beautiful* (Oxford: Oxford University Press, 1998), p. 125.
14. Burke, pp. 125–6; emphasis Burke's.
15. Burke, p. 126.
16. Burke, p. 66.
17. Immanuel Kant, *Critique of Judgment*, trans. by J. H. Bernard (New York: Hafner, 1951), p. 88; italics Kant's.
18. Culler, p. 977.
19. Culler, p. 977.
20. Culler, p. 973.
21. Sara Ahmed, *The Promise of Happiness* (Durham, NC: Duke University Press, 2010), p. 26.
22. For a reading of this dissatisfaction when it manifests as boredom in Mansfield's stories, see Saikat Majumdar, *Prose of the World: Modernism and the Banality of Empire* (New York: Columbia University Press, 2013), pp. 71–99.
23. Cf. the brief commentary on Mansfield's early stories, as they display her 'anger and disgust with the physical traumas and disfigurements of pregnancy', including a view of 'child-bearing [as] the most ignominious of professions', in Lee Garver, 'The Political Katherine Mansfield', *Modernism/modernity*, 8: 2 (2001), pp. 225–43 (p. 228).
24. Halliwell, p. 366.
25. T. S. Eliot, '[The Feminine Voice]', *Katherine Mansfield's Selected Stories* (New York: W. W. Norton and Co., 2006), p. 343.
26. T. S. Eliot, 'Hamlet', *Selected Prose of T. S. Eliot* (New York: Harcourt Brace Jovanovich, 1975), p. 48.
27. Cf. the 'strange beast' of *wanderlust* that 'began to purr' uncannily *from* Vera's bosom in 'A Dill Pickle', *Katherine Mansfield's Selected Stories*, p. 121.

28. Adriana Cavarero, *Inclinations*, trans. by Amanda Minervini and Adam Sitze (Stanford: Stanford University Press, 2016), pp. 5-6.

29. Cavarero, p. 6.

30. Cavarero, p. 6.

31. Cavarero, p. 6.

32. Even though Bertha sometimes sees objects (such as the pear tree) intensely or imagines things in or even as fragments (e.g. the 'piece' of burning sun in her chest), the story shows us, through the various details she does not register, that seeing things in pieces is, of course, not necessarily seeing them in detail.

33. 'The classical senses of ἔκστασις are 'insanity' and 'bewilderment'; but in late Greek the etymological meaning received another application, viz., 'withdrawal of the soul from the body, mystic or prophetic trance'; hence in later medical writers the word is used for trance, etc., generally. Both the classical and post-classical senses came into the modern languages, and in the present figurative uses they seem to be blended.'

'We were a nothingness shot with gleams of what might be. But no more': Katherine Mansfield, Virginia Woolf and the Queer Sublime

Eleri Anona Watson

Edmund Burke argues that the sublime 'comes upon us in the gloomy forest, and in the howling wilderness [. . .]'. To have the sublime 'come upon' or arrive on us, or to come upon or arrive on the sublime ourselves, is to feel the jolt, hit or agitation of what disturbs us – what disarms our security, stability, equilibrium.

Steven Vine[1]

Phenomenology is full of queer moments; moments of disorientation that Maurice Merleau-Ponty suggests involve not only 'the intellectual experience of disorder; but the vital experience of giddiness and nausea, which is the awareness of our contingency, and the horror with which it fills us.' [...] But if we stay with such moments then we might achieve a different orientation toward them; such moments may be the source of vitality as well as giddiness. We might even find joy and excitement in the horror.

Sara Ahmed[2]

From Edmund Burke and Immanuel Kant's dichotomies of 'bounded' beauty and its sublime, 'unbounded' twin, and from William Wordsworth's individualist sublime to the disruptive 'heterogeneous finalities' of Jean-François Lyotard's sublime 'names of history', the sublime has demonstrated its potential for diverse interpretation.[3] Drawn from divergent critical schools and explicating what might, at first glance, seem disparate concepts, Sara Ahmed's phenomenological queer moment and Steven Vine's aesthetic account of Burke's eighteenth-century sublime appear near identical in their evocations of disruptive, dislocating and horrifically 'delightful' moments. The sublime has seemingly been rerendered within a queer framework.

For Michel Foucault, queerness is an affective and cultural relational system, predicated upon ever-mutating models of kinship across differ-ence. Queerness, Foucault contends in 'Social Triumph of the Sexual

74

Will', is a phenomenological 'way of life' that rejects the paucity of relational choices that constitute and sustain heteronormative models of kinship.[4] In turn, it 'yields', as Foucault elaborates in 'Friendship as a Way of Life', 'a culture and an ethics' of its own, entailing the occupation of a 'slantwise position' to the constraints of institutionalised heteronormative culture.[5] Ahmed's queer 'disorientating moments' (p. 9) are arguably figured into Foucault's 'way of life'. Whilst Foucault's queerness is an enduring and 'lived' actuality, Ahmed presents the arrival of a queer-specific 'way of life' within the fleetingness of Maurice Merleau-Ponty's 'queer moment'.

Incorporated into conceptions of 'queer time', the queer moment is established as a rejection of heteronormativity's 'repro time'. The queer moment resists repro time's future-orientated trajectories, rejecting phenomenology's orientating 'straight' lines of continuity and forward-moving directionality. Disrupting such temporalities, the queer moment arrives as a Burkean or Kantian 'jolt'. The sublime moment appears indistinguishable from queer theory's non-linear queer moment. By cutting through heteronormative structures, for José Muñoz, the queer moment has the potential to express a deviant, unrepresentable queerness. As he elaborates, the queer moment provides sublime instants of timeless ecstasy in this aberrant unknowability.[6] Echoing sublime tradition, such moments are none the less suffused with an abject horror, an inherently sublime pain and danger for the queer individual.

The 'sublime' and the 'queer' moment appear a case of 'a rose by any other name'. Despite their apparent parallels, correlations between the queer and sublime moment have been overlooked by scholars of queer theory and aesthetics. Indeed, tracing the evolution of the romantic sublime, Vine's *Reinventing the Sublime* makes only scant reference to the sublime's queer potentialities, noting, for example, the queer novel's capacity to "'represent that which remains unrepresentable [. . . rendering] queer cultural artefacts, at their core, sublime'".[7] Such fleeting allusions overlook the queer moment as the predominant manifestation of sublimity within queer aesthetics, rendering the sublime an unclaimed category of queer expression.

Feminist readings of the sublime provide a possible reasoning for this occlusion.[8] Historically, the sublime has been the territory of masculinist experience, expressing the formation of patriarchal subjectivity and of individual sovereignty (subordinating the threatening other). This misogynist history of the sublime has hindered feminist re-appropriation of the importance of forming a *counter*-sublime. The Wordsworthian 'romantic sublime' as a fundamentally individualist experience ostensibly runs counter to the communitarian aims that represent the cornerstones of feminist theory and the queer 'way of life'. Whilst the sublime might thus appear to be an impossible category for queerness, in overlooking the interrelated nature of the 'queer' and the 'sublime' moment, queer theorists risk obscuring a transgressive facet of queer temporality.

This is, I contend, the case in Katherine Mansfield's 'Prelude' and 'Bliss', and Virginia Woolf's *Mrs Dalloway*. Employing Woolf's representation of the sublime 'moment' in 'A Sketch of the Past' alongside broader theories of sublimity, I propose that Woolf and Mansfield formulate a distinctly 'queer sublime'. In so doing, I ask: what is the queer sublime? How does it manifest and what is its function in Mansfield and Woolf's works? What, if anything, is achieved or realised in the sublimely queer moment? My analysis focuses on three moments: Sally and Clarissa's kiss in *Mrs Dalloway*, and the appearance of the aloe in 'Prelude' and the pear tree in 'Bliss'. Moreover, using theories of queer time and space, I argue that, more than ignoring an act of queer transgression, to neglect the 'queer sublime' is to disregard the sublime nature of the queer moment as the resulting expression of a sapphic 'way of life' in Woolf and Mansfield's fiction.

* * *

In *Phenomenology of Perception*, Merleau-Ponty contends that though the body has no essential 'specific direction' or orientation, one's body adopts a 'verticality' by continually aligning ('straightening') itself to its surroundings (whose level is always already constituted) in order to permit action and extension into space.[9] When one's orientation has adjusted to a position of verticality in symmetry with one's surroundings, one is ' "in line" ' and ' "the right way up" ' (p. 294). 'Disorientation' is therefore to deviate from one's essential verticality and to experience a 'sudden moment' in which 'a subject sees the room in which he is [. . .] "slantwise", things no longer appear "the right way up" ' (p. 294): one is 'out of line' with collective spatio-temporality and one's directionality is ' "wonky" or even "*queer*" ' (Ahmed, p. 66, my emphasis).

In *Queer Phenomenology*, Ahmed locates Merleau-Ponty's orientation and intentionality within affective models: one is 'directed to what we come into contact with: [one is] moved "toward" and "away" from objects' (p. 2). The intentionality of orientation and Merleau-Ponty's 'vertical line' is recognised as collectively constructed. One is orientated according to 'imagined communities [. . .] "going in a certain direction" or facing the same way' (Ahmed, p. 15). A normative model of orientation is thus established, necessitating one's falling into line: *dis*orientation becomes the constitutive other. Ahmed seemingly re-interprets

Merleau-Ponty's 'queerness' (expressed as 'giddiness' or deviation) in terms akin to Foucault's affective queer 'way of life'. Queerness is that which does not follow verticality's 'straight line'; it is bent and crooked. Institutionalised and obligatory, the straight 'line' becomes that of compulsory heterosexuality.

Ahmed's disruptive moment may be clarified within the broader discourses of queer time. Heteronormativity orientates the individual towards an obligatory temporal and spatial directionality: a compulsory heterosexuality. One is thus compelled to maintain one's position on the 'straight and narrow' line. The individual is compulsorily orientated 'away' from the objects of queerness. Situating this temporally, compulsory heterosexuality involves a 'straight' orientation in time as well as space. Straightness is a commitment to patrilinearity and its power to shape one's movement in space and time; it is a social investment in a linear trajectory of 'reproductive futurity'. In Mansfield's 'Prelude', this is aptly expressed by Stanley's investment in land for future financial gains ('you see land about here is bound to become more and more valuable')[10] with the hope of 'passing it on' to his desired male heir; reproductive temporality is one by which values, wealth, goods and morals are passed down through family ties in the assurance of futurity.

In her autobiographical 'A Sketch of the Past', Woolf articulates the experience of temporal conformity. The hegemonic 'line' of compulsory heterosexuality involves spending one's day 'embedded in a kind of nondescript cotton wool. This is always so. A great part of every day is not lived consciously. One walks, eats, sees things, deals with what has to be done.'[11] Compulsory sexuality becomes an embodied habitus. One lives unconsciously in a mode of non-being within a heteronormative world where, as *Mrs Dalloway*'s original title highlights, one is subject to 'The Hours'. Woolf's hegemonic temporality is fundamentally hetero-patriarchal. A centrally looming figure, the phallic Big Ben, reigns panoptically over the novel. Just as the 'clocks of Harley street [. . .] counsel submission, uph[old] authority',[12] Big Ben is anthropomorphised into the policing magistrate 'laying down the law, so solemn, so just', striking the half-hour with 'the direct downright sound' of the gavel (p. 108). Reverberating across London, Big Ben's strict demarcations of linear rhythmic progress are a seemingly totalising 'security apparatus' of this bio-power. The hetero-patrilinear regime inundates both the public and private spheres: 'the sound of Big Ben flood[ing] Clarissa's drawing-room' (p. 99). It is a medicalised temporality: Dr Bradshaw, in a fine-tuned instrumentation of bio-power, is the embodiment of the 'shredding and slicing, dividing and subdividing clock' (p. 86). Carefully measuring his day into strict 'three-quarters of an hour' appointments, he seeks to police the unruly body, to endow it with a comprehension of the 'proportion' within temporal structures (p. 85). That is, the dominant sentiment of temporal 'regulation' within the hetero-patrilinear framework (the proportional measurement of minutes, hours and days) makes 'it impossible for the unfit to propagate their views until they, too, shared his sense of [the] proportion' (p. 84).

The chronopolitics of heteronormativity necessitates a linear orientation marked by milestones that aim towards a reproductive futurity. In orientating one's movement along the 'straight' lines of ideologically constructed markers, one's action is obliged to be followed by a corresponding response as defined within the schema of 'repro time'. Though writing from a distinctly non-queer perspective, Lyotard's notions of historical continuity and the political sublime aptly express the constructed progressive movement of hetero-patrilineary. Lyotard notes that 'the School, the programme, the project – all proclaim that after this sentence comes that sentence, or at least that kind of sentence is mandatory, that one kind of sentence is permitted, while another is forbidden'.[13] Within this scenario, one is certain of the resultant action or milestone, of how one will proceed.

As Woolf's 'Sketch' highlights, it is this constructed sense of progression that constitutes 'the nondescript cotton wool' of heteronormativity in which one 'deals with what *has* to be done' in accordance with its dictatorship (p. 70, my emphasis). One enacts a performed, sexualised temporality in a generational stylised repetition of the Oedipal pattern: 'one's parents giving it into one's hands, this life, to be lived to the end, to be walked with serenely' (*Mrs Dalloway*, pp. 156–7). As the game of 'ladies' in Mansfield's 'Prelude' demonstrates, hetero-patrilinearity is a scripted, inherited performance adopted in childhood. In a cultural configuration, roles of gender and sexuality are strictly designated according to an Oedipal pattern of dualistic binaries; echoing the structures of their own families, the rules of the game dictate that the male ' "Pip can be the father and [Kezia and Lottie] can be all our dear little children" ' (p. 47). Mirroring Stanley's certainty of sequence and ability to contemplate his future in accordance with the inevitability of hetero-patrilinear temporality – 'He began to plan what he would do with his Saturday afternoons and his Sundays' (p. 36) – the game of 'ladies' is one of obligatory adherence to hetero-patrilinear sequentiality and its 'cotton wool'. As Kezia declares, one must follow a strict succession of action: 'you always make us go to church hand in hand and come home and go to bed' (p. 47).

The gendered and sexualised performativity of the hetero-patrilinear endures into adulthood. In 'Bliss', Bertha follows a linear progression, performing actions and reciting words that, Mansfield writes, are 'as it were, *quoted* by her, borrowed [. . .] she'd none of her own'.[14] The institutionally enforced rhythms and habitus of patrilinearity shape the flesh into a culturally acceptable form of temporal embodiment.

However, as Woolf elaborates, the repetition, inevitability and 'non-being' of 'repro time's' 'cotton wool' may be disrupted: 'my days [. . .] contained a large proportion of this cotton wool, this non-being [. . .] nothing made any dint upon me. Then, there was a sudden violent shock; something happened so violently that I have remembered it all my life' ('Sketch', p. 71). In a Merleau-Pontian act of '*queer*' disorientation, 'Sketch' depicts the arrival of 'sudden violent shock[s]' with a 'sledge-hammer force' (p. 72), shocks that powerfully disrupt bodily orientation, dislocating one's 'straight' directionality, forward movement and 'sequence' in an ephemeral 'moment of being'. Woolf's moment may be understood within the lexicon of Burke's sudden, disorientating 'strike', or moreover in Lyotard's politically sublime 'occurrence' – an 'event of fission' that wounds the unity of master discourses.[15] Rejecting temporal progress, this instant is, as Woolf elaborates, a 'space of time' in which one is 'held in place' in a momentary a-temporality ('Sketch', p. 80). This is the 'hush, or solemnity; an indescribable pause; [. . .] before Big Ben strikes' of *Mrs Dalloway* (p. 3). Diverting the individual from the progressive 'lines' of hetero-patrilinearity, the jolting 'moments of being' disrupt linear time. Echoing Septimus's exclamation that 'the word "time" splits its husk' (p. 59), the 'sudden revelation' forces Clarissa's 'world' of measured 'Hours' to 'split its thin skin' (p. 27). In a queer transformation of sublimity's 'jolt', her 'straight' orientation along the phenomenological 'line' is skewed as memories of the sublime moment of Sally, their queer kiss and its 'religious feeling', are relived (p. 30). Clarissa's past inhabits the present in a durational flux, deviating from progressive hetero-temporality. Cast adrift from reproductive futurity, the sublime moment leaves Clarissa suspended within the sublimity of queer time's defining present tense. The sublime moment is temporally queer.

To imply, however, that the sublime solely embodies a temporal queerness distracts from the phenomenological affect of queer sublimity. Mansfield and Woolf's recurring moments of disorientating 'queer sublimity' overturn constructed affective norms. Arriving as interference, their characters are compulsively driven by an unknown gravitational pull 'towards' objects of queerness and its kinships. 'Pulled' under 'pressure' away from linearity's future-orientation, Woolf's Clarissa and Septimus 'f[a]ll a little behind' in temporality, propelled instead through memory towards their respective objects of queer desire in Sally and Evans (p. 30).

Unlike Woolf's retrospective return to a past moment of queer sublimity, Mansfield's sublime instants do not re-animate memories of queer relationality. Rather, 'overcome, suddenly' within the 'drunk and disorderly' disorientation of queer sublimity, Mansfield's women gravitate towards objects of queerness in a present-tense enactment of queer sublimity rather than of return.[16] Just as Linda in 'Prelude' is ostensibly disassociated from her movements, 's[eeing] herself bending forward' (p. 17) towards queer objects in a moment of queer phenomenological 'affect', Bertha is ostensibly ' "pulled" ' toward the bisexual (hermaphroditic) 'pear tree in its fullest, richest bloom' (p. 122). Bertha 'seem[s] to see [the pear tree] on her eyelids' (p. 123), unable to escape this momentary re-orientation and queer pull. Within the queer sublime moment, queer phenomenological affects are irrevocably imprinted upon the body.

* * *

Mansfield and Woolf present protagonists that are embedded within the heteropatriarchal symbolic order. 'Living all the time in relation to certain background rods or conceptions', they inhabit a world of veiled reality, one in which there is an immutable sentiment of 'a pattern hid behind the cotton wool [. . .] of daily life' ('Sketch', p. 73). Elaborated in Mansfield's 'Prelude' and 'At the Bay', there exists the pervasive presence of an 'IT', an alternate reality behind heteronormativity's symbolic order. Lurking 'just behind her, waiting at the door, at the head of the stairs [. . .], ready to dart out at the back door' ('Prelude', p. 7), the 'something else – what was it?'[17] and its 'mysterious important content' permeate the female's surroundings ('Prelude', p. 24). Lingering behind the poppy in the wallpaper as it 'come[s] alive' or in the knowing smile of the bird in the grass, they are seemingly part of the 'secret society' of a heterotopic sphere that exists beyond heterosexuality's symbolic order (p. 24). The moment of queer sublimity is one of exposure, an eruption of the 'IT' of 'the Real'; 'a token', as Woolf writes, 'of some real thing behind appearances' ('Sketch', p. 72). Disrupting the sexualised politics of temporality and overturning 'straight' phenomenological 'affect', the queer sublime initiates moments of exposure.

Erotic desire is exposed in its sublimely ecstatic and disturbing form. We might recall that 'ecstasy' is derived from the Greek, *ekstasis*: that is, to be outside of oneself. Evoking ecstasy's Greek etymology and Martin Heidegger's phenomenological conception of 'being outside oneself in time', Muñoz writes that ecstasy is timeless, 'a thing that is not the linearity of [. . .] straight time' (p. 186). To enter the a-temporality of the queer sublime, to be dislocated 'outside of oneself' in patrilinear time, is to enter a moment of ecstasy. We see this most poignantly in the moment of Sally and Clarissa's kiss in *Mrs Dalloway*. For Clarissa, it is – in a seeming echo of Gian Lorenzo Bernini's *Ecstasy of Saint Teresa* (Lacan's defining symbol of 'the Other or feminine *jouissance*' which occurs outside the symbolic order (Muñoz, p. 186)) – to experience an ecstatic 'radiance burnt through, the revelation' in queer desire and kinship (*Mrs Dalloway*, p. 30). Reaching its apotheosis as the moment 'gushed and poured with an extraordinary alleviation' (p. 27), *Mrs Dalloway*'s queer sublime is an 'eruption' of queer desire, of an orgasmic 'Real' beyond the bounds of compulsory sexuality's relational system of heterosexual kinship, childbearing and futurity.

If the queer sublime allows for the emergence of relationalities and desires beyond the heteronormative order, then it may trouble the broader underpinnings of this naturalised order. Such a reading might permit a queering of Jacques Rancière's sublime, disruptive moment of 'politics'. Emerging, like Lyotard, from the disruption and political 'dislodging' of Paris's May '68 protests, Rancière examines sudden disruptions in history that permit the instigation of 'politics'. Writing in the communitarian tradition of European leftism, Rancière's disruptive moment of politics is defined as a moment of equality in which speech, action and organisations break from the policing state. Understanding the sublime as a dislocating interruption to the dominant symbolic order, announcing the unveiling of 'the Real', Rancière's disruptive moment of politics may also be interpreted within the grammar of queer sublimity. The queer sublime's eruption of sapphic desire presents an interruption to what Rancière terms the natural allotment of the individual's capacities according to the policing state. The sublime initiates the political process of *subjectivation*, through a *recognition* by which, Rancière elucidates, the individual strays from their naturalised positioning, realising capacities beyond those assigned by dominant structures. Mansfield declares that the sublime moment is a ' "kick off" in [her] writing game', of 'joy' and an '*extremely* deep sense of hopelessness', a revolutionary 'occurrence' that 'wounds' the universal validity of compulsory heterosexuality and its related temporality. Its arrival is, Mansfield explains, a sudden and pained 'cry against corruption',[18] a moment of sapphic plight exposing the rigging of naturalised heteronormativity. The sublime unveils the constructedness of the symbolic order, permitting an individual *recognition* of alternate relational capacities in this 'different time'.

If, as Muñoz writes, ' "queerness" time is the time of ecstasy' (p. 186), it is a sublime 'ecstasy' in queer revelation that is none the less tinged with sublimity's inherent abjection. Burke and Kant fundamentally distinguish between the 'beautiful' and the 'sublime', defining beauty as a 'bounded' entity that may be perceived as 'delightful' in one's rational ability to imaginatively conceive of the whole, in a harmonisation of the imagination with reason. In 'Sketch', Woolf depicts the 'delight' of this beautiful 'boundedness'. Echoing Kant's depiction of the bounded, 'beautiful tulip',[19] Woolf perceives beauty in the 'confined' nature of the flower: '[t]hat is whole [. . . and] I was conscious that [. . .] I should in time explain it' ('Sketch', pp. 71-2). As Kant elucidates, 'meeting with a certain finality in its perception', one finds beauty in the delimited object; one's rational faculties can attune with one's imaginative capacity to perceive the whole [20] and, in Woolf's words, one 'should in time explain it' ('Sketch' pp. 71-2). Sublimity, in contrast, and following Kant's distinction, is an unbounded totality, eliciting horrific delight in one's imaginative inability to conceive or present it fully in its indeterminate unboundedness. Unable to marry rational knowledge with its imaginative boundlessness, one is faced with the horrific attraction of the inexpressible.

However, as Woolf writes in 'Sketch', the horrors of the 'the sledge-hammer force' of sublimity might be overturned: 'I make it real by putting it into words. It is only by putting it into words that I make it whole; this wholeness means that it has lost its power to hurt me' (p. 72). Though the sublime may be an unnameable 'IT', by placing the sublime within the defining boundaries of lexicon and the semiotic order, one might 'make it *real*'. By delimiting the sublime within an assured vocabulary of contemporary socio-political intelligibility, Woolf implies that the 'horrific' sublime might conceivably be rendered 'delightfully' beautiful.

Within the context of the queer sublime and of lesbian history, Woolf's premise holds profound significance. Eight years after the publishing of Mansfield's 'Bliss' and three years after that of Woolf's *Mrs Dalloway*, 1928 saw the publication of Radclyffe Hall's *The Well of Loneliness* and Woolf's *Orlando*. 1928 has arguably signified a turning point in the representation and articulation of sapphic kinships. Emerging from World War I's sexual and economic changes for women, sapphism became a progressively coherent category within the lexicon of popular British culture. However, as preceding decades demonstrate, despite the emergence of the 'homosexual person' as a recognisable category within late nineteenth-century psychological and medical discourse, lesbian identity remained vague and its subculture minimal in comparison to that of male homosexuality. As Jeffrey Weeks elucidates, despite the emergence of this New Woman, it would none the less be 'another generation before female homosexuality reached a corresponding level of articulacy'.[21]

Undefined and unarticulated within the proto-lesbian context of Mansfield's 'Bliss' and Woolf's *Mrs Dalloway*, the hetero-patriarchal symbolic order renders sapphic kinships unrecognisable and unintelligible. Positioned outside the bounded purview of the semiotic order, sapphism's unthinkability within contemporary heteronormative discourses seemingly locates such forms of kinship within the unrepresentable unboundedness of the Kantian sublime. For Woolf and Mansfield's women, sapphism involves a kinship that has no name. As Bertha exclaims in 'Bliss', 'Oh, is there no way you can express it?' (p. 117), the articulation of sapphic experience constitutes a hermeneutic lacuna within the constructed logos of the patriarchal heteronorm – their language is empty and incomplete. Yet, might this 'outside' function as a radical zone for meaning-making for the queer individual, a semiotic hub for sapphic expression?

Denoted ambiguously as '*the thing* [. . .] that mattered' in the moment of queer sublimity of the women's remembered kiss (*Mrs Dalloway*, p. 156, my emphasis), the vocabulary of sapphic eroticism is constituted by a rhetoric of uncertainty. Littered with vague qualifiers ('to seem', 'as if', 'as though'), Mansfield and Woolf's women unsuccessfully attempt to grasp at the expression of the sapphic encounter within the context of a linguistic order that occludes its existence. This is a far cry from the 'putting into words' of 'Sketch'. It is, as *Mrs Dalloway*'s Clarissa laments, 'an inner meaning, *almost* expressed' (p. 27, my emphasis). Dwelling outside formal language, the sublime sapphic experience is pre-symbolic. Whilst Lyotard may claim that a realist rhetoric of adequation is totalitarian in nature ('a frenzy to seize reality'),[22] favouring instead the freedom of an undecidable rhetoric of approximation, the bliss of queer sublimity, this 'outside moment', is far from a semiotic hub and distant from Lyotard's undecidable freedom. Possessing none of her own language, Bertha, in Mansfield's 'Bliss', likewise drives toward the creation of a semiotic system, consistently seeking to ' "give a sign" ', an interpretation of the sapphic experience (p. 130). In both texts, attempts at the linguistic delimitation and explanation of the sublime, sapphic moment ultimately fail. Without an established semiotic grammar or recourse to prior example, 'what she meant by [the sign] she did not know' (p. 130). Attempting to grasp at sapphic expression, Bertha ostensibly misplaces ' "the sign" ' of sapphic kinship in her husband's mistress, Pearl Fulton. The queer moment ultimately remains elusive, semiotically 'unthinkable' and unboundedly sublime.

Employing Lyotard's sequentiality, I have argued that to be located beyond the delimiting boundaries of hetero-patrilineary is to exist outside dominant constructions of a logical sequence of action. Lyotard's logic of sequence might equally be applied to linguistic concerns within the context of the queer sublime. By naming and describing, language delimits meaning (rendering the object or experience 'bounded') whilst also placing it within a specific and constructed grammar and syntax. In accordance with hetero-patrilinearity's relational bounds, as expressed in Lyotard's 'after this sentence comes that sentence', the hermeneutic lacuna which restricts Bertha and Clarissa's ability to express the sublime sapphic encounter renders it extra-linguistic and thus unbounded. Bertha can only accumulate the assemblage of sublime experiences as they come upon her, without the capacity to connect or interpret them. Bertha cannot place the queer sublime moment within a bounded grammar of understanding and rules of sequence (x will lead to y). Without this sequential grammar, there exists the possibility, then, as Lyotard notes, 'of nothing happening' beyond the 'momentary'.[23] This lack is marked in Bertha's silences, ellipses and digressions as she attempts to fill the hermeneutic lacuna, to express the ambiguous '*this*' of queer sublimity: '*This*, [...] was so incredibly beautiful' ('Bliss', p. 118). This 'nothingness' and uncertainty engender anxiety, the horrifically sublime feeling that nothing might happen. Expressed in the juxtaposition in the closing lines of 'Bliss', between Bertha's agonising cry of 'What's going to happen now?' and her unaffected sense of her surroundings – 'the pear tree was as lovely as ever and as full of flower and as still' (p. 136) – one might continue to occupy this hermeneutic lacuna without the prospect of making it whole. It is to fear one's inability to include sapphic desire in life's sequentiality, beyond the brevity of the sublime queer moment, of 'waiting', as Linda expresses it in 'Prelude', 'for someone to come who just did not come, watching for something to happen that just did not happen' (p. 25).

Woolf and Mansfield's queer sublime expresses the phenomenological result of the occlusion of sapphism from contemporary discourses of kinship. If, as *Mrs Dalloway*'s Septimus declares, '[c]ommunication is health; communication is happiness' (p. 109), in lacking the hermeneutic means by which to explain and formalise experience, both the 'health' and 'happiness' of the beautiful are fundamentally denied in these texts to both writers' queer women. Just as Radclyffe Hall would plead in 1928 'before the whole world' to 'give us also the right to our existence', Mansfield and Woolf ask, 'Why must you suffer so?' ('Prelude', p. 42), employing the horrors of the queer sublime to express the need for sapphic validation.

* * *

I have proposed that Mansfield and Woolf's sublime queer moment is the phenomenological expression of queerness. Expressing its construction within queerness's embodied alternate temporalities and trajectories, the queer sublime equally expresses sapphism's contemporary exclusion from discourses of kinship. In *The Queer Art of Failure*, Jack Halberstam writes that despite 'the sometimes counterintuitive links between queerness and socialist struggle' (or more specifically, neo-Marxism's portrayal of queerness's 'ludic body politics' as an obstruction to the 'real' work of class and political activism), there exist 'overt connections between communitarian revolt and queer embodiment'.[24] Constructed in opposition to heterosexuality's 'vertical' orientation, queerness is an embodied identity and experience. Within the context in question, the sublime has the power to launch the individual into a space for the enactment of a Foucaultian queer 'way of life' and its potentiality for a collective affect. The sublime, in terms established by Burke and the romantic canon, functions in opposition to collectivism, engaging in an egotistical sublime, involving possession of the other. However, understanding queerness as a collective identity that engenders a group capacity for sublime disruption and disorientation, one might comprehend the queer sublime as a radical form of sublimity, enacting a queering of archetypal sublimity, disrupting its individualist aestheticism.

The queer sublime moment appears as a sudden revelation in which, *Mrs Dalloway*'s Clarissa expresses, one feels 'the world come closer' in a moment of queer intimacy (p. 27). Though located within a heteronormative family setting, the feminine kinships occurring within the sublime moment of Mansfield's 'Prelude' might ostensibly be understood within the bounds of a queer community. Emphasised in 'At the Bay', the sequel to 'Prelude', Mansfield's women live in fear of the masculine temporality embodied in Stanley Burnell's hetero-patrilinearity as the heteronormative regulating agent of patriarchal authority. Anticipating *Mrs Dalloway*'s 'Big Ben', Stanley presides as 'Jehovah, the jealous God, the Almighty', a policing vehicle of bio-political chrononormativity, 'whose eye is upon you, ever watchful, never weary' ('At the Bay', p. 49). Demanding their compliance with a strict schedule of minutes – 'I've only twelve and a half minutes before the coach passes' (p. 10) – Stanley orients women towards a common heteronormative directionality – 'the cold, bright angels will drive you this way and that' (p. 49) – quashing the possibilities of queer time and queer kinship. Linda notes, 'at His coming the whole earth will shake into one ruined grave-yard' ('Prelude', p. 49); his presence re-orientates queer deviance.

Mansfield's Burnells may constitute a heteronormative family structure; however, its women live in 'dread of having children' and are ostensibly driven to reject its chronopolitics and directionality ('At the Bay', p. 26). In a visual rejection of verticality and Merleau-Ponty's natural positioning of straight orientation, the upright figure of Stanley, 'standing firm in the exact centre of a square of sunlight', is juxtaposed with and 'set worlds away from Linda' and her body's deviance from verticality, as she lounges 'on the white tumbled bed' ('Prelude', p. 21). Faced with sublime images of female fecundity in the icon of the flower and its open sexual invitation, Mansfield's women recoil: Beryl shrieks 'No, no' when faced with a male who suggestively 'thrust(s) his head among the [. . .] flowers' and Kezia gazes in abject disgust at the overt fertility of the 'cream white flower [. . .] too full of insects' (pp. 17, 32). Such imagery is echoed across characters; these reverberations inform a psychic connection between women, a collective phenomenological affect. Rather than possessing the other, this is a shared queer directionality. Initiated by the sublimely disruptive moment of coming upon the aloe, Stanley's heteronormative order is disturbed. Unlike the fertile, feminine iconography of the flower, the aloe is intersexual, possessing both the feminine ability to bloom and a phallic 'blind stem cut into the air' (p. 34). It is two in one, fused, a symbolic intersexual power without gendered obligation. Linda vaguely declares that she 'like[s] it more than anything' for 'no reason at all' (p. 61) – the aloe's pull is sublimely incomprehensible. Its disruption to straight orientation moves Mansfield's women towards the queerly intersexual. Though the sublime experience may remain an ambiguous *it*, the aloe's sublime disruption and disorientation none the less have the power to unite Mansfield's women. Linda and Kezia, and later Linda and her mother, are brought together in the face of the aloe in a queer cross-generational community of women, attempting to explain the sublime *it* in a moment of sororal intimacy: ' "Do you feel it, too," said Linda, and she spoke to her mother with the special voice that women use at night to each other' (p. 60).

In *Phenomenology*, Merleau-Ponty perceives disorientation from 'verticality' as a momentary act, emphasising that 'after a few minutes a sudden change occurs: the walls, the man [. . .] become vertical': the momentary slantwise disorientation of queer sublimity is overcome and one returns once more to verticality (p. 289). The disruption of the queer sublime disorients one's progression along the temporal lines of repro time. Rejecting development, the queer sublime arises as an a-temporal moment. In light of Ahmed's assertion that 'lesbian desires create spaces, often temporary spaces that come and go within heteronormative structures' (p.160), one might argue that in functioning as a space of time, the displacing quality of the queer sublime has the potential for the creation of a heterotopic safe space, if only fleetingly. Beyond the boundaries of futurity and heteronormative affect, the queer sublime formulates a functional margin where queerness and its community may, at least briefly, be enacted.

In *Mrs Dalloway*, Clarissa appears to seek spaces beyond those of heteronormativity. Living in strict avoidance of her husband and the heterosexuality of the marital bed, Clarissa inhabits the distant attic. Ascending to the attic, Clarissa perceives herself as becoming desexualised, 'like a nun withdrawing, or a child exploring' (p. 26), seemingly gaining sexual gratification and rapture from the polymorphously perverse experience of the remembered sapphic sublime moment. As Clarissa enters, its solitary 'emptiness' is transformed into a fantastical sphere – an escape-space from heteronormative existence is opened up. Orientating her towards objects of queer desire, the queer sublime returns Clarissa through memory to the moment of queer community: 'the others disappeared; there she was alone with Sally' (p. 30). An instance of tender intimacy, Clarissa is given 'a present' moment existing beyond the temporal, 'wrapped up, and told just to keep it, not to look at it' (p. 30), a momentary sublime space of queer community to which she may safely return in memory.

*   *   *

Beginning with Merleau-Ponty's concept of disorientation, I have explored the possibility and potentialities of the queer sublime. Through examination of aesthetic, queer and phenomenological theorising alongside works by Woolf and Mansfield, I have contended that the re-appropriated queer sublime is a moment that induces queer transgression, disrupting sublimity's individualism. Contextual examination of the sapphic experience demonstrates that the sublime nature of the queer moment is the phenomenological result of an embodied queer experience expressed within Woolf and Mansfield's contexts.

Though it is tempting to view queer sublimity as emancipatory or expressive of the queer experience, the queer sublime none the less represents a failed queerness for Woolf and Mansfield's protagonists. The queer sublime's sapphic expression in Woolf and Mansfield is fleeting. Seemingly unable to be put into words, queerness cannot be rendered beautifully bounded; the sapphic experience cannot be understood or prolonged. Echoing Merleau-Ponty, despite community building and the sublime's momentary ecstasies, the individual returns to heteronormative verticality: Clarissa's remembrance of queer collectivity does not function as the initiation of a new, radical future, an extended queer temporality: Sally straightens to compulsory heteronormativity, to ' "have five enormous boys" '; Clarissa re-aligns herself, becoming the eponymous Mrs Dalloway, engaging in the certain sequence of heteronormative directionality, 'mending her dress as usual, he thought [. . .]; mending her dress; playing about; going to parties' (p. 35). Whilst physical manifestations of collectivity occur in Mansfield's work, as we find in the narratives of the Burnell family in 'Prelude' and 'At the Bay', sublimity is merely collectivist *in potentiality*. Though Kezia and Linda may share a psychic bond, a 'queer sensation' that 'they were members of a secret society' ('Prelude', p. 24), both seeking to identify the 'IT' of sapphic sublimity, this does not extend to all female kinships. The grandmother's irresponsiveness to Linda's query – 'Do you feel it, too[?]' (p. 60) – solely implicates a physical unity and the mere *potential* of psychic unity. In 'At the Bay', for example, despite 'the difference it made to have the man out of the house' (p. 12), Stanley Burnell's return breaks up the sororal heterotopia, instantly instigating a patrilinear clock-time. Though engaging in Rancière's *recognition* and *subjectivation*, Mansfield and Woolf's women cannot complete Rancière's political disruption of the policing state, inhabiting new-found sapphic identifications and kinship possibilities. They cannot instigate their new-found capacities within the present – the moment cannot become a permanent way of life. Whilst Lyotard's sublime implies a horror in the *possibility* that nothing might happen, the queer sublime, as presented in Mansfield and Woolf's contexts, proposes this nothingness as a dreadful certainty. As Mansfield writes, 'But then I remember what we really felt there, the blanks, the silences, the anguish of continual misunderstanding [. . .] We were a nothingness shot with gleams of what might be. But no more.'[25]

We have established a basis for a sapphic sublime in this period, but unanswered questions remain: what happens to the queer sublime in the ensuing contexts of relative lesbian intelligibility? Should we seek a bounded, intelligible queer 'beautiful' or ought we adhere to queerness's openness to play and *différance*? If the latter is the case, should this be through a conscious attempt to extend the sublimely queer moment? Which identities, minorities, politics and histories might we obscure in the penumbras of the sublime's indefinability and uncertainties? In adhering to a post-modern rhetoric of openness to uncertainty and sublime penumbras of Derridean unknowability, such questions of queer sublimity, its benefits and menaces, must become pressing concerns of contemporary queer theory.

Notes

1. Steven Vine, *Reinventing the Sublime* (Eastbourne: Sussex Academic Press, 2013), p. 12.
2. Sara Ahmed, *Queer Phenomenology: Orientations, Objects, Others* (Durham, NC: Duke University Press, 2006), p. 4. All further references are to this edition and will be included parenthetically in the text.
3. Jean-François Lyotard, 'The Sign of History', in *The Lyotard Reader*, ed. by Andrew Benjamin (Oxford: Blackwell, 1989), p. 394.
4. Michel Foucault, 'Social Triumph of the Sexual Will', in *Ethics: Subjectivity and Truth*, ed. by Paul Rabinow, trans. by Robert Hurley (New York: The New Press, 1997), p. 158.
5. Michel Foucault, R. de Ceccaty, J. Danet and J. Le Bitoux, 'Friendship as a Way of Life', in *Ethics: Subjectivity and Truth*, ed. by Paul Rabinow, trans. by John Johnston (New York: The New Press, 1997), p. 138.
6. José Muñoz, *Cruising Utopia: The Then and There of Queer Futurity* (New York: New York University Press, 2009), pp. 186-7. All further references are to this edition and will be included parenthetically in the text.
7. Davin Grindstaff cited in Vine, *Reinventing the Sublime*, pp. 112–113.
8. See Barbara Claire, *The Feminine Sublime: Gender and Excess in Women's Fiction* (Oakland, CA: University of California Press, 1995), and Bonnie Mann, *Women's Liberation and the Sublime* (Oxford: Oxford University Press, 2006).
9. Maurice Merleau-Ponty, *Phenomenology of Perception*, trans. by Colin Smith (London: Routledge, 2002), p. 290. All further references are to this edition and will be included parenthetically in the text.
10. Katherine Mansfield, 'Prelude', in *Bliss and Other Stories* (London: Constable & Company Limited, 1925), p. 18. All further references are to this edition and will be included parenthetically in the text.
11. Virginia Woolf, 'A Sketch of the Past', in *Moments of Being*, ed. by Jeanne Schulkind (Orlando, FL: Harcourt Brace Jovanovich, 1985), p. 70. All further references are to this edition and will be included parenthetically in the text.
12. Virginia Woolf, *Mrs Dalloway* (Oxford: Oxford University Press, 2000), p. 86. All further references are to this edition and will be included parenthetically in the text.
13. Jean-François Lyotard, *The Inhuman: Reflections on Time*, trans. by Geoffrey Bennington and Rachel Bowlby (Stanford, CA: Stanford University Press, 1991), p. 90.
14. Katherine Mansfield, 'Letter to John Middleton Murry [14 March 1918]', in *Letters Between Katherine Mansfield and John Middleton Murry*, ed. by Cherry Hankin (New York: New Amsterdam Books, 1998), p. 130.
15. Lyotard, 'Sign', p. 410.
16. Katherine Mansfield, 'Bliss', in *Bliss and Other Stories* (London: Constable & Company Limited, 1925), p. 116. All further references are to this edition and will be included parenthetically in the text.
17. Katherine Mansfield, 'At the Bay', in *The Garden Party, and Other Stories* (New York: Alfred A. Knopf, 1922), p. 1. All further references are to this edition and will be included parenthetically in the text.
18. Katherine Mansfield, 'Letter to John Middleton Murry [3 February 1918]', in *Letters Between Mansfield and Murry*, p. 107.
19. Immanuel Kant, *The Critique of Judgement*, trans. by James Creed Meredith (Oxford: Clarendon Press, 1964), p. 80.
20. Kant, p. 80.

21. Jeffrey Weeks, *Sex, Politics and Society: The Regulation of Sexuality since 1800* (London: Longman, 1981), p. xi.
22. Jean-François Lyotard, *The Postmodern Condition: A Report on Knowledge,* trans. by Geoff Bennington and Brian Massumi (Minneapolis: University of Minnesota Press, 1984), p. 82.
23. Lyotard, *The Inhuman,* p. 92.
24. Jack Halberstam, *The Queer Art of Failure* (Durham, NC: Duke University Press, 2011), p. 29.
25. Katherine Mansfield, 'Letter to John Middleton Murry [11 October 1922]', in *Letters Between Mansfield and Murry,* p. 371.

Seeking Blissful Ignorance: Katherine Mansfield's Child Protagonists in 'Prelude' and 'Sun and Moon'

Marlene Andresen

In Katherine Mansfield's *Bliss and Other Stories* (1920), family life is often portrayed as a silent battleground. The struggle for each member to maintain their individuality within an already existing social hierarchy forms the crux of some of her most celebrated stories from the collection. The relationship between children and adults, and their vastly different perceptions of the world, presents an intimate, yet imbalanced social dynamic in these texts. In this essay, my aim is to deconstruct Mansfield's fictional universe through the eyes of the child protagonists in 'Prelude' (1917) and 'Sun and Moon' (1918). Concentrating on Kezia and Sun, I will use a comparative and historical framework in order to examine how these children re-engage with romanticism through modernist aesthetics. The stories demonstrate how Mansfield's experimentation with different points of view through *focalisation* creates a critical lens through which the adult world gets scrutinised. By focusing on the child's unique perspective, critics can gain new insight into one of the many ways in which her short stories push the boundaries of conventional narrative forms. As such, the unusual complexity of Mansfield's child protagonists should be considered one of her major literary achievements in the *Bliss* collection – an achievement which marks her as a truly modern writer.

Mansfield's Romantic Legacy

Adrienne E. Gavin sums up the romantics' 'cult of childhood' as 'a lost, idealized, clear-visioned, divinely pure, intuitive, in-tune-with-nature, imaginative stage of life, of whose spirit adults felt the loss and sought to capture in literature'.[1] For the first time in English literature, the child was given tremendous representational value within the artistic imagination. Hence, as Roderick McGillis explains, the child always remained 'more idea than fact'[2] for the romantics; children in the real world were now re-imagined within a *fictional* frame. Not only did this core idea enable poets to let their imagination flourish during the eighteenth century, but the romantic child, as we will see, also continued to inspire the literary imagination in years to come.

By the time *Bliss and Other Stories* was published in 1920, authors and critics had conflicting perceptions about all things pertaining to 'sentimentality'. The child's usefulness as a device for artistic innovation was heavily debated. Still, it is important to acknowledge that the romantic child is not simply a curiosity of the eighteenth century, but an enduring cultural and literary figure which underwent continual renegotiations by the next generation of writers. This is why we see such a longstanding fascination with child protagonists in literature even today; the figure itself continues to evolve in keeping with new social and cultural demands.

On the surface, 'Prelude' and 'Sun and Moon' offer a conceptualisation of the child as a timeless figure. However, by taking a closer look at Mansfield's narrative techniques as she brings these characters to life, we see how she exposes the underlying frailty at the heart of such romanticised ideals. Kezia and Sun are indeed bearers of this longed-for, glorified past in which adults may seek comfort, but as protagonists their function is ultimately to dismantle this very same construct. To appreciate this paradox fully, we need to examine how Mansfield's formal experimentation brings uncertainty to what appears to be a safe world of childhood. This critical approach brings an element of self-scrutiny to her stories, signalling the child figure's subversive potential as a literary device.

Kezia and the 'Innocent Eye'

'Prelude' is not only one of Mansfield's most personal stories from the *Bliss* collection; set in her native New Zealand and inspired by her own memories of being a child, it is also one of her most boundary-breaking texts in terms of formal experimentation. The story's fluctuating narrative perspective depicts the Burnells, a family comprised of what Gérard Genette's narrative theory identifies as *focalising* characters.[3] The narrator's focalisation through Kezia as she explores the garden offers readers a glimpse into a distinctly childlike world. Certain passages echo quintessential qualities of the romantic child, particularly its free-spirited creativity and artistic intuition. Such episodes make Kezia's unique voice instantly recognisable amongst the story's focalising adult characters:

> There were clumps of fairy bells, and all kinds of geraniums, and there were little trees of verbena and bluish lavender bushes and a bed of pelargoniums with velvet eyes and leaves like moths' wings. There was a bed of nothing but mignonette and another of nothing but pansies—orders of double and single daisies and all kinds of little tufty plants she had never seen before. (CW2, p. 72)

The precise classification of each flower according to type and the protagonist's botanical fixation invite readers to immerse themselves in the beauty of the natural landscape. However, there is also a subtle break in the narrative on a structural level which is not consistent with the child's supposed limited knowledge about the world. The precise naming of each flower is a departure from the otherwise childlike and playful associations: some flowers also had 'leaves like moths' wings', and there were 'all kinds of little tufty plants she had never seen before'. Whilst Kezia engages the reader in this game of words, the added botanical knowledge reveals a hidden agenda in the text. We suddenly get a glimpse of something lurking in the background: an educated perspective – a *grown-up's* voice – belonging to a narrator who is likely more knowledgeable in botany than a child of Kezia's age. This shift in focalisation adds another layer to the text. Now, the adult and the child engage in a narratorial exchange where the narrator, presumably an adult, offers *more* information than the child's dominant mode of focalisation would normally allow. This instance of what Genette calls *paralepsis*[4] illustrates how the adult projects romantic attributes onto the child through the text's very structure and narrative situation. This poses a new dilemma to the interpretation of the story: is Kezia simply a representation of an idealising discourse, or does she also confront us with the very impossibility of such escapist fantasies – this modern obsession with an obscure notion of 'childhood innocence'?

Writing in the eighteenth century about the child's way of existing in tune with nature formed part of a reaction against Enlightenment doctrines and increased industrialisation. What we need to recognise, however, is that these literary endeavours did not simply vanish with the modernist movement in the arts; the romantic child maintained its function as a trope well into the twentieth century.[5] Mansfield's technique of variable focalisation places Kezia in opposition to her family, allowing the author to critique the grown-ups' alienation from nature and their fixation upon status and cultural norms. The wonder with which Kezia observes the garden is contrasted by Stanley's economic ambitions: ' "You see land about here is bound to become more and more valuable," ' he boasts. Beryl equates the natural surroundings with social isolation, being ' "pretty certain nobody will ever come out from town to see us' ". For Linda, the countryside merely increases her resentment towards her family: 'She saw herself driving away from them all in a little buggy, driving away from everybody and not even waving' (CW2, pp. 65, 89, 66). Stanley fails to appreciate the land in its natural state, and the women experiences the stillness and remoteness of the countryside as a negative; Beryl is worried about her chances to meet a potential husband so far away from the city, while Linda's desire to escape the demands of marriage and motherhood only intensifies. Overall, the adults fail to perceive their natural surroundings with Kezia's childlike sense of freedom.

If we are to judge Kezia's appeal according to romantic ideals, we grant her a privileged position amongst her family. Tracy Miao argues that much of Kezia's attractiveness within this social unit is a result of her unique ability to derive artistic inspiration from nature.[6] Adopting John Ruskin's theory of 'the innocence of the eye', Miao designates the role of 'child-artist' to the little girl.[7] Inspired by the beautiful flowers in the garden, Kezia decides to make her grandmother a surprise matchbox:

> First she would put a leaf inside with a big violet lying on it, then she would put a very small white picotee, perhaps, on each side of the violet, and then she would sprinkle some lavender on the top, but not to cover their heads. (CW2, p. 72)

Kezia knows exactly what she wants her artwork to look like, planning the flower arrangement with careful precision. As a creative visionary and a giver of gifts, Kezia is presented in a favourable light in the text; both generous and affectionate, she is the romantic child who will share her world with any adult who is willing to partake of it. Her grandmother, whose freedom is constricted by household duties, delightfully accepts and participates in this playful vision: ' "Good gracious, child! How you astonished me!" ' she responds (CW2, p. 73). Seldom able to enjoy the outdoors due to her responsibilities in the household, the grandmother is now offered a miniature representation of the magical garden through Kezia's 'innocent eye'. Similarly, the reader is given a glimpse into this universe through Mansfield's clever use of internal focalisation. As George Shelton Hubbell asserts, 'we interpret everything through [Kezia's] child-mind, free, unsuspicious, unafraid, winged by imagination'.[8] The joyous world offered to both grandmother and reader promises a return to this longed-for state of innocence – before it was replaced by the demands of adulthood. The child suggests there is still hope that such blissful ignorance can – if only temporarily – be regained.

Sun's Imaginative Play

Mansfield's exploration of the child's world through focalisation is also present in 'Sun and Moon'. Similar to Kezia, Sun offers the reader a new lens through which the adult world can be observed and critiqued. Mansfield's technique here, however, differs slightly from that of 'Prelude': first, focalisation is now carried out by a single character throughout. Sun's limited vision – the narrative's *restriction of field*[9] – renders the adult world even more obscure. Second, Mansfield places a much stronger emphasis on the child's unique language. Linda Pillière highlights Sun's wrongful pronunciations, incorrect use of grammar and word boundaries; in sum, his language lacks precision, resulting in an abundance of indeterminates, repetitions and short sentences in the text. Moreover, this tells us something about the child's general incapacity to analyse data correctly.[10] Mansfield's conscious play with an underdeveloped language ensures that the divide between the adult and the child becomes especially prominent.

This story, however, does not deal with the child's connection with nature; the setting is not a garden, but rather the confines of the family home. Sun's creative observations are nevertheless of the same artistic and associative quality as Kezia's, showcasing that the child's creative abilities endure even in a domestic and constricted environment. As such, Sun also mediates the 'innocent eye', and everything around him is perceived with a childish sense of wonder. But just as we will see in 'Prelude' later on, the narrative will soon disrupt his world in disturbing ways.

The opening paragraph in 'Sun and Moon' presents a domestic, as opposed to a natural, scene. Still, the aesthetics remain the same; Sun's world is filled with beautiful and strange things. Immediately, the child-like descriptions make the reader aware of the protagonist's young age:

> In the afternoon the chairs came, a whole big cart full of little gold ones with their legs in the air. And then the flowers came. When you stared down from the balcony at the people carrying them the flower pots looked like funny awfully nice hats nodding up the path. (CW2, p. 136)

Adjectives such as 'little' and 'funny awfully nice' suggest a childlike observer, and Sun's direct address – 'when *you* stared down from the balcony' [my italics] – invites the reader to embrace the child's gaze and join him in the associative play that is unfolding on the page. The sibling relationship between Sun and Moon is then established, as well as Sun's point of view as the oldest of the two: 'Moon thought they were hats. She said: "Look. There's a man wearing a palm on his head." But she never knew the difference between real things and not real ones' (CW2, p. 136). Moon has yet to enter what Pamela Dunbar terms 'the mature world of separate consciousness and symbolic significance';[11] for the younger sibling, anything that can be observed seems plausible and real, while Sun dwells on the border between child and adult consciousness. He partakes in the associative game, yet recognises that what things look like are not necessarily what they *really* are. The opening thus sets up the premise for the rest of the story: the divide between the adult and the child's worlds, the disruptive journey from innocence to experience and the problems of existing in between the two.

Sun's direct addresses to the reader and the fantastical imagery with which ordinary objects are described – even the naming of the characters themselves – infuse the domestic scenery with another romantic fixation: children's fairy tales.[12] This means that Sun experiences the cook's dinner preparations as a magical adventure: 'He made squiggles all over the jellies, he stuck a collar on a ham and put a very thin sort of a fork in it; he dotted almonds and tiny round biscuits on the creams [. . .]' (CW2, p. 137). Sun's limited knowledge and vocabulary mean that he must describe these sensory experiences through imaginative associations. As opposed to Kezia's precise classification of the flowers in the garden, there is no adult perspective lurking in the background to fill in these informational gaps for Sun. However, the attention to and fascination with detail in 'Prelude' is clearly echoed in this passage. Sun may not be able to understand why the household is preoccupied with so many unusual activities, but his ability to construct representative images around a single, miniature phenomenon is the narrative's prime focus throughout:

> Oh! Oh! Oh! It was a little house. It was a little pink house with white snow on the roof and green windows and a brown door and stuck in the door there was a nut for a handle. When Sun saw the nut he felt quite tired and had to lean against Cook. (CW2, p. 137)

The miniature house symbolises the ideal home in all its domestic bliss, but it is the nut that has the most profound effect on Sun, whose overwhelming reaction points to the child's ability to experience artistic pleasure from minute details – details whose significance escapes the adult's busy gaze.

Pillière further suggests that the number of visual details in 'Sun and

Moon' contributes to our notion of the child's limited point of view: the focaliser is 'someone who views the world in a different way from us and is unable to synthesise all that he experiences'.[13] This is certainly true if we look at Sun's reaction to the little nut; he is completely overwhelmed by the fact that this object can signify something completely different when placed in a different context; the nut is no longer a nut, but a door handle! Sun's excitement over this transformation exists on the border between a rite of passage into the symbolic world of adulthood and his current status as an unsuspecting child with a guileless creative vision. The ice pudding is not meant to impress the guests and showcase social status; for Sun, it obtains *intrinsic* value as an aesthetic object.

Ultimately, 'Prelude' and 'Sun and Moon' play with ideas about the romantic child through variable and fixed modes of internal focalisation. In both cases, the child's gaze is drawn to specific objects, whether a matchbox filled with flowers or a little nut imitating a door handle. These are details which escape the adults in the stories, whose lives revolve around acquiring social status, making a profit off real estate, securing good marriages and arranging lavish parties to impress friends. These preoccupations overshadow other aspects of life: the joy derived from little, everyday objects and occurrences, and the pure bliss of existing in the here and now.

Kezia and Sun's worldview is blissfully ignorant and trans-historical, subscribing to a romantic ideology which favours the individual's autonomy, connection with nature, and imagination. Mansfield, however, does not simply create an escapist retreat into an elusive state of childhood innocence. What makes her stories so profound are the ways in which she employs idealising discourses about childhood, only to dismantle them brutally. The shift from romantic escapism through an idealised child figure to a more realist and also subversive discourse can be clearly traced in these two stories. This is precisely why Mansfield should be recognised as one of the most radical modernist authors of the twentieth century.

Modernism and the Dismantling of the Romantic Child

Whilst romantic in origin, Mansfield's child characters share many characteristics with Victorian children. The child was still very much a sentimental figure for the period's realist authors, but children also attained a new – and arguably more progressive – agency. The reader's emotional engagement with literary children became a cry for social change, shedding light on children's often poor 'physical and material circumstances', as Naomi Wood notes.[14] In other words, writers' romantic, *inward* gaze now turned towards *external* issues in the modern world.

The key difference between realist conventions about childhood and Mansfield's short stories, however, lies in her resolute and self-conscious experimentation with literary form. For the modernists, the victimisation of the child could also be conveyed through the very structure of the work itself. Mansfield's modernist aesthetics exploit the child as a metaphor for a new philosophy of art; the child enabled her to be experimental and playful with narrative conventions. Paul March-Russell notes that literary children such as Kezia contributed to 'the Modernist project of renovating language'[15] and, I will argue, to further deconstruct romantic sentimentality in subtle yet brutal ways. The child's emphasis on 'the new' paradoxically becomes an emphasis on 'the old', but the old renegotiated in *new ways* as traditional narrative conventions are discarded. But more than just creating a different aesthetic experience, Mansfield's experimentation also infused her childhood stories with social and ideological critique.

To achieve this, both 'Prelude' and 'Sun and Moon' must take a darker turn. Just as Kezia leaves her grandmother and ventures outside after giving her the matchbox gift, she discovers an elevation in the landscape where 'nothing grew on top except one huge plant with thick, grey-green, thorny leaves' (CW2, p. 73). As opposed to the colourful flowers in the garden, Kezia cannot make sense of this huge, thorny and decaying plant: 'Some of the leaves of the plant were so old that they curled up in the air no longer; they turned back, they were split and broken; some of them lay flat and withered on the ground' (CW2, p. 73). The plant captivates Kezia's gaze much like the flowers in her matchbox did. This time, however, the object triggers confusion and fear. Kezia can neither identify the plant by name nor reconstruct it in a game of imaginative associations: 'Whatever could it be? She had never seen anything like it before' (CW2, p. 73). Until Kezia learns that it is an aloe, the plant belongs to an inaccessible world outside of her limited comprehension. The aloe introduces an uncanny mood in the narrative by removing the child from the safe confines of the garden. She now inhabits a temporal space which is much more uncertain, and this signals the emergence of a future with a much darker potential for Kezia.

Whilst the vibrant flowers in the garden were associated with Kezia's close relationship with her grandmother, the withering aloe links her together with her absent mother in disconcerting ways. As Kezia stares at the plant, Linda comes down the path – the only instance where they share a physical space in the story. The aloe represents the point at which their lives intersect; without it, there would be no communication between mother and child at all. The aloe reconstructs the adult world symbolically as a world of physical and spiritual deterioration – the world her mother inhabits, and the future which Kezia must inevitably face herself. Their shared fascination with the plant suggests an unspoken identification between them, and its decay reminds the reader that childhood may not be so timeless after all. Later, Linda tells her own mother: '"I like that aloe. I like it more than anything here. And I am sure I shall remember it long after I've forgotten all the other things"' (CW2, p. 87). Whilst Linda and Kezia share the creative ability to identify with objects, the attributes which captivate them differ. These two episodes represent two opposite perspectives: Kezia's colourful flowers mediate a romantic world of imagination and creativity, and Linda's identification with the decaying aloe suggests what comes after: old age, patriarchal oppression and, in short, the loss of childhood innocence.

Not only suggesting that the 'innocent eye' is a temporal and illusory state, the aloe also foreshadows a brutal rite of passage later in the story: the beheading of the duck. Pat welcomes the children to partake in what is described as an exciting adventure: '"Come with me,"' he said to the children, '"and I'll show you how the kings of Ireland chop the head off a duck."' He describes the ducks as follows: '"There is the little Irish navy [...] and look at the old admiral there with the green neck and the grand little flagstaff on his tail."' Pip and Rags are excited to participate in Pat's militaristic make-believe game. Isabel, however, has some reservations: '"Do you think we ought to go? [...] We haven't asked or anything. Have we?"' (CW2, pp. 80–1). For one, the children are already somewhat attuned to traditional gender roles; while the boys are excited to witness the violence, the girls are more apprehensive about the idea. Yet, Isabel's concerns also suggest that what they are about to see involves something forbidden for both boys and girls, something which may thwart their innocent worlds permanently. This combination of fear and excitement places them yet again on the border between the safe world of childhood and the unknown and possibly dangerous world of adulthood.

As the beheading commences, the children are immediately overcome with excitement: 'Even Isabel leaped about crying: "The blood! The blood!"' They are described as 'shouting', 'shivering', 'jumping', 'laughing' and 'running' around the duck as it starts to waddle towards the stream – likely in a fit of post-mortem spasms – 'with only a long spurt of blood where the head had been' (CW2, p. 82). Kate Fullbrook describes this scene as 'an adult "rite" of death' and 'a primal fall from innocence'.[16] Dunbar similarly notes: 'In the beheading episode we have not the innocent and idealised children of the early romantics but savage and instinctual twentieth-century beings.'[17] In sum, we witness the splitting of two worlds through imagery of violence and death, wherein the gradual dismantling of Kezia's universe reaches its climax. The beheading also reveals a much darker aspect of nature; not only a source of beauty and creativity, the natural universe can be brutally indifferent to humans' unease with their own mortality. While the natural world offers pleasure and wholesomeness for the individual, it can also bring the most barbaric aspects of the human psyche into the light. This sudden 'hysterical thrill of the sadist', Hubbell remarks, mediates 'the deeply disquieting consciousness of belonging to a society which subsists by such dark, repulsive deeds'.[18] And it is precisely Mansfield's clever use of focalisation which reframes the romantic child through such dark modernist aesthetics, thus unveiling an added interpretative complexity to the two stories.

However, the children's transformation from innocents to 'instinctual twentieth-century beings' is never set in stone. Kezia's subsequent reaction highlights the narrative's ambivalence towards the very dismantling it aspires to provoke:

> But Kezia suddenly rushed at Pat and flung her arms round his legs and butted her head as hard as she could against his knees.
> 'Put head back! Put head back!' she screamed.
> When he stooped to move her she would not let go or take her head away. She held on as hard as she could and sobbed: 'Head back! Head back!' until it sounded like a loud strange hiccup. (CW2, p. 82)

The romantic idealisation of innocence is revealed as a vulnerable construct when Kezia screams in horror at the sight of the duck, and the passage highlights how Mansfield's use of narrative disruptions reveals romanticism's darker potential: namely, its own conceptual impossibility. Kezia wants to reverse time and go back to a state prior to this loss of innocence – to unlearn the knowledge of death and other such unfathomable aspects of adult life. Mansfield does not place the girl in either camp; Kezia cannot *unsee* what she has just seen, she cannot *undo* what has been done, and no one will ever be able to 'put head back'. She is nevertheless unable to process and derive any meaning from this harsh reality, and the scene ends before any insight has been gained. Hence, the reader is now left with more questions than answers.

Mansfield's formal experimentation – the episode's abrupt ending and her refusal to resolve the conflict in the beheading scene – mirrors this unresolved problem of innocence and corruption. The subjective experience of being trapped in a state of stasis corresponds to the abundance of repetitions in the narrative, particularly the phrase 'put head back!' W. H. New argues that repetition in Mansfield's fiction generally 'draws attention not to movement or enterprise or vitality but to a lack of progress, a failure of alteration, an inability to embrace change, a resistance to time'.[19] Kezia's attempt to 'resist time' – to *grow up* – marks another effect of being stuck between two aesthetic modes. To 'resist time', then, is also a refusal to move on from romantic conventions and instead embrace modernity.

We see a similar disruption taking place in 'Sun and Moon' when the siblings sneak downstairs in the middle of the night after the grown-ups' party is over. Again, Mansfield experiments with contrasting perceptions in the narrative, not unlike the juxtaposition between Kezia's joyful exploration of the garden and the uncanny appearance of the aloe plant. Sun is horrified by the sight of the once familiar dining-room:

> And so they went back to the beautiful dining-room. But–oh! oh! what had happened. The ribbons and the roses were all pulled untied.
> The little red table napkins lay on the floor, all the shining plates were dirty and all the winking glasses. The lovely food that the man had trimmed was all thrown about, and there were bones and bits and fruit peels and shells everywhere. There was even a bottle lying down with stuff coming out of it on to the cloth and nobody stood it up again. (CW2, p. 140)

Chaos, disorder and incomprehensibility: this is the child's reaction to what is, in fact, the remnants of a successful, if somewhat rowdy, party. Dunbar identifies the story's central theme as another conflict between innocence and experience: 'The sketch is another rite-of-passage tale; a fable about the inevitable spoiling of perfection and of the child's primal sense of contentment.'[20] 'Sun and Moon' thus continues 'Prelude's' interrogation of childhood innocence; the imagery in Sun's observations suggests a form of violent slaughter similar to what Kezia describes during the beheading of the duck. Sun presents the dining room as an allegorical battlefield where violence has been inflicted upon an otherwise harmonious and perfect world. Not only are decorations and dishes 'untidied' and 'dirty', but everything else has been 'thrown about', and there are 'bones and bits' scattered all over. A particularly disturbing sight for Sun is the 'stuff coming out of' a bottle, a description reminiscent of blood discharging from a dead body. Sun's imaginative game of associations thus takes a much darker turn. Just like Kezia, he concludes – but this time figuratively – that the grown-up world is inherently violent and unsafe.

Like the aforementioned beheading scene in 'Prelude', the focus in

'Sun and Moon' is placed on a specific object. Sun's attention returns to his favourite centrepiece: the house with the little nut for a door handle. Like the duck's head which cannot be 'put back', he witnesses an irreversible act of tearing something apart. The house has also been broken, and when Father asks the children if they want to have a taste, Moon takes the nut off the door and eats it. The rest of the family's greedy gorging then takes on a savage nature:

> 'Have a bit of this ice,' said Father, smashing in some more of the roof. [...] 'Daddy, Daddy,' shrieked Moon. 'The little handle's left. The little nut. Kin I eat it?'
> And she reached across and picked it out of the door and scrunched it up, biting hard and blinking. (CW2, p. 141)

Again, echoing Kezia's 'Head back! Head back!', Sun panics at the sight of his sister eating his favourite decoration, but he is unable to translate this traumatic experience into coherent sentences. Through verbal repetitions, he too communicates an inability to accept that nothing in this world can be eternally fixed: 'Suddenly he put up his head and gave a loud wail. "I think it's *horrid-horrid-horrid!*"' he sobbed (CW2, p. 141, my italics). The adults fail to explain the nature of these events to the child, thus bringing him no consolation or resolution. In this story, we see that adults unknowingly inflict pain and suffering upon the victimised child, who is unable to defend himself from his fragile position within the family's imbalanced power hierarchy. Yet more than anything, as Reinhard Kuhn argues, 'Often the representation of the child is an expression of the bourgeois infatuation with the family as the perfect social unit.'[21] In Mansfield's story, it seems that the function of the miniature house is both to mirror and to critique a seemingly perfect domestic sphere. When this highly symbolic object is destroyed and eaten, Mansfield also breaks apart this romanticised domestic illusion.

When placed within a more extended historical and cultural context, Mansfield's child protagonists and her use of focalisation and narrative disruptions mirror the instability of modernism itself. The breaking apart of childhood innocence leads to a break with the dream of a world built upon romantic illusions. Even if Kezia and Sun lack this understanding, the reader must face the inevitable dissolution of any archaic notion that a simpler, childlike and more in-tune existence with nature can ever be fully retrieved.

Margaret R. Higonnet argues that we need to recognise that the child in modernist literature mediates what Franco Moretti has termed 'the instability of Modernism'.[22] In Mansfield's two stories, the instability lies in our ambivalence to navigate between innocence and experience; the child as a metaphorical device exists somewhere in between a longed-for, romanticised past and a potentially exciting, yet unknown future. Mansfield preserves some of Kezia and Sun's original innocence and invites us to re-engage with our own 'inner child', yet she also reminds us that all of this is but an illusion; like everything else, childhood cannot withstand the test of time. These protagonists are both arrested in time *and* forever changed by the rite of passage into a stage closer to adulthood.

Blissful ignorance, it seems, can be both comforting and deceptive, and Mansfield suggests that the latter reality is something we all must inevitably face. More than anything, these brutal yet incomplete transitions from childhood to adulthood highlight in Mansfield's stories the child protagonist's complexity and stylistic richness – a potential of which the writer knew how to take full advantage.

Notes

1. Adrienne E. Gavin, ed., 'The Child in British Literature: An Introduction', in *The Child in British Literature: Literary Constructions of Childhood, Medieval to Contemporary* (London: Palgrave Macmillan, 2012), pp. 1–18 (pp. 7–8).
2. Roderick McGillis, 'Irony and Performance: The Romantic Child', in Gavin, pp. 101–15 (p. 102).
3. Gérard Genette, *Narrative Discourse: An Essay in Method*, trans. by Jane E. Lewin (Ithaca, NY: Cornell University Press, 1980), p. 186.
4. Genette, pp. 195–7.
5. Cherry A. Hankin, 'Katherine Mansfield and the Cult of Childhood', in *Katherine Mansfield: In from the Margin*, ed. by Roger Robinson (Baton Rouge: Louisiana State University Press, 1994), pp. 25–35 (p. 28).
6. Tracy Miao, 'Children as Artists: Katherine Mansfield's "Innocent Eye"', *JNZL: Journal of New Zealand Literature*, 32 (2014), pp. 143–66 (pp. 150–1).
7. Miao, pp. 144–5.
8. George Shelton Hubbell, 'Katherine Mansfield and Kezia', *Sewanee Review*, 35 (1927), pp. 325–35 (p. 326).
9. Genette, p. 194.
10. Linda Pillière, 'Through the Eyes of a Child: The Language of Katherine Mansfield's Child Narrators', *Anglophonia*, 9 (2001), pp. 143–52 (pp. 144–52).
11. Pamela Dunbar, *Radical Mansfield: Double Discourse in Katherine Mansfield's Short Stories* (London: Macmillan, 1997), p. 150.
12. Dunbar, pp. 150–1.
13. Pillière, p. 151.
14. Naomi Wood, 'Angelic, Atavistic, Human: The Child of the Victorian Period', in Gavin, pp. 116–30 (p. 120).
15. Paul March-Russell, 'Baby Tuckoo among the Grown-Ups: Modernism and Childhood in the Interwar Period', in Gavin, pp. 196–211 (p. 209).
16. Kate Fullbrook, *Katherine Mansfield* (Bloomington and Indianapolis: Indiana University Press, 1986), p. 74.
17. Dunbar, p. 141.
18. Hubbell, p. 331.

19. W. H. New, *Reading Mansfield and Metaphors of Form* (Montreal: McGill-Queen's University Press, 1999), p. 103.
20. Dunbar, p. 150.
21. Reinhard Kuhn, *Corruption in Paradise: The Child in Western Literature* (Hanover, NH: University Press of New England, 1982), p. 66.
22. Margaret R. Higonnet, 'Modernism and Childhood: Violence and Renovation', *Comparatist*, 33: 1 (2009), pp. 86–108 (p. 90).

Of 'Trust' and 'Mistrust':
Reading the Mind of a Predator in
'The Little Governess'

Argha Kumar Banerjee

'Well, I always tell my girls that it's better to mistrust people at first rather than trust them, and it's safer to suspect people of evil intentions rather than good ones ... It sounds rather hard but we've got to be women of the world, haven't we?'[1]

'While the tram swung and jangled through a world full of old men with twitching knees.'[2]

'"The Little Governess" is an uncomfortable depiction of a young girl, journeying alone through Europe, at the mercy of predatory males.'[3]

In her short story 'The Little Governess', Katherine Mansfield pits a young, inexperienced woman against the agile schemes of an old man whom she befriends during the course of a train journey towards Augsburg. Through an exploration of the old man's character, Mansfield meticulously unravels the mind of an abuser, whose intentions and ulterior motives are slowly revealed, becoming clear only by the end of the story. Through an evocative, subtly nuanced psychological exploration, Mansfield also underlines the vulnerability conferred by a sheltered existence to which a woman is conditioned by a patriarchal society.

Mansfield initiates her tale with the conventional admonitions used to ensure conformist female conditioning, with the lady at the Governess Bureau providing a chain of instructions for the governess embarking on her first journey abroad: 'You had better take an evening boat and then if you get into a compartment for "Ladies Only" in the train you will be far safer than sleeping in a foreign hotel' (p. 139). As Bronwen Fetters rightly observes, 'this warning from the woman at the bureau shows the societal expectation for women to close themselves away in order to keep safe', as 'women are charged with not only reactionary but also preventative duty in the case of danger'.[4] The list of do's and don'ts does not end there, as the little governess is bombarded with an extended catalogue of the gender-specific conformities and expectations: 'Don't go out of the carriage; don't walk about the corridors and be sure to lock the lavatory door if you go there' (p. 139). Even the advice for negotiating with occasional hunger on the way is conveyed rather brusquely: 'And when you want anything to eat I would advise you to pop into the nearest baker's and get a bun and some coffee' (p. 139).

Through a close examination of the little governess's anxiety-ridden trip – from a world of seclusion to one of gendered experience and exposure to the public world – Mansfield repeatedly makes her female protagonist react on predictable lines. A probable outcome of her protected lifestyle, the governess would have preferred to avoid commencing her journey at night: 'OH, DEAR, how she wished that it wasn't night-time' (p. 139). However, she did not have much choice in this regard, as her travel plans had already been finalised by the lady at the Governess Bureau, who insisted that she would be safer spending the night on a train, rather 'than sleeping in a foreign hotel' (p. 139). Mansfield here suggests how an oppressive milieu, coupled with a sheltered mode of female existence, tends to constrict the comfort zone of an individual, especially in public spaces of extended social interactions. As the story unfolds, we witness how all these conditioning factors ultimately contribute to the victimisation of the female protagonist in 'The Little Governess'. According to Sydney Janet Kaplan, 'the little governess is not merely an emblem of woman as victim, but a representation of ideology's construction of woman as a target for victimization'.[5]

The initial part of the journey reveals the contrast between the diffident governess and her co-passengers on the boat. As she rests on the 'hard pink-sprigged couches', she observes her 'friendly and natural' co-passengers, who, in sharp contrast to her inhibited and extremely self-conscious existence, are at ease, engaged in spontaneous routine activities: 'pinning their hats to the bolsters, taking off their boots and skirts, opening dressing-cases and arranging mysterious rustling little packages, tying their heads up in veils before lying down' (p. 139). The 'tight bunch of flowers' peeping out from the water bottle 'on a shelf above her head' seems to underline her tentative gaze at the outer world, though she is deeply bound in the ordered claustrophobic conditioning of her existence. Despite these overtures, the little governess seems to enjoy her tentative initiation into the outer world in the relative safety of the gendered segregation of the 'Ladies Cabin' on the boat. However, seeds of anxiety unfold as the boat journey terminates and the governess makes her way up on the deck with the dress basket in one hand and her rug and umbrella in the other, intending to embark on her onward train journey. Her ingrained fears and apprehensions affect her interactions with her co-passengers, especially members of the opposite sex. Indeed, Mansfield makes effective use of images to convey the governess's faltering exposure to the public world – the 'cold', 'strange' flow of the wind, the black 'masts and spars of the ship' pitted against a 'green glittering sky' and the 'strange muffled figures' – all of which portend a world of fear and anxiety. Janka Kascakova refers to the cold wind as a precursor, 'a foreboding of the misfortunes [the little governess] will inadvertently bring upon herself'.[6] Leaving the relative safety of the 'safe, pink, feminine world of the Ladies Cabin, the little governess enters the grim, dark, phallic world where "masts and spars" stand erect before her, the world of which she has been forewarned'.[7]

The first instance of friction that we encounter in the course of her journey occurs with the advent of the intrusive porter 'in a black leather cap', who '*touched* her on the arm', before he 'pounced on her dress basket', imposing himself on her in a 'rude, determined voice', confident of his vulnerable potential target (p. 140). In spite of 'trembling with terror', however, the little governess asserts herself by refusing the porter what he considers his due. As a retaliatory measure and means of reasserting his patriarchal control, the porter takes off the *Dames Seules* label from her compartment door, denying her the comfort and security of the exclusive female space she had previously enjoyed on the boat.

Before her impending train journey, Mansfield portrays the deep anxiety in her central protagonist's mind through a curious mingling of colour symbolism. This anxiety is reflected through a rich diversity of colours ('green', 'red', 'black', 'white'), which conveys the lure of multiple distractions of life for the uninitiated. The engulfing 'strange light from the station lamps' with its deluge of 'green', 'the little boy in red', 'woman in a black alpaca apron' and the 'wreaths of white smoke' conjure up a variegated prelude to a new, unexplored world, where roots of anxiety originate in the governess's mind from the 'four young men in bowler hats', whose presence makes it evident that the protagonist's stress is further exacerbated by interactions with members of the opposite sex. After her stressful encounter with the porter, she spontaneously seems to recoil upon the arrival of the four young men, who ultimately settle in the next compartment of the train. Mansfield's exploration of sexual anxiety surfaces in the governess's perception of proceedings from a 'safe corner':

> She heard them tramping about and then a sudden hush followed by a tall thin fellow with a tiny black moustache who flung her door open.

'If mademoiselle cares to come in with us,' he said, in French. She saw the others crowding behind him, peeping under his arm and over his shoulder, and she sat very straight and still. 'If mademoiselle will do us the honour,' mocked the tall man. One of them could be quiet no longer; his laughter went off in a loud crack. 'Mademoiselle is serious,' persisted the young man, bowing and grimacing. He took off his hat with a flourish, and she was alone again. (p. 141)

The governess's negotiation with the external world, as portrayed during this initial stage, is stereotypically gendered. While it had been a relatively calm experience for the governess in the 'Ladies Cabin' of the boat, her journey into the world beyond instils in her mind a deep sense of anxiety. The personified train suggests the governess's initiation to a dark unknown world:

With a long leap it sprang into the dark. She rubbed a place in the window with her glove but she could see nothing – just a tree outspread like a black fan or a scatter of lights, or the line of a hill, solemn and huge. (p. 142)

From the touch of the imposing porter in his black leather cap, to the jesting of the four young men in bowler hats, Mansfield prepares her readers for the most complex yet traumatic encounter to follow in the form of the governess's interaction with the old man who later joins her in the compartment. The central experience of the governess's encounter with her older co-passenger in the train compartment is portrayed by Mansfield in considerable detail, as she provides an insight into the mind of an old man largely through subtle suggestions and his interactions with his solitary female co-passenger. In *Inside the Minds of Sexual Predators*, Katherine Ramsland and Patrick N. McGrain observe: 'Essentially, a person becomes a predator through mental rehearsal that helps to prepare for opportunities and to empower him or her to act.'[8] In Mansfield's story, the reader is invited to decode the mind of an inveterate predator, indefatigable in his efforts at skilful, manipulative seduction, though he is concealed as an innocuous and dignified old gentleman. We receive an interesting insight into the modus operandi of a disguised perpetrator, especially when it comes to his choice of victim, the approach towards ensnaring his target and the preferred time and mode of execution of the sexual attack.[9] At the very outset, Mansfield understates the old man's entry in the train compartment – an initially forbidden zone. In tune with propriety, the governess's initial reaction to the old man is one of cautious approval: 'I never could have dared to go to sleep if I had been alone' (p. 142). While Mansfield gives us a glimpse of the thought processes of the governess, only the gestures and actions of the old man are presented before us. This requires readers to draw their own inferences from his gestures and interactions, just as the governess does over the course of her journey.

The governess frames her opinions of the old gentleman on the basis of the apparently dignified way he carries himself: 'How spick and span he looked for an old man,' the governess wonders at the outset of the journey, falling for the false mask of respectability: 'He wore a pearl pin stuck in his black tie and a ring with a dark red stone in his little finger; the tip of a white silk handkerchief showed in the pocket of his double-breasted jacket. Somehow, altogether, he was really nice to look at' (p. 142). She is so impressed by the surface sheen that she even discards her predispositions and prejudices towards the elderly: 'Most old men were so horrid. She couldn't bear them doddery – or they had a disgusting cough or something' (pp. 142–3). However, this man seems different and has a clear appeal for the governess: 'But not having a beard – that made all the difference – and then his cheeks were so pink and his moustache so very white' (p. 143). The old man's initial interactions with the governess in the train compartment seem polite, gracious and courteous. From 'bowing graciously' to generously offering 'illustrated papers' to the lady, the old man's conduct perfectly falls in tune with that of the governess's expectations of orthodox conformity as befitting any stranger of his age. His behaviour allows the anxious governess to relax, take off her hat and gloves, settle down comfortably and even read the papers supplied to her. Though apparently there is no overt indication of anything sinister in the old man's behaviour, it is clear from his initial interaction with his co-passenger that he wants to build his trust with the 'little governess'. As psychologist Stanton Samenow observes, such offenders tend to be 'masters of deceit', proficient at chicanery and crafty in masking their true motives and intentions.[10]

Mansfield provides the first clue to the insidious nature of the old man through the description of his surveillance, which tends to hover round the preoccupied governess, occasionally bordering on the zone of deriving intense voyeuristic pleasure:

> How kindly the old man in the corner watched her bare little hand turning over the big white pages, watched her lips moving as she pronounced the long words to herself, rested upon her hair that fairly blazed under the light. Alas! How tragic for a little governess to possess hair that made one think of tangerines and marigolds, of apricots and tortoiseshell cats and champagne! Perhaps that was what the old man was thinking as he *gazed and gazed*, and that not even the dark ugly clothes could disguise her soft beauty. (p. 143)

Mansfield's evocation of 'tangerines', 'marigolds', 'apricots', 'tortoise-shell cats' and 'champagne' to describe the governess's hair is covertly symbolic. The ambiguous nature of the narrative also seems to suggest that the little governess is projecting her desires on to her co-passenger. The citrus tangerine tends to symbolise the infusion of instant energy in the viewer's mind while marigolds (also referred to as 'the herb of the sun') connote strong passions, desires and winning affection from someone. While apricots traditionally signify the rise of renewed hope, champagne ultimately calls for indulgence and a celebration of life. In this context, it is also interesting to note Mansfield's choice of 'tortoise-shell cats', or 'torties' as they are affectionately called – underlying the intrinsic feminine charm associated with the governess's hair – more so, as male tortoiseshells are extremely rare and usually sterile; 'tortoiseshell cats' are exclusively female. In the folklore of many cultures, cats of tortoiseshell coloration tend to possess a distinct personality, accounting for their unique charm and appeal. Through her carefully chosen phrases, Mansfield makes it evident that the old man eroticises the governess's physical attributes. These erotic suggestions seem to serve as a precursor, kindling warm desires in the mind of the beholder, as the authorial voice gradually reveals the true intentions of the governess's co-passenger.

In this context, it is important to consider the old man's choice of the governess as a potential victim. It is in tune with the psychologist's viewpoint that 'vulnerability is all by itself stimulating'.[11] Thus, we as readers might guess that the vulnerable disposition of the solitary governess in itself may have been a factor contributing to the old man's obsession with the little governess. In clinical terms, the old man in Mansfield's story fits the bill of being a 'persuasion-predator', one who is perpetually on the lookout for a 'vulnerable victim', especially an individual who will allow him to be in control:

> Like a shark circling potential prey, the persuasion-predator approaches slowly and watches to see how people react to his advances. He begins a dialogue and with each favourable response he elicits, he circles closer. He makes a small initial investment, a low-risk strategy that allows him to test the waters and move on with nobody the wiser if things don't go well.[12]

In the ensuing conversation, which Mansfield constructs with utmost care, she provides further insight into the predatory mind and the strategy of the old man. After flattering the governess about her fluent German, he manages to flush out significant details about the governess's life, which, on certain occasions, she reveals almost unwittingly. In tune with psychological observation, the process of such a seduction at the initial level 'aims not at passion, but at trust'.[13] In accordance with this, the old man tests her experience, enquiring: ' "You have been in

Germany before, of course?" "Oh no, this is the first time" – a little pause, then – "this is the first time that I have ever been abroad at all"' (p. 143). Subsequently, without wasting much time, he is quick to impose his schemes upon her: ' "But you will like Munich." ' He even weaves a romantic dream world to entice and ensnare his target:

> 'Munich is a wonderful city. Museums, pictures, galleries, fine buildings and shops, concerts, theatres, restaurants – all are in Munich. I have travelled all over Europe many, many times in my life, but it is always to Munich that I return. You will enjoy yourself there.' (p. 144)

Though the governess rejects his proposal, in the process of doing so, she reveals more details about her future plans: ' "I am going to a post as governess to a doctor's family in Augsburg" ' (p. 144). The revelation further encourages the old man in luring her, encouraging her to store up 'pleasant memories' with a brief exploration of the city: ' "But what a pity not to see Munich before you go. You ought to take a little holiday on your way" ' (p. 144). The governess firmly refuses the offer yet again, but further exposes her vulnerability by insisting that such adventures are unwarranted for young women travelling 'alone'. Repeated disapprovals pave the way for an awkward silence in their conversation, as the authorial exploration of the moment takes on a symbolic suggestiveness: 'The train shattered on, baring its dark, flaming breast to the hills and to the valleys. It was warm in the carriage. She seemed to lean against the dark rushing and to be carried away and away' (p. 144). The 'train', usually engendered as a masculine entity, seems to project its 'dark, flaming breast' ambiguously – making its way through the 'hills' and 'valleys' – emblematic of the world of nature. The 'warmth' within the carriage, along with the image of being 'carried away and away' in the darkness rushing outside, seems to connote the strengthening of a passive but strong acquiescence on the part of the Governess.

Undeterred by his recurrent failures to win her trust and confidence, the old man reverts to his protective demeanour, voluntarily offering to protect the governess from the intruding (male) passengers, and even going to the extent of apologising to the young lady for the behaviour of the 'common, vulgar fellows!' in the adjoining compartment. It is this twin-fold lure of consistent amiability and protectiveness that perhaps wins over the mind and confidence of the little governess. Mansfield's subsequent description of the external scenes and the governess's inquisitive reactions to these sights reveal the gradual change in her mindset – from defiant, brusque refusal to a gradual, thoughtful reconciliation:

A cold blue light filled the window-panes. Now when she rubbed a place she could see bright patches of fields, a clump of white houses like mushrooms, a road 'like a picture' with poplar trees on either side, a thread of river. How pretty it was! How pretty and how different! Even those pink clouds in the sky looked foreign. It was cold, but she pretended that it was far colder and rubbed her hands together and shivered, pulling at the collar of her coat because she was so happy. (pp. 144–5)

As the train slows down while crossing a town, Mansfield alludes further to a gradual transformation of the governess's mindset, as she describes the 'taller houses, pink and yellow' gliding by. In the protective company of the old man, the entire townscape, 'fast asleep behind their green eyelids', seemed to be 'guarded by the poplar trees that quivered in the blue air as if on tiptoe, listening' to the secrets of her heart (p. 144), an image reflecting the old man standing guard over the governess. The quivering of the poplars in the 'blue air' reinforces the fact that the governess, in spite of her new-found liberation, is deeply entrenched in a 'man's world' and lacks agency. Her vulnerability and emotional manipulation are further corroborated through the image of the 'pink clouds' that 'looked foreign', signifying her impending status as a susceptible foreigner in an alien land. In the outer world, the sight of a woman opening shutters, flinging 'a red and white mattress across the window frame' while simultaneously glaring at the passing train, seems to unleash an image of contradiction and struggle. The interplay of 'red' and 'white' in this description seems to suggest the tussle between carnality and restraint, wilful submission and resistance, and the warmth of company with the coldness of seclusion.

Mansfield also seems to contrast the sheer naïve innocence of the governess's thought process with the obsessive baleful game plan of the old man accompanying her. The string of pastoral images in the form of a 'flock of sheep', 'the shepherd' in a 'blue blouse and pointed wooden shoes', further enhance the mood of serenity and reconcilement in the governess's mind. As C. A. Hankin observes, 'as long as the little governess's repressed wishes are kept within the realm of "fairy" or "story book", her enjoyment with the old man is unlimited'.[14] The floral imagery further re-affirms the mood of contentment: 'standard roses like bridesmaids' bouquets, white geraniums, waxy pink ones that you would never see out of a greenhouse at home'. While 'white' geraniums conventionally connote purity and innocence, the 'waxy pink' ones traditionally evoke warmth and love. Mansfield's use of floral imagery here is evocative, as it not only indicates the dilemma in the mind of the governess but also portends the forthcoming experiences of traumatic realisations.

The diffident, unsure, inexperienced governess at the start of the journey is now portrayed as an apparently confident young lady gazing at her glass image as one who needed 'nobody else to assure her that she is "quite all right behind"' (p.145). Yet, as W. H. New affirms, 'the little governess has been trained to interpret life according to story-book paradigms, but in practice they do not prove as absolute, as "perfect" as convention declares them to be'.[15] In fact, such a disposition makes her more vulnerable to the designs of the male predator. That the indefatigable old German gentleman has managed to make an impact on her mind is evident when she worries that he may be left behind after a brief halt in the journey. She feels reassured upon his return: 'she dimpled at him as though he were an old accepted friend' (p. 145). This nod of approval paves the way for the old man to exercise a greater hold over his co-passenger, as henceforth he seems to keep track meticulously of the young lady's needs and emotions, taking full control of her vulnerable situation and misplaced trust. As Gavin de Becker observes, 'misplaced trust is the predator's most powerful resource',[16] and by giving the old German such trust, contravening the warning at the Governess bureau, Mansfield paves the way for the impending disaster by contrasting the wonderful nature of the day with the parched void within the little governess: 'Oh, it was daylight – everything was lovely if only she hadn't been so thirsty' (p. 145). Her thirst is satiated by the old man's 'basket of strawberries', which she had earlier desired when the vendor had come by but had to decline due to the exorbitant price. The old man makes it clear that he had bought them exclusively for her, as it has been almost 'twenty years since I was brave enough to eat strawberries' (p. 146). Mansfield again conveys the imposing dominance of the old man over his co-passenger through a rather detailed, sensuous image of the juice of the overtly red, juicy strawberries: 'They were so big and juicy she had to take two bites to them – the juice ran all down her fingers – and it was while she munched the berries that she first thought of the old man as a grandfather' (p. 146). According to Pat Kirkhan, the strawberry evokes contradictory suggestions, being 'culturally coded as both innocent and sexual',[17] and Maria Casado Villanueva adds that as the 'first fruit of the year' it not only suggests innocence but 'its juiciness and freshness has also a voluptuous element' associated with it.[18] The erotic connotation of the scene is obvious, however, as Fetters observes: 'The old man uses the berries in an attempt to awaken the little governess sexually, but as she eats them, she thinks of the man as her grandfather instead of as a lover.'[19]

In spite of failing in his erotic intent to get his desired response from the governess, the old man still succeeds in earning her trust as a surrogate grandfather. Having established a more personal relation-ship, the old man becomes insistent on his plan of taking the governess out for a sightseeing trip of Munich – an offer which she has already firmly discarded earlier. This time, however, he repeats his offer under slightly alleviated circumstances: 'I wonder if you would let me show you a little of Munich today.' Desperate to create an opportune moment of intimate proximity, he further clarifies: 'Nothing much – but just perhaps a picture gallery and the *Englischer Garten* (English Garden).' He almost coaxes his way to gain her consent: 'and you would give an old man a great deal of pleasure' (p. 146).

It is interesting to note that in spite of granting the German a hard-fought consent, the little governess still continues to register her acqui-escence as the outcome of a moral dilemma. As the old man veers the conversation towards the direction of 'travels in Turkey' and the 'attar of roses', 'she wondered whether she had done wrong. After all, she really did not know him' (p. 146). Yet, notwithstanding the nagging doubts and misgivings, the decision tilts in favour of the old man as the governess is perhaps overwhelmed with his protective presence, his apparent kindness and deference. As Hankin acknowledges, she fails 'to distinguish between truth and wish fulfilment'.[20] In fact, given the old man's inveigling and persuasion, there is perhaps no option for her to decline his offer. Mansfield coins yet another image from the world of nature to reveal the state of the governess's mind: 'A drop of sunlight fell into her hands and lay there, warm and quivering' (p. 146). The 'sunlight', emblematic of a new lease of life, infusing warmth and radi-ance, is at the same time described as 'quivering', a word that conveys an impression of uncertainty, doubt, hesitation and indecision. The governess's dilemma is aptly conveyed through this image, having been coerced, or at least persuaded, despite her better judgement, to give her consent due to the carefully manipulated congenial circumstances.

Gaining her consent, the old man furthers sets in motion his agenda, setting afloat yet another gentle request for the lady: 'If I might accom-pany you as far as the hotel' and 'call you again at about ten o'clock' (p. 146). He doesn't stop there; he takes out his pocket book and hands her a visiting card, which has a significant impact on the governess. Now she put all her doubts at rest, feeling deeply convinced about the gentle-man's integrity and reliability, a direct offshoot perhaps of her immatu-rity: 'Herr Regierungsrat . . . He had a title! Well, it was *bound* to be all right!' (p. 146). Her belief that the old man is a government councillor not only grants him instant credibility in her mind, but simultaneously triggers a reckless abandon in the governess's behaviour:

So after that the little governess gave herself up to the excitement of being really abroad, to looking out and reading the foreign advertisement signs, to being told about the places they came to – having her attention and enjoyment looked after by the charming old grandfather – until they reached Munich and the *Hauptbahnhof* (main railway station). (pp. 146-7)

The sequence of events subsequent to her consent proceeds on predictable lines. The protective (indeed, apparently shielding) old man escorts the governess on her onward journey. Searching for a porter, he disposes of his own luggage and guides her 'through the bewildering crowd out of the station'. Mansfield re-evokes the colour imagery, with her emphasis on the 'clean white steps' and the 'white road to the hotel' – underlying the innocence of things in the governess's life which is soon going to change forever (p. 147), perhaps alluding to the governess's virtuousness and virginity. The 'ugly, cold room' of the hotel again asserts the sharp contrast with the warmth of the nascent bonding shared by the old man and the governess. In a remarkable instance of a brilliant inversion in the narrative, Mansfield reminds her readers of the 'cold, strange wind' that the governess confronted following the completion of her boat journey in the relatively secure warmth of the 'Ladies Cabin' at the start of the story. Ironically, largely due to her naïvety and immaturity, the governess wrongly associates the warmth of the 'Ladies Cabin' with the companionship of the old man, rather than the real security and safety of her room in the Hotel Grunewald, in spite of its apparent 'ugly' coldness. The illusory respite from such a cold confinement comes through her escape to the outer world of space, sunshine, congenial company of the 'fairy grandfather' and a taste of freedom. Even here, Mansfield concentrates on the images of innocence by focusing on the colour 'white': 'Over the white streets big white clouds fringed with silver – and sunshine everywhere' (p. 147). In addition, the 'immense fountains', 'noise of laughing', 'coachmen driving fat cabs', 'people laughing and pushing against one another', lush greenery, 'open windows' all combine to suggest a mood of celebration and convivial spirit (p. 147). The 'grandfather' who accompanies the governess seems 'more beautifully brushed than ever', having spruced himself up specifically for the special occasion. He even discards his dull 'brown gloves' for the smarter, brighter 'yellow' ones. Mansfield ironically sums up the ecstatic mood of the governess – overjoyed at her new-found freedom and bliss: 'She wanted to run, she wanted to hang on his arm, she wanted to cry every minute, "Oh, I am so frightfully happy!"' (p. 147). According to Janet Wilson, the childlike behaviour of the little governess signals a resistance to 'adult modes of behaviour': 'These unguarded impulses, savagery and cruelty in sexual love, fear of engulfment, *the desire for security and adult protection*, define the luminal space between childhood and womanhood, *the subject's confusion and hence susceptibility to misinterpreting reality*.'[21] However, with her new-found experience and freedom, time – literally and metaphorically – comes to a grinding halt for the little governess: 'My watch has stopped. I forgot to wind it in the train last night' (p. 148). Similar to Wilson, Villanueva suggests that 'her obliviousness of time and her romantic view of the world around her' are symptomatic of a sentimental personality, 'whose idealising imaginations lead them to misinterpret reality'.[22]

In spite of the wonderful time spent together, the little governess is keen to keep her appointment at the Hotel Grunewald with Frau Arnholdt at six in the evening – intending to return to her hotel at least an hour before her scheduled rendezvous. The old German inevitably tries to delay her plans. Having sneaked a rare moment of physical intimacy during a rain shower, justifying it by proclaiming that in Germany it is customary to do so – ' "if you take my arm, Fraulein. And besides it is the custom of Germany" ' (p. 148) – he makes the seemingly innocuous offer of an ice-cream with an assurance: 'After the ice-cream I shall put you into a cab and you can go there comfortably.' Mansfield describes the eating of chocolate ice-cream with all its sensuous details: 'the chocolate ice-cream melted – melted in little sips a long way down'. However, the joy of the 'shadows of the trees' that 'danced on the tablecloths' makes the governess oblivious of the 'ornamental clock that pointed to twenty-five minutes to seven'. Trapped in her dream world, 'her grateful baby heart glowed with love for the fairy grandfather' as she burst out ironically: 'this has been the happiest day of my life. I have never imagined such a day' (p. 148). Mansfield's choice of words underlines the innocence of the governess's attachment towards the old man. The glow of love that her 'grateful baby heart' radiates is the naïve childlike attachment for her 'fairy grandfather' in an unknown city and country.

It is at the end of the day that the old man reveals his true colours to the governess. Having gained the trust of his targeted victim, he follows the trajectory of the sexual predator by manipulating his victim into 'physical and psychological vulnerability'.[23] Indicating the big buildings in the opposite direction, he informs her that he lives on the third storey of one of them and persuasively invites her to catch a glimpse of his 'bachelor's flat' before boarding a cab for the hotel. Leading the governess through the 'dark' passage, he brings her to his room, making way for an opportune moment to unravel his plans. He chooses a time when the old housekeeper predictably seems to be away: ' "Ah, I suppose my old woman has gone out to buy me a chicken. One moment" ' (p.149). This comment leaves the readers 'to wonder whether the housekeeper ever existed or if she was a fabrication of feminine familiarity, created by the old man to abate the little governess's potential uneasiness with the completely male space of his apartment'.[24] Mansfield carefully leads the reader to the climax of her tale. Amidst the ominous silence, with trembling hands, he pours wine into two pink glasses, requesting the governess to join him. Perhaps sensing something uncanny, the uncomfortable governess strikes a discordant note and tries to escape from the situation by insisting 'I think I ought to go now' (p. 149). Seeing her defiant stand, the old man modifies his position, requesting her just to accompany him for five minutes before parting. Sitting at the edge of the red velvet couch, the governess has no other option but to watch the old man gulp down the wine in honour of her health. Still seeking the governess's acquiescence, the old man makes his final, desperate bid: '"Have you really been happy today?"' (p.149). Mansfield decodes the intimidating body language – especially the close physical proximity – between the old man and the governess: 'so close beside her that she felt his knee twitching against hers' (p. 149). The old man's 'twitching' or trembling is an obvious erogenous manifestation of his agitated state of mind, daring to initiate a sexual relationship with the little governess. Even before the governess can respond to the imposing gesture, 'he held her hands', pleading her for a 'little kiss' before she departed (p. 149). As Hankin points out, the journey from the world of fantasy to one of reality ends in disappointment and disillusionment for the governess, as when 'he attempts to make love to her [. . .] and fantasy threatens to become reality, she reacts with horror and outrage':[25] 'It was a dream! It wasn't true! It wasn't the same old man at all. Ah, how horrible! The little governess stared at him in terror' (p. 149). Interestingly, despite of the rapid unfolding of these alarming developments, the governess is still in a state of denial of the reality. As Villanueva rightly observes, 'not until later will she understand that the idea of the perfect day was the dream, and that, like an evil witch, the man had been feeding her with the intention of making of her his prey afterwards'.[26] On the other hand, this was the culminating moment that the old man had meticulously planned for. As the old man's doggedness and perverse resolve move towards their anticipated goal, Mansfield poignantly contrasts the sheer revulsion and trauma embodied in the little governess:

'No, no, no!' she stammered, struggling out of his hands. 'One little kiss. A kiss. What is it? Just a kiss, dear little Fraulein. A kiss.' He pushed his face forward, his lips smiling broadly; and how his little blue eyes gleamed behind the spectacles! 'Never – never. How can you!' She sprang up, but he was too quick and he held her against the wall, pressed against her his hard old body and his twitching knee and, though she shook her head

117

from side to side, distracted, kissed her on the mouth. On the mouth!
Where not a soul who wasn't a near relation had ever kissed her before
... (p. 149)

Through a very carefully constructed narrative and a dramatic reversal
of situation, Mansfield reveals the traumatised governess's 'brutal awak-
ening to reality', and dramatises how the sexual advance of the old man
'destroys the governess's preconceived idea of how the world should
work'.[27] Yet, throughout the story, since the initiation of the train journey, Mansfield has provided important insights into the mind of an old
man as the quintessential predator. She brilliantly traces the gradual
unfolding of his plan of action, his motives and desires, his relentless
obsessive pursuit of the governess, all of which culminates in the sexual
assault at the end of the story. As the little governess's desperate return
journey to the hotel tends to jangle 'through a world full of old men
with twitching knees', we receive an impression of the psychological
and emotional trauma that afflicts a victim and survivor of sexual assault
(p. 150). In this final part of her trip, she exudes total disenchantment,
as Mansfield inevitably suggests that the abusive traumatic encounter
with the old man would colour all her interactions with the opposite sex
in the future. As Jenny McDonnell observes, Mansfield tricks the reader
'into assuming the veracity of the governess' perspective before unveiling a surprise ending in which the old man that the governess perceives
to be harmless and benevolent proves anything but'.[28] Referring to the
governess as 'little' throughout the story, as Villanueva notes, Mansfield
'underlines the governess's helplessness and serves to infantilise a character who is not a little girl as in the fairy tale, but a woman whose
job should be, paradoxically, taking care of children'.[29] Her childlike
persona underlines her naïvety, clear absence of experience in life and
discomfort in public interactions beyond traditional gendered spaces.
Through the character and experience of the little governess, Mansfield
points to the larger societal lacunae, especially the upbringing and
education of women which dissociate them from the world of reality,
denying the governess the ability to perceive the real motives of the old
man. As the waiter at the Hotel Grunewald conveys the devastating news
of Frau Arnholdt's departure to the governess, we are left with the tragic
lone figure of the young woman, who is 'left violated, jobless and entirely
mistrusting of men'.[30] Significantly, the juicy strawberries which initially
won her consent ironically force Patrick D. Morrow to conclude: 'The
governess was consumed by men just as she consumed the strawberries
given to her on the train.'[31] At the very end of the story, Mansfield, as
she does in some of her other tales in *Bliss*, stages one final confronta-

tion to reinforce her message, this time between the distraught 'little governess' and one of the male waiters in the hotel. This waiter takes delight in informing her that her employer, 'the lady', had come and gone, muttering under his breath "That will show her" (p. 150). The waiter, as a male, gets pleasure from enforcing the hypocritical rules of the patriarchy, while the young governess, whose only mistake has been her naïvety before the advances of an elderly predator, is left shocked, unemployed and terrified.

Notes

1. Katherine Mansfield, 'The Little Governess', in *The Collected Stories of Katherine Mansfield* (London: Wordsworth Classics, 2006), p. 139. Hereafter all references to Mansfield's story are to this edition and page references are placed parenthetically in the text, except for note 2.
2. Mansfield, 'The Little Governess', p. 150.
3. Gerri Kimber, *Katherine Mansfield: The View from France* (Bern: Peter Lang, 2008), p. 117.
4. Bronwen Fetters, 'Patriarchal Pink: Gender Signification in Katherine Mansfield's "The Little Governess"', in *Katherine Mansfield and Psychology*, ed. by Clare Hanson, Gerri Kimber and Todd Martin (Edinburgh: Edinburgh University Press, 2016), pp. 165–71 (p. 166).
5. Sydney Janet Kaplan, *Katherine Mansfield and the Origins of Modernist Fiction* (Ithaca, NY: Cornell University Press, 1991), p. 390.
6. Janka Kascakova, ' "Blue with Cold": Coldness in the Works of Katherine Mansfield', in *Katherine Mansfield and Literary Modernism*, ed. by Janet Wilson, Gerri Kimber and Susan Reid (New York: Bloomsbury, 2011), pp. 188–201 (p. 192).
7. Fetters, p. 167.
8. Katherine Ramsland and Patrick N. McGrain, *Inside the Minds of Sexual Predators* (Oxford: Praeger, Greenwood, 2010), p. 2.
9. Ramsland and McGrain, p. 2.
10. Stanton E. Samenow, 'The Thinking Processes of Sexual Predators', *Psychology Today*, 15 December 2017. Available at <https://psychologytoday.com/us/blog/inside-the-criminal-mind/201712/the-thinking-processes-sexual-predators> (last accessed 19 November 2019).
11. Gavin de Becker, Foreword, in Anna C. Salter, *Predators: Pedophiles, Rapists, and Other Sexual Offenders* (New York: Basic Books, 2003), pp. ix–xiv (p. xi).
12. de Becker, pp. ix–xii (p. xi).
13. de Becker, pp. x–xii (p. xi).
14. C. A. Hankin, *Katherine Mansfield and her Confessional Stories* (London: Macmillan, 1983), p. 100.
15. W. H. New, *Reading Mansfield and Metaphors of Form* (Montreal, Kingston, London and Ithaca, NY: McGill-Queen's University Press, 1999), p. 91.
16. de Becker, pp. x–xii (p. xi).
17. Pat Kirkhan, *The Gendered Object* (Manchester: Manchester University Press, 1996), p. 92.
18. Maria Casado Villanueva, 'The Little Red Governess: Mansfield and the Demythologisation of the Motif of "Little Red Riding Hood" in "The Little Governess"', *Katherine Mansfield Studies* 4 (2012), pp. 5–19 (p. 13).

19. Fetters, p. 168.
20. Hankin, p. 98.
21. Janet Wilson, 'Katherine Mansfield's Stories 1909-1914: The Child and the "Childish"' in *Katherine Mansfield and Continental Europe: Connections and Influences* (Hampshire: Palgrave Macmillan, 2015), p. 224, my emphasis.
22. Villanueva, p. 16.
23. Michele A. Paludi and Ashley Kravitz, 'Sexual Harassment of Adolescent Girls by Peers, Teachers, Employers, and Internet Predators', in *The Psychology of Teen Violence and Victimization*, vol. 1 (Oxford: Praeger, 2011), p. 164.
24. Fetters, p. 169.
25. Hankin, p. 100.
26. Villanueva, p. 17.
27. Villanueva, pp. 16–17.
28. Jenny McDonnell, *Katherine Mansfield and the Modernist Marketplace: At the Mercy of the Public* (Basingstoke: Palgrave Macmillan, 2010), p. 84.
29. Villanueva, p. 12.
30. Fetters, p. 170.
31. Patrick D. Morrow, *Katherine Mansfield's Fiction* (Bowling Green, OH: Bowling Green State University Press, 1993), p. 67.

A NEW STORY

A Mysterious Lost Story by Katherine Mansfield

Martin Griffiths

While researching for my essay 'Katherine Mansfield's Australia',[1] on TROVE – the National Library of Australia online library database aggregator – a potential new short story by Katherine Mansfield, titled 'The Thawing of Anthony Wynscombe' ('TTAW') surfaced.[2] Two versions were published, one in Sydney and one in Warwick, Queensland, the former in Sydney's *Star* on Saturday, 25 June 1910, and signed 'Katharine R. Mansfield'.[3] An extensive search of records, including ancestry, shipping and voter lists, confirmed that no other writer of that name lived in Australia or elsewhere. Hypothetically, use of the middle initial 'R' suggests Katherine Mansfield's continued experimentation with her newly adopted moniker: from 1907 to 1910 her various pseudonyms included K. Mansfield, Katherina Mansfield and Julian Mark. Further, both Katharine and Katherine spellings were used in known stories by Mansfield in 1910 and the middle initial 'R' could be a misreading or mistyping of a 'B' for Beauchamp.

A morality tale set in a coastal English village, 'TTAW' concerns guilt and reconciliation. In the story, an embittered Anthony Wynscombe is the victim of an altercation with rival suitor Frank Selby, to whom a reconciliation is facilitated fifty years later by a benevolent niece, though not before Anthony loses the contest for the love of the Rector's daughter and is blinded by the gun fired by Frank. Surprisingly, the title seems contrived – Anthony remains metaphorically, spiritually and emotionally 'frozen' until the very end of the story – and atypical of Mansfield's style, since even her early writing avoids spelling out the meaning or the message of a text in any given title. However, my initial doubts that the work, dating from about 1908 and full of biblical references, *was* written by the New Zealand-born writer were subdued by overwhelming circumstantial evidence. Yet this evidence needs to be examined before conclusions can be drawn.

As if to reinforce that the story is a morality tale, mentions of water, fire, warmth and sunlight, usually associated with niece Betty, represent the world beyond Anthony's wretched existence. Further, the character Frank Selby is submitted to an epiphany: his response to a choral rendition of a Christmas church anthem is to seek forgiveness from his former friend, Anthony. The closest a known Mansfield text comes to a parable or morality tale is the story 'Mary' (1910), in so far as the message may be, in essence, that one should be kind to a less powerful person than oneself.[4] The story even has references to hymn singing, God and the devil, and significantly, was published only three months before 'TTAW'. Mary, presumably Mansfield herself and named after the mother of Jesus, makes up a short poetic verse: 'I got a yellow frog for a prize, | An' it had china eyes.' Similarly, the narrator of 'TTAW': 'So fine a line is there between the two, | who of us guesses what a smile can do?' Both rhymes juxtapose the artificial with the real; the smile appears benign but it is in fact mocking; the frog's stare is more chilling, more like the devil who 'entered into my soul' than the music of the hymn to which it fails to fit.

Like several of Mansfield's other stories, 'TTAW' has a two-part structure. In the first episode, the conflict of the two protagonists is examined, and in the second, Betty, the intelligent and compassionate relative, steps in and masterminds a reconciliation. Several other early stories by Mansfield have a similar structure, including 'A Little Episode' (1900), 'Millie' (1913), 'The Modern Soul' (1911) and 'Frau Brechenmacher Attends a Wedding' (1910).[5] The characters of Millie and Betty are persuasive young women who intervene in an ugly situations involving gun violence. Although 'Millie' and 'TTAW' are set in New Zealand and England, respectively, and Millie is a more complex, flawed character than Betty, both focus on psychological states rather than situations or narrative.[6]

Further, the story alludes to the tale of Joseph in the Old Testament: niece Betty is unfairly reprimanded by Anthony for the allusion – interpreted by the protagonists as a story of forgiveness and suffering, respectively – when he in fact initiated the discussion. Joseph's ability to dream, or interpret dreams, clearly had a resonance with Mansfield, as she wrote about such talents in her aphorisms 'Bites from the Apple' (1911): 'She wove her thoughts, her desire, her dreams into a long garment of strange | colour [. . .] "I have woven so strongly," said | she, "that the sharp swords of Reality cannot pierce through my garment of | Dreams."'[7] In 'TTAW' Joseph's suffering is represented by the 'iron that enters his soul' from Psalm 105. Mansfield cleverly contrasts this symbolic metaphor for the iron shackles that bound Joseph with the iron gunshot that blinded Anthony.[8] Wynscombe's sister Martha is referred to as 'Martha in the house', the sister of Mary Magdalene or Mary of Bethany whom Jesus visits.[9]

Significantly, around the same time that the story was probably written, the tale of Joseph is evoked in a letter sent by Mansfield to her sister Vera in Sydney, Australia (where Vera had been living for most of 1908); the letter refers to the biblical text, as well as a presumably lost text. Ruth Mantz and John Middleton Murry, as well as Antony Alpers, were aware of the letter and refer to it in their biographies:[10]

> This is going to be only an apology for a letter – I could not allow your last charming Brief to remain unanswered. And firstly – yes – the dedication is to you – please accept it. Thank you immeasurably for your 'Fat' re my work; it is so scarce – I think these are surely the seven lean years of appreciation.[11]

The letter's cryptic remarks refer to Chapters 41–2 of the Old Testament: Genesis, specifically the story of Joseph of Canaan, whose 'lean years' are followed good years in which he reaps the harvest as the 'fat' of the land and who, though sold by his envious brothers into slavery, offers forgiveness to them when they are reunited. Mansfield – who uses the phrase 'fat of the land' in 'Swing of the Pendulum' (CW1, pp. 242–50, p. 246) – marked some of the same chapters in her own Bible, now held in the Alexander Turnbull Library in Wellington.

According to Angela Smith, Mansfield's writing cites scripture from 'Esau and Jacob' (Genesis 27), 'The Gospel of Matthew' (New Testament 7: 24–7) and 'Cain and Abel' (Genesis 4: 1–18).[12] All these occur in the period 1907–10, when 'TTAW' was probably written. CW1 also notes the allusion to the Gospel of John in 'The Advanced Lady' (1911)[13] and the parody of Oscar Wilde's biblical mannerisms in 'Prose' (1909).[14] My research has revealed further biblical references in 'Frau Fischer' (1910), 'At Lehmann's' (1910), 'Bites from the Apple' (1911) and 'Les Deux Étrangères' (1906). Clearly, the Bible provided more than just good copy for Mansfield in these formative years.

Finally, there are phrases and words in 'TTAW' that suggest the hand of Mansfield. Reference is made to an American creeper on a verandah – in 'The Thoughtful Child' (1908) it is a Virginia creeper.[15] There are musical allusions such as 'the same tones – he would have recognised them anywhere, with the peculiar musical timbre which had been pleasant to his ears in the days gone by'. An archaic use of language is found in the same sentence: 'the tones more than the words *smote* on a tender chord' – reminiscent of the biblical style of 'Prose' (1909) and echoing the phrase 'all that he had wished for in her *smote* his heart' from Mansfield's 'The Green Tree' (1911) (CW1, p. 259, my italics).[16] Domestic sanctuaries involving cut flowers feature in 'TTAW':

> Some of the late autumn flowers still lingered, and she gathered a dewy bunch of them for the uncle whom she had not yet seen. It should be her daily cure, she decided, to see that fresh ones were placed in his rooms every day.

and similarly in 'The Wind Blows' (1920): 'Oh, how peaceful it is here. She likes this room. It smells of art serge and stale smoke and chrysanthemums . . . there is a big vase of them on the mantelpiece' (CW2, p. 227). While I could not avoid the conclusion that Mansfield had written or co-written the text, it proved impossible to substantiate. Furthermore, stylometric analysis and expert commentary from Dr Gerri Kimber and Dr Jan Rybicki threw doubt on such authenticity: the story simply did not 'sound' like Mansfield. With conflicting evidence, a third possibility suggested itself. Were there collaborators or a series of editors involved? A comparison of two different versions of 'TTAW', both published in Australia six months apart, confirms that punctuation and spelling were revised and whole words were replaced. This appeared to confirm my alternate theory that a second editorial hand was involved in the story.

A strong argument for authentication concerns locality: 'TTAW' was first published in the same city, Sydney, as Mansfield's poem 'Loneliness'.[17] Further, the *Sun*, which published the poem, and the *Star*, which published the story, were in fact the same newspaper: the publishers chose the new name when they made the move from an afternoon paper to a daily.[18] That the poem was published in London a mere two months before it appeared in Sydney has gone unremarked by any researcher or biographer to date. Perhaps Mansfield intended to publish the poem and 'TTAW' at the same time in Sydney?

Mansfield also had family connections with Sydney, the city where her mother was born. The Lascelles family, with whom Vera stayed during much of 1908, were close relatives. Further, another of Mansfield's poems, 'A Day in Bed', had been published in Sydney's *Lone Hand* magazine (October 1909), and Frank Fox, the editor, also worked as a journalist for the *Sydney Bulletin*. Given that Fox was on the brink of relocating to London, he may have had no compunction in recommending Mansfield to the rival *Star* newspaper, in which the newly discovered text appeared in 1910.[19] Mansfield's artist friend Edie Bendall, with whom she collaborated on a book of children's verse, had recently been studying in Sydney and had several of her drawings published in the *Sydney Mail* in 1905. It is highly possible that she provided Mansfield with contact details for editors who might be interested in her stories.

Candidates for the mystery hand were surprisingly forthcoming. Mansfield's personal circumstances in 1909 (when the story was most likely completed) were fraught and assistance with finding a publisher would not have come from her estranged parents and friends (who had fulfilled the role previously). However, there were several more recent associates and friends who could have helped. For example, a meeting with Elizabeth von Arnim, a famous writer and Mansfield's first cousin, took place in London in early 1909.[20] Von Arnim was born in Sydney, where 'TTAW' was published in the fledgling *Sun* newspaper, and, in a letter to her daughter Evi in 1908, expressed a desire to co-author a work.[21] Then there was Millie Parker, the niece of Mansfield's piano teacher Robert Parker; their friendship was established in Wellington and continued in London between 1908 and 1909. Though Parker was a musician, she had, according to a report in the *New Zealand Herald*, an interest in writing:

> When Miss Millie Parker (Wellington) came to England in July it was her intention to devote her time to music, but she has instead been unexpectedly busy with literary work, and she has just received the appointment of London correspondent for the Encore, the new musical paper published in Melbourne.[22]

Perhaps Parker, who was herself involved in 'literary work', was sending copy from London to Australia and assisting in the editing, posting and perhaps even writing of 'TTAW'.

In the winter and spring of that year Mansfield was still closely associated with at least one of the Trowell twins, Arnold and Garnet. While the latter was not a writer, he was a published researcher and editor, in so far as he worked alongside his brother as a contributor for *Strad* magazine. Arnold was more accomplished than his brother and produced not only a serialised dictionary of cellists for the magazine, but also, as the Brussels correspondent, reviews of concerts. A fabricated news story, published in *Cremona* magazine, refers to the kidnapping, by Māori warriors, of the Trowell twins.[23] Gerri Kimber notes that this story may have inspired Mansfield's 'How Pearl Button was Kidnapped', which was written about this time.[24] Like Mansfield, Tom Trowell had a penchant for mimicry and deception – many of his musical compositions were falsely and deliberately passed off as the work of famous, dead composers. In this context, one could potentially infer the hands of both the Trowells and Mansfield in the fabricated story intriguingly titled 'Children of the Sun God', and more speculatively, one could consider the brothers conspirators in other literature, including 'TTAW.'

The Trowells had an Australian student, Winnie Parsons, living with them in London at the time Mansfield was engaged to Garnet, and it is possible that Winnie's sister Florence assisted Mansfield in forging links with the Sydney press. Florence lived in Sydney from 1898 to 1904, and was in London between July 1904 and October 1905 and then between May 1910 and July 1911. Perhaps it was Frederick, brother of Winnie and Florence – who visited London in February of 1909 – who took copy back with him when he visited Sydney on his way home to Perth in March 1909?[25]

The prospect that Mansfield collaborated with Beatrice Hastings, the then partner of A. R. Orage, on 'TTAW' is also feasible, since they were co-authors of a pastiche of various contemporary writers, published in *New Age*, during1911.[26] As skilled mimics, it would not be surprising if the two had a Victorian author in mind as a model for the style and content of the story. However, in the absence of satire, 'TTAW' seems less than likely to have been co-authored by Hastings and Mansfield. Even in the scenario that a pair of writers from the other side of the world sought to disguise their authorship, surely a newspaper editor with scruples would uncover the ruse and refuse to publish? Perhaps the dissolution of Sydney's *Star*, which occurred less than a week after the publication of 'TTAW', provided the editors with the perfect opportunity to print a cheaply acquired story of dubious provenance; after all, who can sue a paper in the Southern Hemisphere that no longer exists?

In the event that no collaboration occurred, the need for an explanation for the editorial and stylistic variations led me to the staff of Sydney's *Sun* newspaper. Montague Grover, who was a Sydney resident, secretary for the Williamson Opera Company and editor of the *Sun* newspaper (in which the story first appeared) was in London during the winter of 1909–10. Likewise, the aspiring short story writer E. J. Brady was a contributor to the same paper. Despite the fact that Brady's 'discovery' of Mansfield in 1907 occurred in Melbourne, Brady was also a Sydney resident and is known to have sent an unpublished Mansfield manuscript back after his magazine, *Native Companion*, went into liquidation. Perhaps he sent it to his associate, A. G. Stephens, a writer for Wellington's *Evening Post* newspaper for several years from 1907, a time during which Mansfield's 'The Education of Audrey' appeared in the same paper.

Stephens had connections with Edward (Vance) Palmer, who was a 'known associate' of Mansfield's.[27] From September 1910, Palmer lived in London and wrote for the *New Age* – the same magazine that published several of the *German Pension* stories by Mansfield. In November of the same year, he contributed a poem to Stephens's 'The Book

Fellow' in Sydney's *Sunday Sun*, the weekend edition of the *Sun*, which in turn was the evening reincarnation of the morning *Star*. Even more tellingly, a short story by Palmer appeared in the *Warwick Examiner and Times*, the same newspaper that republished 'TTAW'.[28]

Other associates included Frank Morton, editor of both the *Triad* periodicals (Dunedin and Sydney) and first publisher of Mansfield's poem 'Death of a Rose', and Claude McKay, who was, like Montague Grover, a journalist in Sydney connected with the Williamson Opera Company (and by association the elite of the artistic circles in both Australian and New Zealand). Katharine Prichard, short-story writer and close namesake, who travelled from Australia to work as a journalist and writer in London in 1908, seems not to have known Mansfield, though she was aware of, and admired, her work.[29]

Stylistic analysis of 'TTAW' undertaken by Dr Jan Rybicki suggests that three stories by Michel Allison, published in Sydney's *Sun* and *Star*, as well as various other papers in London, Brisbane, Christchurch and Auckland, are almost certainly by the same writer. My own stylometric analysis suggests that there is an overlap, with Allison close to Katharine Prichard, and 'genuine' Mansfield stories close to 'TTAW'.[30] While this does not conclusively determine the authorship of 'TTAW', it does provide a connection with three major 'Empire' countries that were associated with Mansfield, as well as the various editors or ghost writers potentially involved.

The love story 'Cop's Summons' by Michel Allison was published on 1 July 1910, in the very first edition of the *Sun*.[31] The surname of the main character – Rev. Curtis Maitland – recurs in KM's 'The Garden Party: Kitty Maitland is based on Kitty Marchant, daughter of J. W. A Marchant, a neighbour of the Beauchamp family in Tinakori Road.[32] The story itself begins with a concert, featuring '*some* wild Hungarian or Polish music' played by the orchestra. This phrase, in a similarly dismissive tone of voice, is echoed in Mansfield's 'Night Came Swiftly' (1907), where Pearl dreams of conducting '*some* Hungarian Fantasie, *some* Dvorak Serenade' (CW1, p. 72, my italics).

Allison's 'Uncle Jack's Guile' was first published in Preston's *Guardian* in September 1909 and concerns bachelor Jack Murray, whose estate and niece are being pursued by Queen Street lawyer 'Gribber'.[33] Uncle Dick's narration of the story in his West Country English dialect is received by cousin Belle with disdain – a reaction that might suggest she is based on Mansfield's Aunt Bell. A further story by Michel Allison, titled 'The Forgotten Letter', was published in Brisbane in 1910.[34] It is worth noting here that the original first appeared in London in the *Pall Mall Gazette* in January 1910. That Mansfield's poem 'The Pillar Box' appeared in the same magazine the following month, seems more than a coincidence.[35]

The main character in Allison's 'The Forgotten Letter' is Peggy, a writer, or 'scribbler' as she describes herself, who has hit hard times and has to 'earn her bread and butter' by writing. The opening scene involves Peggy and her girlfriends discussing the flirtatious Gilbert Wincott at the tennis party at Grovelands, London. A two-part structure is used. Part one features the tragedy of the death of Peggy's mother and the break-up of Mildred's engagement with Wincott, and part two focuses on the women's renewed friendship. As mentioned previously, this structure is a feature of 'TTAW' and several known Mansfield stories from this period. 'The Forgotten Letter' uses phrases, colours and names found in known Mansfield stories: In 'Brave Love' Mansfield refers to Mildred's 'blue serge dress' and a 'blue veil' (CW1, pp. 400, 407). In 'The Forgotten Letter', Mildred – yes, it is the same name – has 'speedwell blue eyes'. In 'His Sister's Keeper' it is a 'blue cloth dress' and 'blue clocked stockings' (CW1, p. 151). 'A Fairy Story' (1910) refers to the girl as 'slender and dark eyed' while Allison's main character, Peggy, is 'a pretty dark-eyed girl' (CW1, p. 199). Further, Monte Carlo, where Mildred's former lover, Gilbert Wincott, commits suicide, is the same city used in Mansfield's story 'The Young Girl'.[36]

'The Forgotten Letter' and 'TTAW' both refer to 'musical voices' and gardens, an instance of the latter from the Michel Allison story being particularly telling:

> The weather was perfect, and the glamour and glory of May lay over everything. The sunlight flickered down through the young leaves, and at every break in the greenery there were long vistas of masses of pink and white hawthorn, chestnut trees in full bloom, white and purple lilacs, and here and there the yellow tresses of the laburnum.[37]

The species of plants mentioned here almost exactly replicate those in a piece of prose from one of Mansfield's Notebooks from 1907:

> There danced before his eyes a vision of the wonderful Spring of 1893, | marching through the city in green robes, with nodding plumes of lilac and a great | retinue of laburnums bearing lanterns, and chestnuts swinging tapers in | their hundred arms. (CW4, p. 39)

Allison's stories appeared in five major western cities in three different countries, between 1909 and 1910. The four stories by Michel Allison and Katharine R. Mansfield all involve reconciliation and reunion: Cop and Joyce as lovers; Jack Murry and his niece Grace (via his bequest) as friends; Peggy and Mildred as friends; and Anthony Wynscombe and

Frank Selby as friends. Though the Allison stories do not overtly refer to Christian morality, there is a sense that such a moral code is at play.[38]

These stories, as well as others published in Sydney, Auckland, Brisbane and London, may have resulted from collaborations with contributors to newspapers in Australasia, or persons close to Mansfield – associates and friends within Europe, especially those from the year 1909. If this sounds inconclusive, then that is because it is: we simply do not know who wrote this work. If it was not Mansfield, then one might potentially conclude that it was an imposter, perhaps Michel Allison. However, such a person would not have taken the unknown author's name instead of their own: Mansfield's fame began to establish itself only after the publication of *In a German Pension* in 1911, and thereafter grew with two further collections of stories in 1920 and 1922.

Returning to the question of the provenance of 'TTAW', and assuming that the extended Beauchamp family knew about 'TTAW' – despite a relatively small readership, it seems inconceivable that they did not – why was it never acknowledged?[39] Did Mansfield deny writing it? Was she embarrassed by the story? If Mansfield and Ida Baker had kept the letters and diaries from the period in question, this might be easier to determine. Further, the circumstances of Mansfield's multiple affairs and pregnancies, as well as her unconsummated marriage, may have contributed to any subterfuge. The case that Mansfield wrote 'TTAW' and sent it to her sister, who then gave it to A. G. Stephens, who in turn sent it to Sydney's *Star*, is a strong one and not diminished by the likelihood that a ghost writer, editor or co-author (perhaps Stephens, sister Vera or cousin Elizabeth) had a hand in the script.

My search for information has led me to several biographies of Australian writers that blur the distinction between fact and fiction. A similar picture in the world of journalism is painted by Claude McKay, part-time contributor to the *Sun*:

> When, in 1908, the *Sun*, Sydney's evening newspaper, was launched, one of my activities with the J. C. Williamson firm was publicity. The *Sun* was outside the cable combine, and its overseas news was consequently sketchy [. . .] This accounted for Fordyce Wheeler, the *Sun*'s advertising manager, and Monty Grover, its editor, paying me a visit. The object was to ask me to write them a couple of columns of 'cables' a day [. . .] Every morning at nine o'clock I gave them what was happening abroad, or, more truthfully, what wasn't.[40]

The situation was so bad that a bill was introduced to parliament in October 1911 to protect the copyright of works produced outside of Australia.[41] In such a climate it would not be surprising that Mansfield lost editorial control over 'TTAW'.

Mansfield's life, as presented by generations of commentators and scholars, has always been used to contextualise, confirm and inform her fiction. Often, her fiction is used to legitimise her life, or at least our view of it in hindsight. Should 'The Thawing of Anthony Wynscombe' be proven to be a work by Katherine Mansfield, sometimes known as Kathleen Beauchamp or Mrs Middleton Murry, then it is certain that our view of her aesthetic, and her activity during the 'lean years' from 1908 to 1910 and beyond, will have to change.

Notes

1. *Tinakori: Critical Journal of the Katherine Mansfield Society*, Issue 4 (2020).
2. Katharine R. Mansfield, 'A Short Story: The Thawing of Anthony Wynscombe', *Star* (Sydney, NSW), Saturday, 25 June 1910, p. 12. Available at <http://nla.gov.au/nla.news-article228309655> (last accessed 10 June 2019).
3. In the latter version, the spelling of the first name is 'Katherine' with two e's: *Warwick Examiner & Times*, Queensland, on Saturday, 5 November 1910, p. 2. Available at TROVE <http://nla.gov.au/nla.news-article82302493> (last accessed 12 June 2019).
4. CW1, p. 168.
5. While the last two stories are satirical in nature – a feature of the collection *In a German Pension* – 'A Little Episode', 'Millie' and 'TTAW' are more serious.
6. Although 'A Little Episode' and 'TTAW' are set in England, there are inconsistencies: 'Bellevue Avenue' and 'Verandah', respectively, imply possible Australasian or Pacific origins.
7. Chris Mourant, *Katherine Mansfield and Periodical Culture* (Edinburgh: Edinburgh University Press, 2019), pp. 281–4 (p. 282).
8. Psalm 105: 18.
9. Luke 10: 38-42.
10. Ruth Elvish Mantz and J. Middleton Murry, *The Life of Katherine Mansfield* (London: Constable, 1933), p. 314: 'Katherine Mansfield left New Zealand on July 9th, 1908 [. . .] [after which] seven years had to pass; and of those seven years the first three were so bitter in her memory that she seldom spoke of them.' Antony Alpers also refers to a seven-year ordeal: 'Katherine was only to recover the gift that had produced [The Tiredness of] Rosabel, and the power to sustain it, after a seven-year ordeal that itself was only ended by another spiritual upheaval, comparable with that of renouncing her country and returning to London.' Antony Alpers, *Katherine Mansfield* (London: Jonathan Cape, 1954), p. 108. Alpers borrows from Mantz and Murry rather than the letter itself.
11. *Letters* 1, p. 55 (26 June 1908).
12. Angela Smith, *Katherine Mansfield: A Literary Life* (Basingstoke: Palgrave Macmillan, 2000), pp. 24–6.
13. CW1, p. 237. See also 'And God saw that it was good: Katherine Mansfield & the Bible', in Anne Mounic, *Ah, what is it that I Heard?: Katherine Mansfield's Wings of Wonder* (Leiden: Brill, 2014), pp. 39–50.
14. CW1, pp. 146–50.
15. CW1, Appendix B, pp. 531–3. 'Virginia creeper' is also referred to in 'The House' (1912), CW1, pp. 304–11 (p. 304), and 'Maata' (1913), CW1, pp. 344–65 (p. 346).

16. This is also similar to the phrase 'sudden fear smote her heart' from 'Die Einsame' (1904), CW1, pp. 20–2 (p. 21).
17. [Katherine Mansfield], 'Loneliness', *The Sun* (Sydney), 30 July 1912, p. 12. Available at TROVE <https://trove.nla.gov.au/newspaper/article/229969307> (last accessed 10 June 2019).
18. Advertising campaigns promoting Sydney's *Star* reinforced the policy of publishing a short story 'every day'. This policy was discontinued when Sydney's *Sun* was launched.
19. Fox acted as a London correspondent for Sydney's *Star* from 1909.
20. Kathleen Jones, *Katherine Mansfield: The Story Teller* (New York: Penguin Viking, 2010), p. 99.
21. Leslie De Charms, *Elizabeth of the German Garden* (Portsmouth: Heinemann, 1958), p. 126. Von Arnim writes in a letter to her daughter Evi (dated 27 February 1908): 'I'm struggling to write a book [. . .] and I'd love to see yours and there might be things in it that I could put in mine, and then you'd be a collaborator!'
22. 'Personal Items from London', *New Zealand Herald*, 11 January 1909, p. 8. Paperspast, (National Library of New Zealand). Available at <https://paperspast.natlib.govt.nz/newspapers/NZH19090111.2.86> (last accessed 14 June 2019).
23. [Anon.],'Children of the Sun God', *The Cremona*, 1 (March 1907), p. 37.
24. Gerri Kimber, *Katherine Mansfield: The Early Years* (Edinburgh: Edinburgh University Press, 2016), p. 94. It is almost certain that Mansfield was aware of, and had read, Maxim Gorky's play titled 'Children of the Sun' and Mansfield refers to herself as a 'child of the sun', CW4, p. 434.
25. 'List of Visitors', *Daily Post* (Hobart), 8 March 1909, p. 5. Available at TROVE <http://nla.gov.au/nla.news-article181635889> (last accessed 14 September 2019).
26. 'A P.S.A', *New Age*, 9: 4 (May 1911), pp. 95–6.
27. Geoffrey Searle, 'Edward Vivian (Vance) Palmer', in *Australian Dictionary of Biography*, vol. 11 (Melbourne: Melbourne University Press, 1988). Available at <http://adb.anu.edu.au/biography/palmer-edward-vivian-vance-7946> (last accessed 5 October 2019).
28. Vance Palmer, 'Short Story: The Mother', *Warwick Examiner & Times*, Queensland, Wednesday, 27 September 1911, p. 2. Available at TROVE <https://trove.nla.gov.au/newspaper/article/82195293> (last accessed 5 October 2019).
29. Katharine Susannah Prichard, daughter of Australian journalist Tom Prichard, sent stories to E. J. Brady's *Native Companion*, which published 'In the Botanical Gardens' and other prose vignettes by Mansfield.
30. For a detailed methodology see M. Eder, J. Rybicki and M. Kestemont, 'Stylometry with R: A Package for Computational Text Analysis', *The R Journal*, 8: 1 (2016), pp. 107–21.
31. Michel Allison, 'A Short Story: Cop's Summons', *Sun* (Sydney, NSW), Friday, 1 July 1910, p. 7. Available at <http://nla.gov.au/nla.news-article229978188> (last accessed 16 June 2019).
32. Cherry A. Hankin, *Katherine Mansfield and Her Confessional Stories* (London: Palgrave, 1983), p. 236.
33. Storyettes in 'The Preston Guardian', *The Lancashire Daily Post*, 10 June, 1909, p. 4. See also Michel Allison, 'A Short Story: Uncle Jack's Guile', *Star* (Christchurch, NZ), Saturday, 11 December 1909, p. 2. The story was also published in the *New Zealand Herald*, 21 January 1910.
34. Michel Allison, 'The Forgotten Letter', *The Queenslander*, Saturday, 5 March 1910,

p. 44. Available at <https://trove.nla.gov.au/newspaper/page/2493023> (last accessed 16 June 2019).

35. [K. Mansfield], 'The Pillar Box', *Pall Mall Magazine*, 45: 202 (February 1910), p. 300.

36. 'The Young Girl' (1920), CW2, pp. 230–4. The first and last sentences refer to a blue dress.

37. Michel Allison, 'The Forgotten Letter', *The Queenslander*, Saturday, 5 March 1910, p. 44.

38. A feature of Mansfield's style is the declamatory, poetic and musical shaping of the prose. Her style was influenced by the King James Bible (1611), of which she possessed a copy, and which was designed to be used as a spoken text to largely illiterate congregations. An inspection of her copy shows that passages were underlined in the section pertaining to the forgiveness of Joseph's brother, in Chapter 42 of the Book of Genesis, the same story referenced in 'TTAW'.

39. The readership of the *Star* in 1910 was about 15,000. See *Hold Page One: The Memoirs of Monty Grover, Editor* (Loch Haven: Loch Haven Books, 1993), p. 22.

40. Claude McKay, *This is the Life: The Autobiography of a Newspaperman* (Sydney: Angus and Robertson, 1961), p. 76. The launch of the *Sun* was in 1910 rather than 1908, as McKay recalls.

41. 'Radical alterations to the Copyright Act of 1905 are proposed in a bill introduced by Senator M'Gregor in the Senate yesterday, on behalf of the Government. Hitherto the Commonwealth has given copyright only to works first produced in Australia. Other books produced in the Empire have had some scanty protection under the Imperial Copyright Act to which authors have had to refer when they wished copyright in Australia.' 'News of the Week', *The Age* (Melbourne), 5 October 1911, p. 6.

The Thawing of Anthony Wynscombe

Katharine R. Mansfield

I

There were very few who loved Anthony Wynscombe. Even his affliction failed in winning him the sympathy usually offered the blind, and those who knew and lived with him declared he was as hard and jagged as the rocky cliffs[1] which rose up gaunt and grim on the shore which bounded the coast by which he lived.

He was seventy-five now, an old man silvered by time, furrowed by tragedy, nursing an injury with the fostering care of a mother who is long in discovering the true nature of her nursling; and there had been none to tell him, for few in these days knew of it. Something had happened in his earlier years to embitter him, it was said, something which had to do with the cause of his blindness, but no one had learned precisely its nature save the two sisters who lived with him, and they never referred to it even between themselves.

Miss Wynscombe was two years his senior, a good woman, but a very Martha in the house, who looked well to their physical wants, and had small patience with anything savoring of sentiment.

Mrs. Lincoln had been married and widowed before her twenty-fifth year, and had returned with her little son to the old home on Martha's suggestion, where she had remained ever since. The boy had long since grown to man's estate, and had gone with the troops to India, where he had met with his wife, the only child of his commanding officer, a delicate little creature, who had lived but one short year after her marriage with John Lincoln, whom she had left inconsolable with their baby girl, the chief companion of her father in after days.

Mr. Wynscombe was seated in his customary corner under the verandah, where he had been led by his faithful attendant Simmons, seeing nothing of the gorgeous sunset that made the western portion of the heavens[2] aflame with beauty, the mellowed rays filtering through the rich-hued leaves of the American creeper, and but faintly warming the rigid figure who sat alone with his thoughts. A step sounded near, and he knew it was his younger sister who approached. She had not yet attained the ripened age of threescore years and ten, and looked younger than she really was.

'Ah, there you are, Anthony,' she remarked, drawing a light wicker chair nearer to his in its sheltered spot, for the sun was dazzling in its amber splendor.[3] 'You knew I had a letter to-day from John?' she began, tentatively, for Anthony's moods were peculiar, and she wanted to discover the fashion of his present one before committing herself.[4]

'I heard you and Martha talking about it,' he answered tersely.

'Then you probably heard, also, what was said about Betty?'

'You want to have the girl here. Elizabeth, why don't you speak out, and come to the point? You know how I hate beating about the bush.'

'It is John who wishes it, Anthony. There has been a good deal of unrest among the hill tribes lately, which means there will be some fighting. On such occasions Betty has generally remained with Mrs. Forest, but the major is coming home this autumn, and there is no one else with whom he cares to entrust the girl, so he asks if we would mind her coming here until he is able to join her in the spring.'

She paused, and glanced half nervously at the upright figure in the stiff-backed chair, whose stern features relaxed no whit as he snapped out, 'How old is the girl?'

'Eighteen.'

'A silly age,' he snorted, 'when they fancy themselves women, assume all sorts of ridiculous airs, and make fools of the men'.[5]

'Sometimes, doubtless, but it is not every man who permits himself to be duped.' An unfortunate speech, but Elizabeth Lincoln had always been considered the most tactless of women. She recognised her mistake a moment too late.

Anthony Wynscombe's colorless features contracted strangely, and the thin lips straightened into a line.[6] 'She must come, I suppose, if you wish it,' he said, in his most rasping tones. 'I have no desire to play the tyrant, but understand, I keep to my own rooms, and will not have her intruding on my privacy with the inquisitiveness of her sex. Pshaw! the house will be full of women soon.'

As Mrs. Lincoln withdrew into the pleasant little drawing-room where the breezes could not follow, and took up the knitting which invariably shared the twilight with her, a series of incidents came crowding to her mind, summoned, doubtless, by Anthony's cutting allusions to her tactless methods. Fifty years! What a multiplicity of small events had happened in the passing, but tonight[7] they were overshadowed by the memory of that terrible tragedy which had set Anthony for ever apart from his fellows. How handsome he had been in those days, taller than the average, splendidly proportioned, a favorite with all men, among whom he[8] was one whom he had singled out as a sharer of his confidence and affection. They had been at school together, and Anthony was not minded to lose his chum when the sterner duties of life claimed them.

So it happened that Frank Selby came often to the little bay where Anthony lived, and it was soon apparent to most people that his coming was prompted by something that ran deeper than his friendship for Anthony. Elizabeth Wynscombe was fair to look upon, with the simplicity of mind and manner so irresistible with some of the sterner sex. She had lovers galore, and each imagined himself the favored one till she, with capricious suddenness, disillusioned him by accepting a youth, by name John Lincoln, a comparative stranger in the neighborhood.

Of all those who had paid homage at her shrine, Frank Selby was the most badly wounded – not, be it understood, in his heart, but that far more susceptible element, his pride. To be flirted with and cast aside in so summary a fashion was a consummation he had not deemed possible could happen to himself, and he writhed under the knowledge of it as a small boy will when stung by a wasp.

He sought Anthony's interference as guardian of his sister, and Anthony made the irreparable mistake of laughing at him. Selby's ungovernable and almost fantastic rage against the pair of lovers[9] was comic. Alas! ere the play was finished it had turned into tragedy –

So fine a line is there between the two,
Who of us guesses what a smile can do?

Small minds turn quickly to thoughts of revenge, and Selby was not long in discovering a method for punishing Anthony's misplaced mirth. Anthony loved – and Frank knew it – Ruth Leveson, the rector's eldest daughter. Between the two families there had existed an intimacy for many years, but Anthony had told no one of the dream which was yet but a dream. There was time, he said to himself, and they understood one another. Perhaps they did, but it is not always wise to be too certain on such nice points.

Elizabeth would soon be married, and he had reason to believe that Martha would speedily follow her example, then he could take his bride home without the fear of making anyone uncomfortable.

His was a singularly unselfish nature, and his moral code a high one. Nothing mean or shabby could ever be[10] attributed to Anthony Wynscombe. His life was ruled on straight lines, the pity of it was he left religion out of it. Nobody missed it in those days, or imagined his blameless life could be improved by its acceptance.

How Frank discovered his friend's secret never transpired: crafty minds have methods undreamed of by the unsuspicious. Anthony, hedged in by his own rectitude, went on unheeding, and nobody warned him, for nobody knew. Elizabeth was the first to discover the trend of events, perhaps because her volatile nature was likest[11] his, and not dreaming that Anthony had even the vaguest intentions in that quarter, and anxious to make some amends for her conduct to her rejected lover, she worked diligently on his behalf, and did an infinity of mischief with the best intentions.

For a time Ruth refused absolutely to listen or receive any advances from Anthony's good-looking friend. She had liked Frank Selby from the first, his gay, good humor had attracted and amused her, and she had at all times considered him a pleasant companion, but her acquaintance with Anthony was of older date, and a secret hope had long ago dawned in her girlish heart that a closer union would one day unite them. Sometimes she had felt almost sure of his love when his eyes had met hers and a strange fire had kindled there, but it had gone no further; his lips were silent, and hopes within her gave place to doubt. If he loved her what should hinder him telling her so? She knew of no obstacle that would hinder them.

It was at this point Frank began to waver. He found it almost impossible to pass the barrier she had raised between them – such an intangible barrier – when Elizabeth quite unconsciously came to his aid.

It had never occurred to her that Anthony, staid and serious, would ever give his thoughts to such frivolous matters as flirtation, but he had certainly come perilously near it, she believed, with a young lady, sister to Martha's betrothed, with whom he was constantly to be seen, and Frank Selby skilfully turned this piece of information to his own advantage. He contrived that Ruth should hear of it through Elizabeth's garrulity.

There was no one to tell her the truth that the seeming intimacy had reference only to Martha's unhappy wooing, for Ruth shut up the subject in her proud heart, sealing it securely against the inquisitive. She had been mistaken, that was all: Anthony's affection was simply of the brotherly type. She had nothing with which to reproach him and no one guessed at her own smart. Heneforth [*sic*][12] Frank Selby's wooing of the rector's daughter went forward and prospered; in a shorter time than even he had dared to anticipate, she capitulated and gave him the promise for which he had forfeited his honor.

It came as a staggering blow to Anthony, who absolutely refused to credit the truth of it till Ruth's trembling lips confirmed it. The interview was of the briefest between them, but it left a scar upon each which never died out. The rector was disappointed in Ruth's choice. He had made up his mind long before that Anthony was to be his son; but he had no mind to interfere, seeing that Ruth had evidently acted in accordance with her own.

Elizabeth was startled when she saw how Anthony received the news. The placid, even temper which none had ever seen ruffled during the whole of his twenty-five years exploded with a volcanic force that threatened destruction everywhere when he learnt for the first time her own share in the drama. 'I spoke in all innocence. I never imagined you cared for Ruth in that way,' she expostulated, in her own defence. 'If it is true you loved her, why, in the world, did you not tell her so before complications could possibly arise? It is your own stupidity that has wrought this folly. And, after all, Ruth has made her own choice – there has been no compulsion from anyone – which proves that you had never the ghost of a chance.'

But Anthony knew better. He had seen Ruth, had talked with her face to face, had pleaded his passion with an eloquence and force that might have won him distinction at the Bar, but it failed completely with Ruth. He had seen the color ebb and flow in the tell-tale face, had witnessed the love welling up from her soul in response to the outpouring of his, and knew that pride alone forbade her to speak of it. No pressure, no persuasion could win from her pale lips a single word that could bring hope to his troubled heart, and like one bereft of his senses Anthony strode out of her presence away over the fields, he knew not where, and cared less, passion and pain working their will with him. Then, in a lonely spot, with no one near to witness the meeting, he came face to face with his friend. Precisely what happened none ever knew. Probably they were blinded to details themselves; lashed into fury, their strong passions let loose, only evil could result from such an encounter.

Frank carried a gun. He had been amusing himself shooting small game. A struggle undoubtedly ensued, and Anthony Wynscombe was plunged into a darkness from which he would[13] never emerge this side the grave.

The whole village rang with the story of the tragedy, and speculation was rife concerning it, but few ever learned the truth of the matter. Frank went abroad, and Ruth never recovered her spirits; the shock completely shattered her nervous system, and, having no wish to recover, she sank quietly into an early grave from no apparent disease but over-weariness.

Elizabeth married John Lincoln, but Martha's courtship came to an abrupt termination, and with the quiet resolution of a good woman she hid her sorrows in the recesses of her own heart that she might have the more liberty to consider those of others. And thus were matters some fifty years later, when Elizabeth asked permission for her granddaughter Betty to visit them.

II.

'What shall we do, Grannie, dear? It seems heartless to leave him here alone with strangers, when but for him I might have been seriously hurt.'

Mrs. Lincoln looked at the white, still features of the old man and hesitated. What would Martha – what would Anthony say? And yet Betty was right. It was scarcely kind to leave him in this cool fashion after the way in which he had shielded her from injury.

There had been an accident to the train by which Betty had travelled – not a serious one, but several of the passengers had been injured, among them Betty's travelling companion, who, in trying to protect her, had received the crushing blow full on his right arm and had swooned from the excruciating pain. It had happened just outside the station which was Betty's destination, and Mrs. Lincoln was driven quickly to the scene of the disaster.

She had found Betty without much difficulty standing by the prostrate form of an old man whom one of the local surgeons was attending. He looked up as Betty spoke, 'It will be an act of charity if you can take him in for a day or two, Mrs. Lincoln,' he said. 'We shall need all the room our small hospital affords. There are not many serious cases, but several will be incapacitated from pursuing their journey to-night. He is coming too, now. I don't think he will give you much trouble, and I will look in on my way home.'

Martha Wynscombe opened her hospitable doors at once to the sufferer. It was the sort of thing which appealed to her: had she lived in later times it is probable she would have become a trained nurse.

The next morning Betty was up betimes looking round her new home. Some of the late autumn flowers still lingered, and she gathered a dewy bunch of them for the uncle whom she had not yet seen. It should be her daily care, she decided, to see that fresh ones were placed in his rooms every day. And with this purpose she paused before a half-opened door through which Simmons had just emerged.

'Excuse me, Miss, but you mustn't go in there,' he said, suddenly divining her intention and taking fright at it.

140

'And pray why?' she asked, with her hand resting lightly on the handle.

'Because the master will have no one interfering in his room, and –'

'All right, Simmons, I will promise to take no undue liberties, but I am going in to say good morning to my uncle.' And she did so, much to Simmons's amazement.

He was sitting by the window as she entered, a forlorn, pathetic figure, and her warm young heart ached for his solitude. Crossing the room she took the listless fingers in her own that were tingling with life and strength, and pressed a kiss on the withered, shrunken cheek. 'Good morning, dear uncle,' she said. 'I have come to introduce myself! It is less formal, and, as we mean to be friends, we can dispense with ceremony'.

The tones more than the words smote on a tender chord somewhere in that warped nature, and unconsciously he smiled. 'Were you not afraid to come unannounced or unbidden?' he answered[14]. 'I told them they must keep you out of my rooms. You see, my dear, I am not likely to prove a very cheerful companion for a frivolous young creature like you.'

'No! Well, you see, I was never considered frivolous, and as to fear, what is there to cause it? Nothing in you, I am sure. Is not the perfume of these flowers delicious? We had nothing like them in India. It is good to find oneself in dear old much-abused England once again.'

It was an easy conquest. When her grandmother came in quest of the truant she was surprised to hear the animated tones of the girl responded to by the gruff but not unkindly ones of Anthony. From that moment Betty had nothing to fear from the reputed ogre of the household. She read to[15] him, talked to him, walked with him, and the querulous, rasping tones so much dreaded by each member were seldom raised in anger or dispute.

In the meantime the stranger admitted within their gates was found to make but slow progress. The effects of the shock were greater than even the worthy surgeon had anticipated, but some time elapsed before he was able to speak with coherence of his affairs. But Martha had already discovered his name. It was an awkward discovery, and Mrs. Lincoln, when she heard of it, was seized with a fit of nerves.

'Don't be absurd, Elizabeth,' remarked Miss Wynscombe, sternly. 'There is no reason why we should trouble Anthony with the subject. As soon as he is well enough to be moved we will get him away quietly, and there will be an end of it.' But Miss Wynscombe was a trifle out in her calculations.

'Who is the man?' exclaimed Anthony one day, when he had heard the doctor's step go down the gravel path after one of his periodical visits. 'I suppose he has some friends or relatives belonging to him who should be communicated with at once. It is not to be supposed he can remain on here indefinitely.'

To which Betty had answered that she would find out, and in repeating the query to her grandmother was told of the tragedy that had happened in their lives half a century ago.

'We dare not tell your uncle, child; I know not what would happen were he to know that Frank Selby is beneath the very roof which shelters him.'

'Leave it to me,' said Betty, 'I think I can arrange matters without igniting the powder magazine so do not be fearful, Grannie, no harm shall happen to you, I promise you.'

It was a delicate mission which Betty had undertaken, but she proved herself equal to it. 'He has no friends in England, dear uncle,' she said, when, linking her arm in his, she led him gently over the frost-bound earth. 'I remember he told me so when we were journeying down together. He has been abroad for years, and would not have come back now but that he wanted to find out someone to whom he had done a woeful injury when quite a young man. He felt he should never know happiness again till he had gripped that old friend's hand and heard him say he was forgiven.'

Anthony said nothing, but Betty's story haunted him. His thoughts travelled back to the day which had shut him in with his misery and wrongs. Could he so easily forgive if Frank were to come back and plead with him? he asked of himself, and a voice within him whispered – no! He solemnly vowed and declared at the time that he would never, never forgive, and not once during the fifty years had he ever felt tempted to do so. He wished Betty had not recalled it so forcibly to his mind by her tale of another man's wrong.

'It is easy for those who have never suffered to talk idle sentiment,' he said to her one day, 'but let the iron enter into their own soul, and I imagine they will sing to a different tune.'

'That is an expression that had first reference to Joseph, and I think we must all admit he set us an admirable example, and –'

'Pshaw! child, I don't want your Biblical quotations,' he answered, with a testiness rarely evinced towards her. 'I am speaking of human nature.'

Betty's lips curved into a smile, which faded instantly when she looked into the poor, disfigured face. 'I have been told,' she said, shyly, 'it is the malicious who harbor thoughts of resentment; the injured are usually the readiest to forgive.'

The subject was dropped by mutual acquiescence, and no more was said upon it from henceforth. The stranger made such slow progress that no one had ventured to hint at his leaving them. Anthony, hearing and seeing nothing of him, seemed to forget his very presence in the house, but Miss Wynscombe was vigilant and anxious. He had given a name, as soon as he was able to do so, which she at once recognised as his second. It had been his mother's maiden name, but she made no sign, waiting for him to do so. Once when he was sitting by the window, propped up with cushions,[16] she saw him start and a warm tinge of color steal into the pallid cheeks, and following the direction of his eyes she saw Betty, with her arm slipped through Anthony's, guiding his steps down one of the gravelled paths. Then the thin hand went up to his face and hid it from her scrutiny.

It was Sunday morning, and Betty, returning from church with her uncle, had led his steps the longer way round. The stern lips had been telling her the sad story of his wrecked happiness, and following his directions she had led the way to the scene, unvisited by him for half a century.

'I hear the water,' he said: 'it is making the same complaint it did fifty years ago. I remember it well, though I heeded it not at the time; it must have been just about here. There is a little coppice – is there not? – to our left, and the wood grows close to the water's edge.'

Betty stayed their steps, and the old man leaned on his staff. He was living over again the tragedy of that terrible moment, the more realistically because of the darkness which shut out the present. Once again he saw the figure of a young man coming towards him with gun in hand, a pleasant smile on his handsome, boyish face, which later events proved to be the offspring of a vile hypocrisy: then the conflict had begun, and the awful thing had happened which had set him apart from his fellows for ever.

'Forgive him? No, a thousand times – No!'

'Anthony!'

He started, as though his body had been the recipient of a second gun-shot.

'Anthony, I have come back in penitence and sorrow, such sorrow as you, in the innocence of your soul, can never conceive. Come back to hear you say the words for which my soul has thirsted fifty years. You will not refuse to speak them. I did you a great injury, but God knows how I have repented it.'

There was no response, only a curious quivering of the bent frame. The same tones – he would have recognised them anywhere, with the peculiar musical timbre which had been pleasant to his ears in the days gone by – but he would not yield to the impulse that had shaken him – no, he would not!

'I don't deserve your forgiveness, and I certainly have no excuse to offer in defence of my dastardly conduct. I only remembered your noble generosity of soul, the inestimable qualities that made you the man you were, and I ventured to put them to the test – to come in person and crave your forgiveness. Was I wrong?' A pathetic plaint had stolen into the voice that Anthony was quick to detect, but he kept silent.

'Anthony, we are old men; we are told the days of our years are threescore years and ten, and they are passed with both of us. I was never the man you were; your life has ever been blameless, while mine is marred by many a blemish. At one time it seemed scarcely worth preserving, and I was tempted to rid the earth of such an encumbrance, when from a little primitive church near which[17] I had halted, the words of a Christmas anthem floated out on the still air, "Glory to God in the highest; peace on earth, good-will towards men," and I crept in to hear the story of forgiveness that followed it. I could not do so cowardly a deed after that: it was the old story to which we had listened together many a time when we were lads, but it had never seemed a personal matter until then. I resolved to make a fresh start, but it has been uphill work. I was always weak where you were strongest, your moral rectitude of character was a fact which everyone recognised, while I – but I would not urge my weakness as an excuse. I have sinned, and for me there is no forgiveness.'

'Frank.'

A hand was lifted from the staff and thrust out towards the speaker; it was gripped and held as in a vice, and there was silence between them as they bridged the gulf that had separated them for fifty years.

Notes

1. 'hills' in the *Warwick Examiner and Times* (WET) (Warwick, Queensland), Saturday, 5 November 1910, p. 2. Katherine is spelt with two e's in the attribution for this version.
2. 'portion of the heavens' is 'portions of the heaven' in WET.
3. Spelt 'splendour' in WET.
4. A large, slightly off-centre, capital 'K' here in WET.
5. 'fools of *the* men' in WET.
6. 'into line' in WET.
7. 'to-night' in WET.
8. 'among whom *he* was' in WET.
9. Changed to 'jokers' in WET.
10. 'could be' in WET (the word *ever* is absent).
11. 'like to' in WET.
12. Spelling corrected to read 'Henceforth' in WET.
13. Here 'would' instead of 'could' in WET.
14. Corrected to read 'asked' in WET.

15. 'She read *of* him' in WET.
16. Reads 'with *the* cushions' in WET.
17. 'near *by* which' in WET.

CREATIVE WRITING

SHORT STORY

Mari

Paula Morris

My daughter is here from Auckland, loud with chatter and self-importance. She trudged up to the schoolhouse to tell me that the old Queen is dead. The news is weeks old, but we have not heard a peep of it, of course. There are still only muddy tracks into this place, not a road of any description. Here in the valley we're captives, pent in by the hills and the bush and the mist.

The bush is not the forest, nor is it the woods. My father, John Reid, was the steward on a large estate outside London, and there were woods there, luminous with bluebells in the spring. When my sister Mary Ann and I were children we scampered through the trees, swinging from crocked branches. Bush is a thicket so dense and low that only birds that snuffle along the ground can penetrate it. I've lived inside its walls for more than thirty years.

In our little school, where I help teach the Maori children, Victoria is a picture on the wall. The edges curl with damp, a slapped mosquito darkening her arm. Mihi Rihipeti, the children call me – Miss Elizabeth – though I am a married woman.

'We have a king now,' my daughter tells me, breathless with her news. All I can think is: the old Queen is lucky. For years she's been a captive too, under guard in her dank castles and rattling carriages, swaddled in mourning clothes.

The Queen is dead and times, my daughter babbles, will change. Not here, not in the Mangakahia Valley, I want to tell her. The only thing that changes is the colour of the sky.

I have had two lives, one as an English girl, and one as a Maori wife. When I was young, I imagined lives for myself, but I never dreamed of one in this place – an island at the bottom of the world, a drizzle of

149

green on the map.

The man I married told me that I would be no ordinary wife, no ordinary woman. On that faraway island, so much sunnier than my own, I'd be a princess. The Prince of Wales had just married and we were all wild for his Danish princess, pale and thin, her hands delicate, her clothes wafting-white and pure as feathers. I could expect her kind of life, he said, if I followed him across the oceans. I put aside my sewing, and looked into his eyes, and I believed him.

That was what I wanted to believe, forty years ago, when I was still an English girl. The estate in my father's care did not belong to us and never could. After my schooling I was employed in service there, prey for the footmen who brushed too close to me in passageways. I wanted to step across the threshold and see only bowed heads, my crinoline tilting to fit through the doors. Instead I flitted like a ghost from scullery to attic, haunting the back stairs. The only time I spent in the drawing room was on my knees, to set the fire. The highest I could aim was housekeeper, which meant never marrying. When he was younger, my father had gone to sea and roamed the world. I'd heard his stories. I would never be content, I thought, cloistered down someone else's back stairs.

One of the places my father visited on his voyages was New Zealand. He'd met many important people among the natives there, and told us of their ferocious ways – their faces carved with deep grooves, their weapons poised to hack the skulls of their enemies. They wore feathers in their hair – black, with white tips – and wrapped themselves in cloaks made from the skin of dogs. In those days, he said, victors still boiled and devoured the bodies of those they vanquished. They displayed the heads of their enemies, the way heads of traitors were once spiked along London Bridge. Our father's stories might have been inventions, or exaggerations. Mary Ann and I didn't care. We liked to hear of the faraway wild, and of dangers different from the ones on our own streets. We never thought we'd see such a warrior ourselves, not in our own parlour in Marylebone, not in our English-girl lives.

The day I met my husband I should have been at work at the big house, hauling a pail or folding sheets, but I'd been ill with scarlet fever, and they sent me home before anyone else sickened with it. I was not yet robust, though the redness was gone and my throat was no longer swollen. It was summer. The city rotted and stank. Too many people were sick.

My father read in the newspaper of the arrival of a party of Maori chiefs, and he hurried off to visit them in Limehouse, near the docks.

They were staying in an odd place called the Strangers' Home for Asiatics, Africans and South-Sea Islanders, a house for sailors and other itinerants who would not be welcome in the usual lodgings. Back in New Zealand, he'd known the father of one of this Maori party. The old man had been a great warrior chief, he said. So even though my mother was fearful, my father insisted on inviting the young man, Hare Pomare, and all of his kin also present in London, to visit us in Marylebone.

Our strange guests were not quite as fearsome as we'd hoped. All the men wore coats and trousers and boots, with nothing about them made of feathers or dogs. Mr. Hare Pomare was a tall young man, smooth-cheeked and civil, with a shy young wife named Hariata. They were accompanied by four kinsmen. Only two had grooves carved into their skin. One of them was an old man who said very little, and stared at the floor for much of the visit.

The other was a tall man in his middle years, very striking, with great staring eyes and curly black hair. He was the leader of the party, and the only one who spoke any English. His name was Te Hautakiri Wharepapa, words I could not begin to pronounce at the time. His Christian name, given to him by the missionaries who converted him, was Kamariera, the Māori word for Gamaliel. I couldn't say that either. All I could manage was 'Mari', and whenever I said it he smiled.

'Mihi Rihipeti', he said. He was the first to call me this. This was how it began, communicating in signs and smiles, unable to say each other's names. It might have been a warning, perhaps, of other differences. I've learned that not everything can be translated, and not everything can be understood. But it's easy to be wise when you're old and have too much time to think. When you're young, all that matters is the quivering in your belly when a man enters the room, and the tingle along your skin when he touches your hand.

After Mari took his leave, I daydreamed about tracing a soft finger along the grooves in his face – cut with a bone chisel, my father told us, and stained with the gum of a kauri tree. It seemed that Mari was a grand personage indeed on his distant green island. Every line and swirl on his face attested to that. In a way, it was his signature, my father explained. Another language I couldn't read. How impressed I was, in those days, with anything I couldn't understand.

When he visited – and he visited almost every day that August – I sat basking in his smile, the glare of his attention. Mari was a widower. He told us that many Maori people had adopted the English custom, and married in the English way. But others, he said, kept to the old Maori ways. They married, he said, in much the way the lions and the bears marry. I remember my mother shooing us out of the room after that particular conversation.

Mari was only in London for a few weeks before the Maori party moved on to tour other cities, but a few weeks were long enough. Long enough for my father to return to the estate where he had business. Long enough for Mari to call one morning when my mother and sister were not at home. He could piece together sufficient English to tell me that if I returned to New Zealand with him as his wife I would be a great chieftainess, living in state in his beautiful valley, a Queen of his people.

Long enough for certain things to happen, in the manner of lions and bears, to make that future the only one I could choose.

By the new year Mari and his kin were in Birmingham, where they had been making public appearances. I wrote to him almost daily, hoping that he understood English well enough to read what I was telling him. I couldn't hide my condition any longer.

He returned to London in March, and the missionaries arranged our wedding, in St Anne's in Limehouse. My parents would not attend, but they relented a little, after our marriage was formalised. I was permitted to stay with them until we sailed for New Zealand the following month. True, my mother spent much of that time crying, or remonstrating with my father for bringing heathen savages into the house. She would never see me again, she said, when I sailed to the end of the world, and she was right. I have never seen my parents or my sister again.

Our first child, Maria, was born on the voyage, not long after we cleared the Cape of Good Hope and entered the vast waters of the Pacific. It was the largest ocean in the world, I was told, and we were sailing to the bottom of it, where the world ended, and my second life would begin.

The old Queen married beneath herself; that's what some people said, anyway. She married a foreign prince, and he remained a prince even though she was the Queen. She loved him and had many children with him, but it was a political alliance as well. Queen Victoria would not have been permitted to marry a footman, say, even if he'd been a very handsome one, and of the very best character.

It's different with women, of course. We take on the status of our husband, however lowly our origins. And I was a young Englishwoman, from a respectable family; my origins were humble, not lowly. I certainly didn't expect Mari's family to look down at me.

But here were things he hadn't told me in the parlour in Marylebone. To his family, I was a wife who brought with her no dowry and no important relations. I offered no useful political alliances; I would inherit no land. My work in service back in England was beneath me, or beneath him, anyway – slave's work, I heard someone say, when I had learned enough Maori to make sense of the whispers.

And I had to learn Maori very quickly. Mari soon seemed to forget everything he'd learned in England, and after we rode for days through the bush to reach the Mangakahia Valley, I did not meet or speak with another European for almost ten years. The only conversation in English I could have was with my daughters – five of them, one after the other born in a tiny house adrift in the mud, in a settlement so tiny I still wouldn't call it a village.

The days smelled of smoke and rain, of the rotting carcasses of sodden native trees. When I didn't have a broom in my hand, I picked up a hoe to dig in the kumara pits, or carried gourds to the other side of the valley to fetch water. In mutinous moments, I wished that I'd married a footman instead, or simply stayed a maidservant. At least there would have been someone else to cook my meals and mend my boots. I still had to kneel before a fire every day.

The life of a princess, the life of a queen. We'll believe anything, won't we, when someone handsome looks our way?

Mari built a little church and a rich lady in England, a benefactor of the Maori party in Birmingham, sent him a prayer book and a fine altar cloth. Perhaps she thought our churches in New Zealand would be like the sturdy ones in English villages, built from stone to last forever. Our little church was a shanty that soon burned down, though Mari saved the cloth. To him it was a taonga, a treasure, and to me as well, in a different way. It reminded me of the place I'd left behind, and the hours I spent stitching fine things. In New Zealand I learned to strip flax, to roll its coarse strands against my bare knee, so I could weave it into bags and hats.

By the time another European, Dr Fraser, finally turned up in the valley, the sound of English was just a memory. To hear his voice was like hearing a robin sing in the bush, startling and alien, something that didn't belong in the valley. I was relieved to find my own words again, and to help him organise his school, for Dr Fraser had been sent by the government into a Maori area barely speaking a word of the language. Long ago, when Mari was taken to the Isle of Wight to meet the Queen, she had expressed a wish that all Maori children be taught to read and write. But I don't know that she realised how many men on horseback that would take, or how hard it is without books, or slates, or benches, or any of the things I remember from my own school days.

This has been my life for thirty years – first learning to speak again, like a child, and then teaching children much the same thing. Mari gone for long stretches of time, riding to Auckland and getting stuck there, so he always said, for weeks because the winter rain made rough tracks into the Mangakahia Valley impassable.

I've never left this place. My only sight of Auckland was the day our ship docked in 1864. Compared with London, it looked like a toy-town, roads of dust lined with raw wooden buildings, a stream of sewage running down its main street. A rough and ramshackle place, I thought, not knowing what lay in wait for me further north, or how much I would long for the sight of a staircase, or a door that locked, or for the creaking wheels of the rudest cart.

Mari is old now; his whiskers are white. He loves me in his own way, I know, but it's not the way we loved each other during that first sunny, foolish August, or even in the years after he brought me to the valley and built me my tumble-down house. He is still away most of the time. Each time he leaves I wonder if he'll remember to return.

I'm accustomed to this life, familiar with its rhythms, but the news my daughter brings from my old home is unsettling. I wonder if the Queen died on the Isle of Wight, in her palace by the sea. Although this too is an island, the water is distant. We may as well be surrounded by desert. I stand here wearing no shoes, my dirty feet hidden by the drooping hem of my skirt, watching over children who sprawl on the ground. Spindly twigs of light poke through the gaps in the schoolhouse walls, where rain seeps in on wet days and ants trek in and out on hot ones.

I need to find Mari. That's all I can think about now, finding him and telling him what I want. When my daughter goes back to Auckland, I'm going as well. Mari can buy me the thing he promised me long ago, my own palace, or at least a house. Not buried deep in a valley but perched on a hill, where I can see the sea and hear the caw of gulls. I'll gaze out at the ships clustered in the harbour and see the Thames again, its forest of masts, its swarm of sailors, and remember the city I left behind, at the other end of the world.

POETRY

———

Is the Air Always Like This?

I seize on the smallest of details
the heavy feel of the air
as if it were significant in a sketch
of love and loss and embarrassment –
delicately bringing out the distinctions, the levels
in between and up above and below

but the air –
brisk, flagellating/whispering, enticing
holds all the magic, brings the voice into a room
presses down upon our heads
carries that gradual descent to silence
if I say something that misses the tone

then the karaka trees, to be hidden,
broad glossy leaves and shiny fruit – berries –
death-bringers to the uninitiated
should they be held back in a party?
and watch them loom behind the band, over the party-goers' heads?

I feel the hat
with its velvet streamer
a ribbon trailing behind ostentatiously
does it shine more so than the skin glows
from inside, when fresh, gauche youth
has not been tempered by the grubby fingers of six imploring children

I had not been there
and now I have, at Laura's shoulder
gazing at the perfect sleeping fallen
the taste of passion-fruit ice sour under my tongue

ERICA STRETTON

Leslie

You left at the wrong time.
The news burst into a thousand pieces
still floating in the air,
gunpowder on my lips.

Incredulous, I touch your letters
filled with memories,
scent of home, ink
on your fingers.

Your death was not a drill.
The pomegranate spilt seeds on you,
a tin soldier without a fight,
and you lying in that forest,
asleep, while I feel
wind, sea, dawn, life:
I am as dead as you are.

It's useless to cry out. Don't scream!
Hanging in cages
on the dismal wall
we can only
sing, sing.

[*The poem is the author's collaborative translation with Lizzie Davis and Carmel Bird of the Spanish original.*]

GERARDO RODRÍGUEZ-SALAS

Four Hours

She lies on the grass looking up at the sky. She visits me unannounced,
  this Kezia

presenting me the gift of her company. She is mine for four hours.
Her name is chocolate melting on my tongue.
Kee-zia / Ke-zire

lies on the grass and a billion stars shiver. She believes she might touch
  one of them.
Silent, I lie down beside her. We do not touch

her hair, wet from where she swam at the bay, and how she glistened as
  she stepped from the sea, my mermaid. My Kezia

leads me inside and I follow, as though it is her house we enter.
She sits at my kitchen table. Her hand caresses its smoothness. I ache

and she asks for ice.
I bring her diamonds in a crystal flute

and she spoons cubes of them onto the cup of her hand where they
  melt and are gone

and she moves to the doorway and she leaves and I watch her
  diminish,

recalling an old rhyme
Kee-zia's easier /Ke-zire sounds higher

'Kee-zia's easier,' I say as she disappears to nothing.
'Ke-zire rhymes with desire.'

JACKIE DAVIS

157

The Ox

Trapped within the glassed-in veranda,
wings beating to the careless strike of the presentation clock,
they are surrounded by scarlet plush,
the scent of freshly-ground nutmeg,
sticks, umbrellas, sunshades,
leather trunks, old boxes made of tin:

He turns and turns his signet ring.

Brushing past the husks of women knitting,
leaf-like hands waving in greeting,
brandishing an understanding biscuit,
he fetches the grey cobweb of her shawl
which she clasps to her bosom,
crushing dark little violets
which perch on a lepidopterist's pin:

He turns and turns his signet ring.

They sip on tea that tastes of chopped hay
amid the stench of charcoal and swede,
watch the honeymoon couple smile like shimmering fish,
two brimming tubs in the sunshine,
their voices clear as birds laughing,
no glass cage to stem them in:

He turns and turns his signet ring.

He guides her through the rich, rank smell
of fleshy aloes, delicious heliotrope,
a sprig of which she catches in his lapel,
her sickness a gossamer leash
which lures him back to where she sits
under a sky precious as jade.
They creep inside, the dinner bell won't ring:

He turns and turns his signet ring.

In time they dine on eggs and spinach
(to her he is both bread and wine)
then sail upstairs to where their two white beds
float like ships, silvered in moonlight.
He listens to lightning cry like a broken bird,
hears the sound of a piano, a mosquito sing,
hovering in his blue and white pyjamas,
waiting as the rot sets in.

He turns and turns his signet ring.

JESSICA WHYTE

Bertha

She swallows a bright piece of late afternoon sun
breathes it deep into her lungs
observes ecstasy in the dusky mirror
admires a pyramid of floating fruit
a blue dish dipped in milk
the radiance of tangerines
silk-smooth skin of pears
apples stained with strawberry pink.

The cushions come alive;
a pair of cats slink under jade-green sky
the smell of jonquils, drunk on spring
drifts up the stairs
where her baby lies in another woman's arms
the idiocy of civilisation soothed by exquisite toes.

She dresses as a pear
in a white dress, green shoes and stockings
serves an admirable soufflé
to the victims of time and train
who wear socks whiter than the moon
an orange coat, monkeys processing round the hem
a yellow dress of scraped banana skin.

A slender pearl, dressed in silver
fills her up with blissful ardour
before kissing her husband in the hall.

She lives by listening,
her fingers tender as moonbeams.

JESSICA WHYTE

Read the World

Katherine Mansfield would
have loved the web –
she could have sat
as her health deteriorated
& read the world at a glance,
contributed to chat rooms
criticised spelling
added editorial comment,
conversed more immediately
with Middleton Murry –
her horizons expanded
beyond those rooms
where she spent
in troubled pain,
her invalid days.

JULIE KENNEDY

In a Nutshell

When I eat walnuts,
I am Mitochondrial Eve
a small woman
with tennis player's haunches
and opposable thumbs.
I see in colour
speak backwards
        sdrawkcab
or in codes,
too clever by halves
cohabit with cabbage trees
up a salt river
in silence

you have to go days to find.
At night I take off my black caul,
lay out my pretty lobes
in double mirrors
reflections
receding
all the way back to Africa.

When I eat hazelnuts
I am Katherine Mansfield
stranded
in a German pension
hoping for someone to talk to.
With a jeweller's balance
I weigh
strings of uncut amber
twelve-egg *kuchen*
flax and paddocks
European travel.
Nervous bladder
insomniac
lovelorn.

When I eat cashew nuts
I am Suzy Wong
Thai takeaway
succulent cloying colostrum,
hooking in a parlour
in cut-offs
and a boob tube.
Unprotected
I get STDs
like the common cold
douche with sea water
only to fall
first fuck
eight months clean.
Girls rule
men in cars
little sprout.

When I eat brazil nuts
I am Carmen Miranda
muscled
in cherry satin
and violet eye shadow
clicking my teeth
like castanets.
Bits get stuck in my dentures
I am garrulous
break into song
crack jokes, dance.
My trinity –
flesh, shell, oil –
gravid with language.

When I eat almonds
I am Mata Hari
cat-eyed spy
in the house of love.
We drink Cointreau on ice
from gilded glasses
his skin like blossom
and time
flies over the rooftops.

When I eat nuts,
I am Nu:t*
the whole shebang
born of ululation
moisture and fire crackers.
I have no consort
he's outside
drinking
fagging
shooting up
hocking my starry dress
trying to get back up me.
I bear down
without drugs
swallow the night
virgin again
every morning

to make school lunches
and hold up the sky.

* Nu:t is the Egyptian goddess of the sky.

KIRSTEN WARNER

At Katherine's Bay

Water washes over the road
at Eastbourne while

latte spume licks the heels of
city jeeps. The southerly lifts sand

and little blue penguins invade
the investment, once were holiday homes

where Katherine stayed and Stanley Burnell's
children played their part,

native bush and real estate collide
in Sunday kaleidoscope sunshine.

Jonathan Trout isn't shouting out
from the waves nowadays

he sits instead, in the shelter of the boatshed
and watches Stanley catch the ferry.

Linda feasts on eggs florentine
and Beryl's no longer afraid

the Kember's brittle laughter
can be heard over barbecues

and in the bush, if you listen carefully
from somewhere in the shadows

you can hear Jonathan saying,
'It's all wrong, it's all wrong'.

MAGGIE RAINEY SMITH

Your Secret Life

(For Katherine Mansfield)

It's like the day the cat left
and never came back.

You may have seen it surely:
a paw stepping out, a flash of fur

across the street. You had just given
it milk, treated it with utmost kindness.

It was if it were a friend of yours perhaps.
It was part of your life and even,

yes, a new life never begun. It would
happen, oh, about nine times; you were

sure of that, and meanwhile those gentle sounds,
those moments of purring would be the past.

In the future it would be just you and you
alone. But the cat? you ask, well, that was the end.

MARK PIRIE

On Reading the Poems of Katherine Mansfield

A tale found in the pages of a book
Was as bold as the author's fame
A cover bound by the spine of a book
Stood erect as if to claim

Her mind with erstwhile dreams
Where lyrics were her living voice
Where enjoyment spawned the heart's gleams
And her love was the beauty of choice

A Unique Perspective:
Terry Stringer's Sculpted Portraits of
Katherine Mansfield

Robin Woodward

In the late 1960s and 1970s, when Terry Stringer was finding his feet as an artist, New Zealand was breaking traditional ties with 'the mother country'. As part of this transition came the search for New Zealand's own national icons, those which would carry a recognisable sense of nationhood and identity. Stringer lighted upon Katherine Mansfield. In images of Mansfield's sharp and watchful face Stringer saw someone who grew up in New Zealand, who took stock of New Zealanders, and who wrote about them in the cultural heart of the British Empire, England. In his images of Mansfield, Stringer pays homage to this. Ultimately, in a portrait which takes the form of a secular temple, Stringer makes a formal goddess of Mansfield.

Mansfield is the subject of at least five sculpted portraits by Stringer. In addition, there are two of his 'finished' drawings of Mansfield in New Zealand's National Art Gallery at Te Papa Tongarewa (Container of Treasures), and one in a private collection. Stringer's full-length figure, *Homage to Katherine Mansfield* (1977, private collection), and the bronze bust in the collection of the Christchurch Art Gallery Te Puna o Waiwhetu, *Portrait of Katherine Mansfield* (1977), are the earliest known three-dimensional representations of Mansfield. Clearly related to the bust is the Te Papa pencil drawing, *Katherine Mansfield: Study for Sculpture* (1977); a second pencil drawing at Te Papa, *Katherine Mansfield 1916 (Lady Ottoline Morrell)* dates from the same year.[1] In fact, that drawing is taken from Morrell's photograph of Mansfield, the work which initially piques Stringer's interest in Mansfield and leads to this extraordinary run of sculpted portraits.[2] The third sculpture in the series is *Mementoes*, which dates from 1981. In 2009, Stringer's interest in Mansfield was revived when he received an invitation to present a concept for a public monument to Mansfield in Wellington, New

Zealand, conceived by the Katherine Mansfield Society and organised by the Wellington Sculpture Trust. This leads to *Katherine Mansfield as a Temple to her Childhood* (2009) and *The Mind of Katherine Mansfield* (2013).

Any discussion of a portrait of an artist by another artist can be approached from several angles. Portraits can be analysed in relation to the *œuvre* of the sitter and/or the artist. Then there is relevant social and cultural context to be considered, as well as other portraits of the sitter. Questions arise around the purpose and function of the portrait. A discussion that touches on all of these aspects is holistic in approach and addresses the salient features of portrait studies.

All portraits are a complex transaction between the viewer and the subject. What the viewer is responding to is an interpretation of the sitter by an intermediary, in this case a sculptor. In the Stringer/ Mansfield relationship, the connection is distanced because the lives of the sculptor and the writer never overlap. Stringer knows Mansfield only through her writing and through reports and representations by inter-generational intermediaries – writers, photographers and painters. It is these which establish the conditions and circumstances of the image Stringer presents for the viewer. His Mansfield works are therefore an interpretation of others' impressions and afford us a glimpse of the sculptor as well as the sitter. Stringer endows his portraits of Mansfield with the singularity of his intensely personal, creative vision and style.

Consider Stringer's earliest known image of Mansfield, the pencil drawing, *Katherine Mansfield 1916 (Lady Ottoline Morrell)* at Te Papa.[3] In this seated, frontal study Mansfield is presented as a personable young woman who makes eye contact, meets our gaze and has a slight smile for the viewer. The softness of her expression carries through to the flesh of her cheeks and into her hair, where a few wisps float free. The neckline of her dress is rumpled, and this informality is mirrored in the fullness of the large-collared cloak draped over her shoulders. The indistinct cover of the book on her lap merges into the suggestion of each of her hands.

In comparison, in the other Te Papa drawing, which is specified as a study for sculpture, the face, the figure and her book have been translated into the vernacular of Cubism.[4] This drawing is converted directly into Stringer's 1977 bronze portrait bust *Katherine Mansfield* (Figure 2). The face, turned slightly to the side, becomes an exercise in analytical geometry. This angle relieves the bust of complete symmetry and absolute frontality, enlivening and reducing the potential severity of the portrait while retaining the nature of a formal exercise. In their

Fig. 2 Terry Stringer, *Portrait of Katherine Mansfield*, 1977, bronze, Christchurch Art Gallery Te Puna o Waiwhetu. Photographic credit: La Gonda Studio.

turn the pages of the book on Mansfield's lap are regularised and formalised into the straight lines and hard-edged shapes of geometric forms. The differences between the two pencil drawings are at least partially explained by the sub-titles of the works. One is titled *Katherine Mansfield: Study for Sculpture*. The other is inscribed *Katherine Mansfield 1916 (Lady Ottoline Morrell)*.[5]

Fig. 3 Terry Stringer, *Homage to Katherine Mansfield*, 1977, pen and ink, private
collection. Photographic credit: La Gonda Studio.

A photograph is also the inspiration behind Stringer's 1977
full-length standing figure *Homage to Katherine Mansfield* and its related
drawing, a direct compositional copy of Ida Baker's 1920 photograph
of Mansfield standing beneath a parasol on the terrace of the Villa Isola
Bella at Menton.[6] Stringer reduces the figure to a basic silhouette, and
all peripheral detail is simplified into outlines (Figure 3). However,
even this limited narrative and contextual information disappears
in the three-dimensional figure, *Homage to Katherine Mansfield*, which
Stringer sculpts later in the year. Now all that remains is the figure
standing under the parasol. Through this sculpture Stringer makes the
two-dimensional (Ida Baker's photograph) three-dimensional again,

bringing the image full circle; in so doing, the artist is responding to his earliest experience of sculpture.

Growing up in New Zealand in the 1950s, Stringer had an experience of art and art history that was second-hand, acquired through looking at reproductions of artworks in books. Within this context, his earliest art characteristically explores the relationship of two- to three-dimensional form. In the 1970s and early 1980s, for example, much of his work has a Cubist appearance as he examines art historical precedents. Unlike the early twentieth-century Cubists, however, Stringer is not looking to shatter form but rather to accentuate its surface through planes that capture light and shadow.

One manifestation of this is *Mementoes* (Figure 4), comprised of folded and painted aluminium taking the shape of a triangular shelf with figurative elements on it. Of the three sheets of aluminium, one piece is folded at the top and on each side to create the volumetric form of a cube. On to this simple cube of aluminium Stringer paints a three-dimensional shoulder and the head, hair and facial features of Mansfield, creating the effect of a modelled bust. However, any suggestion of modelled form is totally illusionary, as with that other personal memento represented in this work, the portrait photograph. Slotted in behind the bust is a flat piece of aluminium painted to suggest a photograph of Mansfield. Although not a direct copy of a specific photograph, the image shows Mansfield standing in a garden setting; compositionally and contextually, it is akin to photographs taken at her beloved Isola Bella at Menton.[7] Beyond this, even the base on which the head and photograph sit is faux. It is false timber; it too is folded, painted aluminium.

Mementoes stands apart from Stringer's other sculpted portraits of Mansfield in its form and materials: unlike the others, it is neither a bronze nor a modelled volumetric form. It can, however, be regarded in the context of Stringer's series of representations of New Zealand visual artists and writers such as Frances Hodgkins, Rita Angus, Evelyn Page, Lois White, Rick Killeen, Brian Brake and Frank Sargeson. When he returns to Mansfield in 2009 with *Katherine Mansfield as a Temple to her Childhood*, Stringer once again employs a photograph as a point of departure. This work, and *The Mind of Katherine Mansfield* four years later, are visually more complex than the sculptor's earlier representations of Mansfield: the exploration of the *trompe l'œil* effect of sculpted form is taken further in both of them.

While returning to modelled, volumetric form cast in bronze, Stringer simultaneously accords both these works his unique artistic perspective, incorporating features that repay a viewer's investment of time and

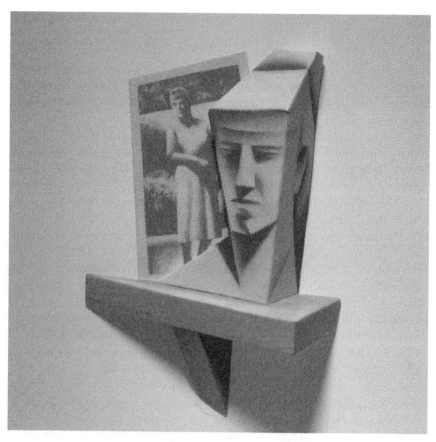

Fig. 4 Terry Stringer, *Mementoes*, 1981, enamel on aluminium, private collection.
Photographic credit: La Gonda Studio.

close observation. Stringer delights in rewarding the viewer who takes
time to engage with his work, and to this end he employs his trademark
innovative multi-viewing point in both of these works. This creates the
effect of 'walk around' artworks which reveal additional images as one
moves around them or turns them on a pivot. In this way the sculpted
works become comparable to the episodic narrative sometimes seen in
painting. A 'walk around' work, with its true three-dimensionality, also
enables communication of more information than a standard bust or
figurative sculpture might.

Katherine Mansfield as a Temple to her Childhood is unremittingly original in concept and composition. Structurally, it references an ancient
trabeated temple with a post and lintel structure of an architrave held
up by three columns. If viewed from one particular viewing point, these

columns form the image of a portrait head of Mansfield (Figure 5). However, there is more to it than that. Move around this piece, or turn the sculpture 45 degrees, and another set of images is revealed (Figure 6). A younger Mansfield emerges: a child wearing spectacles and recognisable from a photograph taken in 1898, *Katherine Mansfield Aged 10*.[8] Accompanied by her muse on the next pillar, this image of childhood is cocooned within a sheltered alcove created by the three columns.

But what of the third column? The accompanying image on this pillar reads as a weeping willow tree – which calls for a re-evaluation of the entire grouping. Close examination reveals that the portrait of Mansfield as a child morphs out of an urn, and her muse is a veiled figure. Is this a funerary figure? In such a reading the internal narrative is memorialising: a mourning female figure, a funerary urn and a weeping willow are a traditional triumvirate in commemorative iconography. However, there are other interpretations. One could read this tableau as a bust of the young Mansfield positioned under a tree and accompanied by an admiring figure – or is this a vision of a figure in her prose? Through an archway between these elements is the glimpse of an arm reaching down to write with a fountain pen. From another direction that element appears to be an arm holding aloft a burning torch.

Clearly, the collection of images can be interpreted in a number of ways. Just as with Mansfield's written observations of people and situations, there is no fixed perspective in Stringer's work. His creative vision offers multiple possibilities and requires intellectual engagement from its audience, calling on the imagination of the viewer to complete a work. In *Katherine Mansfield as a Temple to her Childhood*, beyond the *memento mori* and the notion that there is a child in each one, do these images in Mansfield's head track her life, or more specifically her creative practice? Does the work imply that the essence of creativity lies in one's formative years, or is Stringer conveying something of Mansfield's writing? A vivid sense of childhood shines through much of Mansfield's work, and we know that in 1907 she had planned an illustrated collection of children's stories and poems, which was never published.

Stringer proposed *Katherine Mansfield as a Temple to her Childhood* as Wellington's public monument to Mansfield. In that context there is a synergy between the commemorative and the celebratory. However, the Wellington commission was eventually awarded to Virginia King, whose *Woman of Words* (2013) takes the form of a 3.7 metre figurative sculpture of Mansfield stepping out down Lambton Quay, in Wellington, her childhood home.[9] King's figure is cloaked in phrases selected from Mansfield's writing, affirming her aspiration to be seen as 'a writer first and a woman after'.[10] One further submission to this Wellington

Fig. 5 Terry Stringer, *Katherine Mansfield as a Temple to her Childhood*, 2009, bronze, private collection. Photographic credit: La Gonda Studio.

Sculpture Trust project was Anthony Stones's multi-coloured bust of Mansfield, which now adorns the grounds of the Katherine Mansfield House at 25 Tinakori Road, Wellington.

In its structure, *Katherine Mansfield as a Temple to her Childhood* is designed as three separate forms standing on a communal base. When the three pieces are aligned from a singular viewing point, the profile

Fig. 6 Terry Stringer, *Katherine Mansfield as a Temple to her Childhood*, 2009, bronze, private collection. Photographic credit: La Gonda Studio.

perspective, eye and frontal view of Mansfield's face coalesce into a volumetric three-dimensional head. The sum is greater than its parts. Four years later, in *The Mind of Katherine Mansfield* (Figure 7), there is a similar tripartite configuration minus the intervening space. When this work is viewed from one angle, the face is a reworking of the Ottoline Morrell photographic image; it presents as a monumental mask. Then,

Fig. 7 Terry Stringer, *The Mind of Katherine Mansfield*, 2013, bronze, private collection. Photographic credit: La Gonda Studio.

Fig. 8 Terry Stringer, *The Mind of Katherine Mansfield*, 2013, bronze, private collection. Photographic credit: La Gonda Studio.

as the viewer moves around the sculpture, the image changes and more is revealed (Figure 8). A musing figure (the writer? the sculptor?), head on hand, emerges, followed by a third image, one which is open to multiple interpretations – a doll, a puppet, and that traditional prop for a visual artist, a lay figure. In one reading, this view becomes a hand manipulating a puppet, as if in her mind Mansfield is handling the actions of her characters to fit in with her plotting. There is also a doll-like quality to the figure, bringing to mind both her story 'The Doll's House' and mechanical walking dolls, popular in the early twentieth century.[11] Or is Stringer telling us something about his own creative practice? Is this a lay figure, a jointed manikin of the human body, usually made of wood, which, in the absence of a life model, an artist would use to model figurative representations? Through such a degree of figurative detail numerous stories can be told. Here the head and shoulders of a standard portrait bust are presented as a façade, the physical presence that masks inner thought.

In *Katherine Mansfield as a Temple to her Childhood* we see Mansfield's muse and a picture of her childhood, the source of so much of her imagery and stories. In *The Mind of Katherine Mansfield* we are shown something of her process, which, in its turn, mirrors that of the sculptor. The head-on-hand image suggests thought and contemplation. The jointed manikin, an artist's inanimate substitute for a life model, intimates the opportunity for close observation unaffected by any reciprocated gaze that might challenge or influence. The need for the viewer to spend time with creative works in order to discover varied perspectives, and the dividend this offers, accord also with the depths and nuance of Mansfield's works. They too reward close consideration and repeated reading. The parallels between sculptor and writer are revealed here. Both effectively 'live in their heads': the creative process of each is a solitary activity, and their individual perspectives are a personal vision.

There is no chance that Stringer's portraiture might ever engender Roger Fry's comment that, when looking at a particular portrait, he couldn't see the person for the likeness.[12] In his work Stringer realises something of his sitters' individuality and identity, bringing features to the image which are additional to a basic photographic likeness. His portraits are creative interpretations of his sitters: we always know we are looking at an artwork. However, in the works discussed here we are also aware that we are looking at Mansfield, courtesy of photography. The place of photography in Stringer's creative process, however, is a point of departure rather than a destination. Similarly with art historical conventions of Western portraiture: the genesis of Stringer's portrait works lies in the figurative, either in bust form or representational standing figure. However, his portraits of Mansfield are no social artefacts. The sculptor brings his personal creative process to the table, investing his portraits of Mansfield with a unique perspective. Through this he conveys the particular as well as the general, revealing something of her individual physiognomy, aspects of personality and a cultural context.

Portraiture is not the equal of the sitter, and Stringer does not intend his portraits to be so. Portraiture depends on the artist making something out of the original, drawing on accumulated knowledge of the sitter. Stringer's process includes studying Mansfield's writing, recognising the sources of her inspiration (including her childhood) and how she draws on ideas, experiences and those transient moments that provide fleeting glimpses of something only barely perceived. Then there is Stringer's analogy between a writer's method and the use of an artist's lay figure, a tool in the creative process which assists artists to arrange their ideas and images into a realisable form. Through these, Stringer sculpts a visual diary of Mansfield's life. He presents her as a child, with her muse, in the garden at Garsington with all its Bloomsbury connections, and in turn at Menton with Ida Baker.

Notes

1. Both drawings at Te Papa are dated c.1979 in their online catalogue. The drawings were both purchased and accessioned in 1979. They date from 1977. I am grateful to Penelope Jackson for discussing issues such as this and for sharing her knowledge of portraits of Mansfield.

2. Stringer saw a truncated version of the photograph reproduced in the New Zealand *Listener* (Terry Stringer in conversation with the author, 11 April 2019).

3. Available at <https://collections.tepapa.govt.nz/object/335406> (last accessed 1 October 2019).

4. Available at <https://collections.tepapa.govt.nz/object/40439> (last accessed 1 October 2019).

5. Available at <https://www.npg.org.uk/collections/search/portrait/mw86922/Katherine-Mansfield?LinkID=mp16184&search=sas&sText=Katherine+MAnsfield&OConly=true&role=sit&rNo=2> (last accessed 1 October 2019). There is some inconsistency in documentation of the photograph. The National Portrait Gallery, London, attributes the photograph to Morrell (NPG Ax140568) with the detail 'Place made and portrayed: United Kingdom: England, Oxfordshire (Garsington Manor, Oxfordshire)'. The photograph is in the Lady Ottoline Morrell Album Collection, Album 3, 1914–20 and, in keeping with other annotations in Morrell's photograph albums, is identified as 'Katherine Mansfield' in Morrell's hand. Available at <https://www.npg.org.uk/collections/search/set/183/Lady+Ottoline+Morrell+Collection%2C+Album+3> (last accessed 1 October 2019). With less accuracy, an identical print in Te Puna Mātauranga o Aotearoa National Library of New Zealand (accession number 1/2-002594-F) is documented 'Katherine Mansfield seated, book in hand, in a deck chair in France, 1916. Taken by an unknown photographer'. In Claire Tomalin's *Katherine Mansfield: A Secret Life* (London: Viking, 1997), this photo has the caption '1916: In her St. John's Wood garden'.

6. This photograph is in the collection of the National Library of New Zealand. Available at <https://natlib.govt.nz/records/23149501?search%5Bi%5D%5B_authority_id%5D=77173&search%5Bpath%5D=items> (last accessed 31 October 2019).

7. A number of such photographs are held in the collection of the Alexander Turnbull Library, Wellington. See <https://digitalnz.org/stories/503a962d125757739200523c> (last accessed 1 October 2019).

8. Now in the collection of the Alexander Turnbull Library, Wellington. See <https://natlib.govt.nz/records/23104236> (last accessed 1 October 2019).

9. See Robin Woodward, 'Woman of Words', in *Katherine Mansfield and World War One*, ed. by Gerri Kimber, W. Todd Martin and Delia da Sousa Correa (Edinburgh: Edinburgh University Press, 2014), pp. 160–7.

10. Katherine Mansfield to John Middleton Murry, 3 December 1920, *Letters* 4, p. 133.

11. There is one such doll in the collection at Te Papa. See <https://collections.tepapa.govt.nz/object/66235> (last accessed 1 October 2019).

12. Roger Fry, quoted in Richard Brilliant, *Portraiture* (London: Reaktion Books, 2004), p. 26.

Such 'rich unlawful gold': Mansfield's Semiotic Manœuvres in 'An Indiscreet Journey'

Janet M. Wilson

Biography and Fiction in 'An Indiscreet Journey'

Mansfield's first story about World War I, written between March and May 1915 and published posthumously in the collection *Something Childish and Other Stories* (1924), is based on her clandestine trip to Gray, a town on the River Saône near Dijon in the Zone des Armées (military zone) in February 1915, only six months after the war began.[1] 'An Indiscreet Journey' gives a vital glimpse into the world behind the lines in France at a time when little was known about the realities of war and even less written about its effects on the everyday life of soldiers and citizens, especially from a woman's point of view. Mansfield's daring journey into a territory seventy-five miles behind the trenches, where soldiers were forbidden to receive female visitors, marks the story as not just 'an indiscreet journey', but in fact an illegal narrative written under the radar of official surveillance, testifying to incidents that, as she was aware, were not meant to be reported on. At every stage it displays its deeply transgressive nature. Partly based on her personal account and letters, as recorded in her notebooks, the plotless narrative betrays no sign of the episode's origin in Mansfield's desire for a romantic liaison with the French writer Francis Carco, with whom she spent four nights in Gray from 19 to 23 February, and her anxieties about not being able to write in the weeks leading up to this illicit assignation. The notebook entries nevertheless offer crucial insights into how Mansfield made fiction from a life crisis to produce a unique modernist narrative structure, a distinctively female way of writing about the war that reflects its limited reality for most civilians at that time, in what can be seen as an important transitional story.

The story's evolution from its autobiographical beginnings is traceable in the opening section, in the train travel, arrival and the assignation of the first-person narrator with the 'little corporal', as Carco is described in Mansfield's diary entry for 20 February.[2] Two further sections, set on a subsequent night – either one or two days later – for which no prior written version exists, concern her stay in the unfamiliar town of Gray. The second section takes place in a café that the lovers visit, and depicts the humdrum confusions of war from behind the lines where civilians and soldiers mingle, from the point of view of an outsider. The third section describes their illicit visit to a second café in search of a French plum brandy called mirabelle, using image, simile and symbol to represent a new, decisive stage of Mansfield's search for artistic voice and subject matter. In these sections, through a web of implication transference and repetition, the internal motivations – her prior hopes and anticipations, which have been concealed by the thrill of the illicit adventure – are covertly addressed and refocused in relation to the narrator's sights of war. The heroine's psychic state, her emotional and spiritual responses to her love affair, which mask Mansfield's own struggle with writer's block, as recorded in the diary entries prior to her journey, can be glimpsed behind the scenes of war that she witnesses in the cafés of Gray.

The story has been described by Christiane Mortelier as bringing together 'Katherine Mansfield in love, Mansfield at war and Mansfield at work in a quite extraordinary way',[3] although the elaborate masking of its personal preoccupations through strategies of detachment, impersonation and displacement has resulted in some critical dissension as to how it can be read as a war story: whether Mansfield's encounter with militarism, despite apparently trivialising and aestheticising war, is a convincing one; about the relation of war to the compelling love interest that dominates Mansfield's letters and diaries; and the role of the writing process. Claire Tylee's claim that 'the heroine has discovered the reality of war' is echoed by Josiane Paccaud-Huguet, who argues that Mansfield deals with 'the *real* substance of war experience', while also finding gaps and silences, textual blind spots that indicate the impossibility of narrating this momentous cataclysm. Con Coroneos, by contrast, argues that Mansfield productively resists the model that 'war is always the necessary *real*', suggesting that war is 'an artistic commodity' in a story that is about the intoxication of writing.[4]

Reading the story in relation to the diary, however, allows us to see how Mansfield coded particular images and sights she encountered as reminders and signposts for the fiction, and to become aware of the act of writing that lies at the story's heart. It confirms the indispensability of her diary as an archive, an inspiration and workshop for literary experimentation, as David Manenti remarks.[5] Comparison between the two versions suggests her 'semiotic' approach to her daring escapade by shaping her account into a narrative that is also a commentary on the writing process, and just as illegal an act in its theft from life as the real-life adventure it describes. Mansfield's figuring of the act of writing as a form of alluvial extraction – implied in the image of 'rich unlawful gold' harboured in the bosoms of the houses of Gray (CW1, p. 445) – has implications for reading this story about transgression, found in the mobilising passion of clandestine romance, the illegal visit to a town under military surveillance, and the characters' breaking of the curfew in Gray, described in section three. A semiotic reading, there-fore, indicates that Mansfield rewrote her pre-journey anxieties about love and writing into fiction, independent of any literary models, by cor-relating them with external events and encounters through moments of inspired intensity. In keeping with Sydney Janet Kaplan's view that Mansfield's consciousness is the real centre of her work, I argue that the creative sparks that fly between the documentary account and her story dominate the tone, mood and representation of the mixed civilian and military settings and incidents of 'An Indiscreet Journey', making the narrative at a metafictional level about the rediscovery and liberation of her artistic energies.[6]

Mansfield became attracted to Francis Carco partly because of her growing disillusionment with John Middleton Murry during late 1914, and especially in January 1915, when they were living in Rose Tree Cottage in the Chilterns, about three miles from D. H. and Frieda Lawrence. Like Frieda, who missed her children, Mansfield felt alien-ated from the male camaraderie developing between Murry and Lawrence – then talking of founding an ideal island community called Rananim – while also being frustrated by her inability to write, as evi-denced by feverish petitions in her diary such as 'My God my God let me work, Wasted Wasted'.[7] She had met Carco, a writer and contributor to *Rhythm*, in the winter of 1913–14 when staying with Murry in Paris in the rue de Tournon. She was attracted by his South Seas sensuality, 'his confidence and his warm sensational life [. . .]. I want to laugh and run into the road' (CW4, p. 144).[8] By early January 1915, Carco had enlisted as a postman-corporal for a bakery unit in a cavalry regiment stationed at Gray, and about this time they began corresponding. On the 6th she records, 'he's haunted me all day', continuing, 'I dare not push my thoughts as far as they will go'; she had her photo taken for him and on the 8th sent him a lock of her hair (CW4, p. 149).

Mansfield's growing feelings for Carco, which placed her in a dilemma because of her competing affections for Murry, also emanated from a morbid anxiety about death. She wrote on 2 January: 'I feel really quite past my prime. At times the fear of death is dreadful' (CW4, p. 147–8). The urge to embark on a clandestine love affair manifested in symptoms of ill health and psychic disturbance: a terrible dream about her mother, a violent headache, tiredness, numbness, hands like ice, an attack of flu. By 21 January, as she waited in agony for his letters, her anxiety was such that she felt she was diseased, contaminated, being devoured:

> my anxious heart is eating up my body, eating up my nerves, eating up my brain, now slowly, now at tremendous speed. I feel this poison slowly filling my veins – every particle becoming slowly tainted. Yes love like this is a malady, a fever, a storm. It is almost like hate, one is so hot with it & never never calm. (CW4, p. 154)

This hyper-anxious, hypochondriacal state has elicited psychological explanations such as that she was either self-deluded about Carco or suffering because of the fear of being morally compromised. Murry knew exactly what was going on and did not try to halt her. He noted in his diary,

> she had imagined she had found a deliverer in R. D. [Raoul Duquette]. I was dully aware of it, and sufficiently sensible to make no attempt to disabuse her, although I was curiously aware that she was deceiving herself. [. . .] I had in my head a core of faith that she would return.[9]

Biographers and critics have also treated the affair with scepticism, seeing it as a fiasco in which Mansfield was either indulging in fantasies that led her to be 'deeply hurt', or seeking new material for her art, which is how Carco portrayed her in the character of 'Winnie' in his novel *Les Innocents*: as a ruthless predator searching for copy.[10] Gerri Kimber's account of the relationship cites widely from their correspondence to suggest Carco's duplicity, and discusses their different literary versions of it.[11] Mary Burgan argues that Mansfield's liminal states were symptomatic of a pathology created by a reaction to her transgressive sexual adventures – guilt at her manifestations of bisexuality, an anxiety about infatuations – and that this had 'the effect of relieving her of control and therefore of moral responsibility for her inclinations', so she could not be accused of manipulating others.[12] The rhetoric of illness and death with which Mansfield writes of her erotic desires in her diaries and letters reflects her earlier preoccupation with artistic creativity, the unconscious and the death drive, as in her child-death poems such as 'Die Einsame' (1906). Similar tensions can be discerned in her story: for Paccaud-Huguet, it is the rendezvous with the mutually dependent binary, the love instinct and death drive, Eros and Thanatos, that gives 'An Indiscreet Journey' its contemporary quality.[13] If her extreme emotional state of psychic dis-ease, the 'disease of fragmentation', shows Mansfield's inner life at its most split and divided, then such a discourse of illness and death, caused by her erotic strivings, may also be a necessary form of semiotic coding to signal that her feelings for Carco were inextricable from her turbulent yet resistant creative forces. This may have helped her to start re-assembling herself by moving away from the conventional cultural order represented by Lawrence, Murry, Gordon Campbell and their circle, towards taking a risky journey into the unknown, one that would enable her to express her experience artistically by introducing symbolism, repetition and innuendo.[14]

Mansfield's disequilibrium may be ascribed to repetitive–compulsive urges dominating her psychic processes, of the sort that Burgan defines. The notebook entries of 3 February show her miseries climaxing in a loss of distinction between contrarieties, a sense of life as death, love as hate, hot as cold. In this liminal state of extreme mental and physical disorientation she believed she was on the brink of complete dysfunction unless she could be with Carco:

> But I know I shall go because otherwise I'll die of despair. My head is so hot but my hands are cold. Perhaps I am dead & just pretending to live here. There is at any rate no sign of life in me. (CW4, p. 157)

The autobiographical contexts, therefore, confirm that the erotic idealism that compelled Mansfield to make her journey to Gray was, from the outset, deeply compromised and conflicted. Her compulsion to join him can also be interpreted in terms of its opposite – a framework of death, dissolution and suffering (i.e. of a war-ravaged society) – as she aimed to escape from Murry, capture in fiction the sights and impressions of war, and break the psychological deadlock which immobilised her creativity.

The autobiographical data reveal Mansfield's intention to make artistic capital from her venture: the notebooks contain a brief chronology of her travels that follow her receipt of an urgent summons from Carco, dated 6 February, a diary entry written on 20 February, the day after her arrival in Gray, and two letters that intersperse it, written on the same day. That she transcribed the letters into the notebook indicates that she valued them as resources for her fictional experiment.[15] The three journeys undertaken from the Chilterns to London (where she borrowed £10 from her brother Leslie for the journey on the spurious grounds that she was going to Paris to report on the war), from London to Paris and thence to Gray, from 16 to 20 February, are briefly noted.[16] Her long diary entry for 20 February, begun just after Carco had left for work, 'a terrible moment for a woman', records her feelings after waking up; a letter to Murry follows, written later in the day, stressing how she deceived the military authorities with the fake letter of invitation that Carco had arranged – 'I seem to have just escaped the prison cell, Jaggle dearest'– and her amusement at her new surroundings: the 'large white house [. . .] a most extraordinary room furnished with a bed, a wax apple and an immense flowery clock [. . .]. It would make you laugh, too' (CW4, p. 159). Another letter addressed to Frieda Lawrence also mentions 'dreadful adventures' in a light-hearted way.[17]

The same diary entry then resumes, and retrospectively recounts the events of the previous day (19 February), the journey, arrival in Gray, the meeting with 'le petit corporal' (i.e. Carco) in the room he had found. Mansfield writes, 'It was like an elopement. [. . .] Laughing & trembling we pressed against each other a long, long kiss [. . .] The whole affair seemed somehow so ridiculous and at the same time so utterly natural' (CW4, p. 161). In a similar breathlessly excited mood, she comments that in bed they were so happy 'curled in each other's arms', that '[t]he act of love seemed somehow quite incidental' (CW4, p. 162). There is no further entry for a month, an abrupt termination that is reflected in 'An Indiscreet Journey' by typographical markers representing a new scene or time passing: a line break to introduce the couple's arrival at their white room, and section breaks before parts two and three.

'An Indiscreet Journey', Part One: The Journey to Gray and Arrival

For her journey from Paris to Gray,[18] in Mansfield's story the narrator wears a disguise and she symbolically discards her old self, represented by the 'peg-top with the real seal collar and cuffs', by donning an old Burberry trench-coat as 'the sign and the token of the undisputed venerable traveller' (CW1, p. 439). This also reinforces the device of deception that was crucially required to gain official entry to Gray: a false letter from a fake aunt and uncle, Julie and Paul Boisson, inviting her to visit them urgently because of her aunt's illness.[19] The double impersonation not only suggests that the narrator's speaking voice functions as a performance, but also establishes her as an actor without any past history, lacking motive, cause and effect: in effect, a traveller who is also an observer, receptive to the newness of every sight. Such reckless living for the moment tallies with Mansfield's remark in her diary that 'The curious thing was that I could not concentrate on

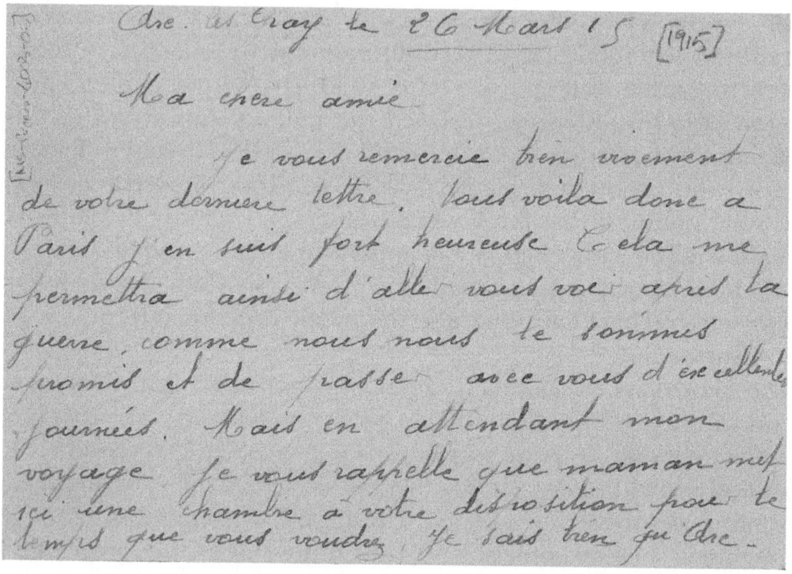

Arc. et Gray le 26 Mars 15 [1915]

Ma chère amie

Je vous remercie bien vivement de votre dernière lettre. Vous voila donc a Paris j'en suis fort heureuse Cela me permettra ainsi d'aller vous voir après la guerre, comme nous nous le sommes promis et de passer avec vous d'excellentes journées. Mais en attendant mon voyage je vous rappelle que maman met ici une chambre à votre disposition pour le temps que vous voudrez. Je sais bien qu'Arc-

Fig. 9 Front of Postcard from Marguerite Bombard (i.e. Francis Carco), 26 Mar 1915. MS-Papers-4003-05-01, Letters to Katherine Mansfield, Feb 1914–Mar 1915, Alexander Turnbull Library, Wellington, NZ.

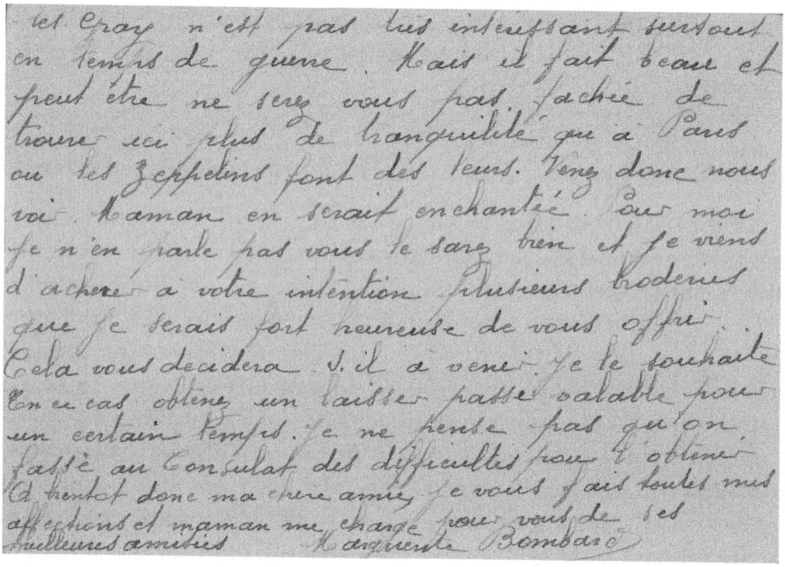

et Gray n'est pas très intéressant surtout en temps de guerre. Mais il fait beau et peut être ne serez vous pas fâchée de trouver ici plus de tranquillité qu'à Paris où les Zeppelins font des leurs. Venez donc nous voir. Maman en serait enchantée. Pour moi je n'en parle pas vous le savez bien et je viens d'acheter à votre intention plusieurs broderies que je serais fort heureuse de vous offrir. Cela vous decidera s'il a venir. Je le souhaite. En ce cas obtenez un laisser passer valable pour un certain temps. Je ne pense pas qu'on fasse au Consulat des difficultés pour l'obtenir. A bientôt donc ma chère amie, je vous fais toutes mes affections et maman me charge pour vous de ses meilleures amitiés

Marguerite Bombard

Fig. 10 Back of Postcard from Marguerite Bombard (i.e. Francis Carco), 26 Mar 1915. MS-Papers-4003-05-01, Letters to Katherine Mansfield, Feb 1914–Mar 1915, Alexander Turnbull Library, Wellington, NZ.

the end of the journey' (CW4, p. 160). In this new space of subjectivity, reality is reduced or defamiliarised, and references to location and temporality are either erased or made uncertain. Indicative of Mansfield's semiotic strategy is the eradication or substitutions of real names: characters are labelled by metonyms or epithets: St Anne is used for the concierge at the place where the narrator stays in Paris; the two colonels who inspect her visa and passport at Gray are God I and God II; a soldier in the Café des Amis is called Blackbeard. Likewise her destinations, the station at Dijon where she changes to a local train for Gray, and Gray itself, are assigned alphabetical codes of X and X.Y.Z. because associated with the war zone, where real meanings have been eradicated.

The narrator has reduced cognitive capacity: she lacks a watch so cannot tell the time, communication is one-sided or blocked as she cannot hear, and her own words in reply to questions are represented by ellipses. Her memory is unreliable: she forgets the names of her fake aunt and uncle in the confusing entanglement of fact and fiction, until reassurance comes from the 'unfamiliar letter written in their familiar handwriting' (CW1, p. 442). A chilling reminder of Mansfield's passionate longing and the risks she is taking comes from the woman seated opposite in the train who delivers a moral caution with a 'strange insulting relish' about the death penalty for soldiers who infringe the rule about bringing women into the military zone. Overweening sexual desire is condemned: '"You know what women are about soldiers [. . .] mad, completely mad,"' while the bird on the woman's hat impersonates her conscience, and interrogates her folly: '"What are *you* going to X for?" said the sea-gull. "What on earth are *you* doing here?"' (CW1, p. 443).

Recent studies of 'An Indiscreet Journey' have noted features of setting and incident that reveal similarities to classical or medieval narrative structures, and the identification of mythic and religious allusions and parallels has led to readings of the story as a rite of passage, a descent into hell or the underworld, or a timeless, medieval mystery play.[20] The journey has been interpreted as having symbolic connotations comparable to the journey in Conrad's *Heart of Darkness* as the narrator's induction into the horrors and realities of war in Gray,[21] and as equivalent to an ancient initiation rite for the transition from this world to the next, for which Mansfield may have drawn on the Greek Orphic mysteries.[22] Such readings give cultural and literary contexts for the mythic motif of the journey but do not always explain the story's aesthetic and artistic principles and the representation of multiple layers of consciousness through Mansfield's semiology by the development of key motifs and concepts, drawn partly from her notebook account, into image and symbol.[23]

The naïve otherworldliness of the narrator's ironic impersonation as the 'venerable traveler' suggests this is a 'straw-man' characterisation that will be overturned by the close-up encounter with harsh reality in Gray depicted in parts two and three, a process that involves verbal repetition and visual coding of meaning through colour symbolism. Her perceptions of a world strangely transformed by war, as the train passes sheds which are makeshift hospitals that shelter wounded soldiers, are based on misunderstandings that oscillate between the superficially comic and the mysterious and numinous: the cemeteries the train passes display not flowers, as the narrator thinks, but ribbons for the dead soldiers; the fighting endeavour is represented by 'a petit soldat, all boots and bayonet' like 'a little comic picture waiting for the joke to be written underneath' (CW1, p. 440), while the 'ridiculous' red and blue uniforms that make the soldiers so glaringly visible provoke the comment about 'la France' – 'Your soldiers are stamped upon your bosom like bright irreverent transfers' (CW1, p. 441). The narrator-as-novice reinforces such under-readings with her incredulity: 'Is there really such a thing as war? [. . .] [H]ave battles been fought in places like these?' (CW1, p. 440), suggesting the need for initiation into more 'authentic' experiences. Her perception of oppositions in combination, of apparent unities, as in the white/ black, light/dark chiaroscuro contrasts of 'These dark woods lighted so mysteriously by the white stems of the birch and the ash' (CW1, p. 440), offers a glimpse into a numinous world both unified yet at odds with itself. This anticipates the mixed society of wounded soldiers and civilians in the cafés of Gray; but the military regimentation and disruptiveness of war also undermine the mysterious order of nature that the narrator marvels at on her journey. The symbolic is still in place (i.e. language is still a coherent system) as people carry on as usual, but society teeters on the edge of the Lacanian Real (the place beyond language, where chaos lies); such a liminal place, where the symbolic order is beginning to break down, recalls Mansfield's positioning between life and death, love and hate, hot and cold, in her fraught reactions to Carco's invitation, and urgent need to move beyond such polarities.[24]

When read alongside the long diary entry for 20 February (CW4, pp. 158, 160–2), the narrator's stress on the glittering, brittle surfaces of things and her oscillation between uncertainty and exhilaration on the journey suggest that Mansfield was primarily reworking her intimacy with Carco by transforming her responses to their lovers' union into little epiphanies, moments of celebration: these balance and contrast with scenes witnessed in Gray that are redolent of the horror and desecration of war.[25] The mask of innocence and superficial gaiety which disguises her heroine's anxieties, as in the deception of the two colonels at Gray concerning the reasons for her visit, transmutes into a more knowing one once the narrator and 'le petit corporal' are united. This first appears in the repetition of whiteness – a metaphoric over-insistence on purity and innocence – in the 'strange white street', the 'quite white' house and white room, and the couple's ironic laughter at the insinuation that their hosts, Aunt Julie and Uncle Paul who have helped them in their deception, 'are as white as snow'.[26]

The first section of the diary (preceding the letters to Murry and Frieda) complicates this overdetermined symbolism of whiteness because her ambiguous comment, 'We spent a queer night', hints at an internal adjustment due to unanticipated sensations: maybe the deflation of her amorous hopes, or the transience of ecstasy, or some other reason. There is no trace of disenchantment in the story, but in her diary Mansfield expresses her misgivings:

> my heart feels rather heavy. I've got a feeling about this prison business which frightens me. I can't bear to think of him in prison – and another feeling, very profound, that he does not love me at all. I find him wonderful. I don't really love him now I know him, but he is so rich and careless – that I love. (CW4, p. 158)

This sobering confession, which may reflect some discrepancy between her performative outer and hidden inner selves, signals the disillusionment that Murry noted when Mansfield returned four days later:

> She was strange, her hair was cut short and she was aggressively defensive. I was not to imagine that she had returned to *me*. She had come simply because there was nowhere else to go. She didn't want to see anybody. I could see that she was bitterly disillusioned.[27]

Mansfield's first night of intimacy with Carco – the immediate goal of her 'indiscreet journey' – might be described as a liminal or threshold moment of initiation, one in which she enters a new phase of life. In narratological terms, this moment of self-awareness is represented as a turning point, as characters try to make sense of external events that are linked to internal changes, and it usually catalyses a sudden change in narrative structure.[28] This moment, and the entire episode, may be read in relation to the significantly coded (by typography and underlining) notebook entry for 19 February:

191

19 FRIDAY
Came to Gray
<u>One night.</u> (CW4, p. 158)

The underlined <u>One night</u> points to Mansfield's technique of suppression and ellipsis; she avoids the potential for plot or denouement that the crisis offers, and silently passes over this crucial moment in her fictional reconstruction, suggesting its presence only by a line break. From this point the story diverges from the known and familiar, whether as recorded in her diaries or in terms of familiar literary models and cultural motifs, and becomes an entirely original creation.

'An Indiscreet Journey', Parts Two and Three: The Café Societies of Gray

Part two opens: 'What an extraordinary thing'. The line break separating the sections also demarcates the narrator's transition from exhilaration to troubling disorientation as she finds herself lost and alone after this first night. Out of touch with her surroundings, she is mired in a sea of mud which she ploughs through in borrowed *sabots*. Both memory and perception fail her as she searches for the café she had earlier visited with her lover; that there were 'no steps, not even a porch' extends earlier misidentifications into a sharper realisation of loss. Mansfield interweaves various strands and motifs thematically, visually and structurally into this section, for which no diary entry exists, and begins to develop, through the colour symbolism hinted at in section one, a distinctive value system that will give credibility to her private quest for literary 'gold'. The driving preoccupation behind her illicit journey and clandestine liaison – her writing impasse – is implied in the view that the underbelly of repression and tension in the town might conceal spiritual riches, with the transferred epithet: the 'unlawful gold' that the houses 'like a company of beggars perched on the hill-side [harbour] in their bosoms' (CW1, p. 445). This, however, can be excavated, it is implied, only by translating the disruption caused by unsettled states of being. As her heroine sits alone in the café observing the soldiers who drift in to play cards under the watchful eye of the Madame and the attention of the waiting-boy, the disorder of its ambience and culture is foregrounded. The café's wallpaper exhibits trees mushrooming to the ceiling, creating the suffocating sense of a dense, thick forest; the young boy's voice is breaking and sometimes 'it boomed up from his throat, deep and harsh', at others 'it broke and scattered in a funny squeaking' (CW2, p. 446); the drip-drip of the wine on to the floor after he accidentally breaks a bottle makes the table look as though it is crying – anticipating the endless drip, drip of tears from the eyes of the soldier who enters, poisoned by tear gas. Almost surreal are hints of bodily contortions and cognitive reversals due to a disturbed temporality: the narrator's 'moment out of time', when years have passed, is signalled by the clock's ticking towards eternity, not marking twenty-four hours. Time jumps across the years into the future, when 'the war is long since over', and registers disappearance: 'there is no village outside at all' (CW2, p. 446). This perception of collapsed human time anticipates the irreverence about time in the next section, when the eight o'clock curfew is disregarded, and the soldiers' blatant lie about the hour when they arrive at Café des Amis.

Mansfield uses repetition and contrast. The three different café settings and images of three proprietresses presiding over scenes of intensifying disorder – the first, at the stop where the narrator boards the train, barely visible as she leans over, 'her breasts in her folded arms' (CW1, p, 441); the second, the scrutinising, scathing Madame, who declares the weeping eyes of the wounded soldier as '*dégoutant*', while arranging 'for the hundredth time a frill of lace on her lifted bosom' (CW1, p. 448); and the 'scrag of a woman in a black shawl' at the Café des Amis, who screams at the company which has arrived unannounced (CW1, p. 450) – are familiar sights in an unknown world that often eludes settled representation. The waiting boy has a counterpart in the 'very pale' (CW1, p. 441) little boy who serves in the green room at the station where she changes trains for Gray, and the first little boy in the coloured socks dancing in front of the Paris Metro at the beginning of her journey. In Gray, however, the Alice in Wonderland vision of the boy who spilt the wine and might have 'brought your dinner turning a Catherine wheel' (CW1, p. 447) both compares with and contrasts to the wounded soldier who has been poisoned by tear gas, constantly mopping with a white cloth his eyes, as pink as a rabbit's, as 'They brimmed and spilled, brimmed and spilled.'[29] The soldier's white face, suggesting trauma and maiming, and the white cloth, suggesting failure to heal or stop corrosion, overturn the earlier symbolism of whiteness, purity and innocence associated with the sexual assignation, while the allusion to the rabbit introduces a hidden discourse on soldiers as sacrificial victims. The transition from courtship to confusion in *les affaires de cœur* that Mansfield's narrator has experienced, as hinted at in the narrator's silence following her first night with her soldier lover and her subsequent physical disorientation, is now iconographically represented. Two paintings, hanging on either side of the clock, suggestively replace the black/white opposites in the grove of trees glimpsed in the train journey to Gray with a more nebulous yellow/black contrast: 'one, a young gentleman in black tights wooing a pear shaped lady in yellow over the back of a garden seat, *Premier Rencontre*; two, the black and yellow in amorous confusion, *Triomphe d'Amour*' (CW1, p. 446).

Part three is dominated by an encounter between the narrator and 'the little corporal', who has by now arrived at the café, and two drunken soldiers: 'the blue-eyed soldier' and 'Blackbeard'. The soldiers' comments on food and alcohol raise questions about the metaphorical relationship between appetite and sexual desire which the narrator has discreetly ignored in section one. This section also presents a second 'indiscreet journey', a search for the liquid ambrosia, mirabelle, an eau de vie made from plums, motivating this group to move to another café (Café des Amis), breaking the curfew and exposing themselves and others to danger. There is a thematic shift – from the illicit consummation of section one which involves the narrator to the illicit consumption (of the alcoholic drink, mirabelle) in which the narrator is more observer than participant – but this consumption, read metaphorically and in terms of Mansfield's semiotics, represents the discovery of her artistic bounty.

In this section Mansfield introduces narrative techniques of substitution and displacement to re-represent the narrator's liaison with her soldier, passed over in section one, to suggest a new 'healing' discourse to counterbalance the images of destruction and disability symbolised by the wounded soldier. The intimacy between the narrator and her lover (recalling the longing and desire recorded in the notebooks) is displaced on to the soldiers' drunken discussion about gustatory and culinary forms of sensual pleasure: Blackbeard desires to eat another mushroom and hopes that the heroine will feed him from her hand, while the blue-eyed soldier longs to drink the elixir mirabelle, which tastes like whiskey but without the hangover. The link between the gold of the dry, white brandy made from plums and the metaphoric 'unlawful gold' buried in the houses of Gray transforms gold into a symbol of the narrator's clandestine appropriation of experience into fiction, for mirabelle is often translated as glorious or marvellous, terms evocative of the religious mystery that Mansfield associated with artistic creation.[30]

Significantly, the narrator appears to have lost her appetite and also to be inexplicably cold – a state of death in life which recalls Mansfield's condition as she languished in unhappy love for Carco in England:

'You are cold,' whispered the little corporal. 'You are cold, *ma fille.*'
'No, really not.'
'But you are trembling.' (CW1, p. 449)

Externally, the scene matches such corporeal disorder and fluctuating temperatures. There are mishaps with food: a bottle of wine is spilt by the young waiter, and there is a 'suffocating smell of onion soup and boots and damp cloth' (CW1, p. 447). If, as Mary Addyman observes, eating or ingesting foreign matter indicates the bodily subject's willing abdication of boundaries between self and world, then these phenomena – the narrator's unusual coldness and recoil from the smells and sounds of food – can be read as resistances to any such incorporation of the external other, whether food, heat or another body.[31] In addition, her fragile, trembling state, which seems to involve a reduction of bodily appetite, is arguably caused by a psychic or emotional disassociation due to the renewal of creative energies as the story begins to reach its finale: that is, it suggests that the eruption of the real is now given representation through Mansfield's experimental fictional language and semiotics. To continue this analogy between food, bodily temperature and writing, Mansfield locates the narrator's appetites, emotions and psychic state within the social rituals of war's material culture, in shaping her oblique response to her 'queer night' with Carco, and her search for creative renewal.

Specific links between ingestion, eating or drinking and the functions of textuality are made through images, similes and metaphors involving food and the consumption of food. These feature in Mansfield's expansion of her diary into fiction, as David Manenti illustrates in his comparison of specific passages:[32] for example, the soldiers' comments on food and appetite can be read as metaphors of sexual desire and hope for consummation; the heads of the two colonels who examine the narrator's visa and fake letter 'rolled on their tight collars, like big over-ripe fruits' (CW1, p. 443). That men might be cannon fodder in war in the same way that rabbits are for the domestic table may lie behind Mansfield's preoccupation with rabbits, as recorded in the diary: a picture on the wall of the room she shared with Carco, of 'the man bringing the rabbit', the story he tells her of 'Le Lapin Blanc', and her visit to the cabinet to see the 'immense ridiculous rabbits' that made her happy again after Carco left for work (CW4, p. 162). All this, however, remains undeveloped in the background. The blue-eyed soldier's acclaim of mirabelle's special property – that it makes you feel 'as gay as a rabbit in the morning' – suggests a healing counterpoint to the wounded soldier's endless weeping from eyes 'as red as a rabbit', rather than any suggestion of violent death.

On occasion, metaphors of taste substitute for the faculties of sight and sound in a form of synaesthesia: the lady opposite the narrator on the train from Paris to Dijon Verdun 'sipped' at a sentence of the letter from her soldier son, 'tasting it'; the blue-eyed soldier's voice 'trickled through the dark' (CW1, pp. 440, 451). The oral forms of speech and taste are elided and speaking is aligned with sampling in the blue-eyed soldier's verbal demonstration of mirabelle's special flavour: he went '*Cluck* [. . .] with his tongue', fragmenting and prolonging the syllables of the word '"E-pa-tant"' ('startling', 'shocking'), then 'rolled the word [mirabelle] round his mouth, under his tongue' (CW1, pp. 448–9). The very name becomes a shifting signifier and its meaning (as brandy/whiskey) is destabilised in his determination to prove to the Englishwoman that '"you'd hardly know it from whiskey, except that it's" – he felt with his hand for the word – "finer, sweeter perhaps, not so sharp"' (CW1, p. 448). In terms of Mansfield's subtext that aligns writing with tasting, this might be seen as an invitation to reconsider her most familiar experiences – to identify where difference lies: that is, where it 'tastes' better – adding yet another layer to mirabelle's symbolism in relation to unlawful gold and her creative juices.

The narrative climax occurs in a doubled moment of seeing and tasting. The glimpse in the Café des Amis of a group of diners, the third and most fleeting of the religious references in the story, evokes the narrator's exclamation: 'How beautiful they are'; they are 'like a family party having supper in the New Testament' (CW1, p. 450), which, in biographical terms, perhaps represents a new vision of Mansfield's own family.[33] This moment of illumination is juxtaposed with the squalid sights of food scraps and peelings in the 'dark smelling scullery', where the soldier discovers the perfect taste of mirabelle, and his 'happy voice' is heard: '"What do you think? Isn't it just as I said? Hasn't it got a taste of excellent *ex-cellent* whiskey?"' (CW1, p. 451). In the story's final transgressive move, these joyful raptures, marking a fulfilment of bodily appetites and, by implication, of Mansfield's rediscovery of her creative forces and her new path in writing, allay the panic caused by breaking the curfew and transcend the characters' sordid wartime surroundings.

Conclusion: Dates, Signs, Meanings

Decoding Mansfield's semiotics shows how she attributes textual value to significant happenings. After Carco's letter on 6 February summoning her urgently, the next three notebook entries are represented typographically as:

15 MONDAY
Went to London with Jack.

16 TUESDAY
Came to Paris.

19 FRIDAY
Came to Gray.
<u>One night.</u> (CW4, p. 158)

In the diary entry that follows that of 20 February, written a month later
and after the return to Murry, the same pattern of three dates appears
to denote Mansfield's next journey from England to Paris:

<u>18 March</u>. Came to Paris again.
<u>19 March</u>. In Paris.
<u>23 March</u>. Kick-off. (CW4, p. 162)

The demarcation of her 'indiscreet journey' between these two sets of
dates about a month apart – and two moments of departure to France
– suggests the importance to Mansfield of her transgressive adventure.
This was her final fling romantically; there was no one else she felt so
passionately about from afar as Carco, and the sensuous liaison seemed
to serve its purpose. Although sexual bliss may have been circumscribed,
her creativity was freed, for as she wrote to Samuel Koteliansky soon
after she returned to England from Gray on 8 March 1915, 'for some
curious reason, I can work. I've been writing quickly and its good'.[34] She
turned back to the relationship with Murry as a companionable refuge[35]
and did not visit Carco or Gray again, though he invited her to do so
on 26 March, including another handwritten, fake letter by which to
gain entry.[36] Instead, she travelled again to Paris a month later to stay in
Carco's flat at 13 quai des Fleurs in preparation for the new 'kick-off':
the beginning of her composition of 'The Aloe'.

Presented as a daring journey to a forbidden war zone, 'An Indiscreet
Journey' is most deceptive when read according to its title, which con-
ceals Mansfield's personal voyage of self-discovery, as risky psychologically as it was physically. It brought her hard up against the divisions in
her own psyche and sexuality as she discovered barriers she erected
against being pushed too far in a direction she did not want to go, but
with a jolt of self-awareness that paradoxically also released her creative
impasse, a moment marked imagistically by an illuminating glimpse
of where her future inspiration lay: the major 'kick-off' was to be in
writing of her own family in New Zealand, as found in 'The Aloe', later
'Prelude', and the other great New Zealand stories for which she is best
known.

Notes

I would like to thank Anna Smith and Austin Gee for reading and commenting on an earlier draft of this essay.

1. Her second is 'The Fly', written at the end of the war; images in other stories, like the dead young man in 'The Garden Party', can also be related to Mansfield's war experiences, although set in c.1898 in New Zealand.

2. Although Mansfield as author and the first-person narrator are separate entities, this article identifies connections between them with reference to the autobiographical writings.

3. Christiane Mortelier, 'The French Connection: Francis Carco', in *Katherine Mansfield: In from the Margin*, ed. by Roger Robinson (Baton Rouge and London: Louisiana State University Press, 1994), pp. 137–57 (p. 139).

4. Claire Tylee, *The Great War and Women's Consciousness: Images of Militarism and Womanhood in Women's Writing, 1914–64* (London: Macmillan, 1990), pp. 90–1, sees the convalescent soldier as being at the heart of the story; Josiane Paccaud-Huguet, '"By what name are we to call death?": The Case of "An Indiscreet Journey"', in *Katherine Mansfield and World War One*, ed. by Gerri Kimber, Todd Martin, Delia da Sousa, Isobel Maddison and Alice Kelly (Edinburgh: Edinburgh University Press, 2014), finds that 'the pulsing substance of the Real oozes through' (pp. 13, 16, 17); Con Coroneos, 'Flies and Violets in Katherine Mansfield', in *Women's Fiction and the Great War*, ed. by Suzanne Rait and Trudi Tate (Oxford: Oxford University Press, 1997), pp. 197–218, argues that its significance as a war story is not in the 'details of gassing, military discipline and war loss' but in 'its ability to rescue itself from the romantic intoxication' of its originating condition, 'by displaying such intoxication as the condition and goal of the writing' (pp. 205, 209, 212); Claire Tomalin argues that Mansfield 'almost banishes the personal and the romantic', but shows 'irreverence for the great theme of war and an insistence on detail'; see 'Dreams and Danger', in *Katherine Mansfield's Selected Stories*, ed. by Vincent O'Sullivan (New York and London: W. W. Norton, 2006), pp. 375–9 (p. 379).

5. David Manenti, 'Indiscreet Journeys: Rewriting Katherine Mansfield', in *Authorial and Editorial Voices in Translation: Editorial and Publishing Practices*, ed. by Hanne Hansen and Ann Wegener (Montreal: Les Editions quebecoises de l'œuvre, 2013), pp. 1–24 (p. 3).

6. Sydney Janet Kaplan, *Katherine Mansfield and the Origins of Modernist Fiction* (Ithaca, NY: Cornell University Press, 1991), p. 183.

7. On 11 and 16 January ('Oh, God, let me work today. Its all I beg'), CW4, p. 152.

8. Carco, born in Nouméa of Corsican parents, was brought up in New Caledonia and moved with his family to France at the age of ten; see Mortelier, p. 139.

9. John Middleton Murry, *Between Two Worlds: An Autobiography* (London: Jonathan Cape, 1935), pp. 320, 321. Alluding to Raoul Duquette, Murry, writing in the 1930s, is referring to the name that Mansfield gave Carco in 'Je ne parle pas français'.

10. See Antony Alpers, *The Life of Katherine Mansfield* (London: Jonathan Cape, 1980), pp. 173–7, 178; Jeffrey Meyers, *Katherine Mansfield: A Biography* (Auckland: Hodder and Stoughton, 1978), pp. 112–14.

11. Gerri Kimber, *Katherine Mansfield: The View from France* (Bern: Peter Lang, 2008), pp. 63–72.

12. Mary Burgan, *Illness, Gender, and Writing: The Case of Katherine Mansfield* (Baltimore: Johns Hopkins University Press, 1994), pp. 46, 53.

13. Paccaud-Huguet, p. 13, n. 7. She argues that the story goes beyond Freud's pleasure principle and touches on Lacan's *'jouissance'*, i.e. that which escapes the realm of the forbidden and the 'nets of the symbolic order of culture' (p. 17, n. 15).
14. Burgan, p. 53.
15. See *Letters* 1, pp. 149–50; CW4, pp. 158–9.
16. Alpers, p. 175.
17. Jaggle is her nickname for Murry.
18. Although Mansfield does not give any place names in recounting the heroine's journey in 'An Indiscreet Journey', they have been provided in this essay to assist the reader.
19. Beatrice Hastings reported that Mansfield had originally planned to pretend she was pregnant: see Meyers, p. 113. As in the story in which the narrator uses a falsified letter, Carco sent Mansfield a postcard posing as a fake aunt using the invented name Marguerite Bombard. He sent the postcard pictured in Figures 9 and 10 to Mansfield in March, which Mansfield was to use to regain entry into Gray for a follow-up tryst; she never used it for this purpose. The postcard reads:

    My dear friend,
    I thank you very much for your recent letter. You are in Paris, for which I am very happy. This will allow me to come and see you after the war, as we promised one another, and to spend some wonderful days with you. In the meantime, I want to remind you that mother is putting a room at your disposal here for as long as you want. I know that Gray is not very interesting, especially during the war. But the weather is nice and you may be happy to find it more tranquil here than in Paris where the zeppelins are always a threat. So, come and see us. Mother would be delighted. As for me, needless to say, I would be very excited; I just bought for you several embroideries that I would be happy to give you. Will this convince you to come? I hope so. If that is the case, get a long-term pass. I do not think that the Consulate would make it difficult to get one. See you soon, then, my dear friend. I send you my affection, and mother sends her warm regards.
    Marguerite Bombard
    Translation kindly provided by Brigitte Martin and Todd Martin.
20. Paccaud-Huguet, pp. 14, 19.
21. Tylee, p. 90.
22. Erica Baldt, '"A god instead of a mortal": Katherine Mansfield and the Orphic Mysteries', in *Katherine Mansfield: New Directions*, ed. by Aimee Gasston, Gerri Kimber and Janet Wilson (London: Bloomsbury, forthcoming).
23. Stressing the impact of the war inadvertently emphasises representations of realism as if the dominant mode. Tylee points to a shift from the 'fragile illusion' of the first half to the 'disgusting reality' of what follows (p. 90). Coroneos argues that the ideals of *Rhythm*, 'disgust, disclosure of the real [. . .] the valorising of pity, brutality, the unsavouriness of truth', underpin the 'ironic indifferentiation of 20th century representations of war', although in its mixed mood and minor epiphanies this story contrasts with Mansfield's *Rhythm* stories like 'The Woman at the Store' (p. 212).
24. Paccaud-Huguet applies Lacan's concept of *jouissance* to the café society of Gray, 'a place of ungendered enjoyment [. . .] where the socially coded values of good and evil have lost relevance', i.e. where soldiers mingle with civilians in ways that imply a breakdown of social and moral order (p. 17, n. 15).
25. Although Gray was well behind the lines and the nearest point of the western front then was Belfort, the noise of battle and gunfire may have been heard. Mansfield's

diary notes the wounded 'coming down the hill [. . .] all bandaged up. One man looked as though he had 2 red carnations over his ears, one man as though his hand was covered in black sealing wax' (CW4, p. 161).

26. The diary entry for 20 February notes: 'a long strange, white street'; 'F. put his arm around me. I know you will like the house. Its quite white & so is the room & the people are'; and 'the white boat' that magically transports the lovers to India, 'to South America, to Marseilles' (CW4, pp. 161–2). Burgan notes that 'innocence is seen as the ultimate form of authenticity in her writing about her own desire', adding that, paradoxically, it can be judged only by one who has experienced corruption (p. 56).

27. Murry, p. 340.

28. Ansgar Nunning, '"With the Benefit of Hindsight": Features and Functions of Turning Points as a Narratological Concept and as a Way of Self-Making', in *Turning Points: Concepts and Narratives of Change in Literature and Other Media*, ed. by Ansgar Nunning and Kai Marcel Sicks (Berlin and Boston: De Gruyter, 2012), pp. 31–58 (p. 37).

29. This refers to the damaging effects of tear gas, which made the eyes weep; chlorine and phosgene gases were not introduced until April and December 1915 (James Patton, Gas in the Great War, Kansas University Medical Center. Available at <http://www.kumc.edu/wwi/medicine/gas-in-the-great-war.html> (last accessed 25 March 2020)). See Gerri Kimber, 'Notes from the Front: Katherine Mansfield's Literary Response to the Great War', in *The Great Adventure Ends: New Zealand and France on the Western Front*, ed. by Nathalie Philippe, John Crawford, Chris Pugsley and Matthias Strohn (Christchurch, NZ: John Douglas Publishing, August 2013), pp. 241–55; Antony Alpers in *The Stories of Katherine Mansfield: Definitive Edition* (Auckland: Oxford University Press, 1984), states that Mansfield may have seen something like this 'very recently, in Paris' (p. 554).

30. See her notebook comment of 31 May 1919: 'Work. Shall I be able to express, one day, my love of work – my desire to be a better writer, my longing to take greater pains. And the passion I feel. It takes the place of religion – it is my religion – of people – I create my people – of "life" – it is Life' (CW4, p. 280).

31. Mary Addyman, '"All else is vain, but eating is real": Gustatory Bodies', in *Food, Drink and the Written Word in Britain, 1820–1945*, ed. by Mary Addyman, Laura Wood and Christopher Yiannitsaros (London: Routledge, 2017), pp. 207–20 (p. 208).

32. Manenti makes a comparison between the texts, noting that various parts of speech are changed to enhance visual representations (pp. 6–8).

33. Other references are to St Anne (whom the narrator's concierge in Paris resembles), and the man with a pail of fish at the stop where she changed to a local train to Gray, 'who looked as though he had escaped from some holy picture' (CW1, pp. 439, 442).

34. *Letters* 1, pp. 152–3.

35. Burgan (p. 58), points out that Mansfield turned away from bisexuality to a 'determined homosexuality' that emphasised companionship rather than sensuality.

36. This is transcribed by Kimber, pp. 70–1, and reproduced above, p. 188, from the manuscript held in the Alexander Turnbull Library, Wellington. English translation provided in note 19.

REVIEW ESSAY

Rhythm, Laughter and Spiritualism: Katherine Mansfield and the Modernist Search for Meaning

Lee Garver

Helen Rydstrand, *Rhythmic Modernism: Mimesis and the Short Story* (London: Bloomsbury, 2019), 247 pp., £96. ISBN 978 1 5013 4341 4.

Jonathan Taylor, *Laughter, Literature, Violence, 1840–1930* (Basingstoke: Palgrave Macmillan, 2019), 258 pp., £59.99, ISBN 978 3 030 11413 8.

Faith Binckes and Carey Snyder, eds, *Women, Periodicals, and Print Culture in Britain, 1890s–1920s* (Edinburgh: Edinburgh University Press, 2019), 476 pp., £150. ISBN 978 1 4744 5064 5.

Roger Lipsey, *Gurdjieff Reconsidered: The Life, the Teachings, the Legacy* (Boulder, CO: Shambhala, 2019), 359 pp., US $24.95. ISBN 978 1 61180 451 5.

When examining the volumes under review in this essay, it quickly becomes clear that Katherine Mansfield was entangled within and gave shape to some of the most important currents in modernist literature. While none of these books focuses specifically on Mansfield, they demonstrate that the New Zealand-born writer shared with many of her contemporaries a deep and profound interest in apprehending and depicting in language the intangible rhythms that she believed underlay human existence and the natural world. They reveal an author who possessed, like Wyndham Lewis, a keenly insightful understanding of laughter, in its most cruel and derisive manifestations, as well as its most visionary and carnivalesque moments. They disclose a diarist and searcher for truth whose posthumous periodical publications have more in common with those of her modernist peers and rivals than has heretofore been realised. Finally, these books make clear that Mansfield's fiction has much more significant ties to the spiritual teachings of G. I. Gurdjieff, and modern spiritualism more generally, than has been commonly understood.

Although Helen Rydstrand's *Rhythmic Modernism: Mimesis and the Short Story* does not break significant new ground in its analysis of Mansfield's fiction, it is a well-written and immensely satisfying study of rhythmic mimesis in the writings of D. H. Lawrence, Katherine Mansfield and Virginia Woolf. Building on the work of scholars such as Michael Golston, William Martin and Kirsty Martin, Rydstrand argues that Lawrence, Mansfield and Woolf were influenced by philosophical and scientific theories that posited the existence of a 'primordial force propelling the universe and underlying all of life's processes: at once metaphysical construct and actual phenomenon' (p. 1). She also claims that these authors were, in crucial ways, concerned with 'epistemic discovery – with bringing these intangible rhythms out of obscurity and into art' (p. 1). In contrast to scholars who characterise literary modernism as anti-mimetic, Rydstrand takes pains to emphasise that Lawrence, Mansfield and Woolf 'considered textual rhythms to function mimetically – quite literally as mimicry of the rhythms of the universe' (p. 1), and in her chapter on Mansfield she makes a compelling case that Mansfield uses textual rhythms in her stories to explore the relationship between individual and world, character and daily routine, and habitual patterns of thought and moments of transcendent understanding.

In her notebooks and letters, as well as the literary manifestoes that she co-wrote with her husband John Middleton Murry for *Rhythm* magazine, Mansfield repeatedly expressed an almost religious veneration for 'life' and suggested that it should be the mission of the artist or writer to depict self and world in all of their everyday detail. She also suggested that a concern with rhythm lay at the heart of any such artistic endeavour and that even the smallest details of existence were part of larger and more enduring patterns of meaning. In a 1915 letter to S. S. Koteliansky, Mansfield offered the following reflection on the importance of detail in her art:

> Do you, too feel an infinite delight and value in *detail* – not for the sake of detail but for the life *in* the life of it. I can never express myself (and you can laugh as much as you please.) But do you ever feel as though the Lord threw you into eternity – into the very exact centre of eternity, and even as you plunged you felt every ripple that flowed out from your plunging – every single ripple floating away and touching and drawing into its circle every slightest thing it touched. (*Letters* 1, 192)

In her analysis of this passage, Rydstrand draws particular attention to Mansfield's use of the word 'ripple', which, she believes, provides a 'rhythmic metaphor' for the underlying waves or pulses of the universe that Mansfield believed tied together the everyday and the numinous, the apparently insignificant and the eternal (p. 106). She also connects the ideas that Mansfield expresses in this passage to 'The Meaning of Rhythm', a manifesto Mansfield co-wrote with Murry for *Rhythm* in 1912. In this piece, Mansfield and Murry equate 'the eternal quest for rhythm' with the highest ideals of art, and Rydstrand argues that the search for a deeper and more spiritual meaning within the rhythms of the everyday is one of the principal goals of Mansfield's mature fiction.

One of the key ways in which Rydstrand believes Mansfield sought to achieve this end was by using textual rhythm to evoke 'the whole, living mind' of a character (p. 110). In introducing this subject, Rydstrand cites a statement Mansfield made about her aesthetic practice in a 1921 letter to her brother-in-law, Richard Murry. In this letter, Mansfield spoke of the extraordinary linguistic care she took to have the language she employed in 'Miss Brill' precisely match the psychological frame of mind and state of being of her titular character:

> In Miss Brill I chose not only the length of every sentence, but even the sound of every sentence – I chose the rise and fall of every paragraph to fit her – and to fit her on that day at that very moment. After I'd written it I read it aloud –numbers of times – just as one would *play over* a musical composition, trying to get it nearer and nearer to the expression of Miss Brill until it fit her. (*Letters* 4, 165)

As this passage makes clear, Mansfield went to enormous lengths to have the rhythms of her sentences mimic or impersonate the rhythms of Miss Brill's mind, mood and physical state of being, and in her analysis of textual mimesis in this story Rydstrand offers a brilliant insight into how Mansfield makes the mental habits of Miss Brill the basis for understanding her character.

Throughout 'Miss Brill', argues Rydstrand, Mansfield uses the 'familiar rhythm of human routine' and its 'arrhythmic' disruptions to portray not only the socially structured sadness and loneliness of her impoverished protagonist but also her self-deceptions and failures of self-recognition (p. 118). Although one of Mansfield's purposes in this story is to 'pay tribute to ordinary marginalized women' and to 'elevate' the importance of her subject through a reverent and almost religious attention to the smallest details of her existence, 'Miss Brill' is, just as importantly for Rydstrand, a searching critique of 'personal inauthenticity' (pp. 117, 120). In Rydstrand's view, the bright, superficially happy tones and rhythms of the story mask from the very beginning a deep, pervasive melancholy, and the tension, or arrhythmia, between these two cognitive or affective registers encourages readers to regard with suspicion the mental habits that prevent Miss Brill from achieving true self-understanding. 'Miss Brill' follows the Sunday afternoon ritual of an elderly unmarried woman who goes each week to a public park to hear a free concert. Using free indirect discourse that Rydstrand describes as 'quick, lively, and controlled' and 'animated diction supported by exclamation points' that is intended to communicate Miss Brill's habit of insisting to herself that she is enjoying herself tremendously, Mansfield reveals the gap between the insistent, practised cheerfulness of the story's language and moments of unacknowledged pain, when, for example, Miss Brill hears a 'faint chill' in the music in the park but fails to connect it to her own unhappiness and isolation (pp. 118, 120). It is not until the story's protagonist overhears a young couple speaking of her in harsh and unflattering terms that she comes to any clear understanding of her social ostracism, and this understanding is represented less by any critical reflection on her part and more by the disruption of routine – in this instance, her failure to purchase a slice of honey-cake on her way home from the concert.

In using textual rhythm to depict 'the whole, living person' in all of their social and psychological complexity, Mansfield, of course, did more than simply examine the relationship between mental habit and personal inauthenticity. For every Miss Brill or Raoul Duquette, the latter of whom, Rydstrand argues, remains tragically trapped 'between artificial pose and genuine emotional response' throughout 'Je ne parle pas français', Mansfield presented a range of characters who achieved at least some level of personal or transcendent understanding (p. 121). Two such characters are sisters Josephine and Constantia from 'The Daughters of the Late Colonel'. While these elderly spinsters are depicted for most of the story as being locked in a series of shared mental rhythms that restrict their capacity to see beyond the socially prescribed limitations placed on single women in the early twentieth century, there is a moment towards the end of the story when, influenced by the musical rhythms of a barrel organ outside the window of their apartment, they become aware of the new-found freedoms they might experience in the aftermath of their tyrannical father's death. The bubbling and spontaneous sounds of the organ, Rydstrand argues, together with the momentary appearance of the sun in their dreary apartment, 'briefly loosens their emotional and mental routines' (p. 130). As she asserts,

It inspires them to consider what else could have happened in their lives, what life is really like, and who they are without the noise and bustle of everyday life, and to edge towards the possibility of a more fulfilling life for themselves in the future. (p. 130).

Although 'force of habit in the form of ingrained social niceties' quickly dissipates this moment of emancipatory revelation, we are left as readers with an awareness of patterns of existence different from those enforced by patriarchy (p. 130).

Other stories that use rhythmic mimesis to gesture towards larger and more emancipatory rhythms include 'Prelude' and 'At the Bay'. In both stories, Rydstrand claims, Mansfield uses textual rhythm as 'an alternate structuring method to conventional plot, one which allows the evocation of atmosphere and other fugitive aspects of everyday experience' (p. 131). In addition to offering what Rydstrand aptly describes as an 'elegiac focus on the gendered quotidian rhythms of domestic space', these stories, she contends, provide insight into our deepest and most universal recesses of being and link the smallest details of everyday life with the universal and the eternal (p. 141). This includes the childlike wonderings of Kezia, whose imaginative sensual experience of nature mimics the rhythms of the natural world. It also includes the private musings of Kezia's mother, Linda Burnell, whose reflections on the 'longer cyclical rhythms of nature' – in particular, the life cycle of the aloe plant in 'Prelude' – stand in stark contrast to the socially structured rhythms of family life (p. 145). Declares Rydstrand,

> For Linda, the otherness of the aloe's life cycle – its rhythmic presence – enables an imaginative expression of her desire for escape from the everyday and especially her family roles. The aloe's flower stem becomes, for the reluctant wife and mother, the mast of a ship that can carry her away. (p. 145)

Something similar takes place in 'At the Bay'. However, instead of depicting the rhythms of nature and the wider universe exclusively through the eyes of various characters, Mansfield periodically punctuates her story with descriptions of the sea in all of its inhuman indifference. In this manner, claims Rydstrand, Mansfield creates a rhythmic structure which, like the aloe in 'Prelude', 'highlights the temporary quality of human existence while simultaneously imbuing the everyday with significance' (p. 147).

In *Laughter, Literature, Violence, 1840–1930,* Jonathan Taylor provides a very different perspective on Mansfield. Examining her alongside Edgar Allan Poe, Edmund Gosse and Wyndham Lewis, Taylor focuses on the complex relationships between laughter, cruelty and violence in

Victorian and modernist literature, and draws a number of fascinating and provocative links between the short stories of Lewis and Mansfield. In taking up this subject, he is particularly concerned with the superiority theory of laughter, as outlined by philosopher Thomas Hobbes. In *Leviathan* (1651), Hobbes famously wrote: '*Sudden Glory*, is the passion which maketh those *Grimaces* called LAUGHTER; and is caused by . . . by the apprehension of some deformed thing in another, by comparison whereof they suddenly applaud themselves' (qtd. in Taylor, p. 8). It is Taylor's belief that Lewis and Mansfield both engage with and comment upon this theory of laughter. It is also his belief that they share a common interest in the cruelty and violence of laughter, and he argues that the modernist short story, as practised by Mansfield, is closely related to the narrative form of the joke.

Lewis's presence in a scholarly monograph of this kind should surprise no one. His work has long been associated with laughter and cruelty, and his stories, memoirs and criticisms, in Taylor's words, 'mingle humour with deadly violence' (p. 6). As Lewis asserts in *The Wild Body* (1927), 'Violence is of the essence of laughter', and as he later argues in *Men Without Art* (1934), laughter finds comedy in 'the contortions of a dying man' or 'the antics of . . . mutilated body-wrecks' (qtd. in Taylor, p. 6). In examining Lewis's fictional and critical engagement with these ideas, Taylor claims that Lewis's treatment of these themes is satirical. 'Lewis's mode of satire', he states, 'makes a reader laugh and then retrospectively exposes the unconscious violence underlying that laughter' (p. 11). While Mansfield's art has little obviously in common with that of Lewis and is rarely discussed in relation to these topics, Taylor makes a persuasive argument that her work is every bit as concerned with laughter and cruelty. In the final chapter of his book, he turns his attention to Mansfield's 'Miss Brill' and argues that the story not only functions like a joke but also engages critically with the superiority theory of laughter.

In Taylor's view, modernist short stories are structured like jokes. Both are scaled-down, compressed narratives that disavow completeness and favour compression. Both also depend in many instances on irony and reversal – that is, something analogous to a punchline – for their effect. In the case of 'Miss Brill', Taylor argues that the story is structured around a distinct moment of anti-climax. In the pages leading up to the scene when a young couple's unkind comments shatter Miss Brill's sense of societal belonging, the story's protagonist, Taylor contends, enjoys a 'visionary' moment of 'participatory, even utopian' laughter (p. 221). Lifted emotionally by the music of the band, Miss Brill forgets momentarily the 'faint chill' she had heard in the music only minutes earlier and imagines that everyone in the park – young, old, wealthy and poor – is about to begin singing, moving and laughing together. While her role in this imagined pageant is more one of 'accompaniment' than actual participation, she finds the idea of singing and laughing in unison with those around her beautiful and tears of joy fill her eyes. It is precisely at this moment in the story, when Miss Brill's imagined laughter and joy reach an emotional crescendo, that Mansfield violently and cruelly punctures Miss Brill's illusion of societal acceptance. A young couple sit down at the opposite end of her park bench, and she overhears the young man refer to her as a 'stupid old thing', and the young woman 'giggle' at her shabby old fur.

While few readers are likely to find this reversal of expectations funny, it is difficult to deny that the story structurally resembles a joke and that the young woman's giggling seems rooted in a Hobbesian sense of sudden glory at the misfortunes of another human being. The shattering of Miss Brill's sense of societal belonging arrives like a swift, cutting punchline, and the young woman's giggling serves, above all other things, to make her feel superior to the poor elderly lady sitting across from her on the bench. Although it is never entirely clear what Taylor thinks Mansfield hoped to achieve in structuring her story in this manner, I believe that Taylor's attention to issues of laughter, cruelty and violence in 'Miss Brill' has considerable value for the field of Mansfield studies. At a minimum, it allows one to see with new-found clarity that Mansfield's fiction dealt unsparingly with illusion and that it did not shy away from examining the cruelty and violence that underlie the most ordinary human interactions. More speculatively, it makes one wonder if Mansfield's ties to Lewis and other satirical modernists, such as Evelyn Waugh and Djuna Barnes, are perhaps deeper, or at the very least more complex, than one might have supposed. But perhaps most importantly, it opens up a fascinating window into the politics of Mansfield's fiction. In identifying a tension between two different kinds of laughter in 'Miss Brill', Taylor brings to light two very different ways of thinking about community, belonging, gender and social change, and I believe the dialectic between these two forms of laughter can tell us something important about Mansfield's political sympathies.

Although it might seem reasonable to draw the conclusion that Miss Brill's imagining of a participatory, utopian laughter that brings together young and old, wealthy and poor is nothing more than the sentimental fantasy of an unhappy social outcast, Taylor goes to considerable length to dispel this idea. In his view, Miss Brill's dream-like vision of the whole world laughing is the necessary counterpart to the laughter of superiority, and while the latter triumphs within the space of the story, the former still exercises an important critical function. 'The visionary moment', he claims

> suggests a much more egalitarian, classless, and communitarian society than the girl's giggle which comes after it. This is a 'carnivalesque' moment, as Mikhail Bakhtin would understand it, which overcomes hierarchies, barriers, and prohibitions, and which would glimpse the 'sphere of utopian freedom', through dance, music and laughter. (p. 221)

In contrast to the young woman's giggle, which Taylor argues is a 'conservative laughter' that 'works within and for the status quo', recycling and reinforcing 'a dominant patriarchal hierarchy, in which the relatively poor, single woman is subordinated to the wealthier, younger, heterosexual couple', Miss Brill's participatory, utopian laughter makes possible the imagining of a 'post-narrational future' in which 'radical equality' might open new forms of human relations (pp. 222, 225). In this respect, however compensatory or unrealistically conceived Miss Brill's vision might have been, it nevertheless offers the closest thing to a statement of Mansfield's political values as can be found in the story.

Women, Periodicals, and Print Culture in Britain, 1890s–1920s, edited by Faith Binckes and Carey Snyder, is an important new collection of essays that significantly broadens our understanding of women's contributions to periodical culture during the late nineteenth and early twentieth centuries. Straddling the fields of feminist periodical studies and modern periodical studies, the volume's twenty-seven contributions open new perspectives on middlebrow and popular magazines, movement-based and radical papers, avant-garde titles and modernist little magazines, as well as the dialogic networks that united and divided these publications. These contributions also bring welcome attention to an extraordinary variety of neglected figures and shine new light on the role that more familiar ones, such as Mansfield, played in shaping conversations about modernism, modernity, gender and social change. Although Mansfield's name is mentioned in only six essays and she is the focus of only one chapter, she is linked to a multiplicity of different periodicals – the *Adelphi, Atalanta's Garland,* the *Athenaeum,* the *Blue Review,* the *Dial,* the *English Review,* the *Nation and the Athenaeum,* the *New Age, Rhythm* and the *Westminster Gazette.* The piece that deals with her directly – Faith Binckes's '"A kind of *minute note-book,* to be published some day": Katherine Mansfield in the *Adelphi,* 1923–1924' – makes a powerful case that Mansfield's posthumous contributions to the *Adelphi* are less editorially compromised and more richly in conversation with other modernists than recent scholarship would lead us to believe.

Mansfield's husband, John Middleton Murry, has come under increasingly harsh criticism for his editing and publication of Mansfield's note-books and papers after her death from tuberculosis in 1923. Murry's presentation of Mansfield's work in the *Adelphi*, a magazine he founded in 1923 and used to showcase his late wife's writings, was marred, in the view of Gerri Kimber, by a 'sycophantic tone', and criticism of the editorial decisions Murry made when constructing the first volume of *The Journal of Katherine Mansfield* (1927) have been severe and unsparing (qtd. in Binckes, p. 259). In their introduction to *The Diaries of Katherine Mansfield: Including Miscellaneous Works* (2016), Kimber and Claire Davison are scathingly critical of Murry's editorial work on *The Journal*:

> It is to JMM's credit as an editor that he was able to create such a seamless text from so many bits and scraps, but this should not detract from the essentially duplicitous nature of his endeavours, which allowed for a false impression of the legacy of KM's personal writing that lasted over three-quarters of a century. (qtd. in Binckes, p. 259)

Like numerous scholars before them, Kimber and Davison find Murry's presentation of Mansfield deceitfully saccharine and sanitised, and they blame him for obscuring Mansfield's ground-breaking contributions to the development of high modernism. Although Binckes does not fun-damentally disagree with these criticisms, she believes that Mansfield's earliest contributions to the *Adelphi* merit reconsideration, and she makes a strong argument that Murry's presentation of her work in the magazine from 1923 to 1924 highlighted, at least as much as it concealed, Mansfield's ties to other modernists.

In developing this argument, Binckes acknowledges that the *Adelphi* was conceived in a very different spirit from previous magazines Murry had edited. In contrast to *Rhythm*, the *Blue Review* or the *Athenaeum*, which were either avant-garde or elitist in outlook, the *Adelphi* sought a broader reading public and, in Binckes's words, 'deliberately took aim at modernism's affiliation with the "ivory tower"' (p. 259). This won the magazine few friends with high modernists such as Ezra Pound, who regarded Murry as a shining example of 'insular dunderness', and it probably did not help matters that the *Adelphi* was modelled on what Binckes describes as 'the miscellaneous or "compendious" magazine', a periodical format that had more in common with a popular publication such as *Tit-Bits* than with the *Dial* or the *Little Review* (p. 260). However, as Binckes is quick to point out, distinctions between modernist maga-zines were rarely as clear-cut in practice as they were in theory, and in her view the *Adelphi* did not so much break with modernism as become more inclusive and eclectic in who it published. While it counted among its contributors such Poundian 'dunderheads' as H. G. Wells,

Arnold Bennett and Frank Swinnerton, it also included in its pages such female modernists as Dorothy Richardson, H. D. and Iris Barry; it is Binckes's belief that the eclectic miscellany format of the magazine, which included in each issue a collection of short pieces written by a 'Contributor's Club', whose members were left free to choose their own subject, as well as a series of shorter, reader-supplied notes and extracts placed at the back of the publication, made the *Adelphi* an unusually effective venue to publish work from Mansfield's notebooks and papers (p. 260).

The format, which privileged heterogeneity and openness over editorial control, discouraged Murry from tampering too overtly with the work of his contributors, and the reader-supplied notes and extracts placed at the rear of the magazine put an emphasis on 'fleeting everydayness' and the 'aesthetics of daily life' that was widely shared by Mansfield (p. 261). Although Binckes faults Murry for introducing Mansfield's work in a manner that speaks of her in 'favoured diminutives', such as 'little' and 'small', and for drawing attention to his 'Boswellian interventions as "Restorer and Preserver"' (p. 266), she believes that 'Mansfield's framing within the *Adelphi* stitched her into the pattern of its concerns', and she points to links between Mansfield's reflections on New Zealand and the stories of South African-born writer Pauline Smith as just one example of the 'two-way contact' between Mansfield and other modernists in the magazine (p. 263). Binckes also argues that Murry took fewer liberties with Mansfield's writings than is commonly assumed during the years 1923–4, and even when he treated separate manuscripts as if they were part of a single notebook, she contends that this 'collation of texts' rarely served to homogenise or sanitise Mansfield and often made 'the differing textures in her writing more, not less, visible' (p. 266). Indeed, she argues that the eclectic miscellany format of the *Adelphi* helped preserve a modernist aesthetic of 'original montage' in which Mansfield's manuscript fragments were treated as finished works of art (p. 269), and in this manner, asserts Binckes, Murry's editorial practice served 'not to separate Mansfield from an emerging canon, but to position her within it' (p. 270).

The last volume under review in this essay is Roger Lipsey's *Gurdjieff Reconsidered: The Life, the Teachings, the Legacy*. Although Lipsey is a well-respected biographer, art historian, editor and translator who has published books about Thomas Merton and Dag Hammarskjöld, this is not a traditional academic study, and it is in few, if any, respects a work of literary criticism. Lipsey has nothing to say about Mansfield's fiction, and Mansfield receives only the briefest mention. Writing instead as a lifelong practitioner of G. I. Gurdjieff's spiritual teachings, and a friend and acquaintance of those who carry on his legacy in the twenty-first century, Lipsey instead uses biography, memoir, personal anecdote and humanistic reflection to offer a spirited defence of this much-maligned Greek–Armenian spiritual teacher. Rejecting vigorously the idea that Gurdjieff was a crank or charlatan, Lipsey laments that 'Gurdjieff and the teaching that bears his name are now all but sealed off from both mainstream history and current concern' and seeks to make him newly accessible to western intellectuals and religious thinkers (p. 1).

Although I do not feel particularly qualified to judge whether Lipsey has succeeded entirely in this last goal, the book has been a revelation to me, and I believe it has a great deal to teach Mansfield scholars. Most academics who write about Mansfield are aware that she was a student of Gurdjieff and spent the last few months of her life at his Institute for the Harmonious Development of Man in Fontainebleau-Avon. If they are at all like me, they have wondered what possessed someone of Mansfield's intelligence and acuity to spend her final days in the company of a spiritual guru and mystic, whose teachings lie so far outside the main-stream. While I am not sure that I am likely to become a convert to his ideas any time soon, Lipsey has succeeded beyond all expectation in making me appreciate the appeal of Gurdjieff to Mansfield and a host of other early twentieth-century modernists. After spending his early adult life travelling across Central Asia and the Middle East and acquiring a wide-ranging knowledge of various eastern religions, Gurdeff settled in Moscow in 1912 and began to attract a small group of followers, includ-ing the composer Thomas de Hartmann, who wrote most of the music for Gurdjieff's 'movements' exercises, and P. D. Ouspensky, the latter of whom would prove critical in recruiting most of Gurdjieff's British disciples. After war and revolution displaced Gurdjieff from Russia, he later moved to France, and it is while established there that he attracted to himself a remarkable range of English-speaking adherents, including Mansfield; *New Age* editor A. R. Orage; *Little Review* editors Margaret Anderson and Jane Heap; author Jean Toomer; architect Frank Lloyd Wright and his wife, dancer Olgivanna Wright; and novelist Kathryn Hulme. All of these individuals played crucial roles in the development and promotion of modernism, and I would like to identify what I think are some of the most important reasons for their interest in Gurdjieff.

In doing so, I want to make clear that I am not proposing to offer any definitive answers. Throughout his book, Lipsey makes it clear that he has no intention of 'expounding' Gurdjieff's teaching, and as a consequence there is a great deal about Gurdjieff's ideas and prac-tices that remain opaque or mysterious to me (p. 48). But in exam-ining Gurdjieff's life and reflecting on the influence he had on his contemporaries, Lipsey has made me see a number of parallels between Gurdjieff and literary modernism, and I believe they can shed light on his appeal to Mansfield. One of the most striking things Lipsey has to say about Gurdjieff, not least because Lipsey never once speaks about modernism in his book, is that Gurdjieff believed, in almost Poundian fashion, that it was 'necessary to start again, to rethink everything, to cultivate values rooted in wise tradition but "renewed"' (p. 24). The appeal of such an outlook to someone like Mansfield, who sought in both her life and her fiction to break with received habit and develop a closer and more authentic relationship to the underlying patterns and rhythms of existence, seems to me obvious, and Lipsey points to a comment by Gurdjieff disciple J. G. Bennett that could almost have been written by Mansfield herself. In speaking of life at the Institute for the Harmonious Development of Man, Bennett suggests that Gurdjieff developed meditative practices and activities that made it possible for his followers to 'see people as they really were behind the habitual masks and patterns of outward behavior' (p. 147). Like Mansfield and many other modernists, Gurdjieff could be fiercely critical of false conscious-ness, and Lipsey remarks at several points upon Gurdjieff's propensity to play 'harmless tricks' on unsuspecting guests, and his severity and occasional cruelty toward 'his pupils and their weaknesses and illusions' (p. 25). While I am uncomfortable defending this behaviour, I am reminded of what Taylor has to say about the joke-like structure of 'Miss Brill', and I believe that Mansfield, like Gurdjieff, probably believed that a certain amount of cruelty was necessary to wake people into a higher state of consciousness. Finally, like Mansfield and a number of her modernist peers, Gurdjieff sought to explore 'deeper dimensions of human being' in a 'new language unheard before in the West' (p. 97). If this connection has been difficult for anyone to see before now, I strongly recommend reading Lipsey's study. It has opened my eyes to connections that I believe merit further discussion and exploration.

Notes on Contributors

Marlene Andresen is a Norwegian-based graduate and holds a Master's Degree with Distinction in Comparative Literature from the University of Oslo. She received a First Class Honours Bachelor's Degree from Falmouth University, UK, in 2015. In her MA thesis, completed in 2017, she researched the role of the child figure in Katherine Mansfield's fiction.

Argha Kumar Banerjee is currently the Dean of Arts, St Xavier's College (Autonomous), Kolkata, Calcutta University. He was previously a Commonwealth Research Scholar at the Department of English, Sussex University, where he wrote his D.Phil. thesis on literature of the First World War. His publications include *Female Voices in Keats's Poetry, Poetry of the First World War 1914–1918: A Critical Evaluation* and *Women's Poetry and the First World War* (1914–1918).

Maurizia Boscagli is a Professor of English and Comparative Literature at the University of California, Santa Barbara. She is the author of *The Eye on the Flesh: Fashions of Masculinity in Early Twentieth-Century Culture,* and of *Stuff Theory: Everyday Objects, Radical Materialism,* translator of Antonio Negri's *Insurgencies: Constituent Power and the Modern State,* co-editor of *Joyce, Benjamin and Magical Urbanism,* and author of many articles on critical theory and modernist cultural studies. She is Director of COMMA, the Center on Modernism, Materialism and Aesthetics at UC Santa Barbara.

Melissa Browne is a poet and fiction writer from New Zealand. She currently lives in Taranaki, with her partner and two young sons. She is currently completing a Master of Arts in Creative Writing (fiction) at the Institute of Modern Letters, Victoria University, Wellington.

Richard Cappuccio has presented papers at the conferences of the Katherine Mansfield Society and the International Virginia Woolf Society. Some of those papers have been expanded and published in *Katherine Mansfield Studies, The Journal of New Zealand Literature, Katherine Mansfield and the Bloomsbury Group* and *Modernism Revisited.*

Jackie Davis lives in Wellington, New Zealand. She holds an MA in Creative Writing and is the author of two novels, published by Penguin Books NZ. She has been published and been awarded fellowships both in New Zealand and internationally. She has also had short fiction broadcast on radio.

Enda Duffy is the Arnhold Presidential Department Chair of English at University of California at Santa Barbara. He is the author of *The Subaltern Ulysses* and of *The Speed Handbook: Velocity, Pleasure, Modernism,* which won the Modernist Studies Association Book Award as the best book in modernist studies, 2010. He is co-editor of *Joyce, Benjamin and Magical Urbanism,* editor of an edition of *Ulysses* and of Katherine Mansfield's short stories, and author of many articles on Joyce, Irish modernism, and on post-colonial and modernist literature and culture.

Lee Garver is Associate Professor of English at Butler University. His research focuses on the politics and culture of early British modernism, and he is currently working on a book project titled *Modernism, Magazines, and Radical Politics: The New Age and British Cultural Conflict 1907–1914.*

Martin Griffiths is a cello teacher and examiner for the New Zealand Music Education Board and principal cellist of Opus Orchestra (NZ), as well as a guest member of *Vox Baroque* and *NZ Barok.* He performed 'Katherine Mansfield, Cellist' at the 2019 Katherine Mansfield Society conference in Krakow, Poland. Martin is editor of the KMS Newsletter and has published in the journals *Tinakori* and *Crescendo.*

Suzanne Herschell lives in Eastbourne, New Zealand. Formerly a teacher of accelerate students, she is an award-winning artist, curator at NZ Academy of Fine Arts, selector and judge of national exhibitions, and an internationally published poet – *Meniscus, A Fine Line, Ghazal Page, Shot Glass Journal, Fib Review* & *Poetry Day* USA.

Julie Kennedy, born in Christchurch, New Zealand, is a Picton-based writer. The Marlborough Sounds and the local landscape inspire both her non-fiction and her poetry. Her book *Katherine Mansfield in Picton* was published by Cape Catley in 2000, and she is working on a collection of her own poetry.

Gerri Kimber, Visiting Professor at the University of Northampton, is co-editor of Katherine Mansfield Studies and Chair of the Katherine

Mansfield Society. She is the deviser and Series Editor of the four-volume *Edinburgh Edition of the Collected Works of Katherine Mansfield,* and together with Claire Davison is currently preparing a new four-volume edition of Mansfield's letters for Edinburgh University Press.

Gaurav Majumdar is an Associate Professor of English at Whitman College. His forthcoming book, provisionally titled *Illegitimate Freedom: Informality in Modernist Literature,* will be published by Routledge. In addition to his first book, *Migrant Form: Anti-Colonial Aesthetics in Joyce, Rushdie, and Ray,* he has published several essays.

Todd Martin is Professor of English at Huntington University and has published articles on John Barth, E. E. Cummings, Clyde Edgerton, Julia Alvarez, Edwidge Danticat, Sherwood Anderson and Katherine Mansfield. He is the co-editor of Katherine Mansfield Studies, editor of *Katherine Mansfield and the Bloomsbury Group,* and editor of the forthcoming *Bloomsbury Handbook on Katherine Mansfield.* He serves as the Membership Secretary of the Katherine Mansfield Society.

Paula Morris, MNZM, is an award-winning fiction writer and essayist of Māori and English descent. Her most recent book is *False River,* a collection of stories and essays around the subject of secret histories. The 2018 Katherine Mansfield Menton Fellow, Paula convenes the Master of Creative Writing programme at the University of Auckland and is the founder of the Academy of New Zealand Literature (www.anzliterature.com).

Mark Pirie is an internationally published New Zealand poet, editor, publisher and archivist for PANZA (Poetry Archive of NZ Aotearoa). In 2016, his selected poems, *Rock & Roll,* were published by Bareknuckle Books, Australia. Other books include *Gallery,* published by Salt, UK. He is a former founder/editor of *JAAM* and publisher for HeadworX, and currently edits *broadsheet: new new zealand poetry.*

Maggie Rainey Smith is a poet, novelist, essayist and short-story writer. Her poetry has appeared in *Essential New Zealand Poems* (Random House), the *Listener, New Zealand Books, 4th Floor Journal, Geometry Mayhem* and Katherine Mansfield Studies. Her novel, *Daughters of Messene,* was a best-seller in translation in Greece.

Marilyn Reizbaum is the Harrison King McCann Professor of English at Bowdoin College. She is the author of *Unfit: Jewish Degeneration and*

217

Modernism and *James Joyce's Judaic Other*, and is co-editor with Kimberly Devlin of *Ulysses: En-gendered Perspectives – Eighteen New Essays on the Episodes*. Her most recent essay in *Textual Practice* is 'Waiting for Godot at *The Mandelbaum Gate*'; her current project is a monograph on Muriel Spark's style – 'Muriel Spark's Art of Ridicule'.

Gerardo Rodríguez-Salas holds an MA in Gender Studies from Oxford University and a PhD from Granada University, where he currently works as a senior lecturer in English Literature. He is the author of three books and several chapters and articles on Katherine Mansfield. His writing career started with the publication of his short-story cycle, *Hijas de un sueño*.

Erica Stretton has recently completed a Master's in Creative Writing at the University of Auckland. She is a librarian and mother of three; she loves to travel.

Kirsten Warner's novel *The Sound of Breaking Glass* won the Hubert Church Prize for Fiction and MitoQ Best First Book Award in the Ockham New Zealand Book Awards in 2019. Her poetry book, *Mitochondrial Eve*, was published in 2018. She lives in Auckland and plays music in a folk blues band.

Eleri Anona Watson is a doctoral student at the Faculty of English, University of Oxford. Her thesis explores women's friendships with gay men in post-war American literature. Eleri is a lecturer and tutor in Women's Studies and English Literature, and has held a Visiting Fellowship at the University of Southern California.

Jessica Whyte has an English and Creative Writing degree from Manchester Metropolitan University and an MA in Modern and Contemporary Literature from the University of Sussex. She is a published poet and writer, and is working on both a novel and a collection of poetry about Katherine Mansfield.

Janet M. Wilson is Professor of English and Postcolonial Studies at the University of Northampton. She has published widely on Katherine Mansfield and other New Zealand diasporic writers such as Janet Frame, Fleur Adcock and Dan Davin. She is co-editor of the *Journal of Postcolonial Writing* and vice-chair of the Katherine Mansfield Society.

Robin Woodward is a Senior Lecturer in Art History at the University of Auckland. She is a specialist in New Zealand art with particular expertise in modern and contemporary sculpture, public art and painting. Robin also acts in an advisory role to arts trusts and civic bodies.

Index

Also available in the series:

www.edinburghuniversitypress.com/series/KMSJ

Join the Katherine Mansfield Society

Patron: Professor Kirsty Gunn

Annual membership starts from date of joining and includes the following benefits:

- Free copy of Katherine Mansfield Studies, the Society's prestigious peer-reviewed annual yearbook published by Edinburgh University Press
- Three e-newsletters per year, packed with information, news, reviews and much more
- Regular email bulletins with the latest news on anything related to KM and/or the Society
- Reduced price fees for all KMS conferences and events
- 20% discount on all books published by Edinburgh University Press
- Special member offers

Further details of how to join are available on our website:
http://www.katherinemansfieldsociety.org/join-the-kms/
or email us:
kms@katherinemansfieldsociety.org

The Katherine Mansfield Society is a Registered Charitable Trust (NZ) (CC46669)